John Miller Dow Meiklejohn

The English language

Its grammar, history and literature

John Miller Dow Meiklejohn

The English language
Its grammar, history and literature

ISBN/EAN: 9783337204587

Printed in Europe, USA, Canada, Australia, Japan

Cover: Foto ©Andreas Hilbeck / pixelio.de

More available books at **www.hansebooks.com**

THE ENGLISH LANGUAGE

THE ENGLISH LANGUAGE

ITS GRAMMAR, HISTORY, AND LITERATURE

WITH CHAPTERS ON

COMPOSITION, VERSIFICATION, PARAPHRASING,
AND PUNCTUATION

BY

J. M. D. MEIKLEJOHN, M.A.

PROFESSOR OF THE THEORY, HISTORY, AND PRACTICE OF EDUCATION
IN THE UNIVERSITY OF ST. ANDREWS

NEW EDITION

LONDON
SIMPKIN, MARSHALL, HAMILTON, KENT, AND CO., Lim.
ST. ANDREWS: A. M. HOLDEN
1890

PREFACE.

THIS book provides sufficient matter for the four years of study required of a pupil-teacher, and also for the first year at his training college. An experienced master will easily be able to guide his pupils in the selection of the proper parts for each year. The ten pages on the Grammar of Verse ought to be reserved for the fifth year of study.

It is hoped that the book will also be useful in Ladies' Colleges and Middle-Class Schools, to candidates for Local Examinations, and to other classes of students.

Only the most salient features of the language have been described, and minor details have been left for the teacher to fill in. The utmost clearness and simplicity have been the aim of the writer, and he has been obliged to sacrifice many interesting details to this aim.

The study of English Grammar is becoming every day more and more historical—and necessarily so. There are scores of inflections, usages, constructions, idioms, which cannot be truly or adequately explained without a reference to the past states of the language—to the time when it was a synthetic or inflected language, like German or Latin.

The Syntax of the language has been set forth in the form of

RULES. This was thought to be better for young learners, who require firm and clear dogmatic statements of fact and duty. But the skilful teacher will slowly work up to these rules by the interesting process of induction, and will—when it is possible—induce his pupil to draw the general conclusions from the data given, and thus to make rules for himself. Another convenience that will be found by both teacher and pupil in this form of *rules* will be that they can be compared with the rules of, or general statements about, a foreign language — such as Latin, French, or German.

It is earnestly hoped that the slight sketches of the History of our Language and of its Literature may not only enable the young student to pass his examinations with success, but may also throw him into the attitude of mind of Oliver Twist, and induce him to "ask for more."

It is also intended that the book shall be useful to Acting Teachers who are preparing for their Certificate Examination.

The Index will be found useful in preparing the parts of each subject; as all the separate paragraphs about the same subject will be found there grouped together.

J. M. D. M.

CONTENTS.

PART I.

PART II.

PART III.

PART IV.

PART I.

THE GRAMMAR OF THE ENGLISH LANGUAGE

INTRODUCTION.

1. What a Language is.—A Language is a **number of con-nected sounds** which convey a meaning. These sounds, carried to other persons, enable them to know how the speaker is feeling, and what he is thinking. More than ninety per cent of all language used is **spoken** language; that which is written forms an extremely small proportion. But, as people grow more and more intelligent, the need of written language becomes more and more felt; and hence all civilised nations have, in course of time, slowly and with great difficulty made for themselves a set of **signs,** by the aid of which the **sounds** are, as it were, indicated upon paper. But it is the sounds that are the language, and not the signs. The signs are a more or less artificial, and more or less accurate, mode of representing the language to the eye. Hence the names **language, tongue,** and **speech** are of themselves sufficient to show that it is the **spoken,** and not the **written,** language that is **the** language,—that is the more important of the two, and that indeed gives life and vigour to the other.

2. The Spoken and the Written Language.—Every civilised language had existed for centuries before it was written or printed. Before it was written, then, it existed merely as a spoken language. Our own tongue existed as a spoken language for many centuries before any of it was committed to writing. Many languages—such as those in the south of Africa—are born, live, and die out without having ever been written down at all. The parts of a spoken language are called **sounds;** the smallest parts of a written language are called **letters.** The science of spoken sounds is called **Phonetics**; the science of written signs is called **Alphabetics.**

3. **The English Language.**—The English language is the language of the English people. The English are a Teutonic people who came to this island from the north-west of Europe in the fifth century, and brought with them the English tongue —but only in its spoken form. The English spoken in the fifth century was a harsh guttural speech, consisting of a few thousand words, and spoken by a few thousand settlers in the east of England. It is now a speech spoken by more than a hundred millions of people—spread all over the world; and it probably consists of a hundred thousand words. It was once poor; it is now one of the richest languages in the world: it was once confined to a few corners of land in the east of England; it has now spread over Great Britain and Ireland, the whole of North America, the whole of Australia, and parts of South America and Africa.

4. **The Grammar of English.**—Every language **grows.** It changes as a tree changes. Its fibre becomes harder as it grows older; it loses old words and takes on new—as a tree loses old leaves, and clothes itself in new leaves at the coming of every new spring. But we are not at present going to trace the growth of the English Language; we are going, just now, to look at it *as it is.* We shall, of course, be obliged to look back now and again, and to compare the past state of the language with its present state; but this will be necessary only when we cannot otherwise understand the present forms of our tongue. A description or account of the nature, build, constitution, or make of a language is called its **Grammar.**

5. **The Parts of Grammar.**—Grammar considers and examines language from its smallest parts up to its most complex organisation. The smallest part of a written language is a **letter**; the next smallest is a **word**; and with words we make **sentences.** There is, then, a Grammar of Letters; a Grammar of Words; and a Grammar of Sentences. The Grammar of Letters is called **Orthography**; the Grammar of Words is called **Etymology**; and the Grammar of Sentences is called **Syntax.**

There is also a Grammar of musically measured Sentences; and this grammar is called **Prosody.**

(i) **Orthography** comes from two Greek words: *orthos*, right; and *graphē*, a writing. The word therefore means **correct writing.**

(ii) **Etymology** comes from two Greek words: *etŭmos*, true; and *logos*, an account. It therefore means **a true account of words.**

(iii) **Syntax** comes from two Greek words: *sun*, together, with; and *taxis*, an order. When a Greek general drew up his men in order of battle, he was said to have them "*in syntaxis.*" The word now means **an account of the build of sentences.**

(iv) **Prosody** comes from two Greek words: *pros*, to; and *ōdē*, a song. It means **the measurement of verse.**

THE GRAMMAR OF SOUNDS AND LETTERS, OR ORTHOGRAPHY.

6. The Grammar of Sounds.—There are two kinds of sounds in our language: (i) the **open** sounds; and (ii) the **stopped** sounds. The open sounds are called **vowels**; the stopped sounds **consonants.** Vowels can be known by two tests—a negative and a positive. The **negative** test is that they do **not** need the aid of **other letters** to enable them to be sounded; the **positive** test is that they are formed by the **continuous** passage of the breath.

(i) **Vowel** comes from Fr. *voyelle;* from Lat. *vōcālis*, sounding.

(ii) **Consonant** comes from Lat. *con*, with; and *sŏno*, I sound.

(iii) **Two** vowel-sounds uttered **without a break** between them are called a **diphthong.** Thus *oi* in *boil; ai* in *aisle* are diphthongs. (The word comes from Greek **dis**, twice; and **phthongē**, a sound.)

7. The Grammar of Consonants: (1) Mutes.—There are different ways of stopping, checking, or penning-in the continuous flow of sound. The sound may be stopped (i) by the **lips**—as in **ib, ip,** and **im.** Such consonants are called **Labials.** Or (ii) the sound may be stopped by the **teeth**—as in **id, it,** and **in.** Such consonants are called **Dentals.** Or (iii) the sound may be stopped in the **throat**—as in **ig, ik,** and **ing.**

These consonants are called **Gutturals.** The above set of sounds are called **Mutes,** because the sound comes to a full stop.

    (i) **Labial** comes from Lat. **labium,** the lip.

    (ii) **Dental** comes from Lat. **dens (dents)** a tooth. Hence also *dentist.*

    (iii) **Guttural** comes from Lat. **guttur,** the throat.

    (iv) **Palatal** comes from Lat. **palātum,** the palate.

8. The Grammar of Consonants : (2) Spirants. Some consonants have a little breath attached to them, do not stop the sound abruptly, but may be prolonged. These are called **breathing letters** or **spirants.** Thus, if we take an ib and breathe through it, we make it an iv—the **b** becomes a **v.** If we take an ip and breathe through it, it becomes an if—the **p** becomes an **f.** Hence **v** and **f** are called **spirant labials.** The following is a complete

TABLE OF CONSONANT SOUNDS.

	MUTES.			SPIRANTS.		
	FLAT (or Soft).	SHARP (or Hard).	NASAL.	FLAT (or Soft).	SHARP (or Hard).	TRILLED.
GUTTURALS	g (in g|g)	k	ng	...	h	...
PALATALS .	j	ch (church)		y (yea)	...	...
PALATAL SIBILANTS }	...	...	...	zh (azure)	sh (sure)	r
DENTAL SIBILANTS }	...	...		z (prize)	s	l
DENTALS .	d	t	n	th (bathe)	th (hath)	...
LABIALS .	b	p	m	v & w	f & wh	...

    (i) The above table goes from the throat to the lips—from the back to the front of the mouth.

    (ii) **b** and **d** are pronounced with less effort than **p** and **t.** Hence **b** and **d,** etc., are called **soft** or **flat;** and **p** and **t,** etc., are called **hard** or **sharp.**

9. The Grammar of Letters.—Letters are **conventional signs** or **symbols** employed to represent sounds to the eye. They have grown out of pictures, which, being gradually pared down, became mere signs or letters. The steps were these: **picture; abridged picture; diagram; sign** or **symbol.** The sum of all the letters used to write or print a language is called its **Alphabet.** Down to the fifteenth century, we employed a set of Old English letters, such as a b c—x g z, which were the Roman letters ornamented; but, from that or about that time, we have used and still use only the plain Roman letters, as a b c—x y z.

The word **alphabet** comes from the name of the first two letters in the Greek language: *alpha, beta.*

10. An Alphabet.—An alphabet is, as we have seen, **a code of signs or signals.** Every code of signs has two laws, neither of which can be broken without destroying the accuracy and trustworthiness of the code. These two laws are:

(i) One and the same sound must be represented by one and the same letter.

Hence: No sound should be represented by more than one letter.

(ii) One letter or set of letters must represent only one and the same sound.

Hence: No letter should represent more than one sound.

Or, put in another way:

(i) One sound must be represented by one distinct symbol.

(ii) One symbol must be translated to the ear by no more than one sound.

(i) The first law is broken when we represent the long sound of **a** in **eight** different ways, as in—**fate, braid, say, great, neigh, prey, gaol, gauge.**

(ii) The second law is broken when we give eight different sounds to the one symbol **ough,** as in—**bough, cough, dough, hiccough** (=cup), **hough** (=hock), **tough, through, thorough.**

11. Our Alphabet.—The spoken alphabet of English contains **forty-three sounds;** the written alphabet has only **twenty-six** symbols or **letters** to represent them. Hence the English al-

phabet is very **deficient**. But it is also **redundant**. For it
contains five **superfluous** letters, *c*, *q*, *x*, *w*, and *y*. The work
of the letter *c* might be done by either *k* or by *s*; that of *q*
by *k*; *x* is equal to *ks* or *gs*; *w* could be represented by *oo*;
and all that *y* does could be done by *i*. It is in the vowel-
sounds that the irregularities of our alphabet are most discern-
ible. Thirteen vowel-sounds are represented to the eye in more
than one hundred different ways.

(i) There are twelve ways of printing a short *i*, as in s*i*t, C*y*ril, bus*y*,
wom*e*n, etc.

(ii) There are twelve ways of printing a short *e*, as in s*e*t, *a*ny, b*u*ry,
br*ea*d, etc.

(iii) There are ten ways of printing a long *ē*, as in m*e*te, mar*i*ne, m*ee*t,
m*ea*t, k*ey*, etc.

(iv) There are thirteen ways of printing a short *u*, as in b*u*d, l*o*ve,
b*e*rth, r*ou*gh, fl*oo*d, etc.

(v) There are eleven ways of printing a long *ū*, as in r*u*de, m*o*ve, bl*ew*,
tr*ue*, etc.

THE GRAMMAR OF WORDS, or ETYMOLOGY.

There are eight kinds of words in our language. These are
(i) **Names** or **Nouns**. (ii) The words that stand for Nouns are
called **Pronouns**. (iii) Next come the **words-that-go-with-
Nouns** or **Adjectives**. (iv) Fourthly, come the **words-that-
are-said-of-Nouns** or **Verbs**. (v) Fifthly, the words that go
with Verbs or Adjectives or Adverbs are called **Adverbs**. (vi)
The words **that-join-Nouns** are called **Prepositions**; (vii)
those **that-join-Verbs** are called **Conjunctions**. Lastly (viii)
come **Interjections**, which are indeed mere sounds without
any **organic** or **vital** connection with other words; and they
are hence sometimes called **extra-grammatical utterances**.
Nouns and Adjectives, Verbs and Adverbs, have distinct, individual, and substantive **meanings**. Pronouns have no meanings in themselves, but merely **refer** to nouns, just like a
in a book. Prepositions and Conjunctions once had independent

meanings, but have not much now: their chief use is to **join** words to each other. They act the part of nails or of glue in language. Interjections have a kind of meaning; but they never represent a **thought**—only a **feeling**, a feeling of pain or of pleasure, of sorrow or of surprise.

NOUNS.

1. A **Noun** is a **name**, or any word or words used as a **name**.

Ball, house, fish, John, Mary, are all **names**, and are therefore **nouns**. "*To walk* in the open air is pleasant in summer evenings." The two words *to walk* are used as the **name** of an action; *to walk* is therefore a **noun**.

The word *noun* comes from the Latin *nomen,* a name. From this word we have also *nominal, denominate, denomination,* etc.

THE CLASSIFICATION OF NOUNS.

2. Nouns are of two classes—**Proper** and **Common.**

3. A **proper noun** is the name of an individual, *as an individual,* and **not** as one of a class.

John, Mary, London, Birmingham, Shakespeare, Milton, are all proper nouns.

The word *proper* comes from the Latin *proprius,* one's own. Hence a *proper noun* is, in relation to *one* person, *one's own name.* From the same word we have *appropriate,* to make one's own; *expropriate,* etc.

(i) Proper nouns are always written with a capital letter at the beginning; and so also are the words derived from them. Thus we write *France, French, Frenchified; Milton, Miltonic; Shakespeare, Shakespearian.*

(ii) Proper nouns, *as such,* have no meaning. They are merely marks to indicate a special person or place. They had, however, originally a meaning. The persons now called *Armstrong, Smith, Greathead,* no doubt had ancestors who were strong in the arm, who did the work of smiths, or who had large heads.

(iii) A proper noun may be *used* as a common noun, when it is employed not to mark an individual, but to indicate *one of a class.* Thus we can say, "He is the *Milton* of his age," meaning by this that he possesses the qualities which all those poets have who are like Milton.

(iv) We can also speak of "the Howards," "the Smiths," meaning a number of persons who are called *Howard* or who are called *Smith.*

4. A **common noun** is the name of a person, place, or thing, considered **not** merely as an individual, but as **one of a class.** *Horse, town, boy, table,* are **common nouns.**

> The word *common* comes from the Lat. *communis,* "shared by several"; and we find it also in *community, commonalty,* etc.

(i) A common noun is so called because it belongs *in common* to all the persons, places, or things in the same class.

(ii) The name *rabbit* marks off, or distinguishes, that animal from all other animals; but it does **not** distinguish one rabbit from another— it is **common** to all animals **of the class.** Hence we may say : a common noun **distinguishes from without;** but it does **not** distinguish **within** its own bounds.

(iii) Common nouns have a meaning; proper nouns have not. The latter *may* have a meaning; but the meaning is generally not appropriate. Thus persons called **Whitehead** and **Longshanks** may be dark and short. Hence such names are merely signs, and not significant marks.

5. Common nouns are generally subdivided into—

> (i) Class-names.
>
> (ii) Collective nouns.
>
> (iii) Abstract nouns.

(i) Under class-names are included not only ordinary names, but also the names of materials—as *tea, sugar, wheat, water.* The names of materials can be used in the plural when **different kinds of the material** are meant. Thus we say "fine teas," "coarse sugars," when we mean *fine kinds of tea,* etc.

(ii) A **collective noun** is the name of a **collection of persons or things,** looked upon by the mind as **one.** Thus we say *committee, parliament, crowd;* and think of these collections of persons as each **one** body.

(iii) An **abstract noun** is the name of a quality, action, or state, **considered in itself,** and as **abstracted** from the thing or person in which it really exists. Thus, we see a number of lazy persons, and think of *laziness* as a quality in itself, abstracted from the persons. (From Lat. *abs,* from ; *tractus,* drawn.)

> (a) The names of arts and sciences are abstract nouns, because they are the names of processes of thought, considered apart and abstracted from the persons who practise them. Thus, *music, painting, grammar, chemistry, astronomy,* are abstract nouns.

(iv) Abstract nouns are (a) derived from adjectives, as *hardness, dulness, sloth,* from *hard, dull,* and *slow;* or (b) from verbs, as *growth, thought,* from *grow* and *think.*

(v) Abstract nouns are sometimes used as collective nouns. Thus we say "the nobility and gentry" for "the nobles and gentlemen" of the land.

(vi) Abstract nouns are formed from other words by the addition of such endings as **ness, th, ery, hood, head,** etc.

6. The following is a summary of the divisions of nouns :—

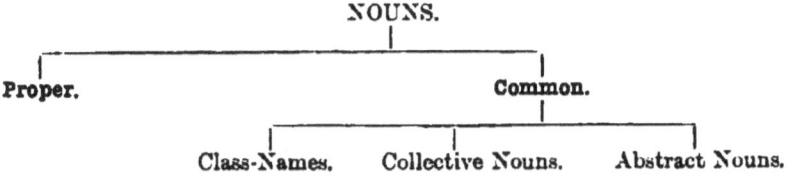

THE INFLEXIONS OF NOUNS.

7. Nouns can be inflected or changed. They are inflected to indicate **Gender, Number,** and **Case.**

We must not, however, forget that differences of gender, number, or case are not always indicated by inflexion.

> *Inflexio* is a Latin word which means *bending*. An inflexion, therefore, is a bending away from the ordinary form of the word.

GENDER.

8. **Gender** is, in grammar, the mode of **distinguishing sex** by the aid of words, prefixes, or suffixes.

The word *gender* comes from the Lat. *genus, generis* (Fr. *genre*); a kind or sort. We have the same word in *generic, general,* etc. (The *d* in *gender* is no organic or true part of the word; it has been inserted as a kind of cushion between the *n* and the *r*.)

(i) **Names of males** are said to be of the **masculine gender,** as *master, lord, Harry.* Lat. *mas,* a male.

(ii) **Names of females** are of the **feminine gender,** as *mistress, lady, Harriet.* Lat. *femina,* a woman. (From the same word we have *effeminate,* etc.)

(iii) Names of **things without sex** are of the **neuter gender,** as *head, tree, London.* Lat. *neuter,* neither. (From the same word we have *neutral, neutrality.*)

(iv) Names of animals, the sex of which is **not indicated,** are said to be of **the common gender.** Thus, *sheep, bird, hawk, parent, servant,* are common, because they may be of **either gender.**

(v) We may sum up thus :—

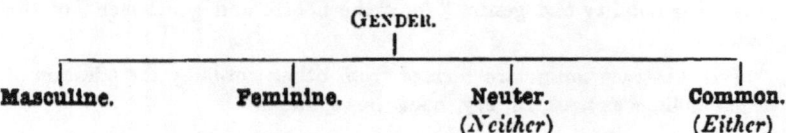

GENDER.

| Masculine. | Feminine. | Neuter.
(Neither) | Common.
(Either) |

(vi) If we *personify* things, passions, powers, or natural forces, we may make them either masculine or feminine. Thus the *Sun*, *Time*, the *Ocean*, *Anger*, *War*, a *river*, are generally made masculine. On the other hand, the *Moon*, the *Earth* ("Mother Earth"), *Virtue*, a *ship*, *Religion*, *Pity*, *Peace*, are generally spoken of as feminine.

(vii) **Sex** is a distinction between **animals**; **gender** a distinction between **nouns**. In Old English, nouns ending in *dom*, as *freedom*, were masculine ; nouns in *ness*, as *goodness*, feminine ; and nouns in *en*, as *maiden*, *chicken*, always neuter. But we have lost all these distinctions, and, in modern English, **gender always follows sex**.

9. There are three ways of marking gender :—

(i) By the use of Suffixes.

(ii) By Prefixes (or by Composition).

(iii) By using distinct words for the names of the male and female.

I. GENDER MARKED BY SUFFIXES.

A. Purely English or Teutonic Suffixes.

10. There are now in our language only two purely English suffixes used to mark the feminine gender, and these are used in only two words. The two endings are **en** and **ster**, and the two words are **vixen** and **spinster**.

(i) **Vixen** is the feminine of *fox;* and **spinster** of *spinner* (*spinder* or *spinther*, which, later on, became *spider*). King Alfred, in his writings, speaks of "the spear-side and the spindle-side of a house"—meaning the men and the women.

(ii) **Ster** was used as a feminine suffix very largely in Old English. Thus, *webster* was a *woman-weaver;* *baxter* (or *bagster*), a *female baker;* *hoppester*, a *woman-dancer;* *redester*, a *woman-reader;* *huckster*, a *female hawker* (travelling merchant) ; and so on.

(iii) In Ancient English (Anglo-Saxon) the masculine ending was **a**, and the feminine **e**, as in *wicca*, *wicce*, witch. Hence we find the names of many Saxon kings ending in **a**, as *Isa*, *Offa*, *Penda*, etc.

B. Latin and French Suffixes.

11. The chief feminine ending which we have received from the French is **ess** (Latin, *issa*). This is also the only feminine suffix with a living force at the present day—the only suffix we could add to any new word that might be adopted by us from a foreign source.

12. The following are nouns whose feminines end in **ess** :—

MASCULINE.	FEMININE.	MASCULINE.	FEMININE.
Actor	Actress.	Host	Hostess.
Baron	Baroness.	Lad	Lass (=ladess).
Caterer	Cateress.	Marquis	Marchioness.
Count	Countess.	Master	Mistress.
Duke	Duchess.	Mayor	Mayoress.
Emperor	Empress.	Murderer	Murderess.

☞ It will be noticed that, besides adding *ess*, some of the letters undergo change or are thrown out altogether.

There are other feminine suffixes of a foreign origin, such as **ine, a,** and **trix.**

(i) **ine** is a Greek ending, and is found in **heroine.** A similar ending in **landgravine** and **margravine,** the feminines of **landgrave** (a German count) and **margrave** (a lord of the *Mark* or of *marches*), is German.

(ii) **a** is an Italian or Spanish ending, and is found in **donna** (the feminine of **Don,** a gentleman), **infanta** (= *the* child, the heiress to the crown of Spain), **sultana,** and **signora** (the feminine of *Signor,* the Italian for *Senior,* elder, which we have compressed into *Sir*).

(iii) **trix** is a purely Latin ending, and is found only in those words that have come to us *directly from Latin;* as *testator, testatrix* (a person who has made a will), *executor, executrix* (a person who carries out the directions of a will).

II. GENDER INDICATED BY PREFIXES (OR BY COMPOSITION).

13. The distinction between the masculine and the feminine gender is indicated by using such words as **man, maid—bull, cow—he, she—cock, hen,** as **prefixes** to the nouns mentioned. In the oldest English, **carl** and **cwen** (=queen) were employed to mark gender; and carl-fugol is = cock-fowl, cwen-fugol = hen-fowl.

14. The following are the most important words of this kind :—

MASCULINE.	FEMININE.	MASCULINE.	FEMININE.
Man-servant	Maid-servant.	Bull-calf	Cow-calf.
Man	Woman (= wife-man).	Cock-sparrow	Hen-sparrrow.
He-goat	She-goat.	Wether-lamb	Ewe-lamb.
He-ass	She-ass.	Pea-cock	Pea-hen.
Jack-ass	Jenny-ass.	Turkey-cock	Turkey-hen.
Jackdaw			

(i) In the time of Shakespeare, *he* and *she* were used as nouns. We find such phrases as "The proudest he," "The fairest she," "That not impossible she."

III. GENDER INDICATED BY DIFFERENT WORDS.

15. The use of different words for the masculine and the feminine does not really belong to grammatical gender. It may be well, however, to note some of the most important :—

MASCULINE.	FEMININE.	MASCULINE.	FEMININE.
Bachelor	Spinster.	Husband	Wife.
Boy	Girl.	King	Queen.
Brother	Sister.	Lord	Lady.
Foal	Filly.	Monk	Nun.
Drake	Duck.	Nephew	Niece.
Drone	Bee.	Ram (or Wether)	Ewe.
Earl	Countess.	Sir	Madam.
Father	Mother.	Sloven	Slut.
Gander	Goose.	Son	Daughter
Hart	Roe.	Uncle	Aunt.
Horse	Mare.	Wizard	Witch.

(i) **Bachelor** (lit., a cow-boy), from Low Lat. *baccalarius*; from *bacca*, Low Lat. for **vacca**, a cow. Hence also *vaccination*.

(ii) **Girl**, from Low German *gör*, a child, by the addition of the diminutive *l*.

(iii) **Filly**, the dim. of *foal*. (When a syllable is added, the previous vowel is often modified : as in *cat, kitten; cock, chicken; cook, kitchen*.)

(iv) **Drake**, formerly *endrake*; *end=duck*, and *rake*=king. The word therefore means *king of the ducks*. (The word *rake* appears in another form in the *ric* of *bishopric*=the *ric* or kingdom or domain of a *bishop*.)

(v) **Drone**, from the *droning* sound it makes.

(vi) **Earl**, from A.S. *corl*, a warrior. **Countess** comes from the French word *comtesse*.

(vii) **Father**=*feeder;* cognate of *fat, food, feed, fodder, foster,* etc.

(viii) **Goose**; in the oldest A.S. *gans;* **Gandr-a** (the *a* being the sign of the masc.). Hence **gander,** the *d* being inserted as a cushion between *n* and *r,* as in *thunder, gender,* etc.

(ix) **Hart**=the horned one.

(x) **Mare,** the fem. of A.S. *mearh,* a horse. Hence also *marshal,* which at first meant horse-servant.

(xi) **Husband,** from Icelandic, *husbondi,* the master of the house. A farmer in Norway is called a *bonder.*

(xii) **King,** a contraction of A.S. **cyning,** son of the kin or tribe.

(xiii) **Lord,** a contraction of A.S. **hláford**—from **hláf,** a loaf, and **weard,** a ward or keeper.

(xiv) **Lady,** a contraction of A.S. **hláefdíge,** a loaf-kneader.

(xv) The old A.S. words were *nefa, nece.*

(xvi) **Woman** = wife · man. The *pronunciation* of *women (wimmen)* comes nearer to the old form of the word. See note on (iii.)

(xvii) **Sir,** from Lat. *senior,* elder.

(xviii) **Madam,** from Lat. **Mea domina** (through the French **Ma dame**) = my lady.

(xix) **Daughter**=milker. Connected with *dug.*

(xx) **Wizard,** from old French *guiscart,* prudent. *Witch* has no connection with *wizard.*

16. All feminine nouns are formed from the masculine, with four exceptions : **bridegroom, widower, gander,** and **drake,** which come respectively from bride, widow, goose, and duck.

(i) **Bridegroom** was in A.S. *brýdguma*=the bride's man. (*Guma* is a cognate of the Lat. *hom-o,* a man—whence *humanity.*)

(ii) **Widower.** The old masc. was *widuwa;* the fem. *widuwe.* It was then forgotten that *widuwa* was a masculine, and a new masculine had to be formed from *widuwe.*

NUMBER.

17. Number is, in nouns, the mode of indicating whether we are speaking of one thing or of more.

18. The English language, like most modern languages, has two numbers : the **singular** and the **plural.**

(i) **Singular** comes from the Lat. *singuli*, one by one; **plural**, from the Lat. *plures*, more (than one).

(ii) Mr Barnes, the eminent Dorsetshire poet, who has written an excellent grammar, called 'Speech-craft,' calls them *onely* and *somely*.

19. There are three chief ways of forming the plural in English :—

      (i) By adding **es** or **s** to the singular.

      (ii) By adding **en.**

      (iii) By changing the vowel-sound.

20. First Mode.—The plural is formed by adding **es** or **s**. The ending **es** is a modern form of the old A.S. plural in *as*, as *stanas, stones.* The following are examples :—

SINGULAR.	PLURAL.	SINGULAR.	PLURAL.
Box	Boxes.	Beef	Beeves.
Gas	Gases.	Loaf	Loaves.
Witch	Witches.	Shelf	Shelves.
Hero	Heroes.	Staff	Staves.
Lady	Ladies.	Thief	Thieves.

(i) It will be seen that *es* in *heroes* does not add a syllable to the sing.

(ii) Nouns ending in **f** change the sharp **f** into a flat **v**, as in *beeves*, etc. But we say *roofs, cliffs, dwarfs, chiefs,* etc.

(iii) An old singular of *lady* was *ladie;* and this spelling is preserved in the plural. But there has arisen a rule on this point in modern English, which may be thus stated :—

    ☞ (*a*) **Y**, with a **vowel before it**, is not changed in the plural. Thus we write **keys, valleys, chimneys, days,** etc.

    (*b*) **Y**, with a **consonant before it**, is changed into **ie** when **s** is added for the plural. Thus we write *ladies, rubies*, and also *soliloquies.*

(iv) **Beef** is not now used as the word for a single ox. Shakespeare has the phrase "beef-witted" = with no more sense than an ox.

21. Second Mode.—The plural is formed by adding **en** or **ne.** Thus we have **oxen, children, brethren,** and **kine.**

(i) **Children** is a double plural. The oldest plural was **cild-r-u,** which became **childer.** It was forgotten that this was a proper plural, and **en** was added. **Brethren** is also a double plural. **En** was added to the old Northern plural **brether**—the oldest plural being **brothr-u.**

(ii) **Kine** is also a double plural of **cow.** The oldest plural was **cý,** and this still exists in Scotland in the form of **kye.** Then **ne** was added.

22. Third Mode.—The plural is formed by **changing the vowel-sound** of the word. The following are examples :—

SINGULAR.	PLURAL.	SINGULAR.	PLURAL.
Man	Men.	Tooth	Teeth.
Foot	Feet.	Mouse	Mice.
Goose	Geese.	Louse	Lice.

(i) To understand this, we must observe that when a new syllable is added to a word, the vowel of the preceding syllable is often weakened. Thus we find **nătion, nătional; fox, vixen.** Now the oldest plurals of the above words had an additional syllable ; and it is to this that the change in the vowel is due.

23. There are in English several nouns **with two plural forms, with different meanings.** The following is a list :—

SINGULAR.	PLURAL.	PLURAL.
Brother	brothers (by blood)	brethren (of a community).
Cloth	cloths (kinds of cloth)	clothes (garments).
Die	dies (stamps for coining)	dice (cubes for gaming).
Fish	fishes (looked at separately)	fish (taken collectively).
Genius	geniuses (men of talent)	genii (powerful spirits).
Index	indexes (to books)	indices (to quantities in algebra).
Pea	peas (taken separately)	pease (taken collectively).
Penny	pennies (taken separately)	pence (taken collectively).
Shot	shots (separate discharges)	shot (balls, collectively)

(i) **Pea** is a false singular. The **s** belongs to the root ; and we find in Middle English "**as big as a pease,**" and the plurals **pesen** and **peses.**

24. Some nouns have the same form in the plural as in the singular. Such are **deer, sheep, cod, trout, mackerel,** and others.

(i) Most of these nouns were, in Old English, neuter.

(ii) A special plural is found in such phrases as : *A troop of horse; a company of foot; ten sail of the line; three brace of birds; six gross of steel pens; ten stone weight,* etc. In fact, the names of numbers, weights, measures, etc., are not put into the plural form. Thus we say, *ten hundredweight, five score, five fathom, six brace.* In Old English we also said *forty year, sixty winter;* and we still say, *a twelvemonth, a fortnight* (= fourteen nights).

25. There are in English several **false plurals**—that is, real singulars which look like plurals. These are **alms, riches,** and **eaves.**

B

(i) **Alms** is a compressed form of the A.S. **aelmesse** (which is from the Greek *cleēmosunē*). We find in Acts iii. 3, "an alms." The adjective connected with it is *eleemosynary.*

(ii) **Riches** comes from the French **richesse.**

(iii) **Eaves** is the modern form of the A.S. **efese**, a margin or edge.

26. There are in English several **plural forms** that are regarded and treated **as singulars.** The following is a list :—

Amends.	Odds.	Smallpox.
Gallows.	Pains.	Thanks.
News.	Shambles.	Tidings.

(i) **Smallpox** = small pocks.

27. There are many nouns that, from the nature of the case, can be used **only in the plural.** These are the names of things (*a*) That consist of **two or more parts**; or (*b*) That are taken **in the mass.**

(*a*) The following is a list of the first :—

Bellows.	Pincers.	Shears.	Tweezers.
Drawers.	Pliers.	Snuffers.	Tongs.
Lungs.	Scissors.	Spectacles.	Trousers.

(*b*) The following is a list of the second :—

Annals.	Dregs.	Lees.	Oats.
Archives.	Embers.	Measles.	Staggers.
Ashes.	Entrails.	Molasses.	Stocks.
Assets.	Hustings.	Mumps.	Victuals.

☞ It must be noticed that several nouns—some of them in the above class—change their meaning entirely when made plural. Thus—

SINGULAR.	PLURAL.	SINGULAR.	PLURAL.
Beef	Beeves.	Iron	Irons.
Copper	Coppers.	Pain	Pains.
Good	Goods.	Spectacle	Spectacles.

28. The English language has adopted many foreign plurals. These, (*a*) when fully naturalised, make their plurals in the usual English way; (*b*) when not naturalised, or imperfectly, keep their own proper plurals.

(*a*) As examples of the first kind, we have—

Bandits, cherubs, dogmas, indexes, memorandums, focuses, formulas, terminuses, etc.

(*b*) As examples of the second, we find—

	SINGULAR.	PLURAL	SINGULAR.	PLURAL.
(1) Latin	Animalculum	Animalcula.	Radix	Radices.
	Datum	Data.	Series	Series.
	Formula	Formulæ.	Species	Species.
	Genus	Genera.	Stratum	Strata.
(2) Greek	Analysis	Analyses.	Ellipsis	Ellipses.
	Axis	Axes.	Parenthesis	Parentheses.
	Miasma	Miasmata.	Phenomenon	Phenomena.
(3) French	Monsieur	Messieurs.	Madam	Mesdames.
(4) Italian	Bandit	Banditti.	Libretto	Libretti.
	Dilettante	Dilettanti.	Virtuoso	Virtuosi.
(5) Hebrew	Cherub	Cherubim.	Seraph	Seraphim.

(i) The Greek plurals *acoustics, ethics, mathematics, optics, politics*, etc., were originally adjectives. We now say *logic*—but *logics*, which still survives in the Irish Universities—was the older word.

29. Compounds attach the sign of the plural to the **leading word,** especially if that word be a noun. These may be divided into three classes :—

(*a*) When the plural sign is added to the Noun, as : *sons-in-law, hangers-on, lookers-on,* etc.

(*b*) When the compound word is treated as one word, as : *attorney-generals, major-generals, court-martials, spoonfuls, handfuls,* etc.

(*c*) When both parts of the compound take the plural sign, as : *men-servants, knights-templars, lords-justices,* etc.

CASE.

30. Case is the **form** given to a noun to show its **relation** to other words in the sentence. Our language has lost most of these forms; but we still use the word **case** to indicate the **function,** even when the **form** has been **lost.**

(i) The word **case** is from the Latin *casus,* and means a falling. The old grammarians regarded the nominative as the *upright case,* and all others as *fallings* from that. Hence the use of the words *decline* and *declension.* (Of course the nominative cannot be a real case, because it is *upright* and not a *falling.*)

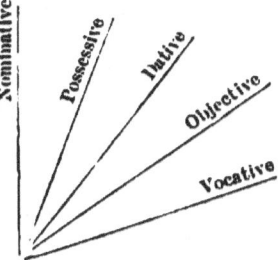

31. We *now* employ five cases; **Nominative, Possessive, Dative, Objective,** and **Vocative.**

(i) In **Nouns,** only one of these is **inflected,** or has a **case-ending**—the Possessive.

(ii) In **Pronouns,** the Possessive, Dative, and Objective are inflected. But the inflexion for the Dative and the Objective is the same. **Him** and **them** are indeed true Datives : the old inflection for the Objective was **hine** and **hi.**

32. The following are the definitions of these cases :—

(1) The **Nominative Case** is the **case of the subject.**

(2) The **Possessive Case** indicates **possession,** or some **similar relation.**

(3) The **Dative Case** is the **case of the Indirect Object,** and also the case governed by certain verbs.

(4) The **Objective Case** is the **case of the Direct Object.**

(5) The **Vocative Case** is the **case of the person spoken to.** It is often called the **Nominative of Address.**

(i) **Nominative** comes from the Lat. *nomināre,* to name. From the same root we have *nominee.*

(ii) **Dative** comes from the Lat *dativus,* given to.

(iii) **Vocative** comes from the Lat. *vocativus,* spoken to or addressed.

33. The **Nominative Case** answers to the question **Who ?** or **What ?** It has always a verb that goes with it, and asserts something about it.

34. The **Possessive Case** has the ending **'s** in the singular; **'s** in the plural, when the plural of the noun ends in **n** ; and **'** only when the plural ends in **s.**

☞ The possessive case is kept chiefly for nouns that are the **names of living beings.** We cannot say "the book's page" or "the box's lid," though in poetry we can say "the temple's roof," etc. There are many points that require to be specially noted about the possessive :—

(i) The apostrophe (from Gr. *apo,* away, and *strophē,* a turning) stands in the place of a lost *e,* the possessive in O.E. having been in many cases **es.** In the last century the printers always put *hop'd, walk'd,* etc., for *hoped, walked,* etc. The use of the apostrophe is quite modern.

(ii) If the singular noun ends in *s*, we often, but not always, write *Moses' rod, for conscience' sake, Phœbus' fire;* and yet we say, and ought to say, *Jones's books, Wilkins's hat, St James's, Chambers's Journal,* etc.

(iii) We find in the Prayer-Book, " For Jesus Christ *his* sake." This arose from the fact that the old possessive in **es** was sometimes written **is**; and hence the corruption into *his.* Then it came to be fancied that 's was a short form of *his.* But this is absurd, for two reasons :—

   (*a*) We cannot say that " the girl's book " is=*the girl his book.*
   (*b*) We cannot say that " the men's tools " is=*the men his tools.*

35. How shall we account for the contradictory forms **Lord's-day** and **Lady-day, Thurs-day** and **Fri-day, Wedn-es-day** and **Mon-day,** and for the curious possessive **Witenagemot ?**

Lady-day and **Friday** are fragments of the possessive of feminine Nouns in O.E., which ended in **an.** Thus, an old possessive of **lady** was **ladyan,** which was shortened into **ladyĕ,** and then into **lady.** So with **Frija,** the Saxon goddess of love. Thus we see that in *Lady-day* and *Friday* we have old feminine possessives. The word **witena-gemot** means the *meet* or *meeting* of the **witan** (=wise men), the possessive of which was **witĕna.**

36. The **Dative Case** answers to the question **For whom ?** or **To whom ?** It has **no** separate **form** for **Nouns ;** and in **Pronouns,** its form is the **same** as that of the **Objective.** But it has a very clear and distinct **function** in modern English. This function is seen in such sentences as—

   (1) He handed the **lady** a chair.
   (2) Make **me** a boat !
   (3) Woe worth the **day** ! (= Woe come to the day !)
   (4) Heaven send the **Prince** a better companion !
   (5) Heaven send the **companion** a better Prince !
   (6)   " Sirrah, knock **me** at this gate,
      Rap **me** here, knock **me** well, and knock **me** soundly."
                    (Shakespeare, " Taming of the Shrew," I. ii. 31.)
   (7) **Methought** I heard a cry ! (= **Meseems.**)
   (8) Hand **me** the salt, if **you** please.

Some grammarians prefer to call this the **Case of the Indirect Object ;** but the term will hardly apply to *day* and *me* in (3) and (7). In all the other sentences, the dative may be changed into an objective with the prep. *to* or *for.*

(i) In the sixth sentence, the **me's** are sometimes called *Ethical Datives.*

(ii) In the seventh sentence, *methought* is = *meseems*, or *it seems to me.* There were in O.E. two verbs—*thincan*, to seem ; and *thencan*, to think.

(iii) In the eighth sentence the phrase *if you please* is = *if it please you*, and the *you* is a dative. If the *you* were a nominative, the phrase would mean *if you are a pleasing person*, or *if you please me.*

37. The **Objective Case** is always governed by an **active-transitive verb** or a **preposition**. It answers to the question **Whom?** or **What?** It is generally placed after the verb. Its form is **different** from that of the Nominative **in pronouns;** but is the **same in nouns.**

(i) The **direct object** is sometimes called the **reflexive object** when the nominative and the objective refer to the same person—as, "*I* hurt *myself;*" "Turn (*thou*) *thee*, O Lord!" etc.

(ii) When the **direct object** is akin with the verb in meaning, it is sometimes called the **cognate object.** The cognate object is found in such phrases as : *To die the death ; to run a race; to fight a fight*, etc.

(iii) A **second direct object** after such verbs as *make, create, appoint, think, suffer*, etc., is often called the **factitive object.** For example : The Queen made *him* a *general ;* the Board appointed *him manager ;* we thought *him* a good *man*, etc.

Factitive comes from the Latin *facĕre*, to make.

38. The difference between the Nominative and the Vocative cases is this : The Nominative case **must** always have a **verb** with it ; the Vocative **cannot** have a **verb.** This is plain from the sentences :—

(i) John did that.
(ii) Don't do that, John !

39. Two nouns that indicate the same person or thing are said to be **in apposition ;** and two nouns in apposition may be in any case.

(i) But, though the two nouns are in the **same case,** only **one** of them has the **sign** or **inflection** of the case. Thus we say, "John the **gardener's** mother is dead." Now, both *John* and *gardener* are in the possessive case; and yet it is only *gardener* that takes the sign of the possessive.

PRONOUNS.

1. A Pronoun is a word that is used instead of a noun.
We say, "John went away yesterday; he looked quite happy."
In this case the pronoun he stands in the place of **John.**

(i) The word **pronoun** comes from the Latin *pro,* for; and *nomen,* a name.

(ii) The above definition hardly applies to the pronoun *I.* If we say *I write,* the *I* cannot have *John Smith* substituted for it. We cannot say *John Smith write.* *I,* in fact, is the universal pronoun for the **person speaking**; and it cannot be said to stand in place of his mere *name.* The same remark applies to some extent to *thou* and *you.*

2. The pronouns are among the oldest parts of speech, and have, therefore, been subject to many changes. In spite of these changes, they have kept many of their inflexions; while our English adjective has parted with all, and our noun with most.

3. There are four kinds of pronouns: **Personal; Interrogative; Relative;** and **Indefinite.** The following is a table, with examples of each:—

PRONOUNS.

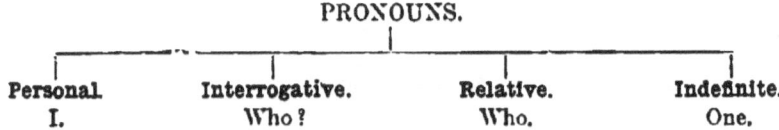

| Personal. | Interrogative. | Relative. | Indefinite. |
| I. | Who? | Who. | One. |

PERSONAL PRONOUNS.

4. There are three Personal Pronouns: The Personal Pronoun of the **First Person**; of the **Second Person**; and of the **Third Person.**

5. The **First Personal Pronoun** indicates the person **speaking**; the **Second Personal Pronoun,** the person **spoken to**; and the **Third,** the person **spoken of.**

6. The **First Personal Pronoun** has, of course, no distinction of gender. It is made up of the following forms, which are fragments of different words:—

	SINGULAR.	PLURAL.
Nominative	I	We.
Possessive	Mine (*or* My)	Our (*or* Ours).
Dative	Me	Us.
Objective	Me	Us.

(i) **We** is not = I + I; because there can be only one *I* in all the world. We is really = I + he, I + you, or I + they.

(ii) *I* can have no vocative as such. If you address yourself, you must say **Thou** or **You**.

(iii) The dative is preserved in such words and phrases as "**Me thinks**" ("it seems *to me*,"—where the *think* comes from *thinean*, to seem, and not from *thencan*, to think); "Woe is **me**;" "Give **me** the plate;" "If **you** please," etc.

7. The **Second Personal Pronoun** has no distinction of gender. It has the following forms :—

	SINGULAR.	PLURAL
Nominative	Thou	You (*or* Ye).
Possessive	Thine (*or* Thy)	Your (*or* Yours).
Dative	Thee	You.
Objective	Thee	You.
Vocative	Thou	You (*or* Ye).

(i) **Ye** was the old nominative plural; **you** was always dative or objective. "Ye have not chosen me ; but I have chosen you."

(ii) **Thou** was, from the 14th to the 17th century, the pronoun of affection, of familiarity, of superiority, and of contempt. This is still the usage in France of *tu* and *toi*. Hence the verb *tutoyer*.

(iii) **My, Thy, Our, Your** are used along with nouns; **Mine, Thine, Ours,** and **Yours** cannot go with nouns, and they are always used alone. **Mine** and **Thine**, however, are used in Poetry and in the English Bible with nouns which begin with a vowel or silent *h*.

8. The **Third Personal Pronoun** requires distinctions of gender, because it is necessary to indicate the sex of the person we are talking of; and it has them.

	SINGULAR.			PLURAL.
	MASCULINE.	FEMININE.	NEUTER.	ALL GENDERS.
Nom.	He	She	It	They.
Poss.	His	Her (*or* Hers)	Its	Their (*or* Theirs).
Dat.	Him	Her	It	Them.
Obj.	Him	Her	It	Them.

(i) **She** is really the feminine of the old demonstrative *se, seo, thaet ;* and it has supplanted the old A.S. pronoun *heo*, which still exists in Lancashire in the form of *hoo*.

(ii) The old and proper dative of **it** is **him**. The old neuter of **he** was **hit**, the **t** being the inflection for the neuter.

(iii) **Him**, the dative, came to be also used as the objective. The oldest objective was **hine**.

9. The Personal Pronouns are often used as **Reflexive Pronouns.** Reflexive Pronouns are (i) **datives ;** or (ii) **objectives ;** or (iii) **compounds** of **self** with the personal pronoun. For example :—

(i) **Dative :** "I press **me** none but good householders," said by Falstaff, in " King Henry IV.," I. iv. 2, 16.

"I made **me** no more ado," I. ii. 4, 223.

"Let every soldier hew **him** down a bough."—Macbeth, V. iv. 6.

(ii) **Objective :** Shakespeare has such phrases as *I whipt me ; I disrobed me ; I have learned me.* In modern English, chiefly in poetry, we have : *He sat him down ; Get thee hence !* etc.

(iii) **Compounds :** *I bethought myself ; He wronged himself ;* etc.

INTERROGATIVE PRONOUNS.

10. The **Interrogative Pronouns** are those pronouns which we use in asking questions. They are **who, which, what,** and **whether.**

(i) The word *interrogative* comes from the Latin *interrogāre*, to ask. Hence also *interrogation, interrogatory,* etc.

11. **Who** is both masculine and feminine, and is used only of persons. Its neuter is **what.** (The **t** in **what,** as in **that,** is the old suffix for the neuter gender.) The possessive is **whose ;** the objective **whom.** The following are the forms :—

SINGULAR AND PLURAL.

	MASCULINE.	FEMININE.	NEUTER.
Nominative	Who	Who	What.
Possessive	Whose	Whose	[Whose.]
Objective	Whom	Whom	What.

(i) **Who-m** is really a dative, like **hi-m**. But we now use it only as an objective.

(ii) **Whose** *may* be used of neuters; but it is almost invariably employed of persons only.

12. Which—formerly *hwilc*—is a compound word, made up of the **wh** in **who**, and **lc**, which is a contraction of the O.E. **lîc** = like. It therefore really means, *Of what sort?* It now asks for **one out of a number**; as, "Here are several kinds of fruits : which will you have?"

13. Whether is also a compound word, made up of **who** + **ther**; and it means, **Which of the two?**

(i) The *ther* in *whether* is the same as the *ther* in *neither*, etc.

RELATIVE OR CONJUNCTIVE PRONOUNS.

14. A Relative Pronoun is a pronoun which possesses two functions : (i) it stands for a noun ; and (ii) it joins two sentences together. That is to say, it is both a pronoun and a conjunction. For example, we say, "This is the man **whose** apples we bought." This statement is made up of two sentences : (i) "This is the man;" and (ii) "We bought his apples." The relative pronoun **whose** joins together the two sentences.

(i) Relative Pronouns might also be called **conjunctive pronouns**.

(ii) **Whose**, in the above sentence, is called **relative**, because it relates to the word *man*. *Man* is called its **antecedent**, or *goer-before*.

The word *antecedent* comes from the Lat. *ante*, before ; and *cedo*, I go.

15. The Relative Pronouns are **that; who, which; what. As** and **but** are also employed as relatives.

(i) **Who, which**, and **what** are also combined with **so** and **ever**, and form **Compound Relatives**; such as **whoso, whosoever, whatsoever,** and **whichsoever**.

(ii) **That** is the oldest of our relative pronouns. It is really the neuter of the old demonstrative adj., *se, seo, thaet.* It differs from *who* in two respects : (*a*) It cannot be used *after* a preposition. We cannot say, "This is the man with that I went." (*b*) It is generally employed to *limit, distinguish*, and *define*. Thus we say, "The house that I built is for sale." Here the sentence *that I built* is an adjective, limiting or defining the noun *house*. Hence it has been called the **defining relative**.

Who or **which** introduces a new fact about the antecedent ; **that** only marks it off from other nouns.

(iii) **Who** has **whose** and **whom** in the possessive and objective—both in the singular and in the plural.

(iv) **Which** is not to be regarded as the neuter of **who**. It is the form used when the antecedent is the name of an **animal** or **thing**. After a preposition, it is sometimes replaced by *where;* as *wherein = in which; whereto = to which.*

(v) **What** performs the function of a compound relative=**that + which**. If we examine its function in different sentences, we shall find that it may be equivalent to—

(*a*) Two Nominatives ; as in ' This is what he is" (=the person that).
(*b*) Two Objectives ; as in "He has what he asked for " (= the thing that).
(*c*) Nom. and Obj.; as in " This is what he asked for " (= the thing that).
(*d*) Obj. and Nom.; as in " I know what he is " (=the person that).

(vi) **As** is the proper relative after the adjectives **such** and **same**. **As** is, however, properly an adverb. "This is the same as I had " is=" This is the same as *that which* I had."

(vii) **But** is the proper relative after a negative ; as "There was no man but would have died for her." Here **but** = **who + not.** (This is like the Latin use of *quin = qui + non*).

INDEFINITE PRONOUNS.

16. An **Indefinite Pronoun** is a pronoun that does not stand in the place of a noun which is the name for a **definite person** or **thing**, but is used vaguely, and without a distinct reference.

17. The chief Indefinite Pronouns are **one, none; any; other; and some.**

(i) **One** is the best instance of an indefinite pronoun. It is simply the cardinal *one* used as a pronoun. In O.E. we used *man;* and we still find one example in the Bible—Zech. xiii. 5 : " Man taught me to keep cattle from my youth." **One,** as an indefinite pronoun, has two peculiarities. It (*a*) can be put in the **possessive case;** and (*b*) can take a plural **form.** Thus we can say : (*a*) " One can do what one likes with **one's** own ;" and (*b*) " I want some big **ones.**"

(ii) **None** is the negative of **one.** " None think the great unhappy but the great." But *none* is always plural. **No** (the adjective) is a short form of *none;* as *a* is of *an;* and *my* of *mine.*

(iii) **Any** is derived from **an,** a form of *one.* It may be used as an adjective also—either with a singular or a plural noun. When used as a pronoun, it is generally plural.

(iv) Other is — **an ther.** The **ther** is the same as that in *either, whether;* and it always indicates that one of two is taken into the mind.

(v) Some is either singular or plural. It is singular in the phrase *Some one;* in all other instances, it is a plural pronoun.

ADJECTIVES.

1. An **Adjective** is a word that **goes with a noun** to describe or point out the thing denoted by the noun—and hence to limit the application of the noun ; or, more simply,—

Adjectives are **noun-marking words.**

(i) Adjectives do not **assert explicitly,** like verbs. They assert **implicitly.** Hence they are **implicit predicates.** Thus, if I say, "I met three old men," I make three statements : (1) I met men ; (2) The men were old ; (3) The men were three in number. But these statements are **not explicitly** made.

(ii) Adjectives **enlarge the content,** but **limit the extent** of the idea expressed by the noun. Thus when we say *"white* horses," we put a **larger content** into the idea of horse ; but, as there are fewer *white* horses than *horses,* we limit the **extent** of the notion.

2. An adjective **cannot stand by itself.** It must have with it a noun either **expressed or understood.** In the sentence "The good are happy," *persons* is understood after *good.*

3. Adjectives are of four kinds. They are (i) **Adjectives of Quality ;** (ii) **Adjectives of Quantity ;** (iii) **Adjectives of Number ;** (iv) **Demonstrative Adjectives.** Or we may say,— Adjectives are divided into

ADJECTIVES

Qualitative. Quantitative. Numbering. Demonstrative.

These four answer, respectively, to the questions—

(i) **Of what sort ?** (ii) **How much ?** (iii) **How many ?** (iv) **Which ?**

4. Qualitative Adjectives denote a quality of the subject or thing named by the noun ; such as *blue, white ; happy, sad ; big, little.*

(i) The word *qualitative* comes from the Lat. *qualis*=of what sort.
(ii) **Most** of these adjectives admit of **degrees of comparison.**

5. Quantitative Adjectives denote either **quantity** or in-definite **number**; and they can go either (i) with the **singular,** or (ii) with the **plural** of nouns, or (iii) with both. The following is a list :—

Any.	Certain.	Few.	Much.	Some.
All.	Divers.	Little.	No.	Whole.
Both.	Enough.	Many.	Several.	

(i) We find the phrases : *Little need; little wool; much pleasure; more sense; some sleep,* etc.

(ii) We find the phrases : *All men; any persons; both boys; several pounds,* etc.

(iii) We find the phrases: *Any man* and *any men; no man* and *no men; enough corn* and *soldiers enough; some boy* and *some boys,* etc.

6. Numbering or **Numeral Adjectives** express the **number** of the things or persons indicated by the noun. They are generally divided into **Cardinal Numerals** and **Ordinal Numerals.** But Ordinal Numerals are in reality Demonstrative Adjectives.

(i) **Numeral** comes from the Lat. *numerus,* a number. Hence also come *numerous, numerical,* and *number* (the *b* serves as a cushion between the *m* and the *r*).

(ii) **Cardinal** comes from the Lat. *cardo,* a hinge.

(iii) **Ordinal** comes from the Lat. *ordo,* order.

7. Demonstrative Adjectives are those which are used to **point out** the thing expressed by the noun ; and, besides indicating a person or thing, they also indicate a **relation** either to the speaker or to something else.

(i) **Demonstrative** comes from the Lat. *demonstro,* I point out. From the same root come *monster, monstrous,* &c.

8. Demonstrative Adjectives are of three kinds : (i) **Articles ;** (ii) **Adjective Pronouns** (often so called) ; and (iii) the **Ordinal Numerals.**

(i) There are two **articles** (better call them **distinguishing adjectives**) in our language : **a** and **the.** **a** is a broken-down form of **ane,** the northern form of *one;* and before a vowel or silent **h** it retains the **n.** In some phrases **a** has its old sense of *one;* as in "two of a trade ;" "all of a size," etc.

"An two men ride on *a* horse, one must ride behind."
Shakespeare (Much Ado about Nothing, III. v. 40).

(ii) We must be careful to distinguish the article *a* from the broken-down preposition *a* in the phrase "twice *a* week." This latter *a* is a fragment of *on;* and the phrase in O.E. was "tuwa on wucan." Similarly, *the* in "the book" is not the same as *the* in "the more *the* merrier." The latter is the old ablative of *thaet;* and is = by that.

(iii) **Adjective Pronouns** or **Pronominal Adjectives** are so called because they can be used either as adjectives **with** the noun, or as pronouns **for** the noun. They are divided into the following four classes :—

(*a*) **Demonstrative Adjective Pronouns** — This, these ; that, those ; yon, yonder.

(*b*) **Interrogative Adjective Pronouns**—Which ? what ? whether (of the two) ?

(*c*) **Distributive Adjective Pronouns**—Each, every, either, neither.

(*d*) **Possessive Adjective Pronouns**—My, thy, his, her, etc. (These words perform a double function. They are adjectives, because they go with a noun ; and pronouns, because they stand for the **noun** or name of the person speaking or spoken of.)

(iv) The **Ordinal Numerals** are : First, second, third, etc.

9. Some adjectives are used **as nouns,** and therefore take a **plural form.** Thus we have *Romans, Christians, superiors, elders, ones, others, nobles,* etc. Some take the form of the **possessive case,** as *either's, neither's.*

(i) The plural of *one* as an adjective is *two, three,* etc. ; of *one* as a noun, *ones.* Thus we can say, "These are poor strawberries, bring me better *ones.*" Other numeral adjectives may be used as nouns. Thus Wordsworth, in one of his shorter poems, has—

> "The sun has long been set ;
> The stars are out by *twos* and *threes* ;
> The little birds are piping yet
> Among the bushes and trees."

(ii) Our language is very whimsical in this matter. We can say *Romans* and *Italians;* but we cannot say *Frenches* and *Dutches.* Milton has (Paradise Lost, iii. 438) *Chineses.*

NUMERALS.

10. Cardinal Numerals are those which indicate numbers alone. Some of them are originally nouns, as *dozen, hundred, thousand,* and *million;* but these may also be used as adjectives.

(i) **One** was in A.S. *an* or *ane*. The pronunciation *wun* is from a western dialect. It is still rightly sounded in its compounds *atone*, *alone*, *lonely*. **None** and **no** are the negatives of *one* and *o* (= *an* and *a*).

(ii) **Two**, from A.S. **twegen** mas.; **twa** fem. The form *twegen* appears in *twain* and *twin*, the *g* having been absorbed.

(iii) **Eleven** = **en** (one) + **lif** (ten). **Twelve** = **twe** (two) + **lif** (ten).

(iv) **Thirteen** = three + ten. The *r* has shifted its place, as in *third*.

(v) **Twenty** = **twen** (two) + **tig** (ten). **Tig** is a noun, meaning "a set of ten." The guttural was lost, and it became *ty*.

(vi) **Score**, from A.S. *sceran*, to cut. Accounts of sheep, cattle, etc., were kept by notches on a stick; and the twentieth notch was made deeper, and was called *the* cut—*the* score.

11. Ordinal Numerals are **Adjectives of Relation** formed mostly from the Cardinals. They are : First, Second, Third, Fourth, etc.

(i) **First** is a contraction of the A.S. *fyrrest* (farthest).

(ii) **Second** is not Eng. but Latin. The O.E. for *second* was **other**. *Second* comes (through French) from the Latin, *secundus*, following— that is, following the first. A following or favourable breeze ("a wind that *follows* fast") was called by the Romans a "secundus ventus." *Secundus* comes from Lat. *sequor*, I follow. Other words from the same root are *sequel*, *consequence*, etc.

(iii) **Third**, by transposition, from A.S. *thridda*. A third part was called a *thriding* (where the *r* keeps its right place) ; as a fourth part was a *fourthing* or *farthing*. *Thriding* was gradually changed into *Riding*, one of the three parts into which Yorkshire was divided.

(iv) In **eigh-th**, as in *cigh-teen*, a t has vanished.

THE INFLEXION OF ADJECTIVES.

12. The modern English adjective has lost all its old inflexions for gender and case, and retains only **two** for **number**. These two are *these* (the plural of *this*) and *those* (the plural of *that*).

(i) The older plural was **thise**—pronounced *these*, and then so spelled. In this instance, the spelling, as so seldom happens, has followed the pronunciation. In general in the English language, the spelling and the pronunciation keep quite apart, and have no influence on each other.

(ii) **Those** was the oldest plural of *this*, but in the 14th century it came to be accepted as the plural of *that*.

13. Most adjectives are now inflected for purposes of **comparison** only.

14. There are **three Degrees** of **Comparison**: the **Positive**; the **Comparative**; and the **Superlative**.

(i) The word *degree* comes from the French *degré*, which itself comes from the Latin *gradus*, a step. From the same root come *grade*, *gradual*, *degrade*, etc.

15. The **Positive Degree** is the **simple form** of the adjective.

16. The **Comparative Degree** is that form of the adjective which shows that the **quality** it expresses has been raised **one step** or **degree** higher. Thus we say *sharp*, *sharper*; *cold*, *colder*; *brave*, *braver*. The comparative degree brings together **only two** ideas. Thus we may speak of "the taller of the two," but not "of the three."

Comparative comes from the Lat. *compăro*, I bring together.

17. The Comparative degree is formed in two ways: either (i) by adding **er** to the positive; or (ii) if the adjective has two syllables (the last ending in a consonant) or more, by placing the adverb **more** before the adjective.

RULES: I. A silent **e** is dropped; as *brave*, *braver*.

II. A **y** after a consonant is changed into i before *er*, etc.; as *happy*, *happier*.

III. A final consonant after a **short vowel** is doubled; as *red*, *redder*; *cruel*, *crueller*.

IV. In choosing between **er** and **more**, sound and custom seem to be the safest guides. Thus we should not say *selecter*, but *more select*; not *infirmer*, but *more infirm*. Carlyle has *beautifullest*, etc.; but his is not an example to be followed.

18. The **Superlative Degree** is that form of the adjective which shows that the quality it expresses has been raised to the **highest degree**. The superlative degree requires that three things, or more, be compared. Thus "He is the tallest of the two" would be incorrect.

Superlative comes from the Lat. *superlatīvus*, lifting up above.

19. The Superlative degree is formed in two ways: either (i) by adding **est** to the positive; or (ii) if the adjective has two syllables (the last ending in a consonant) or more, by placing the adverb **most** before the adjective.

(i) *Happiest.*   (ii) *Most recent; most beautiful.*

20. Some adjectives, from the very nature of the ideas they express, do not admit of comparison. Such are *golden, wooden; left, right; square, triangular; weekly, monthly; eternal, perpetual,* etc.

21. The most frequently used adjectives have **irregular comparisons.** The following is a list :—

PosITIVE.	ComPARATIVE.	SuperLATIVE.	PosITIVE.	ComPARATIVE.	SuperLATIVE.
Bad	worse	worst.	Late	later	latest.
Evil	worse	worst.	Late	latter	last.
Ill	worse	worst.	Little	less	least.
Far	farther	farthest.	Many	more	most.
[Forth]	further	furthest.	Much	more	most.
Fore	former	foremost.	Nigh	nigher	nighest (next).
Good	better	best.	Old	older	oldest.
Hind	hinder	hindmost.	Old	elder	eldest.

[Rathe]   rather   [rathest.]

(i) **Worse** and **worst** come, not from *bad,* but from the root *weor,* evil. (*War* comes from the same root.) The *s* in *worse* is a part of the root; and the full comparative is really *worser,* which was used in the 16th century (Shakespeare, "Hamlet," III. iv. 157). *Worst = worsest.*

(ii) The **th** in **farther** is intrusive. *Farther* is formed on a false analogy with *further;* as *could* (from *can*) is with *would* (from *will*). *Farther* is used of progression in *space; further,* of progression in *reasoning.*

(iii) **Former** was in A.S. **forma** (= first). It is a superlative form with a comparative sense.

(iv) **Better** comes from A.S. *bet* = good—a root which was found in *betan,* to make good, and in the phrase *to boot* = "to the good."

(v) **Later** and **latest** refer to time; **latter** and **last** to position in space or in a series. **Last** is as by assimilation from *latst;* as *best* is from *betst.*

(vi) **Less** does not come from the **lit** in *little;* but from the A.S. **las,** weak. **Least = laesest.**

(vii) **Nighest** is contracted into **next;** as *highest* was into *hext.* Thus **gh + s = k + s = x.**

C

(viii) We say "the **oldest** man that ever lived," and "the eldest of the family." **Older** and **oldest** refer to mere number; **elder** and **eldest** to a family or corporate group.

(ix) **Rathe** is still found in poetry. Milton has "the rathe primrose, that forsaken dies;" and Coleridge, "twin buds too rathe to bear the winter's unkind air." The Irish pronunciation *rayther* is the old English pronunciation.

(x) **Hind** is used as an adjective in the phrase "the hind wheels."

22. The following are **defective comparatives** and **superlatives** :—

POSITIVE.	COMPARATIVE.	SUPERLATIVE.
[Aft]	after	——
[In]	inner	innermost.
[Out]	outer (or utter)	outermost (or uttermost).
——	nether	nethermost.
——	over	——
[Up]	upper	uppermost.

(i) **After**, as an adjective, is found in *aftermath* and *afterthought*.

(ii) **In** is used as an adjective in the word *in-side;* and as a noun in the phrase "the ins and outs" of a question.

(iii) In the inns of law, the **utter-bar** (outer-bar) is opposed to the **inner-bar**.

(iv) The **neth** in *nether* is the same as the **neath** in *beneath*.

(v) The **ov** in *over* is the *ove* in *above*, and is a dialectic form of *up*. It is still found in such names as *Over Leigh* in Cheshire, and *Over Darwen* in Lancashire.

(vi) **Hindmost, uttermost,** are not compounds of **most**, but are double superlatives. There was an old superlative ending **ema**, which we see in Lat. *extrēmus, suprēmus,* etc. It was forgotten that this was a superlative, and **est** or **ost** was added. Thus we had *hindema, midema*. These afterwards became *hindmost* and *midmost*.

THE VERB.

1. The **Verb** is that "part of speech" by means of which we make an assertion.

It is the **keystone of the arch of speech**.

(i) The word **verb** comes from the Lat. *verbum*, a word. It is so called because it is *the* word in a sentence. If we leave the verb out of a sentence, all the other words become mere nonsense. Thus we can say, "I saw him cross the bridge." Leave out *saw*, and the other words have no meaning whatever.

(ii) A verb has sometimes been called a **telling word**, and this is a good and simple definition for young learners.

THE CLASSIFICATION OF VERBS.

2. Verbs are divided into two classes — **Transitive** and **Intransitive**.

3. A **Transitive Verb** denotes an action or feeling which, as it were, **passes over** from the **doer** of the action to the **object** of it. "The boy **broke** the stick;" "he **felled** the tree;" "he **hates** walking."

In these sentences we are able to think of the **action of breaking** and **felling** as *passing over* to the stick and the tree.

Transitive comes from the Lat. verb *transīre*, to pass over.

The more correct definition is this :—

A **Transitive Verb** is a verb that **requires an object**.

This definition covers the instances of *have, own, possess, inherit*, etc., as well as *break, strike, fell*, etc.

4. An **Intransitive Verb** denotes a state, feeling, or action which does **not** pass over, but which **terminates in the doer** or agent. "He sleeps;" "she walks;" "the grass grows."

5. There is, in general, nothing in the look or **appearance** of the verb which will enable us to tell whether it is transitive or intransitive. A transitive verb may be used intransitively; an intransitive verb, transitively. In a few verbs we possess a causative form. Thus we have :—

INTRANSITIVE.	CAUSATIVE	INTRANSITIVE.	CAUSATIVE.
Bite [1]	Bait.	Quoth	Bequeathe.
Deem [1]	Doom (verb).	Rise	Raise.
Drink [1]	Drench.	Sit	Set.
Fall	Fell.	Watch [1]	Wake.
Lie	Lay.	Wring [1]	Wrench.

[1] These are also used transitively.

The following exceptional usages should be diligently noted :—

I. **Intransitive** verbs may be used **transitively**. Thus—

(i) (*a*) He walked to London.   (*b*) He walked his horse.

(*a*) The eagle flew.   (*b*) The boy flew his kite.

(ii) When the intransitive verb is compounded with a preposition either (i) separable, or (ii) inseparable.

(i) (*a*) He laughed.	(*b*) He laughed-at me.
(ii) (*a*) He came.	(*b*) He overcame the enemy.
(iii) (*a*) He spoke.	(*b*) He bespoke a pair of boots.

Such verbs are sometimes called "Prepositional Verbs."

II. **Transitive** verbs may be used **intransitively**—

(i) With the pronoun **itself** understood :—

(*a*) He broke the dish.	(*b*) The sea breaks on the rocks.
(*a*) She shut the door.	(*b*) The door shut suddenly.
(*a*) They moved the table.	(*b*) The table moved.

(ii) When the verb describes a fact perceived by the senses :—

(*a*) He cut the beef.	(*b*) The beef cuts tough.
(*a*) He sold the books.	(*b*) The books sell well.
(*a*) She smells the rose.	(*b*) The rose smells sweet.

The following is a tabular view of the

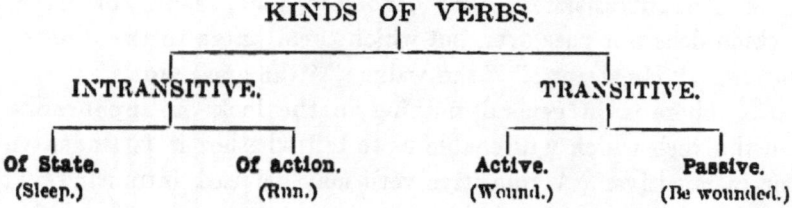

KINDS OF VERBS.

INTRANSITIVE.		TRANSITIVE.	
Of State.	Of action.	Active.	Passive.
(Sleep.)	(Run.)	(Wound.)	(Be wounded.)

THE INFLEXIONS OF VERBS.

6. Verbs are changed or modified for **Voice, Mood, Tense, Number,** and **Person.** These changes are expressed, partly by **inflexion,** and partly by the use of **auxiliary verbs.**

(i) A verb is an **auxiliary verb** (from Lat. *auxilium*, aid) when its own full and real meaning *drops out of sight,* and it aids or helps the verb to which it is attached to express *its* meaning. Thus we say, "He works hard that he *may gain* the prize ; " and here *may* has not its old meaning of *power*, or its present meaning of *permission*. But—

(ii) If we say "He may go," here *may* is not used as an **auxiliary,** but is a **notional** verb, with its full meaning ; and the sentence is = "He has leave to go."

VOICE.

7. Voice is that form of the Verb by which we show whether the **subject** of the statement denotes the **doer** of the action, or the **object** of the action, expressed by the verb.

8. There are two Voices : the **Active Voice,** and the **Passive Voice.**

(i) When a verb is used in the **active voice,**
the **subject** of the sentence stands for
the **doer** of the action.   "He killed the mouse."

(ii) When a verb is in the **passive voice,**
the **subject** of the sentence stands for
the **object** of the action.   "The mouse was killed."

Or we may say that, in the **passive voice**
the **grammatical subject** denotes the **real object.**

(iii) There is in English a kind of **middle voice.**   Thus we can say, "He opened the door" (active); "The door was opened" (passive); "The door opened" (middle).   In the same way we have, "This wood cuts easily ;" "Honey tastes sweet ;" "The book sold well," etc.

9. An Intransitive Verb, as it can have no direct object, cannot be used in the passive voice.   But, as we have seen, we can make an intransitive into a transitive verb by adding a preposition ; and hence we can say :—

ACTIVE.	PASSIVE.
(*a*) They laughed at him.	(*b*) He was laughed-at by them.
(*a*) The general spoke to him.	(*b*) He was spoken-to by the general.

10. In changing a verb in the active voice into the passive, we may make either (i) the **direct** or (ii) the **indirect object** into the **subject** of the passive verb.

ACTIVE.	PASSIVE.
1. They offered her a chair.	(i) A chair was offered her.
	(ii) She was offered a chair.
2. They showed him the house.	(i) The house was shown him.
	(ii) He was shown the house.
3. I promised the boy a coat.	(i) A coat was promised the boy.
	(ii) The boy was promised a coat.

The object after the passive verb is not the real object of that verb, for a passive verb cannot rightly take an object.   It is *left over*, as it were, from the active verb, and is hence sometimes called a **Residuary Object.**

11. The **passive voice** of a verb is formed by using a part of the verb **to be** and the **past participle** of the verb. Thus we say—

ACTIVE.	PASSIVE.	ACTIVE.	PASSIVE.
I beat.	I am beaten.	I have beaten.	I have been beaten.

(i) Some **intransitive** verbs form their perfect tenses by means of the verb *to be* and their past participle, as "I am come ;" "He is gone." But the *meaning* here is quite different. There is no mark of **anything done** to the subject of the verb.

(ii) Shakespeare has the phrases : *is run ; is arrived ; are marched forth ; is entered into ; is stolen away.*

MOOD.

12. The **Mood** of a verb is the **manner** in which the statement made by the verb is presented to the mind. Is a statement made directly? Is a command given? Is a statement subjoined to another? All these are different moods or modes. There are four moods : the **Indicative**; the **Imperative**; the **Subjunctive**; and the **Infinitive**.

(i) **Indicative** comes from the Lat. *indicāre,* to point out.

(ii) **Imperative** comes from the Lat. *imperāre,* to command. Hence also *emperor, empress,* etc. (through French).

(iii) **Subjunctive** comes from Lat. *subjungĕre,* to join on to.

(iv) **Infinitive** comes from Lat. *infinītus,* unlimited ; because the verb in this mood is not limited by *person, number,* etc.

13. The **Indicative Mood** makes a **direct assertion,** or puts a question in a **direct manner.** Thus we say : "John is ill ;" "Is John ill ?"

14. The **Imperative Mood** is the mood of **command, request,** or **entreaty.** Thus we say : "Go !" "Give me the book, please ;" "Do come back !"

(i) The Imperative Mood is the **pure root** of the verb without any inflexion.

(ii) It has in reality only **one person**—the **second.**

15. The **Subjunctive Mood** is that form of the verb which is **used in a sentence** that is **subjoined to a principal**

sentence,—and which does not express a fact directly, but only the **relation** of a fact **to the mind** of the speaker. Most often it expresses both **doubt** and **futurity**. Thus we say : (i) "O that he were here!" (ii) "Love not sleep, lest thou come to poverty." (iii) "Whoever he be, he cannot be a good man."

(i) In the first sentence, the person is *not* here.

(ii) In the second, the person spoken to has *not* come to poverty ; but he may.

(iii) In the third, we do *not* know who the person really is.

(iv) The Subjunctive Mood is rapidly dying out of use in modern English.

16. The **Infinitive Mood** is that form of the verb which **has no reference to any agent,** and is therefore unlimited by person, by number, or by time. It is the verb itself, pure and simple.

(i) The preposition **to** is not an essential part nor a necessary sign of the infinitive. The oldest sign of it was the ending in **an**. After *may, can, shall, will, must, bid, dare, do, let, make, hear, see, feel, need,* the simple infinitive, without **to**, is still used.

(ii) The Infinitive is really a noun, and it may be (*a*) either in the nominative or (*b*) in the obj. case. Thus we have : (*a*) "To err is human ; to forgive, divine ;" and (*b*) "I wish to go."

(iii) In O.E. it was declined like any other noun ; and the dative case ended in **anne**. Then **to** was placed before this dative, to indicate purpose. Thus we find, "The sower went out to sow," when, in O.E. *to sow* was *to sawenne*. This, which is now called the gerundial infinitive, has become very common in English. Thus we have, "I came to see you ;" "A house to let." "To hear him (= on hearing him) talk, you would think he was worth millions."

(iv) We must be careful to distinguish between (*a*) the **pure Infinitive** and (*b*) the **gerundial Infinitive**. Thus we say—
(*a*) I want to see him. (*b*) I went to see him. The latter is the gerundial infinitive—that is, the old dative.
(*c*) The gerundial infinitive is attached (1) to a noun ; and (2) to an adjective. Thus we have such phrases as—
(1) Bread *to eat ;* water *to drink ;* a house *to sell.*
(2) Wonderful *to relate ;* quick *to take offence ;* eager *to go.*

17. A **Gerund** is a **noun** formed from a verb by the addition of **ing**. It may be either (i) a subject ; or (ii) an object ; or

(iii) it may be governed by a preposition. It has two functions : that of a **noun**, and that of a **verb**—that is, it *is* itself a noun, and it *has* the governing power of a verb.

> (i) Reading is pleasant. (ii) I like reading. (iii) He got off by cross-ing the river. In this last sentence, *crossing* is a **noun** in relation to *by*, and a **verb** in relation to *river*.

> *Gerund* comes from the Lat. *gero*, I carry on ; because it *carries on* the power or function of the verb.

> (ii) **The Gerund** must be carefully distinguished from three other kinds of words : (*a*) from the **verbal noun**, which used to end in *ung ;* (*b*) from the **present participle**; and (*c*) from the **infinitive with to.** The following are examples :—

> (*a*) "Forty and six years was this tem-ple in building." Here *building* is a verbal noun.
>
> (*b*) "Dreaming as he went along, he fell into the brook." Here *dreaming* is an adjective agreeing with *he*, and is there-fore a participle.
>
> (*c*) "To write is quite easy, when one has a good pen." Here *to write* is a pres-ent infinitive, and is the nominative to *is*. (It must not be forgotten that the oldest infinitive had no *to*, and that it still exists in this pure form in such lines as "Better *dwell* in the midst of alarms, than *reign* in this horrible place."

> (*a*) "He was punished for robbing the orchard." Here *robbing* is a gerund, be-cause it *is* a noun and also *governs* a noun.
>
> (*b*) "He was tired of dreaming such dreams." Here *dreaming* is a gerund, because it *is* a noun and *governs* a noun.
>
> (*c*) "He comes here to write his letters." Here *to write* is the gerundial infinitive ; it is in the dative case ; and the O.E. form was *to writanne*. Here the *to* has a distinct meaning. This is the so-called "infinitive of purpose ;" but it is a true gerund. In the seventeenth cen-tury, when the sense of the *to* was weak-ened, it took a *for*,—"What went ye out for to see ?"

> (iii) The following three words in *ing* have each a special function :—
> (*a*) He is reading about the *passing* of Arthur (**verbal noun**).
> (*b*) And Arthur, *passing* thence (**participle**), rode to the wood.
> (*c*) This is only good for *passing* the time (**gerund**).

18. A **Participle** is a **verbal adjective.** There are two par-ticiples : the **Present Active** and the **Perfect Passive.** The former (i) has two functions : that of an **adjective** and that of a **verb.** The latter (ii) has only the function of an **adjective.**

> (i) "Hearing the noise, the porter ran to the gate." In this sentence, *hearing* is an **adjective** qualifying *porter*, and a **verb** governing *noise*.

> (ii) Defeated and discouraged, the enemy surrendered.

> ☞ 1. We must be very careful to distinguish between (*a*) the **gerund** in *ing*, and (*b*) the **participle** in *ing*. Thus *running* in a "running stream"

is an adjective, and therefore a participle. In the phrase, "in running along," it is a noun, and therefore a gerund. Milton says—

> " And ever, against eating cares,
> Lap me in soft Lydian airs !"

Here *eating* is an adjective, and means *fretting;* and it is therefore a participle. But if it had meant *cares about eating, eating* would have been a noun, and therefore a gerund. So a *fishing-rod* is not a *rod that fishes; a frying-pan* is not a *pan that fries; a walking-stick* is not a *stick that walks.* The rod is a *rod for fishing;* the pan, a *pan for frying;* the stick, a *stick for walking;* and therefore *fishing, frying,* and *walking* are all gerunds.

2. The word *participle* comes from Lat. *participāre,* to partake of. The participle *partakes of* the nature of the verb. (Hence also *participate.*)

TENSE.

19. Tense is the form which the verb takes to indicate **time.** There are, in human life, three times : past, present, and future. Hence there are in a verb three **chief tenses : Past, Present,** and **Future.** These may be represented on a straight line :—

TENSES.

Past.	Present.	Future.
I wrote.	I write.	I shall write.

(i) The word *tense* comes to us from the French *temps,* which is from the Lat. *tempus,* time. Hence also *temporal, temporary,* etc. (The modern French word is *temps;* the old French word was *tens.*)

20. The tenses of an English verb give not only the **time** of an action or event, but also the **state** or **condition** of that action or event. This state may be **complete** or **incomplete,** or **neither**—that is, it is left **indefinite.** These states are oftener called **perfect, imperfect,** and **indefinite.** The condition, then, of an action as expressed by a verb, or the **condition of the tense** of a verb, may be of three kinds. It may be—

(i) Complete or Perfect, as   Written.
(ii) Incomplete or Imperfect, as   Writing.
(iii) Indefinite, as   Write.

We now have therefore—

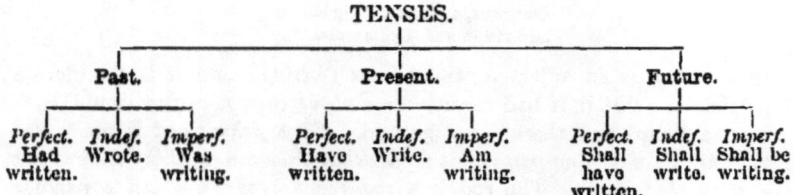

TENSES.

Past.			Present.			Future.		
Perfect.	*Indef.*	*Imperf.*	*Perfect.*	*Indef.*	*Imperf.*	*Perfect.*	*Indef.*	*Imperf.*
Had written.	Wrote.	Was writing.	Have written.	Write.	Am writing.	Shall have written.	Shall write.	Shall be writing.

(i) The only tense in our language that is formed by **inflexion** is the **past indefinite.** All the others are formed by the aid of auxiliaries.

    (*a*) The imperfect tenses are formed by **be + the imperfect participle.**

    (*b*) The perfect tenses are formed by **have + the perfect participle.**

(ii) Besides *had written, have written,* and *will have written,* we can say *had been writing, have been writing,* and *will have been writing.* These are sometimes called **Past Perfect (or Pluperfect) Continuous, Perfect Continuous,** and **Future Perfect Continuous.**

(iii) "I **do** write," "I **did** write," are called **Emphatic forms.**

NUMBER.

21. Verbs are modified for **Number.** There are in verbs **two numbers**: (i) the **Singular** and (ii) the **Plural.**

    (i) We say, "He writes" (with the ending **s**).

    (ii) We say, "They write" (with no inflectional ending at all).

PERSON.

22. Verbs are modified for **Person**—that is, the form of the verb is changed to suit (i) the **first person,** (ii) the **second person,** or (iii) the **third person.**

    (i) "I write."   (ii) "Thou writest."   (iii) "He writes."

CONJUGATION.

23. Conjugation is the name given to the sum-total of all the inflexions and combinations of the parts of a verb.

    The word *conjugate* comes from the Lat. *conjugare,* to bind together.

24. There are two conjugations in English—the **Strong** and the **Weak**. Hence we have: (i) verbs of the **Strong Conjugation**, and (ii) verbs of the **Weak Conjugation**, which are more usually called **Strong Verbs** and **Weak Verbs**. These verbs are distinguished from each other by their way of **forming their past tenses.**

25. The past tense of any verb determines to which of these classes it belongs ; and that by a twofold test—one positive and one negative.

26. (i) The positive test for the past of a **Strong Verb** is that it **changes the vowel of the present.** (ii) The negative test is that it **never adds anything** to the present to make its past tense.

(i) Thus we say **write, wrote,** and change the vowel.

(ii) But in **wrote** there is nothing added to **write.**

27. (i) The positive test for the past tense of a **Weak Verb** is that **d or t is added** to the present. (ii) The negative test is that the **root-vowel of the present** is generally **not changed.**

(i) There are some exceptions to this latter statement. Thus **tell, told; buy, bought; sell, sold,** are **weak** verbs. The change in the vowel does not spring from the same cause as the change in strong verbs. Hence—

(ii) It is as well to keep **entirely** to the **positive** test in the case of weak verbs. However "**strong**" or "**irregular**" may seem to be the verbs **teach, taught; seek, sought; say, said,** we *know* that they are **weak,** because they add a **d** or a **t** for the past tense.

(iii) In many weak verbs there seems to be both a change of vowel and also an absence of any addition. Hence they look *very like* strong verbs. In fact, the **long** vowel of the present is made **short** in the past. Thus we find **meet, met; feed, fed.** But these verbs are not strong. The old past was **mettë** and **feddë** ; and all that has happened is that they have lost the old inflexions **te** and **de.** It was owing to the addition of another syllable that the original long vowel of the verb was shortened. Compare *nation, national ; vain, vanity.*

(iv) The past or passive participle of strong verbs had the suffix **en** and the prefix **ge.** The suffix has now disappeared from many strong verbs, and the prefix from all. But *ge*, which in Chaucer's time had been refined into a *y* (as in *ycomen, yronnen*), is retained still in that form in the one word *yclept.* Milton's use of it in *star-y-pointing* is a mistake.

28. The following is an

ALPHABETICAL LIST OF STRONG VERBS.

(All strong verbs except those which have a *prefix* are monosyllabic.)

The forms in italics are *weak*.

Pres.	Past.	Pass. Part.	Pres.	Past.	Pass. Part.
Abide	abode	abode.	Fly	flew	flown.
Arise	arose	arisen.	Forbear	forbore	forborne.
Awake	awoke	awoke	Forget	forgot	forgotten.
	(*awaked*)	(*awaked*).	Forsake	forsook	forsaken.
Bear	bore	born.	Freeze	froze	frozen.
(bring forth)			Get	got	got, gotten.
Bear	bore	borne.	Give	gave	given.
(carry)			Go	*went*	gone.
Beat	beat	beaten.	Grind	ground	ground.
Begin	began	begun.	Grow	grew	grown.
Behold	beheld	beheld (be-	Hang	hung	hung,
		holden).		(*hanged*)	*hanged.*
Bid	bade, bid	bidden, bid.	Hold	held	held.
Bind	bound	bound.	Know	knew	known.
Bite	bit	bitten, bit.	Lie	lay	lain.
Blow	blew	blown.	Ride	rode	ridden.
Break	broke	broken.	Ring	rang	rung.
Burst	burst	burst.	Rise	rose	risen.
Chide	chid	chidden,	Run	ran	run.
		chid.	See	saw	seen.
Choose	chose	chosen.	Seethe	sod(*seethed*)	sodden.
Cleave	clove	cloven.	Shake	shook	shaken.
(split)			Shine	shone	shone.
Climb	clomb	(*climbed*).	Shoot	shot	shot.
Cling	clung	clung.	Shrink	shrank	shrunk.
Come	came	come.	Sing	sang	sung.
Crow	crew	crown	Sink	sank	sunk,
		(*crowed*).			sunken.
Dig	dug	dug.	Sit	sat	sat.
Do	did	done.	Slay	slew	slain.
Draw	drew	drawn.	Slide	slid	slid.
Drink	drank	drunk,	Sling	slung	slung.
		drunken.	Slink	slunk	slunk.
Drive	drove	driven.	Smite	smote	smitten.
Eat	ate	eaten.	Speak	spoke	spoken.
Fall	fell	fallen.	Spin	spun	spun.
Fight	fought	fought.	Spring	sprung	sprung.
Find	found	found.	Stand	stood	stood.
Fling	flung	flung.	Stave	stove	staved.

Pres.	Past.	Pass. Part.	Pres.	Past.	Pass. Part.
Steal	stole	stolen.	Thrive	throve	thriven
Stick	stuck,[1]	stuck.		(thrived)	(thrived).
Sting	stung	stung.	Throw	threw	thrown.
Stink	stank	stunk.	Tread	trod	trodden,
Stride	strode	stridden.			trod.
Strike	struck	struck.	Wake	woke	(waked).
String	strung	strung.		(waked)	
Strive	strove	striven.	Wear	wore	worn.
Swear	swore	sworn.	Weave	wove	woven.
Swim	swam	swum.	Win	won	won.
Swing	swung	swung.	Wind	wound	wound.
Take	took	taken.	Wring	wrung	wrung.
Tear	tore	torn.	Write	wrote	written.

It is well for the young learner to examine the above verbs closely, and to make a classification of them for his own use. The following are a few suggestions towards this task :—

> (i) Collect verbs with vowels a, e, a ; *like* fall, fell, fallen.
> (ii) Verbs with o, e, o ; *like* throw, threw, thrown.
> (iii) Verbs with i, a, u ; *like* begin, began, begun.
> (iv) Verbs with i, u, u ; *like* fling, flung, flung.
> (v) Verbs with i, ou, ou ; *like* find, found, found.
> (vi) Verbs with ea, o, o ; *like* break, broke, broken.
> (vii) Verbs with i, a, i ; *like* give, gave, given.
> (viii) Verbs with a, o or oo, a ; *like* shake, shook, shaken.
> (ix) Verbs with i (long), o, i (short) ; *like* drive, drove, driven.
> (x) Verbs with ee or oo, o, o ; *like* freeze, froze, frozen; *or* choose, chose, chosen.

29. Weak Verbs are of two kinds : (i) **Irregular Weak** ; and (ii) **Regular Weak**. The Irregular Weak are such verbs as **tell, told; buy, bought.** The Regular Weak are such verbs as **attend, attended; obey, obeyed.**

> (i) The Irregular Weak verbs are, with very few exceptions, mono-syllables, and are almost all of purely English origin.

> (ii) The Regular Weak verbs are entirely of Latin or of French origin. Since the language lost the power of changing the root-vowel of a verb, every verb received into our tongue from another language has been placed in the Regular Weak conjugation.

---

[1] The past tenses of *dig* and *stick* were formerly *weak ;* so were the passive participles of *hide, rot, show, strew, saw.*

(iii) The **ed** or **d** is a shortened form of **did**. Thus, **I loved** is = I love did.

30. Irregular Weak verbs are themselves divided into two classes : (i) those which keep their **ed, d,** or **t** in the past tense ; (ii) those which have lost the **d** or **t**. Thus we find (i) **sleep, slept; teach, taught.** Among (ii) we find **feed, fed,** which was once **fed-dë; set, set,** which was once **set-të.**

It is of the greatest importance to attend to the following changes :—

(i) A sharp consonant follows a sharp, and a flat a flat. Thus **p** in *sleep* is sharp, and therefore we cannot say *sleeped*. We must take the sharp form of **d**, which is **t**, and say *slept*. So also **felt, burnt, dreamt,** etc.

(ii) Some verbs **shorten** their vowel. Thus we have **hear, heard; flee, fled; sleep, slept,** etc.

(iii) Some verbs have different vowels in the present and past: as **tell, told; buy, bought; teach, taught; work, wrought.** But it is not the past tense, it is the **present that has changed.** Thus the o in *told* represents the **a** in *tale*, etc.

(iv) Some have dropped an internal letter. Thus **made** is = **maked; paid = payed; had = haved.**

(v) Some verbs change the **d** of the present into a **t** in the past. Thus we have **build, built; send, sent.**

(vi) A large class have the three parts—present, past, and passive participle—exactly alike. Such are **rid, set,** etc.

The following is an

ALPHABETICAL LIST OF IRREGULAR WEAK VERBS.
CLASS I.

Pres.	Past.	Pass. Part.	Pres.	Past.	Pass. Part.
Bereave	bereft	bereft.	Dwell	dwelt	dwelt.
Beseech	besought	besought.	Feel	felt	felt.
Bring	brought	brought.	Flee	fled	fled.
Burn	burnt	burnt.	Grave	graved	graven.
Buy	bought	bought.	Have	had	had.
Catch	caught	caught.	Hew	hewed	hewn.
Cleave	cleft	cleft.	Hide	hid	hidden.
(split)			Keep	kept	kept.
Creep	crept	crept.	Kneel	knelt	knelt.
Deal	dealt	dealt.	Lay	laid	laid.
Dream	dreamt	dreamt.	Lean	leant	leant.

Pres.	Past.	Pass Part.	Pres.	Past.	Pass. Part.
Learn	learnt	learnt.	Shear	sheared	shorn.
Leap	leapt	leapt.	Shoe	shod	shod.
Leave	left	left.	Show	showed	shown.
Lose	lost	lost.	Sleep	slept	slept.
Make	made	made.	Sow	sowed	sown.
Mean	meant	meant.	Spell	spelt	spelt.
Pay	paid	paid.	Spill	spilt	spilt.
Pen	pent	pent.	Strew	strewed	strewn.
	(penned)		Sweep	swept	swept.
Rap (to	rapt	rapt.	Swell	swelled	swollen.
transport)			Teach	taught	taught.
Rive	rived	riven.	Tell	told	told.
Rot	rotted	rotten.[1]	Think	thought	thought.
Say	said	said.	Tie	tied	tight.[1]
Saw	sawed	sawn.	Weep	wept	wept.
Seek	sought	sought.	Work	wrought	wrought.[1]
Sell	sold	sold.		worked	worked.
Shave	shaved	shaven.			

[1] *Rotten, tight,* and *wrought* are now used as adjectives, and not as passive participles ; cp. *wrought* iron, a *tight* knot, *rotten* wood.

CLASS II.

Pres.	Past.	Pass. Part.	Pres.	Past.	Pass. Part.
Bend	bent	bent.	Meet	met	met.
Bleed	bled	bled.	Put	put	put.
Blend	blent	blent.	Read	read	read.
Breed	bred	bred.	Rend	rent	rent.
Build	built	built.	Rid	rid	rid.
Cast	cast	cast.	Send	sent	sent.
Clothe	clad	clad	Set	set	set.
	(clothed)	(clothed).	Shed	shed	shed.
Cost	cost	cost.	Shred	shred	shred.
Cut	cut	cut.	Shut	shut	shut.
Feed	fed	fed.	Slit	slit	slit.
Gild	gilt	gilt (gilded).	Speed	sped	sped.
	(gilded)		Spend	spent	spent.
Gird	girt	girt.	Spit	spit	spit.
Hear	heard	heard.	Split	split	split.
Hit	hit	hit.	Spread	spread	spread.
Hurt	hurt	hurt.	Sweat	sweat	sweat.
Knit	knit	knit.	Thrust	thrust	thrust.
Lead	led	led.	Wend	wended	wended.
Lend	lent	lent.		or went	
Let	let	let.	Wet	wet	wet.
Light	lit (lighted)	lit (lighted).			

31. Before we can learn the **full conjugation** of a verb, we must acquaint ourselves with all the parts of the **auxiliary verbs—Shall** and **Will; Have** and **Be.**

(i) If **be** means existence merely (as in the sentence GOD IS), it is called a **notional verb**; if it is used in the formation of the passive voice, it is an **auxiliary verb.** In the same way, **have** is a **notional** verb when it means **to possess**, as in the sentence, "I have a shilling."

32. The following are the parts of the verb **Shall** :—

INDICATIVE MOOD.

Present Tense.

Singular.	*Plural.*
1. I shall.	1. We shall.
2. Thou shal-t.	2. You shall.
3. He shall.	3. They shall.

Past Tense.

Singular.	*Plural.*
1. I shoul-*d*.	1. We shoul-*d*.
2. Thou shoul-*d*-st	2. You shoul-*d*.
3. He shoul-*d*.	3. They shoul-*d*.

IMP. MOOD ——.   INF. MOOD ——.   PARTICIPLES ——.

(Should comes from an old dialectic form *shol.*)

33. The following are the parts of the verb **Will** :—

INDICATIVE MOOD.

Present Tense.

Singular.	*Plural.*
1. I will.	1. We will.
2. Thou wil-t.	2. You will.
3. He will.	3. They will.

Past Tense.

Singular.	*Plural.*
1. I would-*d*.	1. We would-*d*.
2. Thou would-*d*-st.	2. You woul-*d*.
3. He woul-*d*.	3. They woul-*d*.

IMP. MOOD ——.   INF. MOOD ——.   PARTICIPLES ——.

(i) **Shall** and **will** are used as **Tense-auxiliaries.** As a tense-auxiliary, **shall** is used only in the **first person.** Thus we say, I **shall** write ; thou **wilt** write ; he **will** write—when we speak merely of **future time.**

(ii) **Shan't** is = shall not. **Won't** is = *wol* not, *wol* being an older form of *will*. We find *wol* also in *wolde*—an old spelling of *would*.

(iii) **Shall** in the 1st person expresses simple **futurity**; in the 2d and 3d persons, **authority**. **Will** in the 1st person expresses **determination**; in the 2d and 3d, only **futurity**.

34. The following are the parts of the verb **Have** :—

INDICATIVE MOOD.

Present Indefinite Tense.

Singular.	*Plural.*
1. I have.	1. We have.
2. Thou ha-st.	2. You have.
3. He ha-s.	3. They have.

Present Perfect Tense.

Singular.	*Plural.*
1. I have had.	1. We have had.
2. Thou hast had.	2. You have had.
3. He has had.	3. They have had.

(i) **Hast** = **havest**. Compare *e'en* and *even*. (ii) **Had** = **haved**.

Past Indefinite Tense.

Singular.	*Plural.*
1. I had.	1. We had.
2. Thou had-st.	2. You had.
3. He had.	3 They had.

Past Perfect (or Pluperfect) Tense.

Singular.	*Plural.*
1. I had had.	1. We had had.
2. Thou hadst had.	2. You had had.
3. He had had.	3. They had had.

Future Indefinite Tense.

Singular.	*Plural.*
1. I shall have.	1. We shall have.
2. Thou wilt have.	2. You will have.
3. He will have.	3. They will have.

Future Perfect Tense.

Singular.	*Plural.*
1. I shall have had.	1. We shall have had.
2. Thou wilt have had.	2. You will have had.
3. He will have had.	3. They will have had.

D

SUBJUNCTIVE MOOD.
Present Indefinite Tense.

Singular.	Plural.
1. I have.	1. We have.
2. Thou have.	2. You have.
3. He have.	3. They have.

Present Perfect Tense.

Singular.	Plural.
1. I have had.	1. We have had.
2. Thou have had.	2. You have had.
3. He have had.	3. They have had.

Past Indefinite Tense.

Same in form as in the Indicative; but with no inflexion in the **second** person.

Past Perfect Tense.

Same in form as in the Indicative; but with no inflexion in the **second** person.

Past Indefinite Tense.

Singular.	Plural.
1. I had.	1. We had.
2. Thou had.	2. You had.
3. He had.	3. They had.

Past Perfect (Pluperfect) Tense.

Singular.	Plural.
1. I had had.	1. We had had.
2. Thou had had.	2. You had had.
3. He had had.	3. They had had.

IMPERATIVE MOOD.—*Singular:* Have! *Plural:* Have!

INFINITIVE MOOD.—**Present Indefinite:** (To) have. **Perfect:** (To) have had.

PARTICIPLES.—**Imperfect:** Having. **Past (or Passive):** Had.

Compound Perfect (*Active*): Having had.

35. The following are the parts of the verb **Be** :—

INDICATIVE MOOD.
Present Indefinite Tense.

Singular.	Plural.
1. I a-m.	1. We are.
2. Thou ar-t.	2. You are.
3. He is.	3. They are.

Present Perfect Tense.

Singular.	*Plural.*
1. I have been.	1. We have been.
2. Thou hast been.	2. You have been.
3. He has been.	3. They have been.

Past Indefinite Tense.

Singular.	*Plural.*
1. I was.	1. We were.
2. Thou wast or wert.	2. You were.
3. He was.	3. They were.

Past Perfect (Pluperfect) Tense.

Singular.	*Plural.*
1. I had been.	1. We had been.
2. Thou hadst been.	2. You had been.
3. He had been.	3. They had been.

Future Indefinite Tense.
I shall be, etc.

Future Perfect Tense.
I shall have been, etc.

SUBJUNCTIVE MOOD.

Present Indefinite Tense.

Singular.	*Plural.*
1. I be.	1. We be.
2. Thou be.	2. You be.
3. He be.	3. They be.

Present Perfect Tense.

Singular.	*Plural.*
1. I have been.	1. We have been.
2. Thou have been.	2. You have been.
3. He have been.	3. They have been.

Past Indefinite Tense.

Singular.	*Plural.*
1. I were.	1. We were.
2. Thou wert.	2. You were.
3. He were.	3. They were.

Past Perfect (Pluperfect) Tense.

Singular.	*Plural.*
1. I had been.	1. We had been.
2. Thou had been.	2. You had been.
3. He had been.	3. They had been.

Past Indefinite (Compound Form).

Singular.	*Plural.*
1. I should be.	1. We should be.
2. Thou should be.	2. You should be.
3. He should be.	3. They should be.

Future Perfect (Compound Form).

Singular.	*Plural.*
1. I should have been.	1. We should have been.
2. Thou should have been	2. You should have been.
3. He should have been.	3. They should have been.

IMPERATIVE MOOD.—*Singular :* Be! *Plural :* Be!

INFINITIVE MOOD.—**Present Indefinite :** (To) be. **Present Perfect :** (To) have been.

PARTICIPLES.—**Present :** Being. **Past :** Been. **Compound :** Having been.

We find the short simple form BE! in Coleridge's line—
" Be, rather than be called, a child of God ! "

(i) It is plain from the above that the verb Be is made up of fragments of three different verbs. As when, in a battle, several companies of a regiment have been severely cut up, and the fragments of those that came out safely are afterwards formed into one company, so has it been with the verb be. Hence the verb ought to be printed thus :—

Am   ———   ———

———   was   ———

———   ———   been.

(ii) **Am** is a different verb from **was** and **been.** The m in am is the same as the m in me, and marks the first person. The t in art is the same as the th in thou, and marks the second person. Compare wil-t and shal-t. Is has lost the suffix th. The Germans retain this, and say ist. Are is not the O.E. plural, which was sind or sindon. The word are was introduced by the Danes. [The Danish word to this day is er, which we have learned to pronounce ar, as we do the er in clerk and Derby.]

(iii) **Was** is the past tense of the old verb **wesan,** to be. In some of the dialects of England it appears as war—the German form.

(iv) **Be** is a verb without present or past tense.

(v) (a) **Be** is a notional or principal verb when it means to exist, as " God is." (b) It is also a principal verb when it is used as a joiner or copula, as in the sentence, " John is a teacher," where the is enables us to connect John and teacher in the mind. In such instances it is called a **Copulative Verb** or **Copula.**

36. The Auxiliary Verbs have different functions.

(i) The verb **Be** is a **Voice** (and sometimes a **Tense**) **Auxiliary.** It enables us to turn the active into the passive voice, and to form the imperfect tenses.

(ii) **May, should, and let are Mood Auxiliaries.** *May* and *should* help us to make the compound subjunctive tenses ; and *let* is employed in the Imperative Mood to form a kind of third person. Thus *Let him go* is = *Go he !*

(iii) **Have, Shall, and Will, are Tense Auxiliaries.** With the aid of *have*, we form the **perfect tenses**; with the help of *shall* and *will*, the **future tenses.**

(iv) **Can** is a defective verb with only one mood, the **Indicative,** and two tenses, the Present and the Past.

> **Present.** I can ; thou canst, etc.
> **Past.** I could ; thou couldst, etc.

Could is a weak form. The *l* has no right there : it has crept in from a false analogy with *should* and *would*. Chaucer always writes *coude* or *couthe*.

(v) **May** is also defective, having only the Indicative Mood and the Present and Past Tenses.

> **Present.** I may ; thou mayest, etc.
> **Past.** I might ; thou mightest, etc.

The O.E. word for **may** was **maegan.** The **g** is still preserved in the **gh** of the past tense. The guttural sound indicated by **g** or **gh** has vanished from both.

(vi) **Must** is the past tense of an old verb **motan,** to be able.

> It is used only in the Indicative Mood, sometimes in the Present, sometimes in the Past Tense ; but the form is the same for both tenses.
> It expresses the idea of *necessity*.

37. The following is the full conjugation of a verb :—

ACTIVE VOICE.

INDICATIVE MOOD.

I. Present Indefinite Tense.
I strike.

Present Imperfect Tense.
I am striking.

Present Perfect Tense.
I have struck.

Present Perfect Continuous.
I have been striking.

II. Past Indefinite Tense.
I struck.

Past Imperfect Tense.
I was striking.

Past Perfect (or Pluperfect) Tense.
I had struck.

Past Perfect (or Pluperfect) Continuous.
I had been striking.

III. Future Indefinite Tense.
I shall strike.

Future Imperfect Tense.
I shall be striking.

Future Perfect Tense.
I shall have struck.

Future Perfect Continuous.
I shall have been striking.

SUBJUNCTIVE MOOD.

I. Present Indefinite Tense.
(If) I, thou, he strike.

Present Imperfect Tense.
(If) I, thou, he be striking.

Present Perfect Tense.
(If) I, thou, he have struck.

Present Perfect Continuous.
(If) I, thou, he have been striking.

II. Past Indefinite Tense.
(If) I, thou, he struck.

Past Imperfect Tense.
(If) I, thou, he were striking.

Past Perfect (or Pluperfect) Tense.
(If) I, thou, he had struck.

Past Perfect (or Pluperfect) Continuous.
(If) I, thou, he had been striking.

III. Future Indefinite Tense.
(If) I, thou, he should strike.

Future Imperfect Tense.
(If) I, thou, he should be striking.

Future Perfect Tense.
(If) I, thou, he should have struck.

Future Perfect Continuous.
(If) I, thou, he should have been striking.

(The **Future Subjunctive**, when not preceded by a Conjunction, is sometimes called the **Conditional Mood.** "I *should strike* him if he were to hurt the child.")

IMPERATIVE MOOD.

I. Present Tense.

Singular. 2. Strike (thou)!   *Plural.* 2. Strike (ye)!

II. Past Tense.
(None.)

III. Future Tense.
2. Thou shalt strike.   2. You shall strike.

INFINITIVE MOOD.

1. **Present Indefinite,** . . (To) strike.
2. **Present Imperfect,** . . (To) be striking.
3. **Present Perfect,** . . . (To) have struck.
4. **Present Perfect Continuous,** (To) have been striking.
5. **Future Indefinite,** . . (To) be about to strike.

PARTICIPLES.

1. **Indefinite** and **Imperfect,** . Striking.
2. **Present Perfect,** . . . . Having struck.
3. **Perfect Continuous,** . . Having been striking.
4. **Future,** . . . . . Going *or* about to strike.

GERUNDS.

1. Striking.   2. To strike.

PASSIVE VOICE.

INDICATIVE MOOD.

I. Present Indefinite Tense.
I am struck.

Present Imperfect Tense.
I am being struck.

Present Perfect Tense.
I have been struck.

Present Continuous.
I am being struck.

II. Past Indefinite Tense.
I was struck.

Past Imperfect Tense.
I was being struck.

Past Perfect Tense.
I had been struck.

Past Continuous.
I was being struck.

III. Future Indefinite Tense.
I shall be struck.

Future Imperfect Tense.
(None.)

Future Perfect Tense.
I shall have been struck.

Future Continuous.
(None.)

SUBJUNCTIVE MOOD.

I. Present Indefinite Tense.

(If) I, thou, he be struck.

Present Imperfect Tense.

(None.)

Present Perfect Tense.

(If) I, thou, he have been struck.

Present Perfect Continuous.

(None.)

II. Past Indefinite Tense.

(If) I, thou, he were struck.

Past Imperfect Tense.

(If) I, thou, he were being struck.

Past Perfect Tense.

(If) I had been struck.

Past Perfect Continuous.

(None.)

III. Future Indefinite Tense.

(If) I, thou, he should be struck.

Future Imperfect Tense.

(None.)

Future Perfect Tense.

(If) I, thou, he should have been struck.

Future Perfect Continuous.

(None.)

(This tense, when used without a preceding conjunction, is sometimes called the **Conditional Mood.** "I *should be struck* were I to go there.")

IMPERATIVE MOOD.

I. Present Tense.

Singular. 2. Be struck !   *Plural.* 2. Be struck !

II. Past Tense.

(None.)

III. Future Tense.

Singular.   *Plural.*

2. Thou shalt be struck.   2. You shall be struck.

INFINITIVE MOOD.

1. **Indefinite,** .   .   .   (To) be struck.
2. **Imperfect,** .   .   .   (None.)
3. **Present Perfect,** .   .   (To) have been struck.

PARTICIPLES.

1. **Indefinite,** .   .   .   Struck.
2. **Imperfect,** .   .   .   Being struck.
3. **Present Perfect,** .   .   Having been struck.
4. **Future,** .   .   .   Going *or* about to be struck.

GERUNDS.

(None.)

ADVERBS.

1. An **Adverb** is a word which goes with a **verb**, with an **adjective**, or with **another adverb**, to modify its meaning :—

(i) He writes badly. Here **badly** modifies the verb **writes.**

(ii) The weather is very hot. Here **very** modifies the adjective **hot.**

(iii) She writes very rapidly. Here **rapidly** modifies **writes,** and **very, rapidly.**

THE CLASSIFICATION OF ADVERBS.

2. Adverbs—so far as their **function** is concerned—are of two kinds : (i) **Simple Adverbs** and (ii) **Conjunctive Adverbs.** (i) A **Simple Adverb** merely modifies the word it goes with. A **Conjunctive Adverb** has two functions: (*a*) it **modifies,** and (*b*) **joins** one sentence with another. Thus, if I say " He came when he was ready," the adverb **when** not only **modifies** the verb **came,** and shows the time of his coming, but it joins together the two sentences " He came " and " he was ready."

3. Adverbs—so far as their **meaning** is concerned—are of several kinds. There are **Adverbs**: (i) **of Time,** (ii) **of Place,** (iii) **of Number,** (iv) **of Manner,** (v) **of Degree,** (vi) **of Assertion,** and (vii) **of Reasoning** :—

(i) **Of Time** : Now, then ; to-day, to-morrow ; by-and-by, etc.

(ii) **Of Place** : Here, there ; hither, thither ; hence, thence, etc.

(iii) **Of Number** : Once, twice, thrice ; singly, two by two, etc.

(iv) **Of Manner** : Well, ill ; slowly, quickly ; better, worse, etc.

(v) **Of Degree** : Very, little ; almost, quite ; all, half, etc.

(vi) **Of Assertion** : Nay, yea ; no, aye ; yes, etc.

(vii) **Of Reasoning** : Therefore, wherefore ; thus ; consequently.

THE COMPARISON OF ADVERBS.

4. Adverbs, like adjectives, admit of **degrees of comparison.** Thus we can say, John works hard ; Tom works harder ; but William works hardest of all.

5. The following are examples of

Positive.	Comparative.	Superlative.
Ill (*or* Badly)	worse	worst.
Well	better	best.
Much	more	most.
Little	less	least.
Nigh (*or* Near)	nearer	next.
Forth	further	furthest.
Far	farther	farthest.
Late	later	last.
	latter	latest.
(Rathe)	rather.	————

(i) **Worse** comes from A.S **weors**, bad.   Shakespeare has *worser*.

(ii) **Much** is an adverb in the phrase *much better*.

(iii) **Little** is an adverb in the phrase *little inclined*.

(iv) **Next** = nighest ; and so we had also **hext** = highest.   **Near** is really the comparative of **nigh.**

(v) **Farrer** would be the proper comparative.   Chaucer has **farrë**, and this is still found in Yorkshire.   The **th** in **farther** comes from a false analogy with **forth, further, furthest.**

(vi) **Late** is an adverb in the phrase *He arrived late.*

(vii) "Till **rathe** she rose, half-cheated in the thought."—Tennyson ('Lancelot and Elaine').

CONNECTIVES.

1. There is, in grammar, a class of words which may be called **joining words** or **connectives.**   They are of two classes :
(i) those which **join nouns** or **pronouns** to some other word ;
and (ii) those which **join sentences.**   The first class are called **Prepositions** ; the second **Conjunctions.**

PREPOSITIONS.

2. A **Preposition** is a word which **connects** a **noun** or pronoun with a **verb**, an **adjective**, or another **noun** or **pronoun.** (It thus shows the relation between things, or between a thing and an action, etc.)

(i) He **stood on** the **table.**   Here **on** joins a **verb** and a **noun.**

(ii) Mary is **fond of music.** Here **of** joins an **adjective** and a **noun.**

(iii) The **man at the door** is waiting. Here **at** joins **two nouns.**

The word **preposition** comes from the Lat. *præ*, before, and *positus*, placed. We have similar compounds in **composition** and **deposition.**

3. The noun or pronoun which follows the preposition is in the **objective case,** and is said to be **governed** by the preposition.

(i) But the preposition may come at the end of the sentence. Thus we can say, "This is the house we were looking **at.**" But **at** still governs **which** (understood) in the objective. We can also say, "Whom were you talking **to** ? "

4. Prepositions are divided into two classes : (i) **simple ;** and (ii) **compound.**

(i) The following are simple prepositions : *at, by, for, in, of, off, on, out, to, with, up.*

(ii) The compound prepositions are formed in several ways :—

(a) By adding a **comparative suffix** to an adverb : *after, over, under.*

(b) By prefixing a **preposition** to an adverb : *above, about, before, behind, beneath, but* (= be-out), *throughout, within,* etc.

(c) By prefixing a **preposition** to a noun : *aboard, across, around, among, beside, outside,* etc.

(d) By prefixing an adverb or adverbial particle to a **preposition** : *into, upon, until,* etc.

(iii) The preposition *but* is to be carefully distinguished from the conjunction *but.* "All were there **but** him." Here *but* is a preposition. "We waited an hour ; **but** he did not come." Here *but* is a conjunction. **But,** the preposition, was in O.E. *be-titan,* and meant on *the outside of,* and then *without :* **but,** the conjunction, was in O.E. *bot.* The old proverb, "Touch not the cat but a glove," means "without a glove."

(iv) **Down** was *adown = of down = off the down or hill.*

(v) **Among** was = *on gemong,* in the crowd.

(vi) There are several compound prepositions made up of separate words : *instead of, on account of, in spite of,* etc.

(vii) Some participles are used as prepositions : *notwithstanding, concerning, respecting.* The prepositions *except* and *save* may be regarded as imperatives.

5. The same words are used sometimes as adverbs, and sometimes as prepositions. We distinguish these words by their **function.** They can also be used as **nouns** or as **adjectives.**

(i) Thus we find the following words used either as

Adverbs	or as	Prepositions.
(1) Stand up !		(1) The boy ran up the hill.
(2) Come on !		(2) The book lies on the table.
(3) Be off !		(3) Get off the chair.
(4) He walked quickly past.		(4) He walked past the church.

(ii) Adverbs are sometimes used as **nouns**, as in the sentences, "I have met him before **now**." "He is dead since **then**."

(iii) In the following we find adverbs used as **adjectives**: "thine **often** infirmities ;" "the **then** king," etc.

(iv) A phrase sometimes does duty as an adverb, as in "from **beyond the sea** ; " "from **over the mountains**," etc.

CONJUNCTIONS.

6. A **Conjunction** is a word that **joins sentences** together.

(i) The word **and**, besides joining sentences, possesses the additional power of joining nouns or other words. Thus we say, "John **and** Jane are a happy pair ;" "Two **and** three are five."

7. Conjunctions are of two kinds : (i) **Co-ordinative**; and (ii) **Subordinative**.

(i) **Co-ordinative Conjunctions** are those which connect co-ordinate sentences and clauses—that is, sentences neither of which is dependent on the other. The following is a list : *And, both, but, either—or, neither —nor.*

(ii) **Subordinative Conjunctions** are those which connect subordinate sentences with the principal sentence to which they are subordinate. The **type** of a subordinative conjunction is **that**, which is really the demonstrative pronoun. "I know **that** he has gone to London " is = " He has gone to London : I know **that**."

(iii) The following is a list of subordinative conjunctions : *After, before ; ere, till ; while, since ; lest ; because, as ; for ; if ; unless ; though ; whether—or ; than.*

INTERJECTIONS.

1. **Interjections** are words which have **no meaning** in themselves, but which give **sudden expression** to an emotion of the mind. They are no real part of language ; they do not enter into the build or organism of a sentence. They have **no grammatical relation** to any word in a sentence, and are there-

fore not, strictly speaking, "parts of speech." Thus we say, **Oh !
Ah ! Alas !** and so on ; but the sentences we employ would be
just as complete—**in sense**—without them. They are extra-
grammatical utterances.

(i) The word *interjection* comes from the Lat. *inter*, between, and
jactus, thrown.

(ii) Sometimes **words with a meaning** are used as interjections. Thus
we say, **Welcome !** for "You are well come." **Good-bye !** for *God be with
you !* The interjection "Now then !" consists of two words, each of
which has a meaning ; but when employed interjectionally, the compound
meaning is very different from the meaning of either.

(iii) In written and printed language, interjections are followed by the
mark (!) of admiration or exclamation.

WORDS KNOWN BY THEIR FUNCTIONS, AND NOT BY THEIR INFLEXIONS.

1. The Oldest English.—When our language first came over
to this island, in the fifth century, our words possessed a large
number of inflexions ; and a verb could be known from a noun,
and an adjective from either, by the mere **look** of it. Verbs
had one kind of inflexion, nouns another, adjectives a third ;
and it was almost impossible to confuse them. Thus, in O.E.
(or Anglo-Saxon) *thunder*, the verb, was *thunrian*—with the
ending *an ;* but the noun was *thunor*, without any ending at
all. Then, in course of time, for many and various reasons,
the English language began to lose its inflexions ; and they
dropped off very rapidly between the 11th and the 15th centuries, till, nowadays, we possess very few indeed.

2. Freedom given by absence of Inflexions.—In the 16th
century, when Shakespeare began to write, there were very
few inflexions ; the language began to feel greater liberty,
greater ease in its movements ; and a writer would use the same
word sometimes as one part of speech, and sometimes as another.
Thus Shakespeare himself uses the conjunction *but* both as a
verb and as a noun, and makes one of his characters say, "But

me no buts!" He employs the adverb *askance* as a verb, and
says, "From their own misdeeds they askance their eyes." He
has the adverb *backward* with the function of a noun, as in
the phrase "The backward and abyss of time." Again, he gives
us an adverb doing the work of an adjective, as in the phrases
"my often rumination," "a seldom pleasure." In the same
way, Shakespeare has the verbs "to glad" and "to mad." Very
often he uses an adjective as a noun; and "a fair" is his phrase
for "beauty," — "a pale" for "a paleness." He carries this
power of using one "part of speech" for another to the most
extraordinary lengths. He uses *happy* for *to make happy;*
unfair for *to deface; to climate* for *to live; to bench* for *to sit;*
to false for *to falsify; to path* for *to walk; to verse* for *to speak
of in verse;* and many others. Perhaps the most remarkable is
where he uses *tongue* for *to talk of*, and *brain* for *to think of.* In
"Cymbeline" he says :—

> "'Tis still a dream ; or else such stuff as madness
> Will tongue, and brain not. . . ."

3. Absence of Inflexions.—At the present time, we have lost
almost all the inflexions we once had. We have only one for
the cases of the noun ; none at all for ordinary adjectives (except to mark degrees) ; a few in the pronoun ; and a few in the
verb. Hence we can use a word sometimes as one part of
speech, and sometimes as another. We can say, "The boys had
a good run;" and "The boys run very well." We can say,
"The train travelled very fast," where *fast* is an adverb, modifying *travelled;* and we can speak of "a fast train." We can
use the phrase, "The very man," where *very* is an adjective
marking *man;* and also the phrase "A very good man," where
very is an adverb modifying the adjective *good.*

4. Function.—It follows that, in the present state of our
language, when we cannot know to what class a word belongs
by its **look**, we must settle the matter by asking ourselves what
is its **function.** We need not inquire what a word *is;* but we
must ask what it *does.* And just as a bar of iron may be used
as a lever, or as a crowbar, or as a poker, or as a hammer, or as

a weapon, so a word may be an adjective, or a noun, or a verb,
—just as it is **used**.

5. Examples.—When we say, "He gave a shilling for the
book," *for* is a preposition connecting the noun *book* with the
verb *gave*. But when we say, "Let us assist them, for our case
is theirs," the word *for* joins two sentences together, and is hence
a conjunction. In the same way, we can contrast *early* in the
proverb, "The early bird catches the worm," and in the sentence
"He rose early." *Hard* in the sentence "He works hard" is an
adverb; in the phrase "A hard stone" it is an adjective. *Right*
is an adverb in the phrase "Right reverend;" but an adjective
in the sentence "That is not the right road." *Back* is an adverb
in the sentence "He came back yesterday;" but a noun in the
sentence "He fell on his back." *Here* is an adverb, and *where*
an adverbial conjunction; but in the line—

> "Thou losest here, a better where to find,"

Shakespeare employs these words as nouns. *The*, in ninety-nine
cases out of a hundred, is an adjective; but in such phrases as
"The more, the merrier," it is an adverb, modifying *merrier* and
more. Indeed, some words seem to exercise two functions at
the same time. Thus Tennyson has—

> "Slow and sure comes up the golden year,"—

where *slow* and *sure* may either be adverbs modifying *comes*, or
adjectives marking *year;* or both. This is also the case with
the participle, which is both an adjective and a verb; and with
the gerund, which is both a verb and a noun.

6. Function or Form ?—From all this it appears that we are
not merely to look at the form of the word, we are not merely
to notice and *observe;* but we must *think*—we must ask ourselves what the word **does**, what is its **function?** In other
words, we must always—when trying to settle the class to which
a word belongs—ask ourselves two questions—

(i) What other word does it go with? *and*

(ii) What does it do to that word?

SYNTAX.

INTRODUCTORY.

1. The word **Syntax** is a Greek word which means **arrangement**. Syntax, in grammar, is that part of it which treats of the **relations of words to each other** in a sentence.

2. Syntax is usually divided into two parts, which are called **Concord** and **Government**.

(i) **Concord** means **agreement**. The chief concords in grammar are those of the **Verb with its Subject**; the **Adjective with its Noun**; one **Noun with another Noun**; the **Pronoun with the Noun** it stands for; the **Relative with its Antecedent**.

(ii) **Government** means the **influence** that one word has upon another. The chief kinds of Government are those of a **Transitive Verb and a Noun**; a **Preposition and a Noun**.

I.—SYNTAX OF THE NOUN.

1.—THE NOMINATIVE CASE.

RULE I.—The **Subject** of a sentence is in the **Nominative Case**.

Thus we say, **I write**; **John writes**: and both *I* and *John*—the subjects in these two sentences—are in the nominative case.

RULE II.—When one noun is used to explain or describe another, the two nouns are said to be **in Apposition**; and they are always in the same case.

Thus we find in Shakespeare's Henry V., i. 2. 188 :—

> " So work the honey-**bees,**
> **Creatures** that by a rule in Nature teach
> The art of order to a peopled kingdom."

Here **bees** is the nominative to work ; **creatures** is in apposition with **bees,** and hence is also in the nominative case. (Of course, two nouns in apposition may be in the objective case, as in the sentence, " We met John the gardener.")

(i) The words in apposition may be separated from each other, as in Cowper's well-known line about the postman :—

> " **He** comes, **the herald** of a noisy world."

RULE III.—The verb **to be,** and other verbs of a like nature, take **two nominatives**—one before and the other after.

Thus we find such sentences as—

> (i) General Wolseley **is** an able soldier.
> (ii) The long-remembered beggar **was** his guest.

In the first sentence **Wolseley** and **soldier** refer to the same person ; **beggar** and **guest** refer to the same person ; and all that the verbs **is** and **was** do is to connect them. They have no influence whatever upon either word. When **is** (or **are**) is so used, it is called the **copula.**

☞ If we call the previous kind of apposition **noun-apposition,** this might be called **verb-apposition.**

RULE IV.—The verbs become, be-called, be-named, live, turn-out, prove, remain, seem, look, and others, are of an appositional character, and take a **nominative case** after them as well as before them.

Thus we find :—

> (i) **Tom** became an **architect.**
> (ii) The **boy** is called **John.**
> (iii) **He** turned out a dull **fellow.**
> (iv) **She** moves a **goddess** ; and **she** looks a **queen.**

On examining the verbs in these sentences, it will be seen that they do not and cannot govern the noun that follows them. The noun before and the noun after designate the same person.

RULE V.—A Noun and an Adjective, or a Noun and a Participle, or a Noun and an Adjective Phrase,—not syntactically

E

connected with any other word in the sentence,—are put in the **Nominative Absolute.**

Thus we have :—

   (i) "She earns a scanty pittance, and at night
        Lies down secure, her **heart** and **pocket light.**"—Cowper.

   (ii) The **wind shifting**, we sailed slowly.

   (iii) "Next Anger rushed, **his eyes on fire.**"—Collins.

   (iv) **Dinner over**, we went up-stairs.

   The word *absolutus* means *freed;* and the absolute case has been freed from, and is independent of, the construction of the sentence.

REMARKS.—1. In the oldest English (or Anglo-Saxon), the absolute case was the **Dative;** and this we find even as late as Milton (1608-1674), who says—

   "**Him destroyed,**
   All else will follow."

2. Caution! In the sentence, "Pompey, having been defeated, fled to Africa," the phrase *having been defeated* is an attributive clause to *Pompey,* which is the noun to *fled.* But, in the sentence, "Pompey having been defeated, his army broke up," *Pompey*—**not** being the **noun** to any **verb**—is in the **nominative absolute.** Hence, if a noun is the **nominative** to a **verb,** it cannot be in the nominative absolute.

Remarks on Exceptions.

1. The pronoun **It** is often used as a **Preparatory Nominative,** or—as it may also be called—a **Representative Subject.** Thus we say, "**It** is very hard to climb that hill," where **it** stands for the true nominative, **to-climb-that-hill.**

2. In the same way, the demonstrative adjective **that** is often used as a **Representative Subject.** "**That** (he has gone to Paris) is certain." **What** is certain? **That.** What is that? The fact that *he has gone to Paris.*

3. Still more oddly, we find both **it** and **that** used in one sentence as a kind of **Joint-Representative Subject.** Thus we have: (i) "**It** now and then happened **that** (he lost his temper) ;" and, in Shakespeare's "Othello"—

    (ii) "**That** (I have ta'en away this old man's daughter)
        It is most true."

What is most true? **It.** What is it? **That.** What is that?[1]
That (I have taken away, etc.) Here the verb **is** has really
three subjects, all meaning the same thing.

> [1] ☞ It must be observed that the demonstrative *that* has by use gained the
> force, and exercises the function, of a conjunction joining two sentences.
> It here joins the two sentences "It is most true," and "I have taken
> away," etc.

4. The nominative to a verb in the Imperative Mood is often
omitted. Thus **Come along!** = Come thou (or *ye*) along!

2.—THE POSSESSIVE CASE.

RULE VI.—When one Noun stands **in the relation** of an
attribute to another Noun, the first of these nouns is put in
the **Possessive Case.**

    (i) The Possessive Case originally denoted mere **possession, as John's
book; John's gun.** But it has gradually gained a wider reference; and
we can say, "The Duke of Portland's funeral," etc.

    (ii) The **objective case** with **of** is = the possessive; and we can say,
"The might of England," instead of "England's might."

RULE VII.—When (i) two or more Possessives are in **apposition,** or (ii) when several nouns connected by **and** are in the
possessive case, the **sign** of the possessive is affixed to the
last only.

    (i) Thus we find : (i) For thy servant David's sake. (ii) Messrs Simp-
kin & Marshall's house.

    ☞ The fact is, that *Messrs Simpkin-&-Marshall*, and other such phrases,
are regarded as one **compound phrase.**

    (ii) The sentence, "This is a picture of Turner's," is = "This is a
picture (one) of Turner's pictures." The *of* governs, not *Turner's*, but
pictures. Hence it is not a double possessive, though it looks like it.

    The phrase, "a friend of mine," contains the same idiom ; only *mine* is used
in place of *my*, because the word *friend* has been suppressed.

3.—THE OBJECTIVE CASE.

1. The **Objective Case** is that case of a noun or pronoun that is " governed by " a transitive verb or by a preposition.

☞ It is only the **pronoun** that has a special **form** for this **case.** The English noun formerly had it, but lost it between the years 1066 and 1300.

2. The **Objective Case** is the case of the **Direct Object;** the **Dative Case** is the case of the **Indirect Object**—and something more.

(i) The Direct Object answers to the question **Whom ?** or **What ?**

(ii) The Indirect Object answers to the question **To whom ? To what ?** or **For whom ? For what ?**

3. The object of an active-transitive verb must always be a **Noun** or the **Equivalent of a Noun.**

RULE VIII.—The **Direct Object** of an **Active-Transitive Verb** is put in the **Objective Case.**

Thus we read: (i) We met the **man** (Noun). (ii) We met **him** (Pronoun). (iii) We saw the **fighting** (Verbal Noun). (iv) I like **to work** (Infinitive). (v) I heard that **he had left** (Noun sentence).

RULE IX.—Verbs of **teaching, asking, making, appointing,** etc., take **two objects.**

Thus we say : (i) He teaches **me grammar.** (ii) He asked **me a question.** (iii) They made **him manager.** (iv) The Queen appointed **him Treasurer.**

☞ In the last two instances the objects are sometimes called **factitive objects.**

RULE X.—Some **Intransitive Verbs** take an objective case after them, if the objective has a **similar** or **cognate** meaning to that of the verb itself.

Thus we find : (i) To die the **death.** (ii) To sleep a **sleep.** (iii) To go one's **way.** To wend one's **way.** (iv) To run a **race.** (v) Dreaming **dreams** no mortal ever dared to dream before.

☞ Such objects are called **cognate objects.**

RULE XI.—The **limitations** of a Verb by words or phrases expressing **space, time, measure,** etc., are said to be in the objective case; as (i) he walked three **miles**; (ii) he travelled all **night**; (iii) the stone weighed three **pounds.**

☞ 1. Because these words limit or **modify** the verbs to which they are attached, they are sometimes called **Adverbial Objects.**

2. The following phrases are **adverbial objects** of the same kind: (i) They bound him **hand and foot.** (ii) They fell upon him **tooth and nail.** (iii) They turned out the Turks, **bag and baggage.** Such phrases are rightly called adverbial, because they modify *bound, fell,* and *turned;* and show **how** he was bound, **how** they fell upon him, etc.

REMARKS ON EXCEPTIONS.

1. The same verb may be either **Intransitive** or **Transitive,** according to its use. Thus—

Intransitive.	Transitive.
(i) The soldier ran away.	(i) The soldier ran his spear into the Arab.
(ii) The man works very hard.	(ii) The master works his men too hard.
(iii) We walked up the hill.	(iii) The groom walked the horse up the hill.

2. An **Intransitive** verb performs the function of a **Transitive** verb when a **preposition** is added to it. Thus—

Intransitive.	Transitive.
(i) The children laughed.	(i) The children laughed at the clown.
(ii) The man spoke.	(ii) The man spoke of wild beasts.

3. The preposition may continue to **adhere** to such a verb, so that it remains even when the verb has been made **passive.**

Thus we can say: (i) He was laughed-at. (ii) Whales were spoken-of. (iii) Prosecution was hinted-at. And this is an enormous convenience in the use of the English language.

4.—THE DATIVE CASE.

1. The **Dative** is the case of the **Indirect Object.**

Thus we say: He handed **her** a chair. She gave it **me.**

2. The **Dative** is also the case of the **Direct Object,** with

such verbs as be, **worth, seem, please, think** (= *seem*); and with the adjectives **like** and **near.**

Thus we have the phrases, **meseems** ; if **you** please (=if it please you); **methought** (=it seemed to me); woe is **me!** and, she is like **him** ; he was near **us.**

"Woe worth the **chase!** woe worth the **day**
That cost thy life, my gallant grey !"
—"Lady of the Lake."

"When in Salamanca's cave
Him listed his magic wand to wave,
The bells would ring in Notre-Dame."
—"Lay of the Last Minstrel."

3. The **Dative** is sometimes the **case of possession** or of **benefit.**

As in, Woe is **me!** Well is **thee!**
" Convey **me** Salisbury into his tent."

RULE XII.—Verbs of **giving, promising, telling, showing,** etc., take two objects ; and the **indirect object** is put in the **dative case.**

Thus we say : He gave **her** a fan. She promised **me** a book. Tell **us** a story. Show **me** the picture-book.

RULE XIII.—When such verbs are turned into the **passive voice,** either the **Direct** or the **Indirect Object** may be turned into the **Subject** of the **Passive Verb.** Thus we can say either—

Direct Object used as **Subject.**	**Indirect Object** used as **Subject.**
(i) A fan was given her.	(i) She was given a fan.[1]
(ii) A book was promised me.	(ii) I was promised a book.[1]
(iii) A story was told us.	(iii) We were told a story.[1]
(iv) The picture-book was shown me.	(iv) I was shown the picture-book.[1]

[1] This has sometimes been called the **Retained Object.** The words **fan,** etc., are in the objective case, not because they are governed by the passive verbs *was given,* etc., but because they still retain, in a latent form, the influence or government exercised upon them by the **active** verbs, **give, promise,** etc.

1. The Dative of the **Personal Pronoun** was in frequent use in the time of Shakespeare, to add a certain liveliness and interest to the statement.

Thus we find, in several of his plays, such sentences as—

(i) "He plucked **me** ope his doublet."
(ii) "Villain, I say, knock **me** at this gate, and rap **me** well."
(iii) "Your tanner will last **you** nine year."

Grammarians call this kind of dative the **ethical dative.**

2. ·The Dative was once the **Absolute Case.**

"**This said,** they both betook them several ways."
—Milton.

II.—SYNTAX OF THE ADJECTIVE.

1. In our Old English—the English spoken before the coming of the Normans, and for some generations after—every adjective agreed with its noun in **gender, number,** and **case ;** and even as late as Chaucer (1340-1400) adjectives had a form for the plural number. Thus in the *Prologue* to the 'Canterbury Tales,' he writes—

"And *smalĕ* fowlës maken melodie,"

where *e* is the plural inflexion.

2. In course of time, partly under the influence of the Normans and the Norman language, all these inflexions dropped off; and there are now only two adjectives in the whole language that have any inflexions at all (except for comparison), and these inflexions are only for the plural number. The two adjectives that are inflected are the demonstrative adjectives **this** and **that,** which make their plurals in **these** (formerly *thise*) and **those.**

(i) **The,** which is a broken-down form of *that,* never changes at all.

(ii) When an adjective is **used as a noun,** it may take a plural inflection ; as *the blacks, goods, equals, edibles, annuals, monthlies, weeklies,* etc.

3. Most adjectives are **inflected** for **comparison.**

4. Every adjective is either an **explicit** or an **implicit** predicate. The following are examples :—

Adjectives used as Explicit Predicates.

1. The way was **long**; the wind was **cold**.
2. The minstrel was **infirm** and **old**.
3. The duke is very **rich**.

Adjectives used as Implicit Predicates.

1. We had before us a **long** way and a **cold** wind.
2. The **infirm old** minstrel went wearily on.
3. The **rich** duke is very niggardly.

5. When an adjective is used as an **explicit predicate**, it is said to be used **predicatively**; when it is used as an **implicit predicate**, it is said to be used **attributively**.

Adjectives used predicatively.

1. The cherries are **ripe**.
2. The man we met was very **old**.

Adjectives used attributively.

1. Let us pluck only the **ripe** cherries.
2. We met an **old** man.

RULE XIV.—An adjective may qualify a noun or pronoun **predicatively**, not only after the verb **be**, but after such intransitive verbs as **look, seem, feel, taste,** etc.

Thus we find : (i) She looked **angry**. (ii) He seemed **weary**. (iii) He felt **better**. (iv) It tasted **sour**. (v) He fell **ill**.

RULE XV.—After verbs of **making, thinking, considering,** etc., an adjective may be used **factitively** as well as **predicatively**.

Thus we can say, (i) We **made** all the young ones **happy**. (ii) All present **thought** him **odd**. (iii) We **considered** him very **clever**.
Factitive comes from the Latin *facio*, I make.

RULE XVI.—An adjective may, especially in poetry, be used as an abstract noun.

Thus we speak of "the **True**, the **Good**, and the **Beautiful** ;" " the **sublime** and the **ridiculous** ;" Mrs Browning has the phrase, " from the depths of God's **divine** ;" and Longfellow speaks of

"A band
Of **stern** in heart and **strong** in hand."

RULE XVII.—An adjective may be used as an adverb in poetry.

Thus we find in Dr Johnson the line—

> "Slow rises worth, by poverty depressed ; "

and in Scott—

> " Trip it deft and merrily ; "

and in Longfellow—

> "The green trees whispered low and mild ; "

and in Tennyson—

> " And slow and sure comes up the golden year."

(i) The reason for this is that in O. E. adverbs were formed from adjectives by adding *e*. Thus brightë was = *brightly*, and deepë = *deeply*. But in course of time the *e* fell off, and an adverb was just like its own adjective. Hence we still have the phrases : "He works hard ; ' " Run quick !" "Speak louder !" " Run fast !" "Right reverend," etc.

(ii) Shakespeare very frequently uses adjectives as adverbs, and has such sentences as : " Thou didst it excellent !' "'Tis noble spoken !" and many more.

RULE XVIII.—A participle is a pure **adjective**, and *agrees* with its noun.

Thus, in Pope—

> " How happy is the blameless vestal's lot,
> The world forgetting, by the world forgot !"

where **forgetting**, the present active participle, and **forgot**, the past passive participle, both **agree** with **vestal** (" the vestal's lot " being = *the lot of the* **vestal**).

(i) But while a participle is a pure adjective, it also retains one function of a verb—the power to govern. Thus in the sentence, "Respecting ourselves, we shall be respected by the world," the present participle *respecting* **agrees** with *we*, and governs *ourselves*.

RULE XIX.—The **comparative** degree is employed when two things or two sets of things are compared ; the **superlative** when three or more are compared.

Thus we say " James is **taller** than I ; but Tom is the **tallest** of the three."

(i) Than is a dialectic form of then. "James is taller ; then I (come)."

(ii) The superlative is sometimes used to indicate **superiority to all others.** Thus Shakespeare says, " A little ere the mightiest Julius fell ;" and we use such phrases as, " Truest friend and noblest foe. This is sometimes called the "superlative of pre-eminence."

(iii) Double comparatives and superlatives were much used in O.E., and Shakespeare was especially fond of them. He gives us such phrases as, "a more larger list of sceptres," "more better," "more nearer," "most worst," "most unkindest cut of all," etc. These cannot be employed now.

RULE XX.—The **distributive** adjectives *each, every, either, neither*, go with **singular** nouns only.

Thus we say : (i) Each boy got an apple. (ii) Every noun is in its place. (iii) Either book will do. (iv) Neither woman went.

Either and **neither** are dialectic forms of **other** and **nother**, which were afterwards compressed into **or** and **nor**.

REMARKS ON EXCEPTIONS.

1. There are some adjectives that cannot be used **attributively**, but only **predicatively.** Such are **well, ill, ware, aware, afraid, glad, sorry**, etc. (But we say "a glad heart," and—in a different sense—"a sorry nag.")

(i) We say " He was **glad** ; " but we cannot say " A **glad** man." Yet Wordsworth has—

" Glad sight whenever new and old
Are joined thro' some dear home-born tie."

We also speak of "glad tidings."

(ii) We say "He was sorry ; " but if we say "He was a sorry man," we use the word in a quite different sense. The **attributive** meaning of the word is in this instance quite different from the **predicative.**

2. The phrase **"the first two"** means *the first and second* in **one** series ; **"the two first"** means the first of **each of two** series.

III.—SYNTAX OF THE PRONOUN.

RULE XXI.—**Pronouns**, whether **personal** or **relative**, must agree in **gender, number,** and **person** with the nouns for which they stand, but **not** (necessarily) in **case.**

Thus we say : "I have lost my **umbrella** : it was standing in the corner."

(i) Here it is neuter, singular, and third person, because umbrella is neuter, singular, and third person.

(ii) Umbrella is in the objective case governed by *have lost;* but it is in the nominative, because it is the subject to its own verb *was standing.*

RULE XXII.—**Pronouns**, whether **personal** or **relative**, take their **case** from the **sentence** in which they stand.

Thus we say : " The sailor *whom* we met on the beach is ill." Here sailor is in the **nominative**, and **whom**, its pronoun, in the **objective**.

(i) **Whom** is in the objective, because it is governed by the verb **met** in its own sentence. " The sailor is ill" is one sentence. " Him (whom=*and him*) we met" is a second sentence.

(ii) The relative may be governed by a preposition, as "The man on whom I relied has not disappointed me."

RULE XXIII.—**Who, whom,** and **whose** are used only of rational beings; **which** of **irrational**; **that** may stand for nouns of any kind.

(i) In poetry, **whose** may be used for *of which.* Thus Wordsworth, in the ' Laodamia,' has—

" In worlds **whose** course is equable and pure."

RULE XXIV.—The possessive pronouns **mine, thine, ours, yours,** and **theirs** can only be used **predicatively**; or, if used as a **subject**, cannot have a noun with them.

Thus we say : " This is mine." " Mine is larger than yours." But **mine** and **thine** are used for **my** and **thy** before a noun in poetry and impassioned prose : " Who knoweth the power of thine anger ? "

RULE XXV.—After **such, same, so much, so great,** etc., the relative employed is not **who,** but **as.**

Thus Milton has—

" Tears such **as** angels weep."

(i) Shakespeare uses **as** even after that—

"**That** kind of fruit **as** maids call medlars."

This usage cannot now be employed.

REMARKS ON EXCEPTIONS.

1. The **antecedent** to the relative may be **omitted.**

Thus we find, in Wordsworth's " Ode to Duty "—

" There are ∧ who ask not if thine eye
Be on them."

And Shakespeare, in " Othello," iii. 3. 157, has—

" ∧ Who steals my purse, steals trash."

And we have the well-known Greek proverb—

" ∧ Whom the gods love, die young."

2. The **relative** itself may be **omitted.**

(i) Thus Shelley has the line—

"Men must reap the things ∧ they sow."

(ii) And such phrases as, "Is this the book ∧ you wanted?" are very common.

3. The word **but** is often used for **who + not.** It may hence be called **the negative-relative.**

Thus Scott has—

"There breathes not clansman of my line
But (= who not) would have given his life for mine."

4. The personal pronouns, when in the dative or objective case, are generally **without emphasis.**

(i) If we say "Give me your hand," the *me* is unemphatic. If we say "Give *me* your hand!" the *me* has a stronger emphasis than the *give*, and means *me*, and **not** any other person.

(ii) Very ludicrous accidents sometimes occur from the misplacing of the accent. Thus a careless reader once read: "And he said, 'Saddle me the ass;' and they saddled *him*." Nelson's famous signal, "England expects every man to do his duty," was once altered in emphasis with excellent effect. A midshipman on board one of H.M.'s ships was very lazy, and inclined to allow others to do his work; and the question went round the vessel: "Why is Mr So-and-so like England?" "Because he expects every man to do *his* duty."

IV.—SYNTAX OF THE VERB.

1.—CONCORD OF VERBS.

We cannot say *I writes*, or *He* or *The man write*. We always say *I write*, *He writes*, and *The man writes*. In other words, certain pronouns and nouns require a **certain form** of a verb to go with them. If the pronoun is of the first person, then the verb will have a certain form; if it is of the third person, it will have a different form. If the noun or pronoun is singular, the verb will have one form; if it is plural, it may have another form. In these circumstances, the verb is said to **agree** with its subject.

All these facts are usually embodied in a general statement, which may also serve as a rule.

RULE XXVI.—A **Finite Verb** must **agree** with its subject in **Number** and **Person**. Thus we say: "He calls," "They walk."

(i) The subject answers to the question **Who?** or **What?**

(ii) The subject of a **finite** verb is always in the **nominative** case.

Or and **nor** are conjunctions which do not add the things mentioned to each other, but allow the mind to take them **separately**—the one **excluding** the other. We may therefore say:—

RULE XXVII.—Two or more singular nouns that are **subjects**, connected by **or** or **nor**, require their verb to be in the singular. Thus we say: "Either Tom **or** John is going." "It **was** either a roe-deer **or** a large goat!"

On the other hand, when two or more singular nouns are connected by **and**, they are **added** to each other; and, just as one and one make two, so two singular nouns are equal to one plural. We may therefore lay down the following rule:—

RULE XXVIII.—Two or more singular nouns that are **subjects**, connected by **and**, require their verb to be in the **plural**. We say: "Tom **and** John are going." "There **were** a roe-deer **and** a goat in the field."

Cautions.—(i) The compound conjunction **as well as** does not require a plural verb, because it allows the mind to take **each** subject **separately**. Thus we say, "Justice, as well as mercy, allows it." We can see the truth of this remark by transposing the clauses of the sentence, and saying, "Justice allows it, as well as mercy [allows it]."

(ii) The preposition **with** cannot make two singular subjects into one plural. We must say, "The Mayor, with his attendants, **was** there." Transposition will show the force of this remark also: "The Mayor was there with his attendants."

RULE XXIX.—**Collective Nouns** take a **singular** verb or a **plural** verb, as the notion of **unity** or of **plurality** is uppermost in the mind of the speaker. Thus we say: "Parliament **was** dissolved." "The committee **are** divided in opinion."

(i) When two or more nouns represent **one idea**, the verb is singular. Thus, in Milton's "Lycidas," we find—

"Bitter constraint and sad occasion dear
Compels me to disturb your season due.

And, in Shakespeare's "Tempest" (v. 104), we read—

> "All torment, trouble, wonder, and amazement
>   **Inhabits** here."

In this case we may look upon the statement as = "A condition which embraces all torment," etc.

(ii) When the verb **precedes** a number of different nominatives, it is often **singular.** The speaker seems not to have yet made up his mind what nominatives he is going to use. Thus, in the well-known passage in Byron's "Childe Harold" we have—

> "Ah! then and there **was** hurrying to and fro,
>   And gathering **tears,** and **tremblings** of distress."

And so Shakespeare, in "Julius Cæsar," makes Brutus say, "There **is** tears for his love, joy for his fortune, honour for his valour, and death for his ambition." And, in the same way, people say, "Where **is** my hat and stick?"

RULE XXX.—The verb **to be** is often **attracted** into the same number as the nominative that **follows** it, instead of agreeing with the nominative that is its true subject. Thus we find : "The wages of sin **is** death." "To love and to admire **has** been the joy of his existence." "A high look and a proud heart **is** sin."

2.—GOVERNMENT OF VERBS.

RULE XXXI.—A **Transitive** Verb in the **active** voice governs its direct object in the **objective case.** Thus we say : "I like **him** ;" "they dislike **her.**"

The following sub-rules are of some importance :—

(i) The **participle,** which is an **adjective,** has the same governing power as the verb of which it is a part—as, "Seeing the rain, I remained at home"—where **seeing** agrees with **I** as an **adjective,** and governs **rain** as a **verb.**

(ii) The **gerund,** which is a **noun,** has the same governing power as the verb to which it belongs. Thus we say : "Hating one's neighbour is forbidden by the Gospel," where **hating** is a **noun,** the nominative to *is forbidden,* and a **gerund** governing *neighbour* in the objective.

RULE XXXII.—Active-transitive Verbs of **giving, promising, offering,** and suchlike, govern the **Direct Object** in the objective case, and the **Indirect Object** in the dative. "I gave **him** an apple." "He promises **me** a book." .

(i) In turning these active verbs into passive, it is the **direct object** that should be turned into the **subject** of the **passive** verb ; and we ought to say, "An apple was given me." But custom allows of either mode of change ; and we also say, "I was given an apple ;" "I was promised a book." Dr Abbott calls the objectives *apple* and *book* **retained objects**, because they are *retained* in the sentence, even although we know that no passive verb can govern an objective case.

RULE XXXIII.—Such verbs as **make, create, appoint, think, believe,** etc., govern **two** objects—the one **direct,** the other **factitive.** Thus we say : "They made **him king** ;" "the king appointed **him governor** ;" "we thought **her** a clever **woman.**"

(i) The second of these objectives remains with the passive verb, when the form of the sentence has been changed ; and we say, "He was made **king** ;" "he was appointed **governor.**"

RULE XXXIV.—One verb governs another in the **Infinitive.** Or,

The **Infinitive Mood** of a verb, being a pure noun, may be the **object** of another verb, if that verb is **active-transitive.** Thus we say : "I **saw** him **go** ;" "we **saw** the ship **sink** ;" "I **ordered** him **to write.**"

(i) In the first two sentences, **him** and **ship** are the **subjects of go** and **sink.** But the **subject** of an **infinitive** is always in the **objective case.** The infinitives **go** and **sink** have a double face. They are **verbs** in relation to their **subjects** *him* and *go ;* they are **nouns** in relation to the **verbs** that govern them.

(ii) In the sentence, "I ordered him to write," **him** is in the dative case ; and the sentence is = "I ordered writing to him." **To write** is the direct object of **ordered.**

(iii) **Conclusion from the above** : An Infinitive is always a noun, whether it be a subject or an object. It is (*a*) a subject in the sentence, "To play football is pleasant." It is (*b*) an object in the sentence, "I like to play football."

RULE XXXV.—Some **Intransitive Verbs** govern the **Dative**

Case. Thus we have *"Methought," "meseems," "Woe worth the day !" "Woe is me !" "If you please !"*

(i) **Worth** is the imperative of an old English verb, *weorthan*, to become. (The German form of this verb is *werden*.)

(ii) Shakespeare even construes the verb *look* with a dative. In "Cymbeline," iii. 5, 32, he has—

She looks us like
A thing more made of malice, than of duty.

3.—MOODS OF VERBS.

1. The **Indicative Mood** is the mood of **direct** assertion or statement, and it speaks of actual facts. The **Subjunctive Mood** is the mood of assertion also, but **with a modification** given to the assertion **by the mind** through which it passes. If we use the term *objective* as describing what *actually exists* independently of our minds, and *subjective* as describing that which *exists in the mind* of the speaker,—whether it really exists outside or not,—we can then say that—

(i) The **Indicative Mood** is the mood of **óbjective assertion.**

(ii) The **Subjunctive Mood** is the mood of **súbjective assertion.**

The Indicative Mood may be compared to a ray of light coming straight through the air ; the Subjunctive Mood to the effect produced by the water on the same ray—the water deflects it, makes it form a quite different angle, and hence a stick in the water looks broken or crooked.

2. The **Imperative Mood** is the **mood of command** or of request.

3. The **Infinitive Mood** is the **substantive mood** or noun of the verb. It is always equal to a **noun** ; it is always either a subject or an object ; and hence it is incapable of making any assertion.

4. The **Subjunctive Mood** has for some years been gradually dying out. Few writers, and still fewer speakers, use it: Good writers are even found to say, "If he was here, I should tell him." But a knowledge of the uses of the subjunctive mood is necessary to enable us to understand English prose and verse anterior to the present generation. Even so late as the year 1817, Jane Austen, one of the best prose-writers of this century, used the subjunctive mood in almost every dependent clause. Not only does she use it after *if* and *though*, but after such conjunctions as *till, until, because,* and others.

RULE XXXVI.—The **Subjunctive Mood** was used—and ought to be used—to express **doubt, possibility, supposition, consequence** (which may or may not happen), or **wish,** all as **moods of the mind** of the speaker.

(i) "If thou **read** this, O Cæsar, thou mayst live." (Doubt.)

(ii) "If he **come**, I will speak to him." (Possibility.)

(iii) "Yet if one heart **throb** higher at its sway,
The wizard note has not been touched in vain." (Supposition.)

(iv) "Get on your night-gown, lest occasion **call** us
And **show** us to be watchers." (Consequence.)

(v) "I would my daughter **were** dead at my foot, and the jewels in her ear!" (Wish.)

☞ In all of the above sentences, the clauses with subjunctives do not state facts, but feelings or notions of what **may** or **might** be.

RULE XXXVII.—The **Subjunctive Mood**, being a *subjoined* mood, is always **dependent** on some other clause antecedent **in thought**, and generally also in expression. The antecedent clause, which contains the **condition**, is called the **conditional clause**; and the clause which contains the **consequence** of the supposition is called the **consequent clause**.

(i) If it were so, it was a grievous fault.
　　Condition.　　*Consequence.*

(ii) If it were done when 'tis done,
　　Condition.

Then 'twere well it were done quickly.
　　Consequence.

REMARKS ON EXCEPTIONS.

1. Sometimes the conditional clause is suppressed. Thus we can say, "I would not endure such language" [if it were addressed to me = conditional clause].

2. The conjunction is often omitted. Thus, in Shakespeare's play of "Julius Cæsar," we find—

" *Were* I Brutus,
And Brutus Antony, there were an Antony
Would ruffle up your spirits."

RULE XXXVIII—The **Simple Infinitive**—without the sign to—is used with auxiliary verbs, such as **may, do, shall, will,** etc.; and with such verbs as **let, bid, can, must, see, hear, make, feel, observe, have, know,** etc.

F

    (i) **Let** darkness **keep** her raven gloss.

    (ii) **Bid** the porter **come.**

    (iii) I **saw** him **run** after a gilded butterfly.

    (iv) We **heard** him **cry.**

    (v) They **made** him **go,** etc., etc.

It was the Danes who introduced a preposition before the infinitive. Their sign was *at*, which was largely used with the infinitive in the Northern dialect.

RULE XXXIX.—The **Gerund** is both a **noun** and a **verb.** As a noun, it **is governed** by a verb or preposition; as a verb, it **governs** other nouns or pronouns.

There are two gerunds—(i) one with **to;** and (ii) one that ends in **ing.**

(i) The first is to be carefully distinguished from the ordinary infinitive. Now the ordinary infinitive **never** expresses a **purpose;** the gerund with *to* almost always does. Thus we find—

"And fools who came **to scoff** remained **to pray.**"

This gerund is often called the **gerundial infinitive.**

(ii) The second is to be distinguished from the present participle in **ing,** and very carefully from the abstract noun of the same form. The present participle in **ing,** as *loving, hating, walking,* etc., is **always** an **adjective,** agreeing with a noun or pronoun. The gerund in **ing** is **always a noun,** and governs an object. "He was very fond of **playing** cricket." Here *playing* is a **noun** in relation to *of;* and a **verb** governing *cricket* in the objective. In the words *walking-stick, frying-pan,* etc., *walking* and *frying* are nouns, and therefore gerunds. If they were adjectives and participles, the compounds would mean *the stick that walks, the pan that fries.*

(iii) The gerund in **ing** must also be distinguished from the verbal noun in **ing,** which is a descendant of the verbal noun in **ung.** "He went a **hunting**" (where a = the old **an** or **on**); "Forty and six years was this temple in **building;**" "He was very impatient during the **reading** of the will." In these sentences **hunting, building,** and **reading** are all verbal nouns, derived from the old verbal noun in **ung,** and are called *abstract nouns.* But if we say, "He is fond of **hunting** deer;" "He is engaged in **building** a hotel;" "He likes **reading** poetry,"—then the three words are gerunds, for they act as verbs, and govern the three objectives, *deer, hotel,* and *poetry.*

RULE XL.—The **Gerundial Infinitive** is frequently construed with nouns and **adjectives.** Thus we say: "A house to sell or let;" "Wood to burn;" "Deadly to hear, and deadly to tell;" "Good to eat."

V.—SYNTAX OF THE ADVERB.

RULE XLI.—The Adverb ought to be as near as possible to the word it modifies. Thus we ought to say, "He gave me **only three** shillings," and not "He only gave me three shillings," because *only* modifies **three**, and not **gave**.

This rule applies also to compound adverbs, such as **at least, in like manner, at random, in part**, etc.

RULE XLII.—**Adverbs** modify **verbs, adjectives,** and other **adverbs**; but they can also modify **prepositions**. Thus we have the combinations **out from, up to, down to,** etc.

In the sentence, "He walked up to me," the adverb **up** does not modify *walked*, but the prepositional phrase *to me*.

VI.—SYNTAX OF THE PREPOSITION.

RULE XLIII.—All prepositions in the English language govern nouns and pronouns in the **objective case**.

The prepositions **save** and **except** are really verbs in the **imperative mood**.

RULE XLIV.—Prepositions generally stand **before** the words they govern; but they may, with good effect, come **after** them. Thus we find in Shakespeare—

"Ten thousand men that fishes gnawed **upon**."

"Why, then, thou knowest what colour jet is **of**."

And, in Hooker, with very forcible effect—

"Shall there be a God to swear **by**, and none to pray **to**?"

RULE XLV.—Certain verbs, nouns, and adjectives require **special** prepositions. Thus we cannot say, "This is different **to** that," because it is bad English to say "This differs **to** that." The proper preposition in both instances is **from**.

The following is a list of some of these

Special prepositions:—

Absolve **from.**
Abhorrence **for.**
Accord **with.**
Acquit **of.**
Affinity **between.**
Adapted **to** (intentionally).
Adapted **for** (by nature).
Agree **with** (a person).
Agree **to** (a proposal).
Bestow **upon.**
Change **for** (a thing).
Change **with** (a person).
Confer **on** (=give to).
Confer **with** (=talk with).
Confide **in** (=trust in).
Confide **to** (=intrust to).
Conform **to.**
In conformity **with.**
Comply **with.**
Convenient **to** (a person).
Convenient **for** (a purpose).
Conversant **with.**
Correspond **with** (a person).
Correspond **to** (a thing).
Dependent **on** (but independent of).

Derogatory **to.**
Differ **from** (a statement or opinion).
Differ **with** (a person).
Different **from.**
Disappointed **of** (what we **cannot** get).
Disappointed **in** (what we **have** got).
Dissent **from.**
Exception **from** (a rule).
Exception **to** (a statement).
Glad **of** (a possession).
Glad **at** (a piece of news).
Involve **in.**
Martyr **for** (a cause).
Martyr **to** (a disease).
Need **of** or **for.**
Part **from** (a person).
Part **with** (a thing).
Profit **by.**
Reconcile **to** (a person).
Reconcile **with** (a statement).
Taste **of** (food).
A taste **for** (art).
Thirst **for** or **after** (knowledge).

VII.—SYNTAX OF THE CONJUNCTION.

RULE XLVI.—The **Conjunction** does not interfere with the action of a transitive verb or preposition, nor with the mood or tense of a verb.

(i) This rule is usually stated thus : " Conjunctions generally connect the same cases of nouns and pronouns, and the same moods and tenses of verbs, as ' We saw him and her,' ' Let either him or me go!' " But it is plain that *saw* governs *her* as well as *him ;* and that *or* cannot interfere with the government of *let.* Such a rule is therefore totally artificial.

(ii) It is plain that the conjunction **and** must make two singulars = one plural, as " He **and** I **are** of the same age."

RULE XLVII.—Certain **adjectives** and **conjunctions** take after them certain **special conjunctions.** Thus, **such** (adj.) requires **as, both** (adj.), **and; so** and **as** require **as; though, yet; whether, or; either, or; neither, nor; nor, nor; or, or.** The following are a few examples :—

(i) "Would I describe a preacher **such as** Paul !"

(ii) "**Though** deep, **yet** clear ; **though** gentle, **yet** not dull."

RULE XLVIII.—The subordinating conjunction **that** may be omitted. Thus we can say, "Are you sure he is here ?" Shakespeare has, "Yet Brutus says he was ambitious ! "

THE ANALYSIS OF SENTENCES.

1. Words are gregarious, and go in **groups**. When a group of words makes **complete** sense, it is called a **sentence**. A sentence is not a chance collection of words; it is a true **organism**, with a heart and limbs. When we take the limbs apart from the central **core** or heart of the sentence, and try to show their relation to that core, and to each other, we are said to **analyse** the sentence. The process of thus taking a sentence to pieces, and naming and accounting for each piece, is called **analysis**.

(i) **Analysis** is a Greek word which means *breaking up* or *taking apart:* its opposite is **Synthesis**, which means *making up* or *putting together.*

(ii) When we **examine** a sentence, and look at its parts, we are said to analyse the sentence, or to perform an act of **analysis**. But when we **make** sentences themselves, we perform an act of **composition** or of **synthesis**.

2. A **sentence** is a statement made about something, as, The horse gallops.

(i) The **something** (horse) is called the **Subject**.

(ii) The **statement** (gallops) is called the **Predicate**.

3. Every sentence consists, and must consist, of at least **two parts**. These two parts are the thing we **speak about** and what **we say** about that thing.

(i) The **Subject** is **what we speak about**.

(ii) The **Predicate** is **what we say** about the subject.

(i) There is a proverb of Solomon which says : "All things are double one against another." So there are the two necessarily complementary ideas of even and odd ;

of **right** and **left**; of **north** and **south**; and many more. In language, the two ideas of **Subject** and **Predicate** are necessarily coexistent; neither can exist without the other: we cannot even *think* the one without the other. They are the two **poles** of thought.

(ii) Sometimes the Subject is **not expressed** in imperative sentences, as in "Go!"="Go you!"

(iii) The Predicate can **never** be suppressed; it must always be **expressed**: otherwise nothing at all would be said.

4. There are **three** kinds of sentences : **Simple, Compound, and Complex.**

(i) A **simple** sentence contains only **one** subject and **one** predicate.

(ii) A **compound** sentence contains two or more simple sentences **of equal rank.**

(iii) A **complex** sentence contains a chief sentence, and one or more sentences that are **of subordinate rank** to the **chief sentence.**

I.—THE SIMPLE SENTENCE.

5. A **Simple Sentence** is a sentence which consists of **one** subject and one predicate.

(i) A Simple Sentence contains, and can contain, only **one finite verb.** If we say, "Baby likes to dance," there are two verbs in this simple sentence. But *to dance* is not a finite verb; it is an **infinitive** ; it is a pure **noun**, and cannot therefore be a predicate.

(ii) If we say, "John and James ran off," the sentence is="John ran off"+"James ran off." It is therefore a compound sentence consisting of two simple sentences, with the predicate of one of them suppressed. Hence it is called a **contracted compound** sentence—**contracted in the predicate.**

(iii) If we say, "John jumped up and ran off," the sentence is = "John jumped up"+"John ran off." It is therefore a compound sentence consisting of two simple sentences, but, for convenience' sake, **contracted in the subject.**

6. The Subject of a sentence is what we **speak about.** What we **speak about** we must **name.**

If we **name** a thing, we must use a **name** or **noun.** Therefore the **subject** must always be either—

(i) A noun; or
(ii) Some word or words **equivalent to a noun.**

7. There are **seven** kinds of Subjects—

   (i) A **Noun**, as, **England** is our home.

   (ii) A **Pronoun**, as, **It** is our fatherland.

   (iii) A **Verbal Noun**, as, **Walking** is healthy.

   (iv) A **Gerund**, as, **Catching** fish is a pleasant pastime.

   (v) An **Infinitive**, as, **To** swim is quite easy.

   (vi) An **Adjective**, with a **noun understood**, as, The **prosperous** are sometimes cold-hearted.

   (vii) A **Quotation**, as, "**Ay, ay, sir!**" burst from a thousand throats.

   (*a*) The verbal noun, as we have seen, originally ended in **ung**.

   (*b*) **Catching** is a gerund, because it is both a **noun** (nominative to *is*) and a **verb**, governing *fish* in the objective.

8. The **Predicate** in a sentence is what we **say** about the subject. If we **say** anything, we must use a **saying** or **telling** word. But a **telling** word is a **verb**.

Therefore the **Predicate** must always be a **verb**, or some word or words **equivalent** to a **verb**.

9. There are **five** kinds of Predicates—

   (i) A **Verb**, as, God is. The stream **runs**.

   (ii) "**To be**" + a **noun**, as, He is a **carpenter**.

   (iii) "**To be**" + an **adjective**, as, They **are idle**.

   (iv) "**To be**" + an **adverb**, as, The books **are there**.

   (v) "**To be**" + a **phrase**, as, She **is in good health**.

10. When the predicate consists of an **active-transitive verb**, it requires an **object** after it to make **complete sense**. This object is called either the **object** or the **completion**. As we must **name** the object, it is plain that it must always, like the subject, be a **noun**, or some word or words **equivalent** to a **noun**.

11. As there are **seven** kinds of **Subjects**, so there are seven kinds of **Objects** or **Completions**. These are :—

(i) A **Noun**, as, All of us love **England**.

(ii) A **Pronoun**, as, We saw him in the garden.

(iii) A **Verbal Noun**, as, We like **walking**.

(iv) A **Gerund**, as, The angler prefers **taking** large fish.

(v) An **Infinitive**, as, We hate **to be idle**.

(vi) An **Adjective** with a noun **understood**, as, Good men love **the good**.

(vii) A **Quotation**, as, We heard his last "Good-bye, Tom!"

12. Verbs of **giving, promising, offering, handing,** and many such, take also an **indirect object,** which is sometimes called the **dative object.**

13. There are **two** kinds of Indirect Objects :—

(i) A **Noun**, We gave the **man** a shilling.

(ii) A **Pronoun**, We offered **him** sixpence.

☞ The indirect or dative object may be construed with **to**. Thus we can say, "We offered it **to him**." But, in such instances, **to him** is still the indirect object and **it** the direct object.

14. The **Subject** or the **Object** is always a **Noun.**

A **Noun** may have going with it any number of **adjectives** or **adjectival phrases**. An adjective or adjectival phrase that goes with a subject or with an object is called, in Analysis, an **Enlargement.**

It is so called because it **enlarges** our knowledge of the subject. Thus, if we say, "The man is tired," we have no knowledge of what kind of *man* is spoken of ; but, if we say, "The poor old man is tired," our notion of the man is **enlarged** by the addition of the facts that he is both *poor* and *old*.

15. There are **seven** kinds of **Enlargements** :—

(i) An **Adjective**—one, two, or more—That **big old red** book is sold.

(ii) A **Noun** (or nouns) **in apposition**, William the Conqueror defeated Harold.

(iii) A **Noun** (or pronoun) in the **Possessive Case,**
His hat flew off.

(iv) A **Prepositional Phrase,** The walk in the fields
was pleasant.

(v) An **Adjectival Phrase,** The boy, **ignorant of his
duty,** was soon dismissed.

(vi) A **Participle** (*a*), or **Participial Phrase** (*b*)—
Sobbing and weeping, she was led from the
room (*a*).   The merchant, **having failed,** gave up
business (*b*).

(vii) A **Gerundial Infinitive**—Anxiety **to succeed** (= of
succeeding) wore him out.   Bread **to eat** (= for
eating) could not be had anywhere.

16. It is plain that all these seven kinds of Enlargements
may go with the **Object** as well as with the **Subject.**

17. An **Enlargement,** being a word or phrase that **goes
with a noun,** must always be **an adjective** or equivalent to
an adjective.

18. The Predicate is always a verb.

The word that goes with a verb is called an **adverb.**

Therefore the word or words that **go with the predicate**
are either **adverbs** or **words equivalent to adverbs.**

19. The adverbs or adverbial phrases that go with the predicate are called, in Analysis, the **Extensions of the Predicate.**

20. There are **six** kinds of **Extensions** :—

(i) An **Adverb,** as, The time went **slowly.**

(ii) An **Adverbial Phrase,** as, Mr Smith spoke **very
well indeed.**

(iii) A **Prepositional Phrase,** as, Mr Smith spoke **with
great effect.**

(iv) A **Noun Phrase,** as, We walked **side by side.**

(v) A **Participial Phrase,** as, The mighty rocks came
bounding down.

(vi) A **Gerundial Phrase,** as, He did it to insult us
(= for insulting us).

☞ Under (v) may come also the **Absolute Participial Phrase,** such
as, "The clock **having struck,** we had to go."

21. Extensions of the predicate are classified in the above
section from the point of view of **grammar;** but they are also
frequently classified from the point of view of **distinction in
thought.**

In this latter way Extensions are classified as extensions of—

(i) **Time,** as, We lived there **three years.**

(ii) **Place,** as, Go home! We came **from York.**

(iii) **Manner,** as, We scatter seeds **with careless hand.**

(iv) **Magnitude,** as, The field measured **ten acres.**

(v) **Cause,** as, The clerk was dismissed **for idleness.**

Under (iv) may also come the idea of **weight** and **price,** as, The parcel weighed
four pounds. It cost **sixpence.**

II.—CAUTIONS IN THE ANALYSIS OF SIMPLE SENTENCES.

22. The following **cautions** are of importance :—

(i) The **Noun** in an **absolute** clause **cannot** be the
Subject of a simple sentence. We can say, "The
train having started, we returned to the hotel."
Here **we** is the subject.

The phrase "the train having started" is an adverbial phrase modifying *returned,* and giving the *reason* for the returning.

(ii) The direct object may be **compound.** Thus we can
say, "I saw the ship sink;" and "the ship sink" is
a **compound direct** object.

If it is necessary to analyse the phrase "the ship sink," then we must
say that **sink** is the direct object of *saw;* and that **ship** is the **subject**
of the infinitive verb **sink.** (In English, as well as in Latin, the subject
of an infinitive is in the **objective or accusative** case.)

(iii) A subject may be **compound,** and may **contain** an
object, as, "To save money is always useful." Here

the subject is **to save money,** and contains the **object** money—the object of the verb to save.

An object may also **contain another** object, which is **not** the object of the sentence. Thus we can say, "I like to **save** money," when the direct object of **like** is to **save,** and **money** is a **part** only of that direct object.

(iv) The **Nominative of address cannot** be the subject of a sentence. Thus, in the sentence, "John, go into the garden," the subject of **go** is not John, but **you** understood.

III.—THE MAPPING-OUT OF SIMPLE SENTENCES.

23. It is of the greatest importance to get the **eye** to help the **mind,** and to present to the **sight** if possible—either on paper or on the black-board—the sentence we have to consider. This is called **mapping-out.**

Let us take two simple sentences :—

(i) "From the mountain-path came a joyous sound of some person whistling."

(ii) "In the Acadian land, on the shores of the Basin of Minas,
    Distant, secluded, still, the little village of Grand-Pré
    Lay in the fruitful valley."

24. These may be mapped out, before analysing them, in the following way :—

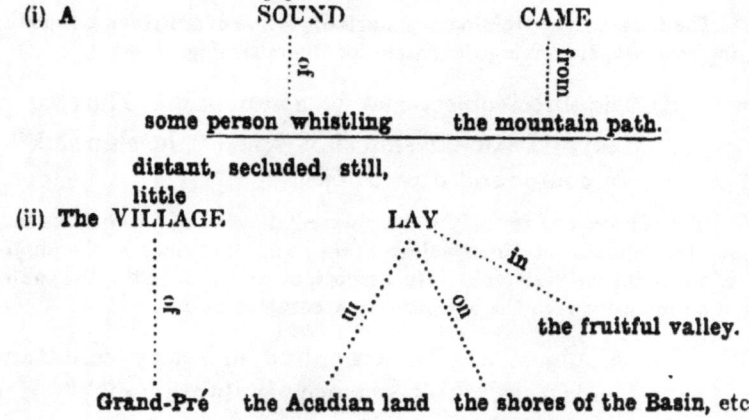

25. Such a mapping-out enables us easily to see, with the bodily as well as with the mind's eye, what is the main purpose of all analysis—to find out which words go with which, and what is the real build of the sentence. Hence, unless we see at a glance the build of the sentence we are going to analyse, we ought, before doing so, to set to work and map it out.

IV.—THE COMPOUND SENTENCE.

26. A **Compound Sentence** is one which consists of two or more **Simple Sentences** packed, for convenience' sake, into one.

Thus, in the "Lay of the Last Minstrel," Sir W. Scott writes :—

"The way was long, the wind was cold,
The minstrel was infirm and old."

He might have put a full stop at **long** and at **cold**, for the sense ends in these places, and, **grammatically**, the two lines form three separate and distinct sentences. But because **in thought** the three are connected, the poet made **one compound** sentence out of the three simple sentences.

27. A Compound Sentence may be **contracted.**

(i) Thus, the famous sentence, "Cæsar came, saw, and conquered" is = three sentences—"Cæsar came," "Cæsar saw," etc., and is therefore **contracted in the subject.**

(ii) In the sentence, "Either a knave or a fool has done this," the sentence is **contracted in the predicate** for the purpose of avoiding the repetition of the verb *has done.*

28. Caution! The relative pronouns **who** and **which** sometimes combine **two co-ordinate sentences** into **one compound sentence.** Thus—

(i) We met a man at the gate, **who** told us the way.

(ii) He was not at home, **which** was a great pity.

Here **who** is = **and he**; **which** is = **and this**; and the two sentences in both instances are of equal rank. Hence both (i) and (ii) are compound sentences.

V.—THE COMPLEX SENTENCE.

29. A **Complex Sentence** is a statement which contains one **Principal Sentence**, and one or more sentences dependent upon it, which are called **Subordinate Sentences.** There are three kinds—and there can only be three kinds—of subordinate sentences—**Adjectival, Noun,** and **Adverbial.**

A subordinate sentence is sometimes called a **clause.**

30. A Subordinate Sentence that **goes with a Noun** fulfils the function of an Adjective, is equal to an Adjective, and is therefore called an **Adjectival Sentence.**

"Darkness, which might be felt, fell upon the city." Here the sub-sentence, "which - might - be - felt," goes with the noun **darkness,** belongs to it, and cannot be separated from it; and this sentence is therefore an adjectival sentence.

31. A Subordinate Sentence that **goes with a Verb** fulfils the function of an Adverb, is equal to an Adverb, and is therefore called an **Adverbial Sentence.**

"I will go whenever you are ready." Here the sub-sentence, "whenever you are ready," is attached to the verb **go,** belongs to it, and cannot be separated from it; and hence this sentence is an adverbial sentence.

32. A Subordinate Sentence that forms the **Subject** of a Predicate, or the **Object,** or that is **in apposition** with a noun, fulfils the function of a **Noun,** and is therefore called a **Noun Sentence.**

"He told me that his cousin had gone to sea." Here the sub-sentence, "his cousin had gone to sea," is the **object** of the transitive verb **told.** It fulfils the function of a **noun,** and is therefore a **noun sentence.**

33. An **Adjectival Sentence** may be attached to—

    (i) The **Subject** of the Principal Sentence; or to

    (ii) The **Object** of the Principal Sentence; or to

    (iii) Any **Noun** whatsoever.

(i) The book that-I-bought is on the table : to the **subject.**

(ii) I laid the book I-bought on the table ; to the **object.**

(iii) The child fell into the stream that-runs-past-the-mill : to the noun **stream**—a noun in an adverbial phrase.

34. An **Adverbial Sentence** may be attached to—

    (i) A **Verb** ;

    (ii) An **Adjective** ; or to

    (iii) An **Adverb.**

(i) To a **Verb.** It does not matter in what position the verb is. It may be (*a*) the Predicate, as in the sentence, "I walk *when I can*." It may be (*b*) an Infinitive forming a **subject**, as, "To get up *when one is tired* is not pleasant." It may be (*c*) a participle as in the sentence, "Having dined *before he came*, I started at once."

(ii) To an **Adjective.** "His grief was **such** *that all pitied him*." Here the sub-sentence "that all pitied him " modifies the adjective **such.**

(iii) To an **Adverb.** " He was so weak *that he could not stand*." Here the sub-sentence "that he could not stand" modifies the adverb **so,** which itself modifies the adjective **weak.**

35. A **Noun Sentence** may be—

    (i) The **Subject** of the Principal Sentence ; or

    (ii). The **Object** of the main verb ; or

    (iii) The **Nominative** after **is** ; or

    (iv) In **Apposition** with another Noun.

(i) "That-he-is-better cannot be denied : " the **subject.** Here the true nominative is **that.** "That cannot be denied." What ? "That = he is better." (From usage, **that** in such sentences acquires the function and force of a conjunction.)

(ii) " I heard that-he-was-better : " the **object.**

(iii) "My motive in going was that-I-might-be-of-use : " **nominative** after **was.**

(iv) " The fact that-he-voted-against-his-party is well known : " **in apposition** with **fact.**

36. Any number of Subordinate Sentences may be attached to the Principal Sentence. The only limit is that dictated by a regard to clearness, to the balance of clauses, or to good taste.

The best example of a very long sentence, which consists entirely of one principal sentence and a very large number of adjective sentences, is "The House that Jack built." "This is the house that-Jack-built." " This is the malt that-lay-in-the-house-that-Jack-built," and so on.

VI.—CAUTIONS IN THE ANALYSIS OF COMPLEX SENTENCES.

37. (i) Find out, **first** of all, the **Principal Sentence.**

(ii) **Secondly,** look for the sentences, if any, that attach themselves to the **Subject** of the Principal Sentence.

(iii) **Thirdly,** find those sentences, if any, that belong to the **object** of the Principal Sentence, or to any other **Noun** in it.

(iv) **Fourthly,** look for the subordinate sentences that are attached to the **Predicate** of the Principal Sentence.

When a subordinate sentence is long, quote only the first and last words, and place dots . . . . between them.

38. The following **Cautions** are necessary :—

(i) A **connective** may be omitted.

> In Shakespeare's "Measure for Measure," Isabel says—
>
> "I have a brother is condemned to die."
>
> Here **who** is omitted, and "**who** . . . **die**" is an adjectival sentence qualifying the object **brother.**

(ii) Do not be guided by the **part of speech** that introduces a subordinate sentence. Thus :—

(*a*) A **relative pronoun** may introduce a **noun sentence,** as, "I do not know who-he-is;" or an **adjectival sentence,** as, "John, who-was-a-soldier, is now a gardener."

(*b*) An **adverb** may introduce a **noun sentence,** as, "I don't know *where it has gone to;*" or an **adjectival sentence,** as, "The spot *where he lies* is unknown." In the sentence, "The reason why so few marriages are happy is because young ladies spend their time in making nets, not in making cages"—the subordinate sentence "why . . . happy" is,—though introduced by an adverb,—in apposition to the noun **reason,** and is therefore a noun sentence.

VII.—THE MAPPING-OUT OF COMPLEX SENTENCES.

39. Complex Sentences should be mapped out on the same

principles as Simple Sentences. Let us take a sentence from Mr Morris's "Jason" :—

> "And in his hand he bare a mighty bow,
> No man could bend of those that battle now."

This sentence may be drawn up after the following plan :—

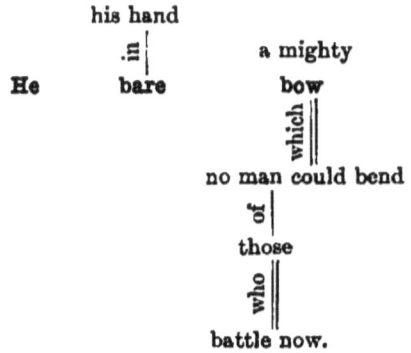

(The single line indicates a preposition ; the double line a conjunction or conjunctive pronoun.)

40. The larger number of subordinate sentences there are, and the farther away they stand from the principal sentence, the larger will be the space that the mapping-out will cover.

Let us take this sentence from an old Greek writer :—

"Thou art about, O king ! to make war against men who wear leathern trousers, and have all their other garments of leather ; who feed not on what they like, but on what they can get from a soil that is sterile and unkindly ; who do not indulge in wine, but drink water ; who possess no figs, nor anything else that is good to eat."

This would be set out in the following way :—

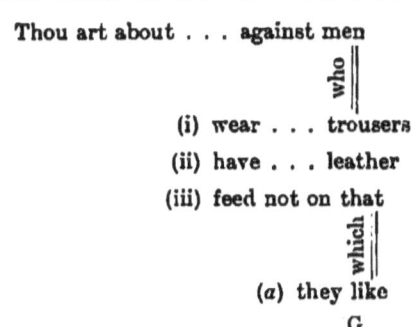

(iv) feed on that

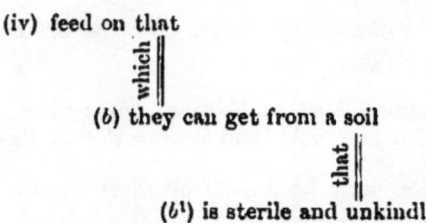

   (*b*) they can get from a soil

      (*b*¹) is sterile and unkindly

(v) do not . . . wine

(vi) drink water

(vii) possess no figs

(viii) possess not anything else

    (*c*) is good to eat.

41. Sentences may also be pigeon-holed, or placed in marked-off spaces or columns, like the following :—

> " Thro' the black Tartar tents he passed, which stood
> Clustering like bee-hives on the low black strand
> Of Oxus, where the summer floods o'erflow
> When the sun melts the snow in high Pamir."

SENTENCES.	KIND OF SENTENCE.	SUBJECT.	ENLARGE-MENT.	PREDI-CATE.	EXTEN-SION.	OBJECT.
A. He passed through the black Tartar tents	A. Prin. sentence.	He		passed	thro' the tents	
(*a*) which clustering like bee-hives stood on the strand of Oxus,	(*a*) Adj. sentence to A.	which	cluster-ing	stood	on the low black strand	
(*b*) [in the place] which the floods o'er-flow	(*b*) Adj. sent. to *place* under-stood	floods	the sum-mer	o'erflow		(which)
(*c*) when . . . melts	(*c*) Adv. sent. to *o'er-flow*	the sun		melts	when in high Pamir	snow

42. There is a kind of **Continuous Analysis,** which may often—not without benefit—be applied to longer passages, and especially to passages taken from the poets.   For example :—

> " Alas ! the meanest herb that scents the gale,
> The lowliest flower that blossoms in the vale
> Even where it dies, at spring's sweet call renews
> To second life its odours and its hues."

1. **Alas !** an interjection, with no syntactical relation to any word in the sentence.
2. **the meanest,** attributive or enlargement to 3.

A
3. **herb,** Subject to 4.
4. **renews,** Predicate to 3.
5. **odours and hues,** Object to 4.
6. **at . . . call,** Extension of *renews,* to 4.
7. **to . . . life,** Extension of *renews,* to 4.

8. **the lowliest,** attributive or enlargement to 9.

B
9. **flower,** Subject to 10.
10. **renews,** Predicate to 9.
11. **odours and hues,** Object to 10.
12. **at . . . call,** Extension to 10.
13. **to . . . life,** Extension to 10.

C
14. **that,** Subject to 15 and connective to 3.
15. **scents,** Predicate to 14.
16. **gale,** Object to 15.

D
17. **that,** Subject to 18 and connective to 9.
18. **blossoms,** Predicate to 17.
19. **in the vale,** Extension to 18.

E
20. **even,** Adverb modifying 21.
21. **where it dies,** Extension to 18.
22. **it,** Subject of 23.
23. **dies,** Predicate of 22.

WORD-BUILDING AND DERIVATION.

1. The **primary element**—that which is the shortest form—of a word is called its **root**. Thus **tal** (which means *number*) is the root of the words **tale** and **tell** and **till** (a box for money).

2. The **stem** is the root + some modification. Thus **love** (= lov + e) is the stem of **lov**.

3. It is to the stem that all inflexions are added, and thus to **love** we add **d** for the past tense.

4. If to the root we add a suffix, then the word so formed is called a **derivative**. Thus by adding **ling** to **dar** (= dear), we make **darling**.

5. In general, we add English prefixes and English suffixes to English words; but this is not always the case. Thus we have **cottage**, where the Latin ending **age** is added to the English word **cot**; and **covetousness**, where the English ending **ness** is added to the Latin word **covetous**. Such words are called **hybrids**.

6. When **two words** are put together to make one, the one word so made is called a **compound**.

7. The adding of prefixes or of suffixes to words, or the making one word out of two, is called **word-formation**.

COMPOUND NOUNS.

8. Compound Nouns are formed by the addition of :—

(i) **Noun** and **Noun**, as—

Bandog (= bond-dog).

Bridal (= bride-ale).

Brimstone (= burn-stone).

Bylaw (= law for a *by* or town).

Daisy (= day's eye).

Evensong.

Garlic (= gar-leek = spear-leek ;
O.E. *gár*, spear).

Gospel (= God's spell = story).

Housetop.

Huzzy (= housewife).

Icicle (= ís-gicel = ice-jag).

Lapwing (= leap-wing).

Nightingale (= night-singer).

Orchard (= ort-yard = wort-yard, *i.e.*,
herb-garden).

Stirrup (= stig-ráp = rising rope).

Tadpole (= toad-head. Pole = poll, a
head, as in poll-tax).

Wednesday (= Woden's day).

(ii) Noun and Adjective, as—

Blackbird.

Freeman.

Midnight.

Midsummer.

Quicksilver.

Twilight (= two lights).

☞ *Black' bird* has the accent on *black*, and is *one* word. A *black' bird* need not be a *black' bird'*.

(iii) Noun and Verb, as—

Bakehouse.

Cutpurse.

Godsend.

Grindstone.

Pickpocket.

Pinfold.

Spendthrift.

Wagtail.

Washtub.

(iv) Noun and Adverb, as offshoot.

(v) Noun and Preposition, as afterthought.

(vi) Verb and Adverb, as—

Castaway.

Welfare.

Drawback.

Farewell.

Income.

Welcome.

COMPOUND ADJECTIVES.

9. There are in the language a great many **compound adjectives**, such as *heart-whole*, *sea-sick*, etc.; and these are formed in a large number of different ways.

Compound adjectives may be formed in the following ways :—

(i) **Noun + Adjective**, as purse-proud, wind-swift, way-weary, sea-green, lily-white.

(ii) **Noun + Present Participle**, as ear-piercing, death-boding, heart-rending, spirit-stirring, sea-faring, night-walking, home-keeping.

(iii) **Noun + Passive Participle**, as moth-eaten, worm-eaten, tempest-tossed, way-laid, forest-born, copper-fastened, moss-clad, sea-girt.

(iv) **Adverb + Present Participle**, as far-darting, everlasting, high-stepping, well-meaning, long-suffering, far-reaching, hard-working.

(v) **Adverb + Passive Participle**, as high-born, "ill-weaved," well-bred, thorough-bred, high-strung, ill-pleased.

(vi) **Noun + Noun + ed,** as hare-brained, dog-hearted, beetle-headed, periwig-pated, club-footed, lily-livered, trumpet-tongued, eagle-eyed.

(vii) **Adjective + Noun + ed,** as evil-eyed, grey-headed, thin-faced, empty-headed, tender-hearted, thick-lipped, two-legged, three-cornered, four-sided, high-minded, bald-pated.

(viii) **Noun + Noun,** as bare-foot, lion-heart, iron-side.

(ix) **Adverb + Noun + ed,** as down-hearted, under-handed.

COMPOUND VERBS.

10. There are not many compound verbs in the English language. The few that there are are formed thus :—

(i) **Verb** and **Noun,** as —

Backbite.	Hamstring.	Hoodwink.
Browbeat.	Henpeck.	Kiln-dry.

(ii) **Verb** and **Adjective,** as—

Dumfound.	Fulfil (=fill full).	Whitewash.

(iii) **Verb** and **Adverb,** as—

Doff (=do off).	Dout (=do out).	Cross-question.
Don (=do on).	Dup (=do up).	Outdo.

THE FORMATION OF ADVERBS.

11. Adverbs are derived from **Nouns,** from **Adjectives,** from **Pronouns,** and from **Prepositions.**

a. Adverbs derived from Nouns are either: (i) **Old Possessives,** or (ii) **Old Datives,** or (iii) **Compounds** of a Noun and a Preposition :—

(i) **Old Possessives : Needs** = of need, or of necessity. The Calendrer says to John Gilpin about his hat and wig—

> " My head is twice as big as yours,
> They therefore **needs** must fit."

Of the same class are : **always, nowadays, betimes.**

(ii) **Old Datives.** These are **seldom** and the old-fashioned **whilom** (= in old times).

(iii) **Compounds : anon** = (in one moment), **abed** (= on bed) **asleep, aloft, abroad, indeed, of a truth, by turns, perchance, perhaps.**

b. Adverbs derived from Adjectives are either: (i) **Old Possessives,** or (ii) **Old Datives,** or (iii) **Compounds** of an Adjective and a Preposition :—

(i) **Old Possessives : else** (ell-es, possessive of *al* = other), **unawares, once** (= ones), **twice, thrice,** etc.

(ii) **Old Datives.** The old English way of forming an adverb was simply to use the dative case of the adjective—which ended in ē. Thus we had **deepē, brightē,** for *deeply* and *brightly*. Then the ē dropped away. Hence it is that there are in English several adverbs exactly like adjectives. These are: *fast, hard, right* (in "Right Reverend"), *far, ill, late, early, loud, high*.

(iii) **Compounds of an Adjective and a Preposition:** on high, in vain, in short, at large, of late, etc.

c. Adverbs derived from Pronouns come from the pronominal stems: **who, the** (or **this**), and **he.** The following is a table, and it is important to note the beautiful correspondences :—

PRONOMINAL STEMS.	PLACE In.	PLACE To.	PLACE From.	TIME In.	MANNER.	CAUSE.
Wh-o	Whe-re	Whi-ther	Whe-nce	Whe-n	Ho-w	Wh-y
Th-e or th-is	The-re	Thi-ther	The-nce	The-n	Th-us	Th-e
He	He-re	Hi-ther	He-nce			

(i) **How** and **why** are two forms of the same word—the instrumental case of **who. How**=in what way? **Why**=with what reason?

(ii) **The,** in the last column, is the adverbial **the** (A.S. thȳ) before a comparative. It is the instrumental or ablative case of *that* or *thaet*. "The more, the merrier"=by that more, by that merrier. That is, the measure of the increase in the number is the measure of the increase in the merriment.

(iii) **Thus** is the instrumental case of *this,* and is=in this manner.

d. Compound Adverbs are formed by adding together—

(i) **Noun and Noun,** as lengthways, endways.

(ii) **Noun and Adjective,** as —

Always.	Head-foremost.	Otherwise.
Breast-high.	Meanwhile.	Sometimes.

(iii) **Preposition and Noun,** as Aboveboard, outside.

(iv) **Adverb and Preposition,** as—

Hereafter.	Therein.	Whereupon.

PREFIXES AND SUFFIXES.

12. The Prefixes used in our language are of English, French, Latin, and Greek origin.

(i) French is only a modified Latin. Hence French prefixes fall naturally under Latin prefixes, as the one is only a form of the other.

13. English Prefixes are divided into **Inseparable** and **Separable**. Inseparable Prefixes are those that have no meaning by themselves and cannot be used apart from another word. Separable Prefixes may be used and are used as independent words.

14. The following are the most important

English Inseparable Prefixes :—

1. **A** (a broken-down form of O.E. **an** = on), as—

Abed.   Aloft (= in the lift or sky).   A-building.
Aboard.   Away.   Athwart (= on the cross).

2. **Be** (an O.E. form of *by*), which has several functions :—

(i) To add an intensive force to transitive verbs, as—

Bedaub.   Beseech   Besmear.
Besprinkle.   (= beseek).   Besmirch.

(ii) To turn intransitive verbs into transitive, as—

Bemoan.   Bespeak.   Bethink.

(iii) To make verbs out of nouns or adjectives, as—

Befriend.   Beguile.   Benumb.   Betroth.
Besiege (= to take a *siege* or seat beside a town till it surrenders).

(iv) To combine with nouns, as—

Behalf.   Bequest.   Bypath.
Behest.   Byname.   Byword.

(v) To form part of prepositions and adverbs, as before, besides, etc.

3. **For** (O.E. *for* = Lat. *per*) means *thoroughly*, and has two functions :—

(i) To add an intensive meaning, as in—

Forbid.   Forget.   Forswear.
Fordone (= ruined).   Forgive.   Forlorn (= utterly lost).

☞ *Forswear* means to *swear out and out*, to swear to anything, hence *falsely*. Compare the Latin *perjurare ;* hence our *perjure*.

(ii) To give a negative meaning, as in *forgo* (wrongly spelled *forego*), to go without.

4. **Fore** = before ; as forebode, forecast.

5. **Gain** (O.E. *gaegn*, back, again), found in gainsay (to speak against) ; gainstand.

6. **Mis** (O.E. *mis*, wrong ; and connected with the verb *to miss*), as in—

Misdeed.	Mislead.	Mistrust.	Mistake.

Caution.—When *mis* occurs in French words, it is a shortened form of *minus*, less ; as in *mischief, mischance, miscount, miscreant* (= non-believer).

7. **Th**, the prefix of the third personal pronoun and its cognates, and indicating something *spoken of*, as in—

Those.	That.	Thither.	They.
This.	There.	Thence.	The.

8. **Un** = not, as

Unholy.	Undo.	Unbind.

9. **Wan** (O.E. *wan*, wanting ; and connected with *wane*), which is found in—

Wanton (= wantowen, lacking education).	Wanhope (= despair). Wantrust.

10. **With** (a shortened form of O.E. *wither* = back or against) is found in—

Withstand.	Withdraw.	Withhold.

☞ It exists also in a *latent* form in the word *drawing-room* = *withdrawing-room*.

15. The following are the most important

English Separable Prefixes :—

1. **After**, which is found in—

Aftergrowth.	Aftermath (*from* mow).	After-dinner.

2. **All** (O.E. *al*, quite), which is found in—

Almighty.	Alone (quite by *one's* self).	Almost.

3. **Forth**, found in forthcoming, forward, etc.

4. **Fro** (a shortened form of *from*), in froward.

5. **In** appears in modern English in two forms, as :—

(i) **In**, in—

Income.	Insight.	Instep.
Inborn.	Inbred.	Inlay.

(ii) **En** or **em** (which is a Frenchified form), in—

Endear.	Entwine.	Embolden.
Enlighten.	Embitter.	

6. **Of** or **off** (which are two spellings of the same word), as—

Offspring.	Offset.
Offshoot.	Offal (that which *falls off*).

7. **On,** as in onset, onslaught, onward.

8. **Out,** which takes also the form of **ut,** as in—

Outbreak.	Outside.	Utter.
Outcast.	Outpost.	Utmost.

9. **Over** (the comparative of the *ove* in *above*), which combines :—

(i) With nouns, as in—

Overcoat.	Overflow.	Overhand.

(ii) With adjectives, as in—

Over-bold.	Over-merry.	Over-proud.

(Shakespeare is very fond of such forms.)

(iii) With verbs, as in—

Overthrow.	Overspread.	Overhear.

10. **Thorough** or **through,** two forms of the same word, as in—

Throughout.　Through-train.　Thorough-bred.　Thoroughfare.

Shakespeare has "thorough bush, thorough brier, thorough flood, thorough fire.

11. **Twi** = two, in twilight, twin, twist, etc.

12. **Under,** which goes :—

(i) With verbs, as in—

Underlie.	Undersell.	Undergo.

(ii) With nouns, as in—

Underhand.	Underground.	Undertone.

(iii) With other words, as in—

Underneath.	Underlying.

13. **Up,** which goes :—

(i) With verbs, as in—

Upbear.	Upbraid.	Uphold.

(ii) With nouns, as in—

Upland.	Upstart.	Upshot.

(iii) With other words, as in—

Upright.	Upward.

16. There are in use in our language many Latin Prefixes; and many of them are of great service. Some of them, as **circum** (about), come to us direct from Latin; others, like **counter** (against), have come to us through the medium of French. The following are the most important

Latin Prefixes :—

1. **A, ab, abs** (Fr. a, av), *away from*, as in—

Avert.	Abjure.	Absent.	Abstain.
Avaunt.	Advantage (which ought to be avantage).		

2. **Ad** (Fr. a), to, which in composition becomes **ac, af, ag, al, an, ap, ar, as, at,** to assimilate with the first consonant of the root. The following are examples of each :—

Adapt.	Affect.	Accord.	Agree.
Aggression.	Allude.	Annex.	Appeal.
Arrive.	Assimilate.	Attain.	Attend.

☞ All these words come straight to us from Latin, except *agree, arrive,* and *attain.* The following are also French : *Achieve* (to bring to a *chef* or head), *amount, acquaint.*

3. **Amb, am** (*ambi*, about), as in—

Ambition.	Ambiguous.	Amputate.

4. **Ante** (Fr. an), before, as in—

Antedate.	Antechamber.	Ancestor (= antecessor).

5. **Bis, bi,** twice, as in—

Bisect.	Biscuit (= biscoctus, twice baked).

6. **Circum, circa,** around, as in—

Circumference.	Circulate.	Circuit.

7. **Cum,** with, in French **com,** which becomes **col, con, cor, coun,** and **co** before a vowel, as in—

Compound.	Collect.	Content.	Correct.
Counsel.	Countenance.	Coeval.	Coöperate.

(i) In *cost* (from *constare*, to "stand"); *couch* (from *collŏco*, I place); *cull* (from *collĕgo*, I collect); and *cousin* (from *consobrīnus*, the child of a mother's sister), the prefix has undergone great changes

(ii) Co, though of Latin origin, can go with purely English words, as in *co-worker, co-understanding.* These are not desirable *compounds.*

8. **Contra** (Fr. **contre**), against, which also becomes **contro** and **counter,** as in—

Contradict.	Controvert.	Counterbalance.

(i) In *counterweigh* and *counterwork* we find it in union with English roots.

(ii) In *encounter* we find it converted into a root.

9. **De** (Fr. **de**), down, from, about, as in—

Decline.	Describe.	Depart.

It has also two different functions.   It is—

   (i) negative in destroy, deform, desuetude, etc.

   (ii) intensive in desolate, desiccate (to dry up), etc.

10. **Dis, di** (Fr. **des, de**), asunder, in two, as in—

Dissimilar.	Disarm.	Dismember.
Differ (s becomes f).	Disease.	Divorce.
Defy.	Defer.	Delay.

   (i) Dis is also joined with English roots to make the hybrids *disown, dislike, distrust, distaste.*

11. **Ex, e** (Fr. **es, e**), out of, from, as in—

Exalt.	Exhale.	Expatriate (*patria*, one's country).
Elect.	Evade.	Educe.

   (i) ex has a privative sense in *ex-emperor*, etc.

   (ii) In *amend* (*emendo*), *astonish* (*étonner*), the e is disguised.

   (iii) In *sample* (short for *example*), *scorch* (O. Fr. *escorcer*), and *special* (for *especial*), the e has fallen away.

12. **Extra**, beyond, as in—

Extraneous.	Extraordinary.	Extravagant.

   (i) In *stranger* (O. Fr. *estranger*, from Lat. *extraneus*) the e has fallen away.

13. **In** (Fr. **en, em**), in, into, which changes into **il, im, ir**, as in—

Invade.	Invent (to *come* upon).	Infer.
Illusion.	Improve.	Immigrate.
Irritate.	Irrigate.	Irradiate.
Enchant.	Endure.	Envoy.

   (i) It unites with English roots to make the hybrids *embody, embolden, endear, entrust, enlighten*, etc.

   (ii) In *ambush* (Ital. *imboscarsi*, to put one's self in a wood), the in is disguised.

14. **In**, not, which becomes **il, im, ir**, and **ig**, as in—

Inconvenient.	Illiberal.	Impious.	Irrelevant.
Incautious.	Illegal.	Impolitic.	Ignoble.

   (i) The English prefix un sometimes takes its place, and forms hybrids with Latin roots in *unable, unapt, uncomfortable.*

   (ii) Shakespeare has *unpossible, unproper*, and many others.

15. **Inter, intro** (Fr. **entre**), between, among—as in

Intercede.	Interpose.	Interfere.
Introduce.	Entertain.	Enterprise.

16. **Male** (Fr. **mau**), ill, as in—

   Malediction, (contracted through French into)

   Malison (opposed to *Benison*).   Maugre.

17. **Mis** (Fr. **mes**, from Latin **minus**), less, as in—

Misadventure.   Mischance.   Mischief.

Caution.—Not to be confounded with the English prefix **mis** in *mistake, mistrust*, etc.

18. **Non**, not, as in—

Nonsense.   Non-existent.   Nonsuit.

(i) The initial n has dropped off in *umpire*, formerly *numpire* = O. Fr. *nonper* = Lat. *nonpar*, not equal.

(ii) The n has fallen away likewise from *norange, napron* (connected with *napkin, napery*), etc., by wrongly cleaving to the indefinite article a.

19. **Ob**, against, becomes **oc, of, op**, etc., as in—

Obtain.   Occur.   Offend.   Oppose.

20. **Pene**, almost, as in—

Peninsula.   Penultimate (the last but one).

21. **Per** (Fr. **par**), through, which becomes **pel**, as in—

Pellucid.   Perform.   Perjure.
Perfect.   Permit.   Pilgrim.

(i) *Pilgrim* comes from *peregrinus*, a person who wanders *per agros*, through the fields,—by the medium of Ital. *pellegrino*.

(ii) *Perhaps* is a hybrid.

22. **Post**, after, as in—

Postpone.   Postdate.   Postscript.

(i) The *post* is much disguised in *puny*, which comes from the French *puis né* = Lat. *post natus*, born after. A "puny judge" is a junior judge, or a judge of a later creation.

23. **Præ, pre** (Fr. **pré**), before, as in—

Predict.   Presume.   Pretend.   Prevent.

(i) It is shortened into a pr in *prize, prison, apprehend, comprise* (all from *prehendo*, I seize).

(ii) It is disguised in *provost* (*prepositus*, one placed over), in *preach* (from *prædico*, I speak before), and *provender* (from *præbeo*, I furnish).

24. **Præter**, beyond, as in—

Preternatural.   Preterite (beyond the present).   Pretermit.

25. **Pro** (Fr. **pour**), which becomes **pol, por, pur**, as in—

Pronoun.   Proconsul.   Procure.   Protest.
Pollute.   Portrait.   Pursue.   Purchase.

26. **Re** (Fr. **re**), back, again, which becomes **red**, as in—

Rebel.   Reclaim.   Recover.   Refer.
Redeem.   Redound.   Readmit.   Recreant.

(i) It is much disguised in *rally* (= re-ally), in *ransom* (a shortened Fr. form of *redemption*), and in *runagate* (= *renegade*, one who has denied—*negavit*—his faith).

(ii) It combines with English roots to form the hybrids *relay, reset, recall*.

27. **Retro**, backwards—as in retrograde, retrospect.

(i) It is disguised in *rear-guard* (Ital. *retro-gardia*), *rear*, and *arrears*.

28. **Se** (Fr. **sé**), apart, which becomes **sed**, as in—

Secede.   Seclude.   Seduce.   Sedition.

29. **Sub** (Fr. **sous** or **sou**), under, which becomes **suc, suf, sud, sum, sup, sur,** and **sus,** as in—

Subtract.   Succour.   Suffer.   Suggest.
Summon.   Supplant.   Surrender.   Suspend.

(i) **Sub** is disguised in *sojourn* (from O. Fr. *sojorner*, from Low Latin *subdiurnâre*), and in *sudden* (from Latin *subitaneus*).

(ii) It combines with English roots to form the hybrids *sublet, subworker, sub-kingdom,* etc.

30. **Subter**, beneath—as in subterfuge.

31. **Super** (Fr. **sur**), above, as in—

Supernatural.   Superpose.   Superscription.
Surface (superficies).   Surname.   Surtout (over-all).

(i) It is disguised in *sovereign* (which Milton more correctly spells *sovran*), from Low Latin *superanus*.

32. **Trans** (Fr. **trés**), beyond, which becomes **tra**, as in—

Translate.   Transport.   Transform.   Transitive.
Tradition.   Traverse.   Travel.   Trespass.

(i) It is disguised in *treason* (the Fr. form of *tradition*, from *trado* (=*transdo*), I give up), in *betray* and *traitor* (from the same Latin root), in *trance* and *entrance* (Latin *transitus*, a passing beyond), and in *trestle* (from Latin diminutive *transtillum*, a little cross-beam).

33. **Ultra**, beyond, as in—

Ultra-Liberal.   Ultra-Tory.   Ultramontane.

(i) In *outrage* (O. Fr. *oultrage*) the *ultra* is disguised.

34. **Unus**, one, which becomes **un** and **uni**, as in—

Unanimous.   Uniform.   Unicorn.

35. **Vice** (Fr. **vice**), in the place of, as in—

Viceroy.   Vicar.   Vice-chancellor.   Viscount.

17. Our language possesses also a considerable number of prefixes transferred from the Greek language, many of which are very useful. The following are the most important

Greek Prefixes:—

1. **An, a** (ἀν, ἀ), not, as in—
Anarchy.   Anonymous.   Apteryx (the wingless).   Atheist.

2. **Amphi** (ἀμφί), on both sides, as in—
Amphibious.   Amphitheatre.

3. **Ana** (ἀνά), up, again, back, as in—
 Anatomy. Analysis. Anachronism.

4. **Anti** (ἀντί), against or opposite to, as in—
 Antidote. Antipathy. Antipodes. Antarctic.

5. **Apo** (ἀπό), away from, which also becomes **ap**, as in—
 Apostate. Apostle. Apology. Aphelion.

6. **Arch, archi, arche** (ἀρχή), chief, as in—
 Archbishop. Archangel. Architect. Archetype.

7. **Auto** (αὐτός), self, which becomes **auth**, as in—
 Autocrat. Autograph. Autotype. Authentic.

8. **Cata, cat** (κατά), down, as in—
 Catalogue. Catapult. Catechism. Cathedral.

9. **Dia** (διά), through, across, as in—
 Diameter. Diagram. Diagonal.

 (i) This prefix is disguised in *devil*—from Gr. *diabŏlos*, the accuser or slanderer, from Gr. *diaballein*, to throw across.

10. **Dis, di** (δίς), twice, as in—
 Dissyllable. Diphthong. Dilemma.

11. **Dys** (δυς), ill, as in—
 Dysentery. Dyspeptic (contrasts with Eupeptic).

12. **Ec, ex** (ἐκ, ἐξ), out of, as in—
 Eccentric. Ecstasy. Exodus. Exotic.

13. **En** (ἐν), in, which becomes **el** and **em**, as in—
 Encyclical. Encomium. Ellipse. Emphasis.

14. **Epi, ep** (ἐπί), upon, as in—
 Epitaph. Epiphany. Epoch. Ephemeral.

15. **Eu** (εὖ), well, which also becomes **ev**, as in—
 Euphemism. Eulogy. Evangelist.

16. **Hemi** (ἡμί), half, as in—
 Hemisphere. Hemistich (half a line in poetry).

17. **Hyper** (ὑπέρ), over and above, as in—
 Hyperborean. Hyperbolé. Hypercritical. Hypermetrical.

18. **Hypo, hyp** (ὑπό), under, as in—
 Hypocrite. Hypotenuse. Hyphen.

19. **Meta, met** (μετά), after, changed for, as in—
 Metaphor. Metamorphosis. Metonymy. Method.

20. **Mono, mon** (μόνος), alone, as in—
 Monogram. Monody. Monad. Monk.

21. **Pan** (πᾶν), all, as in—

    Pantheist.   Panacea.   Panorama.   Pantomime.

22. **Para** (παρά), by the side of, which becomes **par**, as in—

    Paradox.   Parallel.   Parish.   Parody.

23. **Peri** (περί), round, as in—

    Perimeter.   Period.   Perigee.   Periphery.

24. **Pro** (πρό), before, as in—

    Prophet.   Prologue.   Proboscis.   Problem.

25. **Pros** (πρός), towards, as in—

    Prosody.   Proselyte.

26. **Syn** (σύν), with, which becomes **syl**, **sym**, and **sy**, as in—

    Syntax.   Synagogue.   Syllable.
    Sympathy.   Symbol.   System.

18. The Suffixes employed in the English language are much more numerous than the Prefixes, and much more useful. Like the Prefixes, they come to us from three sources—from Old English (or Anglo-Saxon); from Latin (or French); and from Greek.

19. The following are the most important

English Suffixes to Nouns:—

1. **Ard** or **art** (=habitual), as in—

    Braggart.   Coward.   Drunkard.   Dullard.
    Laggard.   Niggard.   Sluggard.   Wizard.

2. **Craft** (skill), as in—

    Leechcraft (=medicine).   Priestcraft.   Witchcraft.
    Woodcraft.   Rimecraft (old name for *Arithmetic*).

3. **D, t** or **th** (all being dentals), as in—

    (i) Blood (from *blow*, said of flowers).   Blade (from the same).   Deed (do).
        Flood (flow).   Seed (sow).   Thread (throw).

    (ii) Drift (drive).   Drought (dry).   Draught (draw).
        Flight (fly).   Height (high: Milton uses *highth*).   Shrift (shrive).
        Rift (rive).   Theft (thieve).   Weft (weave).

    (iii) Aftermath (mow).   Berth (bear).   Dearth (dear).
        Death (die).   Earth (ear=plough).   Health (heal).
        Mirth (merry).   Sloth (slow).   Tilth (till).

4. **Dom** (O.E. **dôm**=doom), power, office, from *deman*, to judge, as in—

Dukedom.   Kingdom.   Halidom (=holiness).
Christendom.   Thraldom.   Wisdom.

(i) In O.E. we had *bisceopdóm* (=bishopdom); and Carlyle has accustomed us to *rascaldom* and *scoundreldom*.

5. **En** (a diminutive), as in—

Chicken (cock).   Kitten (cat).   Maiden.

(i) The addition of a syllable has a tendency to modify the preceding vowel—as in *kitchen* (from *cook*), *vixen* (from *fox*), and *national* (from *nation*).

6. **Er**, which has three functions, to denote—

(i) An **agent**, as in—

Baker.   Dealer.   Leader.   Writer.

(ii) An **instrument**, as in—

Finger (from O.E. *fangan*, to take).   Stair (from *stigan*, to mount).

(iii) A **male agent**, as in—

Fuller (from *fullian*, to cleanse).   Player.   Sower.

☞ The ending *er* has become disguised in *beggar* and *sailor* (not *sailer*, which is a ship). Under the influence of Norman-French, an *i* or *y* creeps in before the *r*, as in *collier* (from *coal*), *lawyer*, *glazier* (from *glass*), etc.

7. **Hood** (O.E. **hâd**), state, rank, person, as in—

Brotherhood.   Childhood.   Priesthood.   Wifehood.

(i) In *Godhead*, this suffix takes the form of *head*.

8. **Ing** (originally=*son of*) part, as in—

Farthing (*fourth*).   Riding (*trithing*=*thirding*).   Tithing (tenth).

(i) This suffix is found as a patronymic in many proper names, such as *Browning*, *Harding*; and in *Kensington*, *Whittington*, etc.

(ii) *Lording* (=the son of a lord) and *whiting* (from *white*) are also diminutives.

(iii) This *ing* is to be carefully distinguished from the *ing* (=*ung*) which was the old suffix for verbal nouns, as *clothing*, *learning*, etc.

9. **Kin** (a diminutive), as in—

Bodkin.   Firkin (from *four*).   Lambkin.   Mannikin.

(i) It is also found in proper names, as in *Dawkins* (=*little David*), *Jenkins* (=son of *little John*), *Hawkins* (=son of *little Hal*), *Perkins* (=son of *little Peter*).

10. **Ling** = 1 + **ing** (both diminutives), as in—

Darling (from *dear*).   Duckling.   Gosling (*goose*).
Firstling.   Hireling.   Nestling.

(i) Every diminutive has a tendency to run into depreciation, as in *groundling*, *underling*, *worldling*, etc.

(ii) In some words, *ing* has been weakened into *y* or *ie*, as in *Johnnie*, *Billy*, *Betty*, etc.

H

11. **Le** or **l**, as in—

Beadle (from *beodan*, to bid).   Bundle (bind).   Saddle (seat).
Settle (seat).   Nail.   Sail.

12. **Lock** (O.E. **lâc**, gift, sport), which also becomes **ledge**, as in—
Knowledge.   Wedlock.   *Feohtlâc* (battle).

(i) This is not to be confused with the *lock* and *lick* in the names of plants, which in O.E. was *leac*, and which we find in *hemlock, charlock; gurlick* (=*spear plant*) and *barley* (=*berelic*).

13. **Ness** forms abstract nouns from adjectives, as in—
Darkness.   Holiness.   Weakness.   Weariness.

(i) *Witness* differs from the above in two respects: (*a*) it comes from a verb—*witan*, to know; and (*b*) is *not* always an abstract noun.

(ii) This English suffix combines very easily with foreign roots, as in *acuteness, commodiousness, gracefulness, remoteness*, and many others.

14. **Nd** (which is the ending of the present participle in O.E.), found in—

Friend (=the loving one).   Fiend (=the hating one).
Errand.   Wind (from a root *vâ*, to blow).

15. **Ock** (a diminutive), as in—
Bullock.   Hillock.   Ruddock (=redbreast).

(i) In *hawk* (=the seizer, from *have*) this suffix is disguised.

(ii) It is also found in proper names, as in—
Pollock (from *Paul*).   Maddox (from *Matthew*).   Wilcox (from *William*).

16. **M** or **om**, which forms nouns from verbs, as in—
Bloom (from *blow*).   Qualm (from *quell*).
Gloom (from *glow*).   Seam (from *sew*).
Gleam (from *glow*).   Team (from *tow*).

(i) This suffix unites with the Norman-French word *réal* (*royal*) to form the hybrid *realm*.

17. **Red** (mode, fash on—and also counsel), as in—
Hatred.   Kindred.   Sibrede (relationship).

(i) This ending is also found in proper nouns. Thus we have *Mildred=mild in counsel; Ethelred=noble in counsel*, called also *Unrede*, which does not mean *unready*, but *without counsel*.

18. **Ric** (O.E. **rice**, power, dominion)—as in bishopric.

(i) In O.E. we had *abbotric, hevenricke*, and *kingric*.

19. **Ship** (O.E. **scipe**, shape or form), which is also spelled **scape** and **skip**, makes abstract nouns, as in—

Fellowship.   Friendship.   Lordship.
Landscape.   Workmanship.   Worship (=worthship).

(i) Milton writes *landskip* for *landscape*.

20. **Stead** (O.E. **stéde**, place), as in—

Bedstead.   Homestead.   Hampstead.   Berkhamstead.

21. **Ster** was originally the feminine of **er**, the suffix for a male agent : it has now two functions :—

   (i) It denotes an **agent**, as in—

      Huckster (hawker).   Maltster.   Songster.   Roadster.

   (ii) It has an element of **depreciation** in—

      Gamester.   Punster.   Oldster.   Youngster.

   (iii) We had, in Old English, *baxter* (fem. of *baker*), *webster* (*weaver*), *brewster*, *fithelstre* (*fiddler*), *seamestre* (*sewer*), and even *belleringestre* (for female bellringer). Most of these are now used as proper names.

   (iv) **Spinster** is the feminine of *spinner*, one form of which was *spinder*, which then became *spider*.

22. **Ther, der,** or **ter** denotes the agent—with the notion of *duality*—as in—

Father.   Mother.   Sister.   Brother.
Bladder (*blow*).   Rudder (*row*).   Water (*wet*).   Winter (*wind*).

23. **Wright** (from **work,** by metathesis of the **r**), as in—

Shipwright.   Wainwright (=waggonwright).   Wheelwright.

24. **Ward,** a keeper, as in—

Hayward.   Steward (=*sty-ward*).   Woodward.

(i) *Ward* has also the Norman-French form of *guard*.
(ii) In *steward*, the word *stige* or *sty* meant *stall* for horses, cows, etc.

20. The following are the most important

English Suffixes to Adjectives :—

1. **Ed** or **d,** the ending for the passive participle, as in—

Cold (=chilled).   Long-eared.   Lauded.   Talented.

2. **En,** denoting material, as in—

Golden.   Silvern.   Flaxen.   Hempen.
Oaken.   Wooden.   Silken.   Linen (from *lin*, flax)

3. **En,** the old ending for the passive participle, as in—

Drunken.   Forlorn.   Molten.   Hewn.

4. **Ern,** denoting quarter, as in—

Eastern.   Western.   Northern.   Southern.

5. **Fast** (O.E. **faest,** firm), as in—

Steadfast.   Rootfast.   Shamefast (wrongly *shamefaced*).

6. **Fold** (O.E. **feald**), as in—

Twofold.   Threefold.   Manifold.

(i) *Simple*, from Lat. *simplex*, has usurped the place of *anfeald* = *onefold*.

7. **Ful** =: **full**, as in—

Hateful.   Needful.   Sinful.   Wilful.

8. **Ish** (O.E. **isc**) has three functions ; it denotes :—

(i) Partaking in the **nature of**, as in—

Boorish.   Childish.   Churlish.   Waspish.

(ii) A **milder** or sub-form of the **quality**, as in—

Blackish.   Greenish.   Whitish.   Goodish.

(iii) A **patrial relation** as in—

English.   Irish.   Scottish.   Welsh (= *Wylisc*).

9. **Le**, with a diminutive tendency, as in—

Little (*lyt*).   Brittle (from *break*).   Fickle (*unsteady*).

10. **Less** (O.E. **leâs**), loose from, as in—

Fearless.   Helpless.   Sinless.   Toothless.

11. **Like** (O.E. **lîc**), softened in **ly**, as in—

Childlike.   Dovelike.   Wifelike.   Warlike.
Godly.   Manly.   Womanly.   Ghastly (= ghostlike).

12. **Ow** (O.E. **u** and **wa**), as in—

Narrow.   Callow.   Fallow.   Yellow.

(i) *Fallow* is connected with the adjective *pale*, and *yellow* with the *yol* in *yolk*.

13. **Right**, with the sense of *direction*, as in—

Forthright.   Downright.   Upright.

14. **Some** (O.E. **sum**, a form of *same*, like), as in—

Buxom (from *bugan*,   Gladsome.   Lissom (=lithesome):
    to bend).
Irksome.   Gamesome.   Winsome.

15. **Teen** (O.E. **tyne**) = ten by addition, as in—

Thirteen.   Fourteen.   Fifteen.   Sixteen.

(i) In *thirteen* = three + ten, the r has changed its place by metathesis.
(ii) In *fifteen*, the hard *f* has replaced the soft *v*.

16. **Ty** (O.E. **tig**) = tens by multiplication, as in—

Twenty (= *twain*-ty).   Thirty (= *three*-ty).   Forty.

17. **Ward** (O.E. **weard**, from **weorthan**, to become), denoting **direction**, as in—

Froward (from).   Toward.   Untoward.
Awkward (from *awk*,   Homeward.   Seaward.
    contrary).

(i) This ending, **ward**, has no connection with *ward*, a keeper. It is connected with the verb *worth* in the line, "Woe *worth* the chase, woe *worth* the day !"

18. **Wise** (O.E. **wis**, mode, manner), as in—

Righteous (properly *rightwise*).   Boisterous (O.E. *bostwys*).

(i) The English or Teutonic ending *wise* has got confused with the Lat. ending *ous* (from *osus* = full of).

19. **Y** (O.E. **ig**, the guttural of which has vanished) forms adjectives from nouns and verbs, as in—

Bloody.	Crafty.	Dusty.	Heavy (heave).
Mighty.	Silly (soul).	Stony.	Weary.

21. The following are the most important

English Suffixes for Adverbs :—

1. **Ere**, denoting **place in**, as in

Here.   There.   Where.

2. **Es** or **s** (the old genitive or possessive), which becomes **se** and **ce**, as in—

Needs.	Besides.	Sometimes.	Unawares.
Else.	Hence.	Thence.	Once.

(i) "I must *needs* go" = *of need*.

3. **Ly** (O.E. **lice**, the dative of **lic**), as in—

Only (=*onely*).   Badly.   Willingly.   Utterly.

4. **Ling, long**, denotes **direction**, as in—

Darkling.   Grovelling.   Headlong.   Sidelong.

(i) *Grovelling* is not really a present participle; it is an adverb, and was in O.E. *gruflynges*.

(ii) We once had also the adverbs *flatlings* and *noselings*.

5. **Meal** (O.E. **maelum** = at times), as in—

Piecemeal.   Limbmeal.

(i) Shakespeare, in "Cymbeline," has the line—

"O that I had her here, to tear her limbmeal."

(ii) Chaucer has *stound-meal* = hour by hour; King Alfred has *stykkemaelum* = stick-meal, or here and there.

6. **Om** (an old dative plural), as in—

Whilom (= in old times).   Seldom (from *seld*, rare).

7. **Ther**, which denotes **place to**, as in—

Hither.   Thither.   Whither.

8. **Ward** or **wards**, which denotes **direction**, as in—

Homeward.   Homewards.   Backwards.   Downwards.

9. **Wise** (O.E. **wis**, manner, mode), as in—

Anywise.   Nowise.   Otherwise.   Likewise.

"Some people are wise; and some are otherwise."

22. The following are the most important

English Suffixes for Verbs :—

1. **Le or l** has two functions :—

   (i) **Frequentative,** as in—

      Dabble (*dab*).   Grapple (*grab*).   Waddle (*wade*).
      Dribble (*drip*).   Drizzle (from *dreósan*, to fall). Jostle.

   (ii) **Diminutive,** as in—

      Dazzle (*daze*).   Dibble (*dip*).   Dwindle.
      Gabble.   Niggle.   Sparkle.

2. **Er or r** adds a frequentative or intensive force to the original verb, as in—

    Batter (*beat*).   Chatter.   Glitter (*glow*).   Flutter (*flit*).
    Glimmer (*gleam*). Clatter.   Sputter (*spit*).
    Stagger.   Stammer.   Stutter.   Welter.

    Er has also the function of making **causative verbs** out of adjectives, as *linger* (*long*), *lower*, *hinder*.

3. **En or n** makes **causative verbs** out of nouns and adjectives, as in—

    Brighten.   Fatten.   Lighten.   Lengthen.
    Broaden.   Gladden.   Soften.   Sweeten.

4. **K** has a **frequentative** force, as in—

    Hark (*hear*).   Stalk (*steal*).   Talk (*tell*).

5. **S or se** has a **causative** force, as in—

    Cleanse (*clean*).   Curse.   Rinse (from *hreinn*).

23. The Suffixes of Latin origin are of great importance ; and they have been of great use for several centuries. Many of them—indeed, most of them—have been influenced by passing through French mouths, and hence have undergone considerable change. The following are the chief

Latin and French Suffixes for Nouns :—

1. **Age** (Lat. **aticum**), which forms either **abstract** or **collective** nouns, as in—

    Beverage.   Courage.   Carnage.   Homage.
    Marriage.   Personage. Vassalage. Vintage.

    (i) It unites easily with English roots to form hybrids, as in *bondage, mileage, tonnage, poundage, tillage, shrinkage*.

2. **An, ain,** or **ane** (Lat. **ānus**), connected with, as in—

    Artisan.   Pagan.   Publican.   Roman.
    Chaplain.   Captain.   Humane.   Mundane.

    (i) The suffix is disguised in *sovereign* (O. Fr. *soverain*), which has been wrongly supposed to have something to do with *reign;* in *warden, citizen, surgeon*, etc. Milton always spells *sovereign, sovran*.

3. **Al** or **el** (Lat. **ālis**), possessing the quality of, as in—

Animal.	Cardinal.	Canal.	Channel.
Hospital.	Hostel.	Hotel.	Spital.

(i) *Canal* and *channel* are two different forms—doublets—of the same. So are *cattle* and *chattels* (capitalia).

(ii) Hospital, spital, hostel, hotel, are four forms of the one Latin word *hospitalium*. (*Ostler* is a shorter form of *hosteller*, with a dropped *h*.)

4. **Ant** or **ent** (Latin **antem** or **entem**), denotes an **agent**, as in—

Assistant.	Servant.	Agent.	Student.

5. **Ance, ancy,** or **ence, ency** (Lat. **antia, entia**), form abstract nouns, as in—

Abundance.	Chance.	Distance.	Brilliancy.
Diligence.	Indulgence.	Constancy.	Consistency.

(i) *Chance* comes from late Lat. *cadentia*=an accident. *Cadence* is a doublet.

6. **Ary, ry,** or **er** (Lat. **arium**), a place where a thing is kept, as in—

Apiary (*apis*, a bee).	Armoury.	Granary.	Sanctuary.
Treasury.	Vestry.	Larder.	Saucer.

(i) The ending **ry** unites freely with English words to form hybrids, as in *cookery, piggery, robbery*.

(ii) In *Jewry, jewellery* (or *jewelry*), *poultry, peasantry, cavalry*, the *ry* has a collective meaning.

7. **Ary, ier, eer,** or **er** (Lat. **arius**), denotes a person engaged in some trade or profession, as in—

Commissary.	Notary.	Secretary.	Statuary.
Brigadier.	Engineer.	Mountaineer.	Mariner.

(i) This ending is disguised in *chancellor* (*cancellarius*), *vicar, butler* (=*bottler*), *usher* (*ostiarius*, a doorkeeper), *premier*, etc.

8. **Ate** (Lat. **atus**, past participle ending), becoming in French **e** or **ée**, denotes—

(i) An **agent**, as in—

Advocate.	Curate.	Legate.	Private.

(ii) The **object** of an action, as in—

Grantee.	Legatee.	Trustee.	Vendee.

☞ In *grandee* the passive signification is not retained.

9. **Ce** (Lat. **cium, tium,** or **tia**) forms **abstract** nouns, as—

Benefice.	Edifice.	Sacrifice.
Hospice.	Palace.	Grace.

10. **El, le** or **l** (Lat. **ŭlus, ellus,** etc.), a diminutive, as in—

Angle (a little corner).   Buckle (from *bucca*, the cheek).

Castle.	Chapel.	Libel.	Pommel.	Title.	Seal.

(i) A *buckle* used to have a cast of the human face.

(ii) *Castle*, from Lat. *castellum*, a little fort, from *castrum*, a fort.

(iii) *Libel*, from Lat. *libellus*, a little book (*liber*).

(iv) *Pommel*, from Lat. *pomum*, an apple.

(v) *Seal* from Lat. *sigillum*.

11. Ern (Lat. **erna**), denoting **place**, as in—

Cavern.	Cistern.	Lantern.	Tavern.

12. Et, ette, and **let** (Fr. **et, ette**) all diminutives, as in—

Bassinette.	Buffet.	Chaplet.	Coronet.
Goblet.	Gibbet.	Lancet.	Leveret.
Puppet.	Trumpet.	Ticket.	Turret.

(i) The *let* is =l + *et*, and is found in *bracelet, fillet, cutlet,* etc. It also unites with English words to form hybrids—as in *hamlet, leaflet, ringlet, streamlet,* etc.

(ii) This ending is disguised in *ballot* (a small *ball*), *chariot* (*car*), *parrot* (=*perroquet*), etc.

13. Ess (late Lat. **issa**), a female agent, as in—

Empress.	Governess.	Marchioness.	Sorceress.

(i) It unites with English words to form the hybrids *murderess, sempstress* (The last is a double feminine, as *seamestre* is the old word.)

14. Ice, ise, or **ess** (Lat. **tia**; Fr. **esse**), as in—

Avarice.	Cowardice.	Justice.	Merchandise.
Distress.	Largess.	Noblesse.	Riches.

(i) It is a significant mark of the carelessness with which the English language has always been written, that the very same ending should appear in three spellings in *largess, noblesse, riches.*

(ii) *Riches* is a false plural: it is an *abstract* noun, the French form being *richesse.*

15. Ice (Lat. **icem** acc. of nouns in **x**), which has also the forms of **ise, ace,** as in—

Chalice.	Pumice.	Mortise.	Furnace.

(i) The suffix is much disguised in *radish* (=the *root*, from *radicem*).

(ii) It is also disguised in *partridge* and *judge* (*judicem*).

16. Icle (Lat. **iculus, ellus, ulus**), which appears also as **cel** and **sel,** a diminutive, as in—

Article (a little *joint*).	Particle.	Receptacle.	Versicle.
Parcel (*particella*).	Morsel (from *mordeo*, I bite).		
Damsel (*dominicella*, a little lady).			

(i) The ending is disguised in *rule* (*regula*), *carbuncle* (from *carbo*, a coal), *uncle* (*avunculus*), and *vessel* (from *vas*).

(ii) *Parcel* and *particle* are doublets.

17. Ine or **in** (Lat. **inus**) related to, as in—

Divine (noun).	Cousin.

(i) *Cousin* is a contraction—through French—of the Latin *consobrinus*, the child of a mother's sister.

(ii) The ending is disguised in *pilgrim*, from *peregrinus* = from *per agros*, through the fields.

18. Ion (Lat. **iōnem**), which appears also as **tion, sion,** and, from French, as **son, som,** denotes an **action**, as in—

Action.	Opinion.	Position.	Vacation.
Potion.	Poison.	Benediction.	Benison.
Redemption.	Ransom.	Malediction.	Malison.

(i) *Potion, poison*, and the three other pairs are doublets — the first having come through the door of books straight from the Latin, the second through the mouth and ear, from French.

(ii) *Venison (hunted* flesh, from *venationem), season* (*sationem*, the *sowing* time), belong to the above set.

19. **Ment (Lat. mentum)** denotes an **instrument** or an **act**, as in—

Document. Instrument. Monument. Ornament.

(i) It combines easily with English words to make hybrids, as *atonement, acknowledgment, bewitchment, fulfilment.*

20. **Mony (Lat. monium)** makes abstract nouns, as—

Acrimony. Matrimony. Sanctimony. Testimony.

21. **Oon or on (Fr. on; Ital. one)**, an augmentative, as in—

Balloon.	Cartoon.	Dragoon.	Saloon.
Flagon.	Million.	Pennon.	Glutton.
Clarion.	Galleon.	Trombone.	Truncheon.

(i) Augmentatives are the opposite of diminutives. Contrast *balloon* and *ballot ; galleon* and *galliot* (a small galley).

(ii) A *balloon* is a large ball ; a *cartoon* a big carte ; a *dragoon* a large dragon ; a *saloon* a large hall (*salle*) ; *flagon* (O. Fr. *flascon*), a large flask ; *million*, a big thousand (*mille*) ; *pennon*, a large *pen* or feather ; *galleon*, a large *galley ; trombone*, a large *trump-et ; truncheon*, a large staff (or *trunk*) of office.

22. **Ory, (Lat. orium)**, which appears also as **or, our**, and **er**, and denotes **place**, as in—

Auditory.	Dormitory.	Reféctory.	Lavatory.
Mirror.	Parlour.	Dormer.	Manger.

(i) *Mirror* is contracted by the French from *miratorium ; parlour* from *parlatorium ; manger* from *manducatorium*=the eating-place. *Dormer* is short for *dormitory*, from *dormitorium.*

23. **Our (Lat. or; Fr. eur)**, forms **abstract** or **collective** nouns, as in—

Ardour. Clamour. Honour. Savour.

(i) The ending resumes its French form in *grandeur.*

(ii) It forms a hybrid in *behaviour.*

24. **Or or our (Lat. orem; Fr. eur)** denotes an **agent**, as in—

Actor. Governor. Emperor. Saviour.

(i) This ending is disguised in *interpreter, labourer, preacher*, etc.

(ii) A large number of nouns which used to end in *our* or *or*, took *er* through the influence of the *English* suffix *er*. They were "attracted" into that form.

25. **T** (Lat. **tus**—the ending of the past participle) indicates a **completed act,** as in—

> Act.   Fact.   Joint.   Suit.

(i) The t in Latin has the same origin and performs the same function as the d in English (as in *dead, finished,* and other past participles, etc.)

(ii) The ending is disguised in *feat,* which is a doublet of *fact,* in *fruit* (Lat. *fruct-us*), *comfit* (= *confect*), *counterfeit* (= *contrafact-um*).

26. **Ter** (Lat. **ter**) denotes a **person,** as in—

> Master (contracted from *magister*).   Minister.

(i) *Magister* comes from *magis,* more, which contains the root of *magnus,* great; *minister* from *minus,* less.

27. **Tery** (Lat. **terium**) denotes **condition,** as in—

> Mastery.   Ministry.

28. **Trix** (Lat. **trix**) denotes a **female agent,** as in—

> Executrix.   Improvisatrix.   Testatrix.

(i) This ending is disguised in *empress* (Fr. *impératrice* from Lat. *imperatrix*); and in *nurse* (Fr. *nourrice,* Lat. *nutrix*).

29. **Tude** (Lat. **tudinem**), denotes **condition,** as in—

> Altitude.   Beatitude.   Fortitude.   Multitude.

(i) In *custom,* from Lat. *consuetudinem,* the ending is disguised.

30. **Ty** (Lat. **tatem**; Fr. **té**) makes **abstract** nouns, as in—

> Bounty.   Charity.   Cruelty.   Poverty.
> Captivity.   Frailty.   Fealty.   Vanity.

(i) *Bounty* (*bonté*), *poverty* (*pauvreté*), *frailty,* and *fealty* come, not directly from Latin, but through French.

31. **Ure** (Lat. **ura**) denotes an **action,** or the **result** of an action, as in—

> Aperture.   Cincture.   Measure.   Picture.

32. **Y** (Lat. **ia**; Fr. **ie**) denotes **condition** or **faculty,** as in—

> Company.   Family.   Fury.   Victory.

(i) This suffix unites easily with English words in *er*—as *bakery, fishery, robbery,* etc.

(ii) It stands for Lat. **ium** in *augury, remedy, study, subsidy,* etc.

(iii) It represents the Lat. ending **atus** in *attorney, deputy, ally, quarry.*

24. The Latin (or French) suffixes employed in our language to make **Adjectives** are very useful. The following are the chief

Latin Suffixes for Adjectives.

1. **Aceous** (Lat. **aceus**) = **made of,** as in—

> Argillaceous (*clayey*).   Farinaceous (*floury*).

2. **Al** (Lat. **ālis**) = **belonging to**, as in—

Legal.   Regal.   Loyal.   Royal.

(i) *Loyal* and *royal* are the same words as *legal* and *regal*; but, in passing through French, the hard *g* has been refined into a *y*.

3. **An, ane**, or **ain** (Lat. **anus** and **aneus**) = **connected with**, as in—

Certain.   Human (*homo*).   Humane.   Pagan (*pagus*, a district).

(i) This ending disguises itself in *mizzen* (*medianus*); in *surgeon* (*chirurgianus*); and in *sexton* (contracted from *sacristan*).

(ii) In *champaign* (*level*), and *foreign* (*foraneus*), this ending greatly disguises itself. In *strange* (*extraneus*), still more. All have been strongly influenced in their passage through the French.

4. **Ant, ent** (Lat. **antem, entem**, acc. of pres. part.), as in—

Current (*curro*, I run).   Distant.   President.   Discordant.

5. **Ar** (Lat. **āris**) which appears also as **er** = **belonging to**, as in—

Regular.   Singular.   Secular.   Premier.

(i) *Premier* (Lat. *primarius*), has received its present spelling by passing through French.

6. **Ary** (Lat. **ārius**), which also takes the *secondary* formations of **arious** and **arian** = **belonging to**, as in—

Contrary.   Necessary.   Gregarious.   Agrarian.

7. **Atic** (Lat. **āticus**) = **belonging to**, as in—

Aquatic.   Fanatic (*fanum*).   Lunatic.

8. **Able, ible, ble** (Lat. **ābilis, ēbilis, ibilis**) = **capable of being**, as in—

Amiable.   Culpable.   Flexible.   Movable.

(i) *Feeble* (Lat. *flebilis*, worthy of being wept over), comes to us through the O. Fr. *floible*.

(ii) This suffix unites easily with English roots to form hybrids, like *eatable*, *drinkable*, *teachable*, *gullible*. Carlyle has also *doable*.

9. **Ple, ble** (Lat. **plex**, from **plico**, I fold) = the English suffix—**fold**, as in—

Simple (=*onefold*).   Double.   Triple.   Treble.

10. **Esque** (Lat. **iscus**; Fr. **esque**) = **partaking of**, as in—

Burlesque.   Grotesque (*grotto*).   Picturesque.

(i) This ending is disguised in *Danish*, *French*, etc.; and in *morris* (*dance*) = *Moresco* (or *Moorish*).

11. **Ic** (Lat. **icus**) = **belonging to**, as in—

Gigantic.   Metallic.   Public (*populus*).   Rustic.

(i) This ending is disguised in *indigo* (from *Indicus* [colour] = *the Indian colour*.)

12. Id (Lat. **Idus**) = **having the quality of,** as in—

Acid.   Frigid.   Limpid.   Morbid.

13. Ile, Il (Lat. **Ilis**), often used as a *passive* suffix, as in—

Docile.   Fragile.   Mobile.   Civil.

(i) *Fragile,* in passing through French, lost the *g*—which was always *hard*—and became *frail.*

(ii) The suffix *ile* is disguised in *gentle* and *subtle.*

(iii) *Gentile, gentle,* and *genteel,* are all different forms of the same word.

(iv) *Kennel* (= *canile*) is really an adjective from *canis.*

14. Ine (Lat. **Inus**) = **belonging to,** as in—

Canine.   Crystalline.   Divine.   Saline.

(i) In *marine,* the ending, by passing through French, has acquired a French pronunciation.

15. Ive (Lat. **Ivus**) = **inclined to,** as in—

Abusive.   Active.   Fugitive.   Plaintive.

(i) This ending appears also as *iff,* by passing through French, as in *caitiff* (= *captivus*); and in the nouns *plaintiff* and *bailiff.*

(ii) It also disguises itself as a *y* in *hasty, jolly, testy,* which in O. Fr. were *hastif, jollif, testif* (= *heady*).

(iii) It unites with the English word *talk* to form the hybrid *talkative.*

16. Lent (Lat. **lentus**) = **full of,** as in—

Corpulent.   Fraudulent.   Opulent (*opes*).   Violent (*vis*).

17. Ory (Lat. **ōrius**) = **full of,** as in—

Amatory.   Admonitory.   Illusory.

18. Ose, ous (Lat. **ōsus**) = **full of,** as in—

Bellicose.   Grandiose.   Verbose.   Curious.

(i) The form in *ous* has been influenced by the French ending *eux.*

19. Ous (Lat. **us**) = **belonging to,** as in—

Anxious.   Assiduous.   Ingenuous.   Omnivorous.

(i) It unites with English words to form the hybrids *wondrous, boisterous, righteous* (which is an imitative corruption of the O.E. *rihtwis*).

20. Und (Lat. **undus**) = **full of,** as in—

Jocund.   Moribund.   Rotund.

(i) *Rotund* has been shortened into *round. Second* is, through French, from Lat. *secundus* (from *sequor,* I follow)—the number that *follows* the first. *Ventus secundus* is a favourable wind, or a "wind that *follows* fast."

(ii) This ending is slightly modified in *vagabond* and *second.*

21. Ulous (Lat. **ūlus**) = **full of,** as in—

Querulous (full of *complaint*).   Sedulous.

25. The following are the chief

Latin Suffixes for Verbs.

1. **Ate** (Lat. **atum**, supine), as in—

    Complicate.   Dilate.   Relate.   Supplicate.

    (i) *Assassinate* (from the Arabic *hashish*, a preparation of Indian hemp, whose effects are similar to those of opium) is a hybrid.

2. **Esce** (Lat. **esco**), a **frequentative** suffix, as in—

    Coalesce (to grow together).   Effervesce (to boil up).

3. **Fy** (Lat. **fico** ; Fr. **fie**—from Lat. *facio*) = **to make**, as in—

    Beautify.   Magnify.   Signify.

4. **Ish** (connected with Lat. **esco**) = **to make**, as in—

    Admonish.   Establish.   Finish.   Nourish.

5. **Ete, ite, t** (Lat. **itum, etum, tum**), with an **active** function, as in—

    Complete.   Delete.   Expedite.   Connect.

26. The suffixes which the English language has adopted from Greek are not numerous ; but some of them are very useful. Most of them are employed to make nouns. The following are the chief

Greek Suffixes.

1. **Y** (Gr. *ια*), makes **abstract** nouns, as in—

    Melancholy.   Monarchy.   Necromancy.   Philosophy.

    (i) **Fancy** is a compressed form of **phantasy** (*phantasia* = imagination).

    (ii) The *Iliad* is the story of *Ilion* (Troy), written by Homer.

2. **Ic** (Gr. *ικός*) = **belonging to**, as in—

    Aromatic.   Barbaric.   Frantic.   Graphic.
    Arithmetic.   Schismatic.   Logic.   Music.

    (i) With the addition of the Latin *alis*, adjectives are formed from some of these words, as *logical, musical*, etc.

    (ii) The *plural* form of some adjectives also makes nouns of them, as in *politics, ethics, physics*. In Ireland we find also *logics*.

    (iii) *Arithmetic, logic,* and *music* are from Greek *nouns* ending in *ikē*.

3. **Sis** (Gr. *σις*) = **action**, as in—

    Analysis.   Emphasis.   Genesis.   Synthesis.

    (i) In the following words *sis* has become *sy*, as *hypocrisy, poesy, palsy* (short for *paralysis*).

    (ii) In the following the *is* has dropped away altogether—*ellipse, phase.*

4. **Ma** or **m** (Gr. μα), **passive** suffix, as in—

Diorama.	Dogma.	Drama (*something done*).	Schism.
Baptism.	Barbarism.	Despotism.	Egotism.

(i) In *diadem* and *system* the *a* has dropped off; in *scheme* and *theme* it has been changed into an *e*.

(ii) *Schism* comes from *schizo*, I cut. The ending in *ismos* is most frequent.

(iii) This ending unites freely with Latin words to form hybrids, as in *deism, mannerism, purism, provincialism, vulgarism,* etc.

5. **St** (Gr. στης) = **agent,** as in—

Baptist.	Botanist.	Iconoclast (image-breaker).

(i) This suffix has become a very useful one, and is largely employed. It forms numerous hybrids with words of Latin origin, as *abolitionist, excursionist, educationist, journalist, protectionist, jurist, socialist, specialist, royalist.*

6. **T** or **te** (Gr. της) = **agent,** as in—

Comet.	Planet.	Poet.	Apostate.

(i) *Comet* means a *long-haired star; planet,* a *wanderer; poet,* a *maker* (in Northern English poets called themselves "Makkers"); an *apostate,* a person who has *fallen away.*

(ii) This ending is also found in the form of *ot* and *it,* as in *idiot, patriot, hermit.*

7. **Ter** or **tre** (Gr. τρον), denotes an **instrument** or **place,** as in—

Metre.	Centre.	Theatre.

8. **Isk** (Gr. ισκος), a **diminutive,** as in—

Asterisk (a little star).	Obelisk (a small spit).

9. **Ize** or **ise** (Gr. ιζω) makes **factitive** verbs, as in—

Baptise.	Criticise.	Judaize.	Anglicize.

(i) This ending combines with Latin words to form the hybrids *minimise, realise,* etc.

WORD - BRANCHING.

WHEN our language was young and uninfluenced by other languages, it had the power of **growing** words. These words, like plants, grew from a **root**; and all the words that grew from the same root had a family likeness. Thus **byrn-an**, the old word for *to burn*, gave us **brimstone, brown** (which is the *burnt* colour), **brunt, brand, brandy,** and **brindle.** These we might represent to ourselves, on the blackboard, as growing in this way.

But, unfortunately, we soon lost this power. From the time when the Normans came into this country in 1066, the language became less and less capable of growing its own words. Instead of producing a new word, we fell into the habit of simply taking an old and **ready-made** word from French, or from Latin, or from Greek, and giving it a place in the language. Instead of the Old English word **fairhood**, we imported the French word **beauty**; instead of **forewit**, we adopted the Latin word **caution**; instead of **licherest**, we took the Greek word **cemetery.** And so it came about that in course of time we lost the power of growing our own new words. The Greek word **asterisk** has prevented our making the word **starkin**; the Greek name **astronomy** has kept out **star-craft**; the Latin word **omnibus** has stopped our even thinking of **folkwain**; and the name **vocabulary** is much more familiar to our ears than **word-hoard.** Indeed, so strange have some of our own native

1287GRAMMAR OF THE ENGLISH LANGUAGE.

English words become to us, that sentences composed entirely of English words are hardly intelligible; and, to make them quickly intelligible, we have to translate some of the English words into Greek or into Latin. It is well, however, for us to become acquainted with those pure English words which grew upon our own native roots, and which owe nothing whatever to other languages. For they are the purest, the simplest, the most homely and the most genuine part of our language; and from them we can get a much better idea of what our language once was than we can from its present very mixed condition. The following are the most important

ENGLISH ROOTS AND BRANCHES (OR DERIVATIONS).

Ac, an oak—acorn, Acton, Uckfield.

Bac-an, to bake—baker, baxter [1] (a woman baker), batch.

Ban-a, a slayer—bane, baneful; ratsbane, henbane.

Bead-an, to pray — bedesman; beadle; bead ("to bid one's beads" was to say one's prayers; and these were marked off by small round balls of wood or glass —now called *beads* — strung upon a string); *forbid*.

Beat-an, to strike — beat, bat (a short cudgel): battle; beetle (a wooden bat for beating clothes with); batter (a kind of pudding).

Beorg-an, to shelter—burrow, bury (noun in Canterbury — and verb); burgh, burgher; burglar (a house-robber); harbour, Cold Harbour; [2] harbinger (a person sent on in front to procure lodgings); borrow (to raise money on *security*).

Bér-an, to bear—bear, bier, bairn; birth, berth; brood, brother, breed, bird; [3] burden; barrow.

Bét-an, to make good—better, best; boot (in "to boot"="to the good"), bootless.

Bind-an, to bind—band, bond, bondage; bundle; *wood*bine; blind*weed*.

Bit-an, to bite—bit; beetle; bait; bitter.

Bla'w-an, to puff—bladder, blain (chilblain), blast, blaze (to proclaim), blazon (a proclamation), blare (of a trumpet); blister; blot, bloat.

Blow-an, to blossom—blow (said of *flowers*); bloom, blossom; blood, blade; blowsy.

Brec-an, to break—break, breakers; brake, bracken; breach, brick: break-*fast*; brook (=the water which breaks up through the ground); brittle (=brickle or breakable); bray (where the hard guttural has been absorbed).

Breow-an, to brew—brew, brewer; broth, brose; bread (perhaps).

---

[1] Compare *brewster*, a woman brewer, *spinster*, *webster*, and others. *Brewster, Baxter,* and *Webster* are now only used as proper names.

[2] Cold Harbour was the name given to an inn which provided merely shelter without provisions. There are fourteen places of this name in England. Many of them stand on the great Roman roads; and they were chiefly the ruins of Roman villas used by travellers who carried their own bedding and provisions. See Isaac Taylor's 'Words and Places,' p. 256.

[3] Brid or bird was originally the young of any animal.

Bug-an, to bend—bow, elbow ;[1] bough ;
bight ; buxom (O.E. bocsum, flexible or
obedient). The hard g in *bigan* appears
as a w in *bow*, as a gh in *bough*, as a y
in *buy*, as a k in *buxom=buk-som*.

Byrn-an, to burn—burn, brown ; brunt,
brimstone ; brand, brandy ; brindled.

Catt, a cat—catkin ; kitten, kitling ; caterpillar (the hairy cat, from Lat. *pilosus*,
hairy), caterwaul.

Ceapi-an, to buy—cheap, cheapen ; chop
(to exchange) ; a chopping sea ; chap,
chapman ; chaffer ; Eastcheap, Cheapside, Chepstow (=the market *stow* or
place), Chippenham.[2]

Cenn-an, to produce—kin, kind, kindred ;
kindly ; kindle.

Ceow-an, to chew—chew ; cheek ; jaw
(=chaw) ; jowl ; chaw-*bacon* ; cud (=the
chewed). Compare *seethe* and *suds*.

Cleov-an, to split—cleave, cleaver ; cleft ;
clover (split grass).

Clifi-an, to stick to — cleave ; clip (for
keeping papers together) ; claw (by
which a bird *cleaves to* a tree) ; club (a
set of men who *cleave* together).

Cnáw-an, to know—ken, know (= ken-ow
—*ow* being a dim.) ; knowledge.

Cnotta, a knot—knot, knit, net (the *k*
having been dropped for the eye, as well
as for the ear).

Cunn-an, to know or to be able—can, con ;
cunning ; uncouth.

Cweth-an, to say—quoth ; bequeath.

Cwic, alive—quick, quicken ; quickset ;
quicklime ; quicksilver ; *to cut to the
quick*.

Dáel-an, to divide—deal (verb and noun),
dole, deal (*said of wood*) ; dale, dell (the
original sense being *cleft*, or separated).

Dem-an, to judge—deem, doom ; dempster (the name for a *judge* in the Isle of
Man) ; doomsday ; *kingdom*.

Deór, dear—dearth ; darling ; endear.

Dóan, to act—do ; don, doff, dup (=do
up or op-en) ; dout (=do out or put out) ;
deed. Compare mow, mead ; sow, seed.

Drag-an, to draw — drag, draw, dray
(three forms of the same word) ; draft
(draught) ; drain ; dredge ; draggle ;
drawl.

Drif-an, to push—drive ; drove ; drift,
adrift.

Drige, dry—dry (*verb and adj.*) ; drought ;
drugs (originally *dried plants*).

Drinc-an, to soak—drink ; drench (to
make to drink). Compare sit, set ; fall,
fell, etc.

Drip-an, to drip — drip, drop, droop ;
dribble, driblet.

Dug-an, to be good for—do (in "How
do you do?" and "That will do") ;
doughty.

Eác, also—eke (verb and adv.) ; ekename
(which became a *nickname* ; the n having dropped from the article and clung
to the noun).

Eáge, eye—Egbert (=*bright-eyed*) ; daisy
(=*day's eye*) ; window (=wind-eye).

Eri-an, to plough—ear (the old word for
plough) ; earth (= the ploughed).

Far-an, to go or travel—far, fare ; welfare,
fieldfare, thoroughfare ; ferry ; ford.

Feng-an, to catch—fang, finger, new-
fangled (catching eagerly after new
things).

Feówer, four—farthing ; firkin ; fourteen ;
forty.

Fleóg-an, to flee—fly, flight ; flea ; fledged.

Fleót-an, to float—fleet (noun, verb, and
adj.) ; float ; ice-floe ; afloat ; flotsam[3]
(*things found* floating on the water after
a wreck).

Fód-a, food—feed ; food, fodder, foster ;
fath-er ; forage (=foddcrage), forager ;
foray (an excursion to get food).

Freón, to love—freond = friend (the pres.
part.) a lover ; Fri-day (the day of Friya,
the goddess of love) ; friendship, etc.

Gal-an, to sing—gale, yell ; nightingale.[4]

Gang-an, to go — gang, gangway ; ago.
(The words *gate* and *gait* do not come
from this verb, but from *get*.)

Gnag-an, to bite — gnaw (the *g* has be-

---

[1] Elbow=ell-bow. The ell was the forepart of the arm.

[2] The same root is found in the Scotch *Kippen* and the Danish *Copenhagen*=Mer-
chants' Haven.

[3] "Flotsam and jetsam" mean the floating things and the things thrown over-
board from a ship. Jetsam comes from Old Fr. *jetter*, to throw. (Hence also "*jet* of
water" ; *jetty*, etc. *Jetsam* is a hybrid—*sam* being a Scandinavian suffix.

[4] The n in *nightingale* is no part of the word. It is intrusive and non-organic ; as
it also is in *passenger*, *messenger*, *porringer*, etc.

I

come a tr); gnat; nag (to tease). connected with nail.

Graf-an, to dig or cut—grave, groove, grove (the original sense was a lane cut through trees); graft, engraft; engrave, engraver; carve (which is another form of the verb grave).

Grip-an, to seize — grip, gripe; grasp; grab; grope.

Gyrd-an, to surround—gird, girdle; garden, yard, vineyard, hopyard.

Hael-an, to heal — hale; holy, hallow, All-hallows; health; hail; whole,[1] wholesome; wassail (= Waes hâl ! = Be whole !)

Hebb-an, to raise—heave, heave-offering; heavy (=that requires much heaving); heaven.

Hláf, bread—loaf; lord (hláford = loaf-ward); lady (= hláf-dige, from dig-an, to knead); Lammas (=Loaf-mass, Aug. 1; a loaf was offered on this day as the offering of the first-fruits).

Leác, a leek—house-leek; garlic; hemlock.

Licg-an, to lie—lie; lay, layer; lair; outlay.

Loda, a guide—lead (the verb); lode-star, lode-stone (also written loadstone).

Mag-an, to be able—may, main (in "might and main"), might, mighty.

Mang, a mixture—a-mong; mongrel; mingle; cheesemonger.

Maw-an, to cut—mow; math, aftermath; mead, meadow (the places where grass is mowed).

Món-a, the moon—month; moonshine. (This word comes from a very old root, ma, to measure. Our Saxon forefathers measured by moons and by nights, as we see in the words fortnight, se'nnight.)

Naeddrë, a snake — adder. The n has dropped off from the word, and has adhered to the article. Compare apron, from naperon (compare with napkin, napery); umpire, from numpire. The opposite example of the n leaving the article and adhering to the noun, is found in nag, from an äg; nickname from an ekename.

Nasu, a nose—nose, naze, ness (all three different forms of the same word, and found in the Naze, Sheerness, etc.); nostril = nose-thirl (from thirlian, to bore a hole), nozzle; nosegay.

Penn-an, to shut up or enclose—pen, pin (two forms of the same word); pound, pond (two forms of the same word): impound.

Pic, a point—pike, peak (two forms of the same word); pickets (stakes driven into the ground to tether horses to); pike, pickerel (the fish); peck, pecker.

Ráed-an, to read or guess—rede (advice); riddle; Ethelred (=noble in counsel); Unready (=Unrede, without counsel); Mildred (=mild in counsel).

Reáf, clothing, spoil; reáf-an, to rob—rob, robber; reave, bereave; reever; robe.

Ripe, ripe—reap (to gather what is ripe).

Scád-an, to divide — shed (to part the hair); watershed.

Sceap-an, to form or fashion—shape; ship (the suffix in friendship, etc.); scape (the suffix in landscape, etc.)

Sceót-an, to throw — shoot, shot, shut (=to shoot the bolt of the door); sheet (that which is thrown over a bed); shutter, shuttle; scud.

Scér-an, to cut—shear, share, sheer, shire, shore (all forms of the same word); scar, scare; score (the twentieth notch in the tally, and made larger than the others); scarify, sharp; short, shirt, skirt (three forms of the same word); shred, potsherd (the same word, with the r transposed); sheriff (=scir-geréfa, reeve of the shire); scrip, scrap, scrape. The soft form sh belongs to the southern English dialects: the hard forms, sc and sk, to the northern.

Scuf-an, to push—shove, shovel, shuffle; scuffle; sheaf; scoop.

Sett-an, to set, or make sit—set, seat: settle, saddle; Somerset, Dorset.

Slag-an, to strike—slay (the hard g has been refined into a y), slaughter; slog, sledge (in sledge-hammer).

Slip-an, to slip—slop; slipper, sleeve (into which the arm is slipped).

Snic-an, to crawl — sneak, snake, snail (here the hard guttural has been refined away).

Spell, a story or message—spell (= to give

---

[1] The w in whole is intrusive and non-organic, as in whoop, and in wun (=one, so pronounced, but not so written). Before the year 1500 whole was always written hole; and in this form it is seen to be a doublet of hale. Holy is simply hole+y.

an account of or tell the story of the letters in a word); spell-bound; gospel (= God's spell).

Stearc, stiff—stark; strong (a nasalised form of *stark*); string (that which is *strongly* twisted); strength; strangle.

Stede, a place—stead, instead, homestead, farm-steading; steady; steadfast; bestead; Hampstead.

Stic'i-an, to stick—stick, stitch (two forms of the same word), stake, stock, stockade; stock-dove; stock-fish (fish dried to keep *in stock*); stock-still.

Stig-an, to climb—stair; stile; stirrup (= *stigráp,* or rope for rising into the saddle); sty (in pig-sty).

Stow, a place—bestow; stowage, stowaway; *Chepstow* (= the place where a *cheap* or market is held); *Bristol* (the l and w being interchangeable).

Stýr-an, to direct—steer, stern; steerage.

Sundri-an, to part—sunder; sundry; asunder. (Compare *sever* and *several.*)

Sweri-an, to declare—swear, answer (= andswerian, to declare in opposition or in reply to), forswear.

Taec-an, to show—teach, teacher; token (that which is shown); taught (when the hard c reappears as a gh).

Tell-an, to count or recount—tell; tale,[1] talk; toll; teller.

Teoh-an (or teón), to draw—tow, tug (two forms of the same word, the hard guttural having been preserved in the one); wanton (= without right upbringing). Compare wanhope = despair; wantrust = mistrust.

Thaec, a roof—thatch; deck.

Tred-an, to walk—tread, treadle; trade; tradesman, trade-win.

Truwa, good faith—true, truth, troth, betroth.

Twá, two—two, twin, twain; twelve (= two + lufan, ten); twenty; between; twig; twiddle; twine, twist, etc.

Waci-an, to be on one's guard—wake, watch (two forms of the same word); awake, wakeful.

Wad-an, to go—wade; waddle; Watling Street (the road of the pilgrims). The Eng. word *wade* is of the same origin as the Lat. *vade* in *evade, invade,* etc.

Wana, a deficiency—wan, wane; want, wanton; wanhope (the old word for *despair*).

Wef-an, to weave—weave, weaver; web, webster (a woman-weaver); cobweb; woof, weft (v, b, and f, being all labials).

War, a state of defence—war, wary, aware (= on one's guard); warfare (*going to war*); ward, guard (a Norman-French doublet of ward); warden, guardian (the same).

Wit-an, to know—wit, to wit; wise, wisdom; wistful; witness; Witena-gemote (= the Meeting of the Wise); y-wis (the past participle, wrongly written I *wis*).

Wraest-an, to wrest—wrest, wrestle; wrist.

Wring-an, to force—wring, wrong (that which is *wrung* out of the right course).

Wyrc-an, to work—work, wright (the r shifts its place).

Wyrt, a herb or plant—wort; orchard (= wort-yard); wart (on the skin); St John's wort, etc.

LATIN ROOTS.

Those words with (F.) after them have not come to us directly from Latin; but, indirectly, through French.

Acer (acris), *sharp;* acrid, acrimony, vinegar (sharp wine, F.), eager (F.)

Ædes, *a building;* edifice, edify.

Æquus, *equal;* equality, equator, equinox, equity, adequate, iniquity.

Ager, *a field;* agriculture, agrarian, peregrinate.

Ago (actum), *I do, act;* act, agent, agile, agitate, cogent.

Alo, *I nourish;* aliment, alimony.

Alter, *the other of two;* alternation, subaltern, altercation.

Altus, *high;* altitude, exalt, alto (It.), altar.

---

[1] " And every shepherd tells his tale (= counts his sheep) Under the hawthorn in the dale.' —MILTON: *Il Penseroso.*

Ambulo, *I walk;* amble, perambulator.

Amo, *I love;* amity, amorous, amiable (F.), inimical.

Angulus, *a corner;* angle, triangle, quadrangle.

Anima, *life;* animal, animate, animation.

Animus, *mind;* magnanimity, equanimity, unanimous, animadvert.

Annus, *a year;* annual, perennial, biennial, anniversary.

Aperio (apertum), *I open;* aperient, aperture, April (the opening month).

Appello, *I call;* appeal, appellation, appellant, peal (of bells).

Aqua, *water;* aqueduct, aquatic, aqueous, aquarium.

Arcus, *a bow;* arch, arc, arcade (Fr. It.)

Ardeo, *I burn;* ardent, ardour, arson (F.)

Ars (artis), *art;* artist, artisan (F.), artifice, inert.

Audio, *I hear;* audience, audible, auditory.

Augeo (auctum), *I increase;* augment, author, auctioneer.

Barba, *a beard;* barb, barber, barbel (all through F.).

Bellum, *war;* rebel, rebellious, belligerent, bellicose.

Bis, *twice;* biscuit, bissextile, bisect, bicycle.

Brevis, *short;* brevity, abbreviate, brief (F.), breviary, abridge (F.)

Cado (casum), *I fall;* casual, accident.

Cædo (cæsum), *I cut, kill;* precise, excision, decide.

Candeo, *I shine;* candidus, *white;* candid, candidate, candle.

Cano (cantum), *I sing;* cant, canticle, chant (F.), incantation.

Capio (captum), *I take;* captive, accept, reception (F.), capacity.

Caput, *the head;* capital, captain, cape, chapter (F.)

Caro (carnis), *flesh;* carnal, carnival, carnivorous, carnation.

Causa, *a cause;* causative, accuse (F.), excuse (F.)

Cavus, *hollow;* cavity, cave, excavate, concave.

Cedo (cessum), *I go, yield;* proceed (F.), ancestor (F.), secede.

Centrum (Gr. κεντρον = a point), *centre;* centralise, centripetal, eccentric.

Centum, *a hundred;* century, centurion, cent.

Cerno (cretum), *to distinguish;* discern, discretion, discreet.

Cingo (cinctum), *I gird;* cincture, succinct, precinct.

Cito, *I call or summon;* citation, recite (F.), excite (F.), incite (F.)

Civis, *a citizen;* city (F.), civic, civil, civilise, civilian.

Clamo, *I shout;* claim (F.), clamour, reclaim (F.), proclamation.

Clarus, *clear;* clarify, declare, clarion, claret (F.)

Claudo (clausum), *I shut;* clause, close (F.), exclude, seclusion.

Clino, *I bend;* incline, decline, recline.

Colo (cultum), *I till;* cultivate, arboriculture, agriculture.

Cor (cordis), *the heart;* courage (F.), cordial (F.), discord, record.

Corona, *a crown;* coronet, coroner, coronation, corolla.

Corpus, *the body;* corps, corpse (F.), corpulent, corporation.

Credo, *I believe;* credibility, credence (F.), miscreant (F.), creed, creditor.

Creo, *I create;* create, creation, recreation, creature.

Cresco, *I grow;* increase, decrease, increment.

Crux (crucis), *a cross;* crucial, crucifix, cruise (F.)

Cubo, *I lie down;* cubit, incubate, recumbent.

Culpa, *a fault;* culprit, culpable, exculpate, inculpate.

Cura, *cure;* curate, curator, accurate, secure, incurable.

Curro (cursum), *I run;* current, recur, excursion, cursory, course (F.), occur.

Decem, *ten;* decimal, December, decimate.

Dens (dentis), *a tooth;* dentist, dental, indent, trident.

Deus, *God;* deity, deify, divine.

Dico (dictum), *I say;* verdict, dictionary, dictation, indictment, ditto.

Dies, *a day;* diary, diurnal, meridian.

Dignus, *worthy;* dignity, dignify, indignant, deign (F.)

Do (datum), *I give;* date, data, donor, tradition.

Doceo (doctum), *I teach;* docile, doctor, doctrine.

Dominus, *a lord;* domineer, dominion, dominant, dame (F.), damsel (F.), madame (F.)

Domus, *a house;* domestic, domicile.

Dormio, *I sleep;* dormitory, dormant, dormouse.

Duco (ductum), *I lead;* induct, education, duke (F.), produce.

Duo, *two;* dual, duel, duplex, double (F.)

Emo (emptum), *I buy;* exemption, redeem.

Eo (itum), *I go;* exit, transit, circuit (F.), ambition, perish (F.)

Erro, *I wander;* err, error, aberration.

Facies, *a face;* facial, facet (F.), superficial.

Facio (factum), *I make;* manufacture, factor, faction, fashion (F.), feature (F.), fact, feat (F.)

Fero (latum), *I carry;* infer, suffer, reference, difference; relative, correlative.

Fido, *I trust;* confide, diffident, infidel.

Filum, *a thread;* file, defile, profile, fillet (F.)

Finis, *the end;* finish, finite, infinite, infinitive.

Firmus, *firm;* infirm, affirm, confirm.

Flecto (flexum), *I bend;* inflect, inflection, flexible.

Flos (floris), *a flower;* floral, flora, floriculture.

Fluo (fluxum), *I flow;* fluent, fluid, flux, affluent.

Folium, *a leaf;* foliage, foil (F.), portfolio, trefoil (F.)

Forma, *a form;* form, formal, reform, conformity.

Fortis, *strong;* fortify, fortitude, fortress, force (F.)

Frango (fractus), *I break;* fragile (F.), fragmentary, infraction, infringe.

Frater, *a brother;* fraternal, fratricide, friar (F.)

Frons (frontis), *the forehead;* front, frontal, frontier, frontispiece.

Fugio, *I flee;* fugitive, refugee, subterfuge.

Fundo (fusum), *I pour;* fount (F.), foundry, funnel, fusible, diffusion.

Fundus, *the bottom;* foundation, profound (F.), founder.

Gens (gentis), *a race, people;* gentile, genteel (F.), gentle, congenial.

Gero (gestum), *I bear, carry;* gesture, suggestion, indigestion.

Gradus, *a step;* gradior (gressus), *I go;* grade, degrade, graduate; progress (F.), gradient.

Gratia, *favour,* pl. *thanks;* gratitude, ingratiate, gratis.

Gravis, *heavy;* grave, gravity, grief (F.), aggrieve (F.)

Habeo (habitum), *I have;* habit, able, exhibit, prohibition.

Hæreo (hæsum), *I stick;* adhere, adherent, cohesion.

Homo, *a man;* homicide, homage (F.), human, humane.

Ignis, *fire;* ignite, igneous.

Impero, *I command;* imperative, imperial, empire, emperor (F.)

Initium, *a beginning;* initiate, initial.

Insula, *an island;* isle, insular, peninsula.

Jacio (jectum), *I throw;* adjective, project, injection, object, subject.

Judex (judicis), *a judge;* judgment (F.), judicial.

Jungo (junctum), *I join;* junction, juncture, conjoin (F.), adjunct.

Jus (juris), *right;* justice (F.), jury, injury.

Labor (lapsus), *I glide;* lapse, relapse, collapse.

Lapis (lapidis), *a stone;* lapidary, dilapidated.

Laus (laudis), *praise;* laud, laudable, laudation, allow (F.)

Lego (lectum), *I gather, read;* collect, elector, select; lecture (F.), legend, legible.

Lego (legatum), *I send;* legate, delegate, legacy.

Levis, *light;* levity, alleviate, relief (F.), lever, leaven.

Lex (legis), *a law;* legal, legislate, legitimate.

Liber, *free;* liberal, liberty, libertine.

Liber, *a book;* library, librarian.

Ligo, *I bind;* ligament, religion, oblige (F.), liable (F.)

Linquo (lictum), *I leave;* relinquish, relict, relics.

Litera, *a letter;* literal, literary, literature.

Locus, *a place;* local, allocate, dislocate, locomotive.

Loquor (locutus), *I speak;* loquacious, elocution, colloquy.

Ludo (lusum), *I play;* elude, illusion, interlude, ludicrous.

Lumen, *light;* illuminate, luminous, luminary.

Luna, *the moon;* lunar, sublunary, lunacy.

Luo (lutum), *I wash;* ablution, dilute, antediluvian.

Lux (lucis), *light;* lucid, elucidate, pellucid.

Magnus, *great;* magnitude, magnify, magnificent, magnanimous.

Malus, *bad;* malady, malice (F.), malaria, malevolent.

Maneo (mansum), *I remain;* manse, mansion, permanent.

Manus, *the hand;* manuscript, manual, manufacture, amanuensis.

Mare, *the sea;* marine, mariner, maritime.

Mater, *a mother;* maternal, matricide, matron, matriculate.

Maturus, *ripe;* mature, immature, premature.

Medius, *the middle;* medium, mediate, immediate, Mediterranean.

Memini, *I remember;* memor, *mindful;* memory, memoir (F.), commemorate, immemorial.

Mens (mentis), *the mind;* mental, demented.

Mergo (mersum), *I dip;* emerge, immersion, emergency.

Merx (mercis), *goods;* merchandise (F.), commerce (F.), merchant (F.)

Miles (militis), *a soldier;* military, militant, militia.

Miror, *I admire;* admirable, miracle, mirage (F.)

Mitto (missum), *I send;* commit, missile, mission, remittance.

Modus, *a measure;* mood, modify, accommodate.

Moneo (monitum), *I advise;* monition, monitor, monument.

Mons (montis), *a mountain;* amount (F.), dismount (F.), promontory, ultramontane.

Mors (mortis), *death;* mortify, mortal, immortality.

Moveo (motum), *I move;* mobile (F.), promote, motor, motive.

Multus, *many;* multitude, multiple, multiply.

Munus (muneris), *a gift;* munificent, remunerate, municipal.

Muto, *I change;* mutable, transmute.

Nascor (natus), *to be born;* nascent, natal, nativity, nature.

Navis, *a ship;* navy, naval, navigate, nave.

Necto (nexum), *I tie;* connect, connection, annex.

Nego (negatum), *I deny;* negative, negation, renegade (Sp.)

Noceo, *I injure;* noxious, innocuous, innocent.

Nomen, *a name;* nominal, cognomen, nomination.

Novus, *new;* novel, renovate, novelty, innovation.

Nox (noctis), *night;* nocturnal, equinoctial, equinox.

Nudus, *naked;* nude, denude, denudation.

Numerus, *a number;* numeration, innumerable, enumerate.

Octo, *eight;* octave, octagon, October.

Omnis, *all;* omnibus, omnipotent, omniscient.

Opus (operis), *work;* operation, co-operate, opera.

Ordo (ordinis), *order;* ordinal, ordinary, ordinance.

Oro, *I pray;* oration, orator, peroration.

Pando (pansum or passum), *I spread;* expand, expanse, compass, pace.

Pareo, *I appear;* appearance, apparent, apparition.

Paro (paratum), *I prepare;* repair (F.), apparatus, comparison (F.)

Pars (partis), *a part;* particle, partition, partner, parcel (F.)

Pasco (pastum), *I feed;* pastor, repast, pasture.

Pater, *a father;* paternal, parricide (F.), patrimony.

Patior (passus), *I suffer;* impatient, passive, passion.

Pax (pacis), *peace;* pacify, pacific.

Pello (pulsum), *I drive;* repel, expel, expulsion, impulsive.

Pendeo (pensum), *I hang;* pendant, depend, suspend, suspense, appendix.

Pes (pedis), *the foot;* pedal, impede, pedestrian, biped.

Peto (petitum), *I seek;* petition, petulant, compete, appetite.

Planus, *level;* plan (F.), plane, plain, explain.

Plaudo (plausum), *I clap the hands;* applaud, plausible (F.), explode.

Pleo (pletum), *I fill;* complete, completion, supplement.

Plico (plicatum), *I fold;* complicated, pliable (F.), reply (F.), display (F.), simple.

Pœna, *punishment;* penal, repent, penalty, penitent, penance.

Pono (positum), *I place;* deponent, position, imposition, post.

Pons (pontis), *a bridge;* pontiff, transpontine.

Porto, *I carry;* export, deportment, report, portmanteau (F.)

Possum, *I am able;* potens, *able;* possible, potency (F.), impotent.

Prehendo (prehensum), (Fr. *prendre, pris*), *I take;* prehensile, comprehend, apprise, comprise, apprentice (F.)

Primus, *first;* primary, primitive, primrose.

Probo, *I try, prove;* probe, probable, improve (F.), approve (F.)

Proprius, *one's own;* proper, property, appropriation.

Pungo (punctum), *I prick;* pungent, expunge, punctual, poignant (F.)

Puto (putatum), *I cut, think;* compute, count (F.), amputate, reputation.

Quatuor, *four;* quadra, *a square;* quart, quarter, quarry (F.), quadrant.

Radix, *a root;* radical, eradicate, radish (F.)

Rapio (raptum), *I seize;* rapture, rapine, surreptitious.

Rego (rectum), *I rule; rex* (regis), *a king;* regal, regulate, regent, rector, interregnum, royal (F.), realm (N.-Fr. *réal*).

Rideo (risum), *I laugh;* ridicule (F.), deride, ridiculous (F.), risible.

Rogo (rogatum), *I ask;* rogation, interrogation, derogatory.

Rota, *a wheel;* rotary, rotation, rotund —contracted into round (F.)

Rumpo (ruptum), *I break;* rupture, eruption, disruption.

Sacer, *sacred;* sacrament, sacrilege (F.), sacerdotal, sexton (contracted from *sacristan*).

Salio (saltum), *I leap;* sally (F.), assail (F.), salient, salmon.

Sanctus, *holy;* sanctuary, sanctify, saint (F.)

Scando (scansum), *I climb;* scala, *a ladder;* scan, scale, descent, ascension.

Scio, *I know;* science, scientific, conscience, omniscient.

Scribo (scriptum), *I write;* scribe, scribble, scripture, inscription, postscript.

Seco (sectum), *I cut;* bisect, dissect, insect, section.

Sedeo (sessum), *I set, sit;* sediment, subside, see (F.), residence (F.), insidious.

Sentio, *I feel;* sense, sentiment, sensual, scent (F.)

Septem, *seven;* septennial, September.

Sequor (secutus), *I follow;* sequence (F.), sequel, consequent, prosecute.

Servio, *I serve;* service (F.), servant, sergeant (F.)

Signum, *a sign;* signify, significant, designation, ensign (F.)

Similis, *like;* similar, similitude, resemble (F.)

Socius, *a companion;* social, society, association.

Solus, *alone;* solitude, sole, solo (It.)

Solvo (solutum), *I loose;* dissolve, resolve, absolute, resolution.

Specio (spectum), *I see;* aspect, spectator, specimen, spectre.

Spero, *I hope;* despair (F.), desperate.

Spiro, *I breathe;* inspire, aspire, conspiracy.

Statuo, *I set up;* sto (statum), *I stand;* statue, statute, stature, institute.

Stringo (strictum), *I bind;* stringent, constrain (F.), district.

Struo (structum), *I build;* structure, construct, obstruct, construe.

Sumo (sumptum), *I take;* assume, consume, assumption.

Tango (tactum), *I touch;* tangible, tangent, contact, contagious.

Tego (tectum), *I cover;* integument, detect, tile (F.); from Lat. *tegula.*

Tempus (temporis), *time;* temporal, contemporary, extempore.

Tendo (tensum), *I stretch;* contend, extend, attend, tense (F.), tendon.

Teneo (tentum), *I hold;* tenant, tenet, tendril, detain (F.), retentive.

Terminus, *an end, boundary;* terminate, term, interminable.

Terra, *the earth;* subterranean, terrestrial, Mediterranean.

Terreo, *I frighten;* terror, terrify, deter.

Texo (textum), *I weave;* textile, text, texture, context.

Timeo, *I fear;* timid, timorous.

Torqueo (tortum), *I twist;* torture, torment, contortion, retort.

Traho (tractum), *I draw;* traction, subtract, contraction, tract.

Tres (tria), *three;* trefoil, trident, trinity.

Tribuo, *I give;* tribute, tributary, contribution.

Tumeo, *I swell;* tumulus, *a swelling or mound;* tumult, tumour, tomb (F.)

Unus, *one;* union, unit, unite, uniform, unique (F.)

Urbs, *a city;* suburb, urbanity, urbane.

Valeo, *I am strong;* valour, valiant (F.), prevail (F.)

Vanus, *empty;* vanity, vanish, vain (F.)

Veho (vectum), *I convey;* vehicle, conveyance (F.), convex.

Venio, *I come;* venture, advent, convene, covenant (F.)'

Verbum, *a word;* verb, adverb, verbose, verbal, proverb.

Verto (versum), *I turn;* convert, revert, divert, versatile.

Verus, *true;* verity, verify, aver, verdict.

Via, *a way;* deviate, previous, trivial.

Video (visum), *I see;* vision, provide, visit (F.), revise (F.)

Vinco (victum), *I conquer;* victor, convict, victory, convince.

Vitium, *a fault;* vice (F.), vitiate, vicious (F.)

Vivo (victum), *I live;* vivid, revive, viands (F.), survive.

Voco (vocatum), *I call;* vocal, vowel (F.), vocation, revoke, vociferate.

Volo, *I wish;* volition, voluntary, benevolence.

Volvo (volutum), *I roll;* revolve, involve, evolution, volume.

Voveo (votum), *I vow;* vote, devote, vow (F.)

Vulgus, *the common people;* vulgar, divulge, vulgate.

GREEK ROOTS.

Agōn, *a contest;* agony, antagonist

Allos, *another;* allopathy, allegory.

Angelos, *a messenger;* angel, evangelist.

Anthrōpos, *a man;* misanthrope, philanthropy.

Archo, *I begin, rule;* monarch, archaic, archbishop, archdeacon.

Arithmos, *number;* arithmetic.

Aster or astron, *a star;* astronomy, astrology, asteroid, disaster

Atmos, *vapour;* atmosphere

Autos, *self;* autocrat, autograph.

Ballo, *I throw;* symbol, parable.

Bapto, *I dip;* baptise, baptist.

Baros, *weight;* barometer, baritone.

Biblos, *a book;* Bible, bibliomania.

Bios, *life;* biography, biology, amphibious.

Cheir, *the hand;* surgeon [older form, chirurgeon].

Cholē, *bile;* melancholy, choler.

Chrio, *I anoint;* Christ, chrism.

Chronos, *time;* chronology, chronic, chronicle, chronometer.

Daktūlos, *a finger;* dactyl, pterodactyl, date (*the fruit*).

Deka, *ten;* decagon, decalogue, decade.

Dēmos, *the people;* democrat, endemic, epidemic.

Dokeo, *I think;* doxa and dogma, *an opinion;* doxology, orthodox, heterodox, dogma, dogmatic.

Drao, *I do;* drama, dramatic.

Dunāmis, *power;* dynamics, dynamite.

Eidos, *form;* kaleidoscope, spheroid.

Eikon, *an image;* iconoclast.

Electron, *amber;* electricity, electrotype.

Ergon, *a work;* surgeon (=chirurgeon), energy, metallurgy.

Eu, *well;* eucharist, euphony, evangelist.

Gamos, *marriage;* bigamy, monogamist, misogamy.

Gē, *the earth;* geography, geometry, geology.

Gennao, *I produce;* genesis, genealogy, hydrogen, oxygen.

Grapho, *I write;* gramma, a letter; graphic, grammar, telegraph, biography, diagram.

Haima, *blood;* hæmorrhage, hæmorrhoid.

Haireo, *I take away;* heresy, heretic.

Hecaton, *a hundred;* hecatomb, hectometre.

Helios, *the sun;* heliograph, heliotype.

Hemi, *half;* hemisphere.

Hieros, *sacred;* hierarchy, hieroglyphic.

Hippos, *a horse;* hippopotamus, hippodrome.

Hodos, *a way;* method, period, exodus.

Homos, *the same;* homœopathy, homogeneous.

Hudor, *water;* hydraulic, hydrophobia, hydrogen.

Ichthus, *a fish;* ichthyology.

Idios, *one's own;* idiom, idiot, idiosyncrasy.

Isos, *equal;* isochronous, isobaric (of equal weight), isosceles.

Kalos, *beautiful;* caligraphy, kaleidoscope.

Kephalē, *the head;* hydrocephalus.

Klino, *I bend;* clinical, climax, climate.

Kosmos, *order;* cosmogony, cosmography, cosmetic.

Krino, *I judge;* critic, criterion, hypocrite.

Kuklos, *a circle;* cycle, cycloid, cyclone.

Kuon (kun-os), *a dog;* cynic, cynicism.

Lēgo, *I say, choose;* eclectic, lexicon.

Lithos, *a stone;* lithograph, aerolite.

Lōgos, *a word, speech;* logic, dialogue, geology.

Luo, *I loosen;* dialysis, analysis, paralysis.

Mētēr, *a mother;* metropolis, metropolitan.

Metron, *a measure;* metre, metronome, diameter, thermometer, barometer.

Mōnos, *alone;* monastery, monogram, monosyllable, monopoly, monarch.

Morphē, *shape;* amorphous, dimorphous, metamorphic.

Naus, *a ship;* nautical, nausea.

Nekros, *a dead body;* necropolis, necromancy.

Nōmos, *a law;* autonomous, astronomy, Deuteronomy.

Oikos, *a house;* economy, economical.

Onōma, *a name;* anonymous, synonymous, patronymic.

Optōmai, *I see;* optics, synoptical.

Orthos, *right;* orthodoxy, orthography.

Pais (paid-os), *a boy;* pedagogue [lit. *a boy-leader*].

Pan, *all;* pantheist, panoply, pantomime.

Pathos, *feeling;* pathetic, sympathy.

Pente, *five;* pentagon, pentateuch, Pentecost.

Petra, *a rock;* petrify, petrel, Peter.

Phainōmai, *I appear;* phenomenon, phantasy, phantom, fantastic, fancy.

Phero, *I bear;* periphery, phosphorus [=the light-bearer].

Phileo, *I love;* philosophy, Philadelphia, philharmonic.

Phōnē, *a sound;* phonic, phonetic, euphony, symphony.

Phōs (phōt-os), *light;* photometer, photograph.

Phusis, *nature;* physics, physiology, physician.

Poieo, *I make;* poet, poetic, pharmacopœia.

Polis, *a city;* Constantinople, metropolis.

Polus, *many;* polytheist, Polynesia, polyanthus, polygamy.

Pous (pŏd-os), *a foot;* antipodes, tripod.

Protos, *first;* prototype, protoplasm.

Pur, *fire;* pyrotechnic, pyre.

Rheo, *I flow;* rhetoric, catarrh, rheumatic.

Skōpeo, *I see;* microscope, telescope, spectroscope, bishop [from *episkopos,* an overseer].

Sophia, *wisdom;* sophist, philosophy.

Stello, *I send;* apostle, epistle.

Stratos, *an army;* strategy, strategic.

Strēpho, *I turn;* catastrophe, apostrophe.

Technē, *an art;* technical.

Tēlē, *distant;* telegraph, telescope, telephone, telegram.

Temno, *I cut;* anatomy, lithotomy.

Tetra, *four;* tetrachord, tetrarch.

Theāomai, *I see;* theatre, theory.

Theos, *a god;* theist, enthusiast, theology.

Thermē, *heat;* thermal, thermometer, isotherm.

Tithēmi, *I place;* thēsis, *a placing;* synthesis, hypothesis.

Treis, *three;* triangle, trigonometry, tripod, trinity, trichord.

Trēpo, *I turn;* trophy, tropic, heliotrope.

Tupos, *the impress of a seal;* type, stereotype.

Zōon, *an animal;* zoology, zodiac.

WORDS DERIVED FROM THE NAMES OF PERSONS, ETC.

Argosy, from the name of the ship **Argo,** in which Jason and his companions sailed to the Black Sea to find the Golden Fleece. Used by Shakespeare, in the "Merchant of Venice," i. 1. 9, in the sense of *trading vessel.*

Assassins, the name of a fanatical Syrian sect of the thirteenth century, who, under the influence of a drug prepared from hemp, called *haschisch,* rushed into battle against the Crusaders, and slaughtered many of their foes.

Atlas, one of the Titans, or earlier gods, who was so strong that he was said to carry the world on his shoulders.

August, from Augustus Cæsar, the second Emperor of Rome.

Bacchanalian, from the festival called *Bacchanalia;* from **Bacchus,** the Roman god of wine.

Boycott (to), from Captain Boycott, a land-agent in the west of Ireland, who was "sent to Coventry" by all his neighbours; they would neither speak to him, buy from him, or sell to him—by order of the "Irish Land League."

Chimera, a totally imaginary and grotesque image or conception; from **Chimæra,** a monster in the Greek mythology, half goat, half lion.

Cicerone, a guide; from **Cicero,** the greatest Roman orator and writer of speeches that ever lived. (Guides who described antiquities, etc., were supposed to be as "fluent as Cicero.")

Cravat, from the **Croats** or **Crabali** of Croatia, who supplied an army corps to Austria, in which long and large neck-ties were worn by the soldiers.

Dahlia, from **Dahl,** a Swedish botanist, who introduced the flower into Europe.

Draconian (code), a very severe code; from Draco, a severe Athenian legislator, who decreed death for every crime, great or small. His laws were said to have been "written in blood."

Dunce, from **Duns Scotus,** a great philosopher (or "schoolman") of the Middle Ages, who died 1308. The followers of Thomas Aquinas called "Thomists," looked down upon those of Duns, who were called "Scotists," and in course of time "Dunces."

Epicure, a person fond of good living ; from **Epicurus,** a great Greek philosopher.   His enemies misrepresented him as teaching that pleasure
   was the highest or chiefest good.

Euphuistic (style), a style of high-flown refinement ; from **Euphues** (the
   well-born man), the title of a book written in the reign of Elizabeth,
   by John Lyly, which introduced a too ingenious and far-fetched way
   of speaking and writing in her Court.

Fauna, the collective name for all the animals of a region or country ; from
   Faunus, a Roman god of the woods and country.   (The **Fauni** were
   minor rural deities of Rome, who had the legs, feet, and ears of a goat,
   and the other parts of the body of a human shape.)

Flora, the collective name for all the plants and flowers of a region or
   country ; from **Flora,** the Roman goddess of flowers.

Galvanism, from **Galvani,** an Italian physicist, lecturer on anatomy at
   Bologna, who discovered, by experiments on frogs, that animals are
   endowed with a certain kind of electricity.

Gordian (knot), the knot tied by Gordius a king of Phrygia, who had been
   originally a peasant.   The knot by which he tied the draught-pole
   of his chariot to the yoke was so intricate, that no one could untie it.
   A rumour spread that the oracle had stated that the empire of Asia
   would belong to him who should untie the Gordian knot.   Alexander
   the Great, to encourage his soldiers, tried to untie it ; but, finding
   that he could not, he cut it through with his sword, and declared that
   he had thus fulfilled the oracle.

Guillotine, an instrument for beheading at one stroke, used in France.
   It was invented during the time of the Revolution by **Dr Guillotin.**

Hansom (cab), from the name of its inventor.

Hector (to), to talk big ; from **Hector,** the bravest of the Trojans, as
   Achilles was the bravest of the Grecian chiefs.

Hermetically (sealed), so sealed as to entirely exclude the outer air ;
   from **Hermes,** the name of the Greek god who corresponds to the
   Roman god Mercury.   Hermes was fabled to be the inventor of
   chemistry.

Jacobin, a revolutionist of the extremest sort ; from the hall of the
   Jacobin Friars in Paris, where the revolutionists used to meet.
   Robespierre was for some time their chief.

Jacobite, a follower of the Stuart family ; from James II. (in Latin
   Jacobus), who was driven from the English throne in 1688.

January, from the Roman god **Janus,** a god with two faces, "looking
   before and after."

Jovial, with the happy temperament of a person born under the influence
   of the star Jupiter or **Jove** ; a term taken from the old astrology.
   (Opposed to *saturnine,* gloomy, because born under the star Saturn.)

July, from **Julius,** in honour of Julius Cæsar, the great Roman general,
   writer, and statesman—who was born in this month.

Lazarettor or **Lazar-house,** from **Lazarus,** the beggar at the gate of

Dives, in Luke xvi. The word is corrupted into *lizard* in **Lizard-point,** where a lazar-house once stood, for the reception of sick people from on board ship.

Lynch-law, from a famous Judge Lynch, of Tennessee, who made short work of his trials, and then of his criminals.

Macadamise, to make roads of fragments of stones, which afterwards cohere in one mass ; from John Loudon **Macadam,** the inventor, who, in 1827, received from the Government a reward of £10,000 for his plan.

March, from Mars, the Roman god of War.

Martinet, a severe disciplinarian, with an eye for the smallest details ; from General **Martinet,** a strict commander of the time of Louis XIV. of France.

Mausoleum, a splendidly built tomb ; from **Mausōlus,** King of Caria in Asia Minor, to whom his widow erected a gorgeous burial-chamber.

Mentor, an adviser ; from **Mentor,** the aged counsellor of Telémăchus, the son of Ulysses.

Mercurial, of light, airy, and quick-spirited temperament, as having been born under the planet **Mercury** (compare *Jovial, Saturnine,* etc.)

Panic, a sudden and unaccountable terror ; from **Pan,** the god of flocks and shepherds. He was fabled to appear suddenly to travellers.

Parrot (= *Little Peter,* or *Peterkin*), from the French **Perrot** = *Pierrot,* from *Pierre,* Peter. Compare *Magpie* = *Margaret Pie ; Jackdaw ; Robin-redbreast ; Cuddy* (from *Cuthbert*), a donkey, etc.

Petrel, the name of a sea-bird that skims the tops of the waves in a storm, the diminutive of **Peter.** It is an allusion to Matthew xiv. 29. These birds are called by sailors "Mother Carey's chickens."

Phaeton, a kind of carriage ; from Phäethon, a son of Apollo, who received from his father permission to guide the chariot of the Sun for a single day.

Philippic, a violent political speech directed against a person ; from the orations made by Demosthenes, the great Athenian orator, against **Philip** of Macedon, the father of Alexander the Great.

Plutonic (rocks), igneous rocks (created by the action of fire)—in opposition to sedimentary rocks, which have been formed by the depositing action of water ; from **Pluto,** the Roman god of the infernal regions.

Protean, assuming many shapes ; from **Proteus,** a sea-deity, who had received the gift of prophecy from Neptune, but who was very difficult to catch, as he could take whatever form he pleased.

Quixotic, fond of utterly impracticable designs ; from **Don Quixote,** the hero of the national Spanish romance, by Cervantes. Don Quixote is made to tilt at windmills, proclaim and make war against whole nations by himself, and do many other chivalrous and absurd things.

Simony, the fault of illegally buying and selling church livings ; from **Simon Magus.** (See Acts viii. 18.)

Stentorian, very loud and strong ; from **Stentor,** whom Homer describes as the loudest-voiced man in the Grecian army that was besieging Troy.

Tantalise, to tease with impossible hopes ; from **Tantalus,** a king of Lydia in Asia Minor.   He offended the gods, and was placed in Hadés up to his lips in a pool of water, which, when he attempted to drink it, ran away ; and with bunches of grapes over his head, which, when he tried to grasp them, were blown from his reach by a blast of wind.

Tawdry, shabby — a term often applied to cheap finery ; from **St Ethelreda,** which became **St Audrey :** originally applied to clothes sold at St Audrey's fair.   (Compare *Tooley* from *St Olave ; Ted* from *St Edmund ;* etc.)

Volcano and **Vulcanite,** from the Roman god of fire and smiths, **Vulcanus.** A volcano was regarded as the chimney of one of his workshops.

WORDS DERIVED FROM THE NAMES OF PLACES.

Academy, from **Academia,** the house of **Acadēmus,** a friend of the great Greek philosopher Plato, who was allowed to teach his followers there. Plato taught either in Academus's garden, or in his own house.

Artesian (well), from **Artois,** the name of an old province in the north-west of France, the inhabitants of which were accustomed to pierce the earth for water.

Bayonet, from **Bayonne,** in the south of France, on the Bay of Biscay. (Compare *Pistol* from *Pistoia,* a town in the north of Italy.)

Bedlam, the name for a lunatic asylum—a corruption of the word **Bethlehem** (Hospital).

Cambric, the name of the finest kind of linen ; from **Cambray,** a town in French Flanders, in the north-west of France.

Canter, an easy and slow gallop ; from the pace assumed by the **Canterbury** Pilgrims, when riding along the green lanes of England to the shrine of Thomas à Becket.

Carronade, a short cannon ; from **Carron,** in Stirlingshire, Scotland, where it was first made.

Cherry ; from **Cerasus,** a town in Pontus, Asia Minor, where it was much grown.

Copper and **Cypress** ; from the island of **Cyprus,** in the Mediterranean.

Currants, small dried grapes from **Corinth,** in Greece, where they are still grown in large quantities. They are shipped at the port of Patras.

Damson, a contraction of **damascene**; from **Damascus** — the Damascus plum. (Hence also *damask.*)

Dollar, a coin—the chief coin used in America ; from German **Thaler** (= *Daler,* or something made in a *dale* or valley). The first coins of this sort were made in St Joachimsthal in Bohemia, and were called *Joachim's thaler.*

Elysian (*used with* fields *or* bliss), from **Elysium,** the place to which the souls of brave Greeks went after death.

Ermine, the fur worn on judges' robes ; from **Armenia,** because this fur is "the spoil of the Armenian rat."

Florin, a two-shilling piece ; from **Florence.** Professor Skeat says : " Florins were coined by Edward III. in 1337, and named after the coins of Florence."

Gasconading, boasting ; from Gascony, a southern province of France, the inhabitants of which were much given to boasting. One Gascon, on being shown the Tuileries—the palace of the Kings of France—remarked that it reminded him to some extent of his father's stables, which, however, were somewhat larger.

Gipsy, a corrupt form of the word **Egyptian.** The Gipsies were supposed to come from Egypt. (The French call them *Bohemians.*)

Guinea, a coin value 21s. now quite out of use, except as a name—made of gold brought from the **Guinea Coast,** in the west of Africa.

Hock, the generic term for all kinds of Rhine-wine, but properly only the name of that which comes from **Hochheim,** a celebrated vineyard.

Indigo, a blue dye, obtained from the leaves of certain plants ; from the Latin adjective **Indicus**=belonging to India.

Laconic, short, pithy, and full of sense ; from **Laconia, a** country in the south of Greece, the capital of which was Sparta or Lacedæmon. The Laconians, and especially the Spartans, were little given to talking, unlike their lively rivals, the Athenians.

Lilliputian, very small ; from **Lilliput,** the name of the imaginary country of extremely small men and women, visited by Captain Lemuel Gulliver, the hero of Swift's tale called 'Gulliver's Travels.'

Lumber, useless things ; from **Lombard,** the Lombards being famous for money-lending. The earliest kind of banking was pawnbroking ; and pawnbrokers placed their pledges in the " Lombard-room," which, as it gradually came to contain all kinds of rubbish, came also to mean and to be called "lumber-room." In America, timber is called *lumber.*

Meander (to), to "wind about and in and out ;" from the **Mæander,** a very winding river in the plain of Troy, in Phrygia, in the north-west of Asia Minor.

Magnesia and **Magnet,** from **Magnesia,** a town in Thessaly, in the north of Greece.

Milliner, originally a dealer in wares from **Milan,** a large city in the north of Italy, in the plain of the Po.

Muslin, from **Mosul,** a town in Asiatic Turkey, on the Tigris.

Palace, from the Latin **palatium,** a building on Mons **Palatinus,** one of the seven hills of Rome. This building became the residence of Augustus and other Roman emperors ; and hence *palace* came to be the generic term for the house of a king or ruling prince. *Palatinus,* itself comes from **Pales,** a Roman goddess of flocks, and is connected with the Lat. *pater,* a father or feeder.

Peach, from Lat. **Persicum** (*malum*), the Persian apple, from **Persia.** The *r* has been gradually absorbed.

Pheasant, from the **Phasis,** a river of Colchis in Asia Minor, at the eastern end of the Black Sea, from which these birds were first brought.

Port, a wine from **Oporto,** in Portugal. (Compare *Sherry* from *Xeres*, in the south of Spain.)

Rhubarb, from **Rha barbarum,** the wild Rha plant. *Rha* is an old name for the Volga, from the banks of which this plant was imported.

Solecism, a blunder in the use of words; from **Soli,** a town in Cilicia, in Asia Minor, the inhabitants of which used a mixed dialect.

Spaniel, a sporting-dog remarkable for its sense ; from **Spain.** The best kinds are said to come from **Hispaniola,** an island in the West Indies, now called Hayti.

Stoic, from **Stoa** Poikílé, the Painted Porch, a porch in Athens, where Zeno, the founder of the Stoic School, taught his disciples.

Utopian, impossible to realise ; from **Utopia** (= Nowhere), the title of a story written by Sir Thomas More, in which he described, under the guise of an imaginary island, the probable state of England, if her laws and customs were reformed.

WORDS DISGUISED IN FORM.

WHEN a word is imported from a foreign language into our own, there is a natural tendency among the people who use the word to give it a native and homely dress, and so to make it look like English. This is especially the case with proper names. Thus the walk through St James's Park from Buckingham Palace to the House of Commons was called *Bocage Walk* (that is, shrubbery walk); but, as *Bocage* was a strange word to the Londoner, it became quickly corrupted into Birdcage Walk, though there is not, and never was, any sign of birdcages in the neighbourhood. *Birdcage* is a known word, *Bocage* is not—that is the whole matter. In the same way, our English sailors, when they captured the French ship *Bellerophon*, spoke of it as the *Billy Ruffian;* and our English soldiers in India mentioned Surajah Dowlah, the prince who put the English prisoners into the Black Hole, as *Sir Roger Dowler.* The same phenomenon is observed also in common names—and not infrequently. The following are some of the most remarkable examples :—

Alligator, from Spanish **el lagarto,** *the* lizard. The article **el** (from Latin *ille*) has clung to the word. Lat. *lacerta,* a lizard. (The Arabic article *al* has clung to the noun in *alchemy, algebra, almanac,* etc.)

Artichoke (no connection with *choke*), from Ital. **articiocco;** from Arabic *al harshaff,* an artichoke.

Atonement, a hybrid—*atone* being English, and *ment* a Latin ending. *Atone=to bring or come into one.* Shakespeare has "Earthly things, made even,' atone together."

Babble, from **ba** and the frequentative **le;** it means "to keep on saying " **ba.**

Bank, a form of the word **bench,** a money-table.

Belfry (nothing to do with *bell*), from M. E. **berfray;** O. Fr. *berfroit,* a watch-tower.

Brimstone, from *burn*. The **r** is an easily moved letter—as in *three, third; turn, trundle*, etc.

Bugle, properly *a wild ox*. *Bugle*, in the sense of a musical instrument, is really short for *bugle-horn*. Lat. *buculus*, a bullock, a diminutive of *bos*.

Bustard, from O. Fr. **oustarde**, from Lat. *avis tarda*, the tardy or slow bird.

Butcher, from O. Fr. **bocher**, a man who slaughters he-goats; from **boc**, the French form of *buck*.

Butler, the servant in charge of the **butts** or casks of wine. (The whole collection of butts was called the **buttery**; a little butt is a **bottle**.)

Buxom, stout, healthy; but in O. E. obedient. "Children, be buxom to your parents." Connected with *bow* and *bough*. From A. S. *bugan*, to bend; which gives also *bow, bight, boat*, etc.

Carfax, a place where four roads meet. O. Fr. *carrefourgs;* Latin *quatuor furcas*, four forks.

Carouse, from German **gar aus**, quite out. Spoken of emptying a goblet.

Caterpillar = hairy-cat, from O. Fr. *chate*, a she-cat, and O. Fr. *pelouse*, hairy, Lat. *pilosus*. Compare *woolly-bear*.

Causeway (no connection with *way*), from Fr. **chausée**; Lat. *calceata via*, a way strewed with limestone; from Lat. *calx*, lime.

Clove, through Fr. **clou**, from Lat. **clavus**, a nail, from its resemblance to a small nail.

Constable, from Lat. **comes stabuli**, count of the stable; hence Master of the Horse; and, in the 13th century, commander of the king's army.

Coop, a cognate of **cup**; from Lat. **cupa**, a tub.

Cope, a later spelling of **cape**. *Cap, cape*, and *cope* are forms of the same word.

Costermonger, properly *costard-monger;* from **costard**, a large apple.

Counterpane (not at all connected with *counter* or with *pane*, but with *quilt* and *point*), a coverlet for a bed. The proper form is *contrepointe*, from Low Lat. **culcita puncta**, a punctured quilt.

Country-dance, (not connected with *country*), a corruption of the French *contre-danse;* a dance in which each dancer stands *contre* or *contra* or *opposite* his partner.

Coward, an animal that drops his tail. O. Fr. **col and ard**; from Lat. *cauda*, a tail.

Crayfish, (nothing to do with *fish*), from O. Fr. *escrevisse*. This is really a Frenchified form of the German word *Krebs*, which is the German form of our English word *crab*. The true division of the word into syllables is *crayf-ish;* and thus the seeming connection with *fish* disappears.

Custard, a misspelling of the M. E. word *crustade*, a general name for pies made with crust.

Daisy = day's eye. Chaucer says: "The dayes eye or else the eye of day."

Dandelion = dent de lion, the lion's tooth ; so named from its jagged leaves.

Dirge, a funeral song of sorrow. In the Latin service for the dead, one part began with the words (Ps. v. 8) **dirige**, Dominus meus, in conspectu tuo vitam meam, "Direct my life, O Lord, in thy sight ; " and **dirige** was contracted into **dirge**.

Drawing-room = withdrawing-room, a room to which guests retire after dinner.

Dropsy (no connection with *drop*), from O. Fr. **hydropisce**, from Gr. *hudōr*, water. (Compare *chirurycon*, which has been shortened into *surgeon; example*, into *sample; estate*, into *state*.)

Easel, a diminutive of the word **ass**, through the Dutch **ezel**; like the Latin *asellus*.

Farthing = fourthing. (*Four* appears as *fir* in firkin ; and as *for* in *forty*.)

Frontispiece (not connected with *piece*), that which is seen or placed in front. Lat. *specio*, I see.

Gadfly = goad-fly (sting-fly).

Gospel = God-spell, a narrative about God.

Grove, originally a lane cut through trees. A doublet of *groove*, and *grave*, from A. S. *grafan*, to dig.

Haft, that by which we **have** or hold a thing.

Hamper, old form, **hanaper**; from Low Latin **hanaperium**, a large basket for keeping drinking-cups (*hanapi*) in.

Handsel, money given into the hand ; from A. S. *sellan*, to give.

Hanker, to keep the mind **hanging** on a thing. **Er** is a frequentative suffix, as in *batter, linger*, etc.

Harbinger, a man who goes before to provide a **harbour** or lodging-place for an army. The **n** is intrusive, as in *porringer, passenger*, and *messenger*. (The ruins of old Roman villas were often used by English travellers as inns. Such places were called "Cold Harbours." There are fourteen places of this name in England—all on the great Roman roads.)

Hatchment, the escutcheon, shield, or coat-of-arms of a deceased person, displayed in front of his house. A corruption (by the intrusion of **h**) of **atch'ment**, the short form of *atchievement*, the old spelling of *achievement*, which is still the heraldic word for *hatchment*.

Hawthorn = hedge-thorn. *Haw* was in O. E. *haga ;* and the hard g became a **w**; and also became softened, under French influence, into dg. **Haha**, older form *Hawhaw*, is a sunk fence.

Heaven, that which is **heaved** up ; **heavy**, that which requires much **heaving**.

Horehound (not connected with *hound*), a plant with stems covered with white woolly down. The M. E. form is **hoar-hune** ; and the second syllable means scented. The syllable *hoar* means *white*, as in *hoar-frost*. The final d is excrescent or inorganic—like the d in *sound, bound* (= ready to go), etc.

Humble-bee (not connected with the adjective *humble*), from M. E. **hummelen**, to keep humming — a frequentative; the **b** being inorganic.

Humble-pie (not connected with the adjective *humble*), pie made of **umbles**, the entrails of a deer.

Husband, (not connected with *bind*), from Icelandic **husbuandi**, *buandi*, being the pres. participle of *bua*, to dwell ; and **hus**, house.

Hussif (connected with *house*, but not with *wife*), a case containing needles, thread, etc. From Icelandic, **húsi**, a case, a cognate of **house**. The f is intrusive, from a mistaken opinion that the word was a short form of *housewife*.

Hussy, a pert girl ; a corruption of **housewife**.

Icicle, (the ending *cle* is not the diminutive) a hanging point of ice. The A. S. form is **isgicel**, a compound of *is*, ice, and *gicel*, a small piece of ice ; so that the word contains a redundant element. (The *ic* in icicle is entirely different from the *ic* in *art-ic-le* and in *part-ic-le*.)

Intoxicate, to drug or poison ; from Low Lat. *toxicum*, poison ; from Gr. *toxon*, a bow, plural *toxa*, bow and arrows—arrows for war being frequently dipped in poison.

Island (not connected with *isle*) = water-land, a misspelling for **iland** (the spelling that Milton always uses). The **s** has intruded itself from a confusion with the Lat. *insula*, which gives *isle*.

Jaw, properly **chaw**, the noun for *chew*. Cognates are *jowl* and *chaps*.

Jeopardy, hazard, danger. M. E. **jupartie**, from O. Fr. **jeu parti**, a game in which the chances are even, from Low Lat. *jŏcus partitus*, a divided game.

Jerusalem artichoke (not at all connected with *Jerusalem*), a kind of sunflower. Italian **girasole**, from Lat. *gyrus*, a circle, and *sol*, the sun. (In order to clench the blunder contained in the word *Jerusalem*, cooks call a soup made of this kind of artichoke "Palestine soup !")

Kickshaws, from Fr. **quelquechose**, something. There was once a plural —*kickshawses*.

Kind, the adjective from the noun **kin**.

Ledge, a place on which a thing lies. Hence also *ledger*.

Line (to line garments) = to put **linen** inside them. (*Linen* is really an adjective from the M. E. *lin*, just like *woollen*, *golden*, etc.)

Liquorice (not connected with *liquor*), in M. E. **licoris** ; from Gr. *glykyrrhiza*, a sweet root. (For the loss of the initial *g*, compare *Ipswich* and *Gyppenswich ; enough* and *genoh ;* and the loss of ge from all the past participles of our verbs.)

Mead, meadow = a place **mowed**. Hence also *math, aftermath*, and *moth* (= the biter or eater).

Nostrils = nose-thirles, nose-holes. **Thirl** is a cognate of *thrill, drill, through*, etc. (For change of position of **r**, compare *turn, trundle ; work, wright ; wort, root ; bride, bird,* etc.)

Nuncheon, a corruption of M. E. **none-schencke**, or noon-drink. Then this word got mixed up with the provincial English word **lunch**, which means a lump of bread; and so we have **luncheon**.

Nutmeg, a hybrid compounded of an English and a French word. *Meg* is a corruption of the O. Fr. *musge,* from Lat. *muscum*, musk.

Orchard = wort-yard, yard or garden for roots or plants. *Wort* is a cognate of *wart* and *root.*

Ostrich, from Lat. **avis struthio**. Shakespeare spells it *estridge* in "Antony and Cleopatra," iii. 13. 197, "The dove will peck the estridge." (*Avis* is found as a prefix in *bustard* also.)

Pastime = that which enables one to **pass** the **time**.

Pea-jacket (not connected with *pea*), a short thick jacket often worn by seamen; from the Dutch **pije**, a coarse woollen coat. Thus the word *jacket* is superfluous. In M. E. *py* was a coat; and we find it in Chaucer combining, with a French adjective, to make the hybrid *courtepy*, a short coat.

Peal (of bells), a short form of the word **appeal**; a call or summons. (Compare *penthouse* and *appentis; sample* and *example; scutcheon* and *escutcheon; squire* and *esquire;* etc.)

Penthouse (not connected with *house*), in reality a doublet of **appendage**, though not coming from it. O. Fr. **appentis**, from Lat. *appendicium*, from *appendix*, something *hanging* on to. (*Pendēre*, to hang.)

Periwinkle, a kind of evergreen plant; formed, by the addition of the diminutive **le**, from Lat. **pervinca**, from *vincīre*, to bind.

Periwinkle, a small mollusc with one valve. A corruption of the A. S. **pinewincla**, that is, a winkle eaten with a pin.

Pickaxe (not connected with *axe*), a tool used in digging. A corruption of M. E. *pickeys*, from O. Fr. *picois;* and connected with *peak, pike,* and *pick.*

Poach = to put in the **poke, pocket,** or **pouch.** So *poached eggs* are eggs dressed so as to keep the yoke in a *pouch.* Cognates are *pock, small-pox* (=*pocks*), etc.

Porpoise (not connected with the verb *poise*); from Lat. **porcum**, a pig, and **piscem**, a fish.

Posthumous (work), a work that appears after the death of the author; from Lat. **postumus**, the last. The **h** is an error; and the word has no connection with the Lat. *humus*, the ground.

Privet, a half-evergreen shrub. A form of **primet**, a plant carefully cut and trimmed; and hence **prim.** (For change of **m** into **v** (or **p**), compare *Molly* and *Polly; Matty* and *Patty,* etc. **V** and **p** are both labials.)

Proxy, a contraction of **procuracy**, the taking care of a thing for another. Lat. *pro* for, and *cura*, care.

Quick, living. We have the word in *quicklime, quicksand, quicksilver;* and in the phrase "the quick and the dead."

Quinsy, a bad sore throat, a contraction of O. Fr. **squinancie**, formed, by the addition of a prefixed and strengthening **s**, from Gr. *kynanchē*, a dog-throttling.

Riding, one of the three divisions of Yorkshire. The oldest form is **Trithing** or **Thrithing** (from *three* and *ing,* part; as in *farthing*=fourth part, etc.) The *t* or *th* seems to have dropped from its similarity and nearness to the *th* in *north* and the *t* in *east;* as in *North-thrithing, East-trithing,* etc.

Sexton, a corruption of **sacristan,** the keeper of the sacred vessels and vestments; from Lat. *sacer,* sacred. But the sexton is now only the grave-digger. (In the same way, *sacristy* was shortened into *sextry.*)

Sheaf a collection **shoved** together. *Shove* gives also *shovel;* and the frequentatives *shuffle* and *scuffle.*

Soup, a cognate of **sop** and **sup.**

Splice (to join after *splitting*), a cognate form of *split* and *splinter.*

Squirrel, from O. Fr. **escurel;** from Low Lat. *scuriolus;* from Gr. *skia,* a shadow, and *oura,* a tail. Hence the word means "shadow-tail."

Starboard, the **steering** side of a ship—the right, as one stands looking *to* the bow.

Stew, the verb corresponding to **stove.**

Steward, from A. S. **stiward,** from the full form *stigweard;* from *stige,* a sty, and *weard,* a keeper. Originally a person who looked after the domestic animals.

Stirrup, modern form of A. S. **stigrap,** from *stigan,* to climb, and *ráp,* a rope. Cognates are *sty, stile, stair.*

Straight, an old past participle of *stretch.* (*Strait* is a French form of the word *strict,* from Lat. *strictus,* tied up.)

Strong, a nasalised form of **stark.** Derivatives are *strength, strengthen, string,* etc.

Summerset (not connected either with *summer* or with *set*), or **somersault,** a corruption of Fr. **soubresault,** from Lat. *supra,* above, and *saltum,* a leap. (There is a connection between the b and the m—the one sliding into the other when the speaker has a cold.)

Surgeon (properly a *hand-worker*), a contraction of **chirurgeon;** from Gr. *cheir,* the hand, and *ergein,* to work.

Tackle, that which *takes* or grasps, holding the masts of a ship in their places. The **le** is the same as that in *settle* (a seat), *girdle,* etc.

Tale, from A. S. **talu,** number. Derivatives are *tell* and *till* (box for money), but not *talk,* which is a Scandinavian word.

Tansy, a tall plant, with small yellow flowers, used in medicine; from O. F. *athanasie;* from Gr. *athanasia,* immortality.

Thorough, a doublet of **through,** and found in *thorough-fare, thorough-bred,* etc. (The *dr, thr,* or *tr* is also found in *door, thrill, trill, drill, nostril,* etc.)

Treacle, from M. E. **triacle,** a remedy; from Lat. *theriaca,* an antidote against the bite of serpents; from Gr. *thērion,* a wild beast or poisonous animal. Milton has the phrase "the sovran treacle of sound doctrine." (For the position of the **r,** compare *trundle* and *turn; brid* and *bird;* etc.)

Truffle, an underground edible fungus; from Italian **tartufola**; tar being = Lat. *terræ*, of the ground, and *tuföla* = *tuber*, a root. *Trifle* is a doublet of *truffle*.

Twig, a thin branch of a tree. The **tw** here is the base of *two*, and is found also in *twin, twilight, twice, twine;* and probably also in *tweak*, *twist, twinkle,* etc. (*Twit* is not in this class; it comes from *at-witan*, to throw blame on.)

Verdigris (not connected with *grease*), the rust of brass or copper. From Lat. **viride aeris**, the green of brass. (The **g** is intrusive, and has not yet been accounted for.)

Walrus, a kind of large seal; from Swedish **vallross** = a whale-horse. The older form of *ross* is found in Icelandic as *hross*, which is a doublet of the A. S. *hors*. The noise made by the animal somewhat resembles a neigh.

Wassail, a merry carouse; from A. S. **wes haél** = Be well! **Wes** is the imperative of *wesan* to be (still existing in *was*); and **hael** is connected with *hail! hale* (Scand.), *whole* (Eng.), and *health*.

Whole, a misspelling, now never to be corrected, of *hole*, the adjective connected with *hale, heal, health, healthy,* etc. The **w** is probably an intrusion from the S.-W. of England, where they say *whoam* for *home*, *woat* for *oat*, etc. If we write *whole*, we ought also to write *wholy* instead of *holy*.

WORDS THAT HAVE GREATLY CHANGED IN MEANING.

Abandon, to proclaim openly; to denounce; then to cast out. (From Low Lat. *bannus*, an edict.) The earlier meaning still survives in the phrase, "banus of marriage."

Admire, to wonder at.

Allow, to praise (connected with *laud*).

Amuse, to cause to muse, to occupy the mind of. "Camillus set upon the Gauls, when they were amused in receiving their gold," says a writer of the sixteenth century.

Animosity, high spirits; from Lat. *animosus*, brave.

Artillery (great weapons of war), was used to include bows, crossbows, etc., down to the time of Milton. See P. L. ii. 715; and 1 Sam. xx. 40.

Awkward, going the wrong way. From M. E. **awk**, contrary. "The awk end" was the wrong end. "With awkward wind "=with contrary wind.

Babe, doll. Spenser says of a pedlar—
"He bore a truss of trifles at his back,
As bells, and babes, and glasses in his pack."

Blackguard, the band of lowest kitchen servants, who had to look after the spits, pots, and pans, etc.

Bombast (an inflated and pompous style of speaking or writing), cotton-wadding.

Boor (a rough unmannerly fellow), a tiller of the soil; from the Dutch *boawen*, to till. (Compound **neighbour**.) In South Africa, a farmer is still called a *boer*.

Brat (a contemptuous name for a child), a Celtic word meaning rag. In Wales it now means a *pinafore*.

Brave, showy, splendid.

By-and-by, at once.

Carpet, the covering of tables as well as of floors.

Carriage (that which *carries*) meant formerly *that which was carried*, or baggage. See Acts xxi. 15.

Cattle, a doublet of chattels, property. Lat. *capitalia*, heads (of oxen, etc.) Chaucer says, "The avaricious man hath more hope in his catel than in Christ."

Censure (blame) meant merely opinion; from the Lat. *censeo*, I think. Shakespeare, in Hamlet i. 3. 69, makes Polonius say: "Take each man's censure, but reserve thy judgment."

Charity (almsgiving) meant *love*; from Lat. *carus*, dear, through the French.

Cheat (to deceive for the purpose of gain) meant *to seize upon a thing as* **escheated** or forfeited.

Cheer, face. "Be of good cheer "=" Put a good face upon it." "His cheer fell" =" His countenance fell."

Churl (an uncourteous or disobliging person) meant a countryman. Der. churlish. (Shakespeare also uses the word in the sense of a *miser*.)

Clumsy, stiff with cold. "When thou *clomsest* with cold," says Langland (14th century) = art benumbed. (Cognates, *clamp, cramp.*)

Companion, low fellow. Shakespeare has such phrases as " Companions, hence !"

Conceit (too high an opinion of one's self) meant simply **thought.** Chaucer was called "a conceited clerk" = "a learned man full of thoughts." From Lat. *conceptus,* a number of facts brought together into one general *conception* or idea. Shakespeare has the phrase "passing all conceit" = beyond all thought.

Count (to number) meant **to think** (2 with 3, &c.) with; from Lat. *compūto,* I compute or think with. **Count** is a doublet, through French, of **compute.**

Cunning, able or skilled. Like the word *craft,* it has lost its innocent sense.

Danger, jurisdiction, legal power over. The Duke of Venice says to the Merchant, "You stand within his danger, do you not?" M. V. iv. 1. 180.

Defy, to pronounce all bonds of faith dissolved. Lat. *fides,* faith.

Delicious, too scrupulous or finical. A writer of the seventeenth century says that idleness makes even "the soberest (most moderate) men delicious."

Depart, part or divide. The older version of the Prayer-Book has "till death us *depart*" (now corrupted into *do part*).

Disaster, an unfavourable star. A term from the old astrology.

Disease, discomfort, trouble. Shakespeare has, "She will *disease* our bitter mirth ;" and Tyndale's version of Mark v. 35, is, "Thy daughter is dead : why *diseasest* thou the Master any further?"

Duke, leader. Hannibal was called in old English writers, "Duke of Carthage."

Ebb, shallow. "Cross the stream where it is *ebbest,*" is a Lancashire proverb. (The word is a cognate of *even.*)

Essay, an attempt. The old title of such a book was not "Essay on" but "Essay at." From Lat. *exagium,* a weighing.

An older form is *Assay.* Shakespeare has such phrases as "the assay of arms."

Explode, to drive out by clapping of the hands. The opposite of **applaud.** Lat. *plaudo,* I clap my hands.

Explosion, a hissing a thing off the stage.

Firmament, that which makes *firm* or strong. Jeremy Taylor (seventeenth century) says, "Custom is the firmament of the law."

Fond, foolish. The past participle of A. S. fonnan, to act foolishly.

Frightful, full of fear. (Compare the old meaning of *dreadful.*)

Garble, to sift or cleanse. Low Lat. garbellare, to sift corn.

Garland, a king's crown ; now a wreath of flowers.

Gazette (Italian), a magpie. Hence the Ital. *gazettare,* to chatter like a magpie; to write tittle-tattle. (It was also the name of a very small coin, current in Venice, etc.)

Generous, high-born. Lat. *genus,* race. Compare the phrases "a man of family ;" "a man of rank." Shakespeare has "the generous citizens" for those of high birth.

Gossip, sib or related in God ; a godfather or godmother. It now means such *personal talk* as usually goes on among such persons. (Compare the French *commère* and *commérage.*)

Handsome, clever with the hands.

Harbinger, a person who prepared a harbour or lodging.

Heathen, a person who lives on a heath. (Cf. *pagan,* person who lives in a *pagus,* or country district.)

Hobby, an easy ambling nag.

Idiot (Gr. *idiōtes*), a private person ; a person who kept aloof from public business. Cf. *idiom ; idiosyncrasy;* etc.

Imp, an engrafted shoot. Chaucer says: "Of feeble trees there comen wretched impes."
Spenser has "Well worthy impe."

Impertinent, not pertaining to the matter in hand.

Indifferent, impartial. "God is indifferent to all."

Insolent, unusual. An old writer praises Raleigh's poetry as "insolent and passionate."

Kind, born, inborn; natural; and then loving.

Knave, boy. "A knave child "=a male child. Sir John Mandeville speaks of Mahomet as "a ponre knave."

Lace, a snare. Lat. *laqueus,* a noose.

Livery, that which is given or delivered, Fr. *livrer;* from Lat. *liberare,* to free. It was applied both to food and to clothing. "A horse at livery" still means a horse not merely kept, but also *fed.*

Magnificent, doing great things; large-minded. Bacon says, "Bounty and magnificence are virtues very regal."

Maker, a poet.

Manure, to work with the hand; a doublet of manœuvre. (Lat. *manus,* the hand.)

Mere, utter. Lat. *merus,* pure. Shakespeare, in "Othello," speaks of "the mere perdition of the Turkish fleet." "Mere wine" was unmixed wine.

Metal, a mine.

Minute, something very small. Lat. *minutus,* made small; from *minus,* less. Cognates, *minor; minish; diminish;* etc.

Miscreant, an unbeliever. Lat. *mis* (from *minus*), and *credo,* I believe; through O. Fr. mescréant.

Miser, a wretched person. Lat. *miser,* miserable.

Nephew, a grandchild. (Lat. *nepos.*)

Nice, too scrupulous or fastidious. Shakespeare, in "K. John," iii. 4. 138, says—
"He that stands upon a slippery place,
Makes nice of no vile hold to stay him up."

Niece, a grandchild. Lat. *neptis.*

Novelist, an innovator.

Offal, that which is allowed to fall off.

Officious, obliging. In modern diplomacy, an *official* communication is one made in the way of business; an *officious* communication is a friendly and irregular one. Burke, in the eighteenth century, speaks of the French nobility as "very officious and hospitable."

Ostler=hosteller. The keeper of a hostel or hotel. (A comic derivation is that it is a contraction of *oatstealer*).

Painful, painstaking. Fuller, in the seventeenth century, speaks of Joseph as "a painful carpenter."

Palliate, to throw a cloak over. Lat. *pallium,* a cloak.

Pencil, a small hair brush. Lat. *penecillus,* a little tail.

Peevish, obstinate.

Perspective, a glass for seeing either near or distant things.

Pester, to encumber or clog. From Low Lat. *pastorium,* a clog for horses in a pasture.

Plantation, a colony of men planted.

Plausible, having obtained applause. "Every one received him plausibly," says a seventeenth-century writer.

Polite, polished. A seventeenth-century writer has "polite bodies as looking-glasses."

Pomp, a procession.

Preposterous, putting the last first. Lat. *pro,* before; and *post,* after.

Prevaricate, to reverse, to shuffle. Lat. *prævaricari,* to spread the legs apart in walking.

Prevent, to go before. Lat. *pro,* before, and *venio,* I come. The Prayer-Book has, "Prevent us, O Lord, in all our doings."

Prodigious, ominous. "A prodigious meteor," meant a meteor of bad omen.

Punctual, attending to small points of detail. Lat. *punctum;* Fr. *point.*

Quaint, skilful. Prospero, in the "Tempest," calls Ariel "My quaint Ariel!"

Racy, having the strong and native qualities of the race. Cowley says of a poet that he is—
"Fraught with brisk racy verses, in which we
The soil from whence they come, taste, smell, and see."

Reduce, to lead back.

Resent, to be fully sensible of. **Resentment,** grateful recognition of.

Restive, obstinate, inclined to *rest* or stand still. "To turn rusty" (=resty) is to turn obstinate.

Retaliate, to give back benefits as well as injuries.

Room, space, place at table. Luke xiv. 8.

Rummage, to make room.

Sad, earnest.

Sash, a turban.

Secure, free from care. Ben Jonson says: "Men may securely sin; but safely, never."

Sheen, bright, pure. Connected with *shine.*

Shrew, a wicked or hurtful person.

Silly, blessed.

Sincerity, absence of foreign admixture.

Soft, sweetly reasonable.

Spices, kinds—a doublet of **species.** (A grocer in French is called an *épicier.*)

Starve, to die. Chaucer says, "Jesus starved upon the cross."

Sycophant, "a fig-shower" or informer against a person who smuggled figs. Gr. *sukon,* a fig; and *phaino,* I show.

Table, a picture.

Tarpaulin, a sailor; from the tarred canvas suit he wore. Now shortened into *tar.*

Thews, habits, manners.

Thought, deep sorrow, anxiety. Matthew vi. 25. In "Julius Cæsar," ii. 1. 187, we find, "Take thought, and die for Cæsar."

Trivial, very common. Lat. *trivia,* a place where three roads meet.

Tuition, guardianship. Lat. *tuitio,* looking at.

Uncouth, unknown.

Union, oneness; or a pearl in which size, roundness, smoothness, purity, lustre, were united. See "Hamlet," v. 2. 283. A doublet is *onion*—so called from its shape.

Unkind, unnatural.

Urbane, living in a city. Lat. *urbs,* a city.

Usury, money paid for the use of a thing.

Varlet, a serving-man. Low Lat. *vassalettus,* a minor vassal. *Varlet* and *valet* are diminutives of *vassal.*

Vermin was applied to noxious animals of whatever size. "The crocodile is a dangerous vermin." Lat. *vermis,* a worm.

Villain, a farm-servant. Lat. *villa,* a farm.

Vivacity, pertinacity in living; longevity. Fuller speaks of a man as "most remarkable for his vivacity, for he lived 140 years."

Wit, knowledge, mental ability.

Worm, a serpent.

Worship, to consider worth, to honour.

Wretched, wicked. A. S. *wrecca,* an outcast.

PART II.

COMPOSITION, PUNCTUATION, PARAPHRASING,
AND PROSODY.

HINTS ON COMPOSITION.

1. Composition is the art of putting sentences together.

(i) Any one can make a sentence; but every one cannot make a sentence that is both clear and neat. We all speak and write sentences every day; but these sentences may be neat or they may be clumsy— they may be pleasant to read, or they may be dull and heavy.

(ii) Sir Arthur Helps says: "A sentence should be powerful in its substantives, choice and discreet in its adjectives, nicely correct in its verbs; not a word that could be added, nor one which the most fastidious would venture to suppress; in order, lucid; in sequence, logical; in method, perspicuous."

2. The manner in which we put our sentences together is called **style**. That style may be good or bad; feeble or vigorous; clear or obscure. The whole purpose of style, and of studying style, is to enable us to present our thoughts to others in a clear, forcible, and yet graceful way.

"Style is but the order and the movement that we put into our thoughts. If we bind them together closely, compactly, the style becomes firm, nervous, concise. If they are left to follow each other negligently, the style will be diffuse, slipshod, and insipid."—BUFFON.

3. Good composition is the result of three things: (i) clear thinking; (ii) reading the best and most vigorous writers; and (iii) frequent practice in writing, along with careful polishing of what we have written.

(i) We ought to read diligently in the best poets, historians, and essayists,—to read over and over again what strikes us as finely or nobly or powerfully expressed,—to get by heart the most striking passages in a good author. This kind of study will give us a large stock of appropriate words and striking phrases; and we shall never be at a loss for the right words to express our own sense.

Ben Jonson says : " For a man to write well, there are required three necessaries : let him read the best authors ; observe the best speakers ; and have much exercise of his own style."

(ii) " My mother forced me, by steady daily toil, to learn long chapters of the Bible by heart ; as well as to read it every syllable through, aloud, hard names and all, from Genesis to the Apocalypse, about once a-year: and to that discipline,—patient, accurate, and resolute,—I owe, not only a knowledge of the book, but much of my general power of taking pains, and *the best part of my taste in literature*."—JOHN RUSKIN.

(iii) But, though much reading of the best books and a great deal of practice in composition are the only means to attain a good and vigorous style, there are certain directions—both general and special—which may be of use to the young student, when he is beginning.

GENERAL DIRECTIONS.

4. We must know the subject fully about which we are going to write.

(i) If we are going to tell a story, we must know all the circumstances ; the train of events that led up to the result ; the relations of the persons in the story to each other ; what they said ; and the outcome of the whole at the close.   These considerations guide us to

Practical Rule I.—Draw up on a piece of paper a **short skeleton** of what you are going to write about.

(i) Archbishop Whately says : "The more briefly this is done, so that it does but exhibit clearly the heads of the composition, the better ; be-cause it is important that the whole of it be placed before the eye and mind in a small compass, and be taken in, as it were, at a glance ; and it should be written, therefore, not in *sentences*, but like a table of contents. Such an outline should not be allowed to *fetter* the writer, if, in the course of the actual composition, he find any reason for deviating from his original plan,—it should serve merely as a *track* to mark out a path for him, not as a *groove* to confine him."

(ii) Cobbett says : "Sit down to write *what you have thought*, and not *to think what you shall write*."

5. Our sentences must be written in **good English**.

Good English is simply the English of the best writers ; and we can only learn what it is by reading the books of these writers. Good writers of the present century are such authors as Charles Lamb, Jane Austen, Scott, Coleridge, Landor, Macaulay, Thackeray, Dickens, Matthew Arnold, Froude, Ruskin, and George Eliot.

6. Our sentences must be written in **pure English.**

(i) This rule forbids the use of obsolete or old-fashioned words, such as *erst, peradventure, hight, beholden, vouchsafe, methinks,* etc.

(ii) It forbids also the use of slang expressions, such as *awfully, jolly, rot, bosh, smell a rat, see with half an eye,* etc.

(iii) It forbids the employment of technical terms, unless these are absolutely necessary to express our meaning ; and this is sure to be the case in a paper treating on a scientific subject. But technical terms in an ordinary piece of writing, such as *quantitative, connotation, anent, chromatic,* are quite out of place.

(iv) In obedience to this rule, we ought also carefully to avoid the use of foreign words and phrases. Affectation of all kinds is disgusting ; and it both looks and is affected to use such words as *confrère, raison d'être, amour propre, congé,* etc.

(v) This recommendation also includes the **Practical Rule :** " When an English-English (or ' Saxon ') and a Latin-English word offer themselves, we had better choose the Saxon."

(vi) The following is from an article by Leigh Hunt : " In the Bible there are no Latinisms ; and where is the life of our *language* to be found in such *perfection* as in the *translation* of the Bible ? We will *venture* to *affirm* that no one is *master* of the English *language* who is not well read in the Bible, and *sensible* of its *peculiar excellences.* It is the *pure* well of English. The taste which the Bible *forms* is not a taste for big words, but a taste for the *simplest expression* or the *clearest medium* of *presenting* ideas. *Remarkable* it is that most of the *sublimities* in the Bible are *conveyed* in *monosyllables.* For *example,* 'Let there be light : and there was light.' Do these words want any life that Latin could lend them ? . . . The best *styles* are the freest from Latinisms ; and it may be almost laid down as a *rule* that a good writer will never have *recourse* to a Latinism if a Saxon word will *equally serve* his *purpose.* We cannot *dispense* with words of Latin *derivation ;* but there should be the *plea* of *necessity* for *resorting* to them, or we wrong our English."

(vii) At the same time, it must not be forgotten that we very often are compelled by necessity to use Latin words. Even Leigh Hunt, in the above passage, has been obliged to do so while declaiming against it. This is apparent from the number of words printed in italics, all of which are derived from Latin. This is most apparent in the phrase *equally serve his purpose,* which we could not now translate into " pure " English.

7. Our sentences must be written in **accurate English.** That is, the words used must be **appropriate** to the sense we wish to convey. Accuracy is the virtue of using "the right word in the right place."

(i) "The attempt was found to be impracticable." Now, *impracticable* means impossible of accomplishment. Any one may *attempt* anything; carrying it out is a different thing. The word used should have been *design* or *plan*.

(ii) "The veracity of the statement was called in question." *Veracity* is the attribute of a person ; not of a statement.

(iii) Accurate English can only be attained by the careful study of the different shades of meaning in words ; by the constant comparison of synonyms. Hence we may lay down the

Practical Rule II.—Make a collection of **synonyms,** and compare the meanings of each couple (i) in a dictionary, and (ii) in a sentence.

The following are a few, the distinctions between which are very apparent :—

Abstain	Forbear.	Custom	Habit.
Active	Diligent.	Delay	Defer.
Aware	Conscious.	Difficulty	Obstacle.
Character	Reputation.	Strong	Powerful.
Circumstance	Event.	Think	Believe.

8. Our sentences should be perfectly **clear.** That is, the reader, if he is a person of ordinary common-sense, should not be left for a moment in doubt as to our meaning.

(i) A Roman writer on style says : "Care should be taken, not that the reader may understand if he will, but that he shall understand whether he will or not."

(ii) Our sentences should be as clear as "mountain water flowing over a rock." They should "economise the reader's attention."

(iii) Clearness is gained by being **simple,** and by being **brief.**

(iv) **Simplicity** teaches us to avoid (*a*) too learned words, and (*b*) roundabout ways of mentioning persons and things.

(*a*) We ought, for example, to prefer—

Abuse	*to* Vituperation.	Neighbourhood	*to*	Vicinity.
Begin	„ Commence.	Trustworthy	„	Reliable.
Commence	„ Initiate.	Welcome	„	Reception.

(*b*) We ought to avoid such stale and hackneyed phrases as the "Swan of Avon" for Shakespeare; the "Bard of Florence" for Dante; "the Great Lexicographer" for Dr Johnson.

(v) **Brevity** enjoins upon us the need of expressing our meaning in as few words as possible.

Opposed to brevity is **verbosity,** or wordiness.   Pope says—

> " Words are like leaves; and, where they most abound,
> Much fruit of sense beneath is rarely found."

(vi) Dr Johnson says : " Tediousness is the most fatal of all faults."

9. Our sentences should be written in **flowing English.** That is, the rhythm of each sentence ought to be pleasant to the ear, if read aloud.   This axiom gives rise to two rules :—

Practical Rule III.—Write as you would speak !

(i) This, of course, points to an antecedent condition—that you must be a good reader.   Good reading aloud is one of the chief conditions of good writing.   "Living speech," says a philosophic writer, "is the corrective of all style."

Practical Rule IV.—After we have written our piece of composition, we should **read it aloud** either to ourselves or to some one else.

Thus, and thus only, shall we be able to know whether each sentence has an agreeable rhythm.

Practical Rule V.—" Never write about any matter you do not well understand.   If you clearly understand all about your matter, you will never want thoughts; and thoughts instantly become words."—COBBETT.

> " Seek not for words; seek only fact and thought,
> And crowding in will come the words, unsought."—HORACE.
> " Know well your subject; and the words will go
> To the pen's point, with steady, ceaseless flow."—PENTLAND.

10. Our sentences should be **compact.**

(i) That is, they ought not to be loose collections of words, but firm, well-knit, nervous organisms.

(ii) A sentence in which the complete sense is suspended till the close is called a **period.**   Contrasted with it is the loose sentence.

(*a*) **Loose Sentence.**—The Puritans looked down with contempt on the rich and the eloquent, on nobles and priests.

(*b*) **Period.**—On the rich and the eloquent, on nobles and priests, the Puritans looked down with contempt.

(iii) The following is a fine example of a loose sentence: " Notwithstanding his having gone, in winter, to Moscow, where he found the cold excessive, and which confined him, without intermission, six weeks to his room, we could not induce him to come home." This no more makes a sentence than a few cartloads of bricks thrown loosely upon the ground constitute a house.

EMPHASIS.

One object in style is to call the attention of the reader in a forcible and yet agreeable way to the most important parts of our subject—in other words, to give **emphasis** to what is emphatic, and to make what is striking and important strike the eye and mind of the reader. This purpose may be attained in many different ways; but there are several easy devices that will be found of use to us in our endeavour to give weight and emphasis to what we write. These are :—

1. The ordinary grammatical order of the words in a sentence may be varied ; and emphatic words may be thrown to the **beginning** or to the **end** of the sentence. This is the device of **Inversion.**

Thus we have, "Blessed is he that cometh in the name of the Lord." "Jesus I know, and Paul I know: but who are ye?" "Some he imprisoned ; others he put to death." "Go he must !" "Do it he shall !" "They could take their rest, for they knew Lord Strafford watched. Him they feared, him they trusted, him they obeyed." "He that tells a lie is not sensible how great a task he undertakes ; for, to maintain one, he must invent twenty more." In the last sentence, the phrase *to maintain one* gains emphasis by being thrown out of its usual and natural position. But

Caution 1.—Do not go out of your way to invert. It has a look of affectation. Do not say, for example, "True it is," or "Of Milton it was always said," etc. And do not begin an essay thus : "Of all the vices that disfigure and degrade," etc.

2. The **Omission of Conjunctions** gives force and emphasis.

Thus Hume writes: "He rushed amidst them with his sword drawn, threw them into confusion, pushed his advantage, and gained a complete victory." We may write: "You say this; I deny it."

3. The use of the **Imperative Mood** gives liveliness and emphasis.

Thus we find the sentence: "Strip virtue of the awful authority she derives from the general reverence of mankind, and you rob her of half her majesty." Here *strip* is equal to *If you strip;* but is much more forcible.

4. Emphasis is also gained by employing the **Interrogative Form.**

(i) Thus, to say "Who does not hope to live long?" is much more forcible and lively than "All of us hope to live long."

(ii) This is a well-known form in all impassioned speech. Thus, in the Bible we find: "Your fathers, where are they? And the prophets, do they live for ever?"

5. The device of **Exclamation** may also be employed to give emphasis; but it cannot be frequently used, without danger of falling into affectation.

Thus Shakespeare, instead of making Hamlet say, "Man is a wonderful piece of work," etc.—which would be dull and flat—writes, "What a piece of work is man!" etc.

6. **Emphasis** may be gained by the use of the device of **Periphrasis.**

(i) Thus, instead of saying "John built this house," or "This house was built by John," we can say: "It was John who built this house;" "It was no other than John who," etc.

7. **Repetition** is sometimes a powerful device for producing emphasis; but, if too frequently employed, it becomes a tiresome mannerism.

(i) Macaulay is very fond of this device. He says: "Tacitus tells a fine story finely, but he cannot tell a plain story plainly. He stimulates till stimulants lose their power." Again: "He aspired to the highest —above the people, above the authorities, above the laws, above his country."

(ii) Its effect in poetry is sometimes very fine :—

> " By foreign hands thy dying eyes were closed;
> By foreign hands thy decent limbs composed;
> By foreign hands thy humble grave adorned;
> By strangers honoured, and by strangers mourned."

8. The device of **Suspense** adds to the weight and emphasis of a statement; it keeps the attention of the reader on the stretch, because he feels the sense to be incomplete.

(i) The suspense in the following sentence gives a heightened idea of the difficulty of travelling: "At last, with no small difficulty, and after much fatigue, we came, through deep roads, storms of wind and rain, and bad weather of all kinds, to our journey's end."

(ii) This device is frequent in poetry. Thus Keats opens his "Hyperion" in this way :—

> " Deep in the shady sadness of a vale,
> Far sunken from the healthy breath of morn,
> Far from the fiery noon and eve's one star—
> Sat grey-haired Saturn, quiet as a stone."

Here the verb is kept to the last line.

9. Antithesis always commands attention, and is therefore a powerful mode of emphasising a statement. But antithesis is not always at one's command; and it must not be strained after.

Macaulay employs this device with great effect. He has: "The Puritans hated bear-baiting, not because it gave pain to the bear, but because it gave pleasure to the spectators." Swift was very fond of it. Thus he says: "The two maxims of a great man at court are, always to keep his countenance, and never to keep his word." Dr Johnson has this sentence: "He was a learned man among lords, and a lord among learned men." "He twice forsook his party; his principles never."

10. A very sharp, sudden, and unexpected antithesis is called an **Epigram**.

(i) Thus Lord Bacon, speaking of a certain procession in Rome, says that "The statues of Brutus and Cassius were conspicuous by their absence." Macaulay says of the dirt and splendour of the Russian Ambassadors: "They came to the English Court dropping pearls and vermin."

(ii) The following are additional instances of truths put in a very striking and epigrammatic way: "Verbosity is cured by a large vocabulary" (because when you have a large stock of words, you will be able to choose the fittest). "We ought to know something of everything, and everything of something." "He was born of poor but dishonest parents." "When you have nothing to say, say it." "He had nothing to do, and he did it." "The better is the enemy of the good." "One secret in education," says Herbert Spencer, "is to know how wisely to lose time." "Make haste slowly." "They did nothing in particular ; and did it very well."

(iii) But no one should strain after such a style of writing. Such an attempt would only produce smartness, which is a fatal vice.

DISTINCTNESS OF STYLE.

1. One great secret of a good and striking style is the art of **Specification.**

Professor Bain gives us an excellent example of a vague and general, as opposed to a distinct and specific style :—

(*a*) **Vague.**—"In proportion as the manners, customs, and amusements of a nation are cruel and barbarous, the regulation of their penal codes will be severe."

(*b*) **Specific.**—"According as men delight in battles, bull-fights, and combats of gladiators, so will they punish by hanging, burning, and crucifying."

2. Specification or distinctness of style may be attained in two ways: (i) by the use of **concrete terms**; and (ii) by the use of **detail.**

3. A **concrete** or **particular term** strikes both the feelings and imagination with greater force than an abstract or general term can do.

(i) Let us make a few contrasts :—

ABSTRACT.	CONCRETE.
Quadruped.	Horse.
Building materials.	Bricks and mortar.
Old age.	Grey hairs.
Warlike weapons.	Sword and gun.
Rich and poor.	The palace and the cottage.
A miserable state.	Age, ache, and penury.
"I have neither the necessaries of life, nor the means of procuring them."	"I have not a crust of bread, nor a penny to buy one."

(ii) Campbell says : "The more general the terms are, the picture is the fainter ; the more special, the brighter." "They sank *like lead* in the mighty waters" is more forcible than "they sank like metal."

4. Details enable the reader to form in his mind a vivid picture of the event narrated or the person described ; and, before beginning to write, we ought always to draw up a list of such details as are both striking and appropriate — such details as tend to throw into stronger relief the chief person or event.

The following is a good example from the eloquent writer and profound thinker Edmund Burke. He is speaking of the philanthropist Howard :—

"He has visited all Europe to dive into the depths of dungeons; to plunge into the infections of hospitals ; to survey the mansions of sorrow and pain ; to take the gauge and dimensions of misery, depression, and contempt ; to remember the forgotten, to attend to the neglected, to visit the forsaken, and to compare and collate the distresses of all men in all countries."

GENERAL CAUTIONS.

1. Avoid the use of threadbare and hackneyed expressions. Leave them to people who are in a hurry, or to penny-a-liners.

INSTEAD OF	WRITE
At the expiration of four years.	At the end, etc.
Paternal sentiments.	The feelings of a father.
Exceedingly opulent.	Very rich.
Incur the danger.	Run the risk.
Accepted signification.	Usual meaning.
Extreme felicity.	Great happiness.
A sanguinary engagement.	A bloody battle.
In the affirmative.	Yes.

2. Be very careful in the management of pronouns.

(i) Cobbett says : "Never put an *it* upon paper without thinking well what you are about. When I see many *it's* in a page, I always tremble for the writer." See also 2 Kings, xix. 35 : "And when *they* arose early in the morning, behold *they* were all dead corpses."

(ii) Bolingbroke has the sentence : "They were persons of very moderate intellects, even before they were impaired by their passions." The last *they* ought to be *these*.

(iii) The sentence, "He said to his patient that if he did not feel better in half an hour, he thought he had better return," is a clumsy sentence, but clear enough ; because we can easily see that it is the *patient* that is to take the advice.

3. Be careful not to use mixed metaphors.

(i) The following is a fearful example : "This is the arrow of conviction, which, like a nail driven in a sure place, strikes its roots downwards into the earth, and bears fruit upwards."

(ii) Sir Boyle Roche, an Irish member, began a speech thus : "Mr Speaker, I smell a rat, I see him floating in the air ; but, mark me, I shall yet nip him in the bud." A similar statement is : "Lord Kimberley said that in taking a very large bite of the Turkish cherry the way had been paved for its partition at no distant day."

4. Be simple, quiet, manly, frank, and straightforward in your style, as in your conduct. That is : Be yourself !

SPECIAL CAUTIONS.

1. Avoid tautology.

Alison says : "It was founded mainly on the *entire* monopoly of the *whole* trade with the colonies." Here *entire* and *whole* are tautological ; for *monopoly* means *entire possession*, or *possession of the whole*. "He appears to enjoy the universal esteem of all men." Here *universal* is superfluous.

2. Place the adverb as near the word it modifies as you can.

"He not only found her employed, but also pleased and tranquil." The *not only* belongs to *employed*, and should therefore go with it.

3. Avoid circumlocution.

"Her Majesty, on reaching Perth, partook of breakfast." This should be simply *breakfasted*. But the whole sentence should be recast into : "On reaching Perth, the Queen breakfasted in the station."

4. Take care that your participles are attached to nouns, and that they do not run loose.

"Alarmed at the news, the boat was launched at once." Here *alarmed* can, grammatically, agree with *boat* only. The sentence should be : "The men, alarmed at the news, launched their boat at once."

5. Use a present participle as seldom as possible.

(i) "I have documents proving this" is not so strong as "to prove this."

(ii) "He dwelt a long time on the advantages of swift steamers, thus accounting for the increase," etc. The phrase "thus accounting" is very loose. Every sentence ought to be neat, firm, and compact.

6. Remember that **who = and he** or **for he;** while **that** introduces a merely adjectival clause.

"I heard it from the doctor, who told the gardener that-works-for-the-college." Here *who=and he;* and *that* introduces the adjectival sentence.

7. Do not change the Subject of your Sentence.

(i) Another way of putting this is : "Preserve the unity of the sentence !"

(ii) "Archbishop Tillotson died in this year. He was exceedingly beloved both by King William and Queen Mary, who nominated Dr Tenison to succeed him." The last statement about *nominating* another bishop has no natural connection with what goes before.

(iii) "After we came to anchor, they put me on shore, where I was welcomed by all my friends, who received me with the greatest kindness." This sentence ought to be broken into two. The first should end with *on shore;* and the second begin "Here I was met and, etc."

8. See that **who** or **which** refers to its proper **antecedent.**

"Shakespeare married Anne Hathaway, the daughter of a yeoman, to whom he left his second-best bed." Here the grammatical antecedent is *yeoman;* but the historical and sense-antecedent is certainly *daughter.*

9. Do not use **and which for which.**

(i) "I bought him a very nice book as a present, and which cost me ten shillings." The *and* is here worse than useless.

(ii) If another *which* has preceded, of course *and which* is right.

10. Avoid exaggerated or too strong language.

Unprecedented, most extraordinary, incalculable, boundless, extremely, awfully, scandalous, stupendous, should not be used unless we know that they are both true and appropriate.

11. Be careful not to mix up **dependent** with principal sentences.

"He replied that he wished to help them, and intended to give orders to his servants." Here it is doubtful whether *intended* is co-ordinate with *replied* or with *wished.* If the former is the case, then we ought to say *he intended.*

12. Be very careful about the right position of each phrase or clause in your sentence.

The following are curious examples of dislocations or misplacements : "A piano for sale by a lady about to cross the Channel in an oak case with carved legs." "I believe that, when he died, Cardinal Mezzofanti spoke at least fifty languages." "He blew out his brains after bidding his wife good-bye with a gun." "Erected to the memory of John Phillips, accidentally shot, as a mark of affection by his brother." "The Board has resolved to erect a building large enough to accommodate 500 students three storeys high." "Mr Carlyle has taught us that silence is golden in thirty-seven volumes."

PUNCTUATION.

1. Certain signs, called **points**, are used in sentences to mark off their different parts, and to show the relation of each part to the organic whole.

(i) Putting in the right points is called **punctuation**, from the Latin *punctum*, a point. From the same word come *punctual* and *punctuality*.

2. These points are the **full stop**, the **colon**, the **semicolon**, the **dash**, and the **comma**.

3. The **full stop** (.) or **period** marks the close of a sentence.

4. The **colon** (:) introduces (i) a new statement that may be regarded as an **after-thought**; or (ii) it introduces a **catalogue** of things; or (iii) it introduces a formal speech.

(The word *colon* is Greek, and means *limb* or *member*.)

(i) "Study to acquire a habit of accurate expression : no study is more important."

(ii) "Then follow excellent parables about fame : as that she gathereth strength in going ; that she goeth upon the ground, and yet hideth her head in the clouds ; that in the day-time she sitteth in a watch-tower, and flieth most by night."—BACON.

(iii) "Mr Wilson rose and said : 'Sir, I am sorry,' etc."

5. The **semicolon** is employed when, for reasons of sound or of sense, two or more simple sentences are thrown into one.

(*Semicolon* is Greek, and means *half a colon*.)

(i) "In the youth of a state, arms do flourish ; in the middle age of a state, learning ; and then both of them together for a time ; in the declining age of a state, mechanical arts and merchandise."—BACON.

> (ii) Learn from the birds what foods the thickets yield ;
> Learn from the beasts the physic of the field ;
> Thy arts of building from the bee receive ;
> Learn of the mole to plough, the worm to weave."—POPE.

6. The **dash** is used (i) to introduce an amplification or explanation ; and (ii) two dashes are often employed in place of the old parenthesis.

(i) "During the march a storm of rain, thunder, and lightning came on—a storm such as is only seen in tropical countries."

(ii) "Ribbons, buckles, buttons, pieces of gold-lace—any trifles he had worn—were stored as priceless treasures."

7. The **comma** is used to indicate a **strong pause**, either of sense or of sound.

(i) It is true that the comma is the weakest of all our stops ; but there are many pauses which we ought to make in reading a sentence aloud that are not nearly strong enough to warrant a comma.

(ii) It is better to understop rather than to overstop. For example, the last part of the last sentence in the paragraph above might have been printed thus : "there are many pauses, which we ought to make, in reading a sentence aloud, that are not nearly strong enough to warrant a comma." This is the old-fashioned style ; but such sprinkling of commas is not at all necessary.

(iii) Two things are all that are required to teach us the use of a comma : (*a*) observation of the custom of good writers ; and (*b*) careful consideration of the sense and build of our own sentences.

(iv) The following are a few special uses of the comma :—

> (*a*) It may be used in place of *and* :—
>> "We first endure, then pity, then embrace."
>
> (*b*) After an address : "John, come here."
>
> (*c*) After certain introductory adverbs, as *however, at length, at last*, etc. . "He came, however, in time to catch the train."

8. The **point of interrogation** (?) is placed at the end of a question.

9. The **point of admiration** (!) is employed to mark a statement which calls for surprise or wonder ; but it is now seldom used.

FIGURES OF SPEECH.

1. The mind naturally tends, especially when in a state of excitement, to the use of what is called **figurative language**. It is as if we called upon all the things we see or have seen to come forward and help us to express our overmastering emotions. In fact, the external shows of nature are required to express the internal movements of the mind ; the external world provides a language for the internal or mental world.   Hence we find all language full of **figures of speech**.   Though we do not notice them at the time, we can hardly open our mouths without using them.   As Butler says in his famous poem :—

> "For Hudibras,—he could not ope
> His mouth, but out there flew a trope." [1]

We speak of a town being *stormed ;* of a *clear* head ; a *hard* heart ; *wingëd* words ; *glowing* eloquence ; *virgin* snow ; a *torrent* of words ; the *thirsty* ground ; the *angry* sea.   We speak of God's Word being a *light* to our feet and a *lamp* to our path.

2. This kind of language has been examined, classified, and arranged under heads ; and the chief figures of speech are called **Simile, Metaphor, Personification, Allegory, Synecdoché, Metonymy,** and **Hyperbolé.**

3. A **Simile** is a comparison that is limited to one point. "Jones fought like a lion."   Here the single point of likeness between Jones and the lion is the bravery of the fighting of each.

(*Simile* comes from the Latin *similis*, like.)

(i) "His spear was like the mast of a ship."   "His salté terés striken down like rain," says Chaucer.   "Apollo came like the night," says Homer.   "His words fell soft, like snow upon the ground," are the words used by Homer in speaking of Ulysses.   "It stirs the heart like the sound of a trumpet" said Sir Philip Sidney in speaking of the ballad of "Chevy Chase."   Tennyson admirably compares a miller covered with flour to "a working-bee in blossom-dust."

---

[1] *A trope*—from Greek *trópos*, a turning.   A word that has been *turned* from its ordinary and primary use.   From the same root come *tropics* and *tropical*.

4. A Metaphor is a simile with the words *like* or *as* left out. Instead of saying "Roderick Dhu fought like a lion," we use a metaphor, and say "He *was* a lion in the fight."

(*Metaphor* is a Greek word meaning *transference*.)

(i) All language, as we have seen, is full of metaphors. Hence language has been called "fossil poetry." Thus, even in very ordinary prose, we may say, "the wish is *father* to the thought;" "the news was a *dagger* to his heart;" or we speak of the *fire* of passion; of a *ray* of hope; a *flash* of wit; a thought *striking* us; and so on.

(ii) By frequent use, and by forgetfulness, many metaphors have lost their figurative character. Thus we use the words *provide* (to see beforehand), *edify* (to build up), *express* (to squeeze out), *detect* (to unroof), *ruminate* (to chew the cud), without the smallest feeling of their metaphorical character.

(iii) We must never *mix* our metaphors. It will not do to say : "In a moment the *thunderbolt* was on them, *deluging* the country with invaders." "I will now *embark* upon the *feature* on which this *question* mainly *hinges*."

(iv) Metaphors and similes may be mixed. Thus Longfellow :—

Metaphor,.. { The day is done ; and the darkness
              Falls from the wings of night,

Simile,...... { As a feather is wafted downward
               From an eagle in his flight.

(v) A metaphor is a figure in which the objects compared are treated by the mind as *identical* for the time being. A simile simply treats them as *resembling* one another ; and the mind keeps the two carefully apart.

5. Personification is that figure by which, under the influence of strong feeling, we attribute life and mind to impersonal and inanimate things.

(i) Thus we speak, in poetic and impassioned language, of *pale* Fear ; *gaunt* Famine ; *green-eyed* Jealousy ; and *white-handed* Hope. The morning is said to *laugh;* the winds to *whisper;* the oaks to *sigh;* and the brooks to *prattle*.

(ii) Milton, in the 'Paradise Lost,' ix. 780, thus describes the fall of Eve :—

"So saying, her rash hand in evil hour
Forth reaching to the fruit, she plucked, she ate !
Earth *felt* the *wound;* and Nature, from *her* seat,
Sighing through all her works, gave signs of *woe*
That all was lost."

Shelley's '**Cloud**' is one long personification.

(iii) When the personified object is **directly** addressed, the figure is called **Apostrophé**. Thus we have, "O Death, where is thy sting? O Grave, where is thy victory?"

6. An **Allegory** is a continuous personification in the form of a story.

(i) The **genus** is personification; the **differentia**, a story; and the **species** is an allegory.

(ii) Milton's "Death and Sin," in the tenth book of the 'Paradise Lost,' is a short allegory. Spenser's 'Faerie Queene' and Bunyan's 'Pilgrim's Progress' are long allegories.

(iii) A short allegory is called a **Fable**.

7. Synecdoché is that figure of speech by which a **part** is put for the **whole**. Thus we say, in a more striking fashion, *bread* instead of *food ;* a *cut-throat* for a *murderer;* fifty *sail* for fifty *ships;* all *hands* at work.

(i) Lear, in the height of his **mad rage** against his daughters, shouts, "I abjure all *roofs !*"

(ii) The name of the **material**—as a part of the whole production—is sometimes used for the thing made : as *cold steel* for the *sword;* the *marble* speaks ; the *canvas* glows.

8. Metonymy is that figure of speech by which a thing is named, not with its own name, but by some **accompaniment.** Thus we say, the *crown* for the *king;* the *sword* for *physical force.*

(The word *metonymy* is a Greek word meaning *change of names.*)

We write *the ermine* for *the bench of judges; the mitre* for *the bishops ; red tape* for *official routine; a long purse* for a *great deal of money ; the bottle* for *habits of drunkenness.*

9. Hyperbolé or **Exaggeration** is a figure by which much more is said than is literally true. This is of course the result of very strong emotion.

(i) Milton says :—

"So frowned the mighty combatants, that hell
Grew darker at their frown."

(ii) Scott, in 'Kenilworth,' has this passage : "The mind of England's Elizabeth was like one of those ancient Druidical monuments called rocking-stones. The finger of Cupid, boy as he is painted, could put her feelings in motion; but the *power of Hercules* could not have destroyed their equilibrium."

10. The following is a summary of the chief of the above statements :—

1. A Figure of Speech employs a vivid or striking image of something **without** to express a feeling or idea **within.**
2. A Simile uses an external image with the word **like.**
3. A Metaphor uses the same image **without** the word **like.**
4. A Personification is a metaphor taken from a **person** or living being.
5. An allegory is a **continuous personification.**

PARAPHRASING.

1. Paraphrasing is a kind of exercise that is not without its uses. These uses are chiefly two : (i) to bind the learner's attention closely to every word and phrase, meaning and shade of meaning; and (ii) to enable the teacher to see whether the learner has accurately and fully understood the passage. But no one can hope to improve on the style of a poem by turning the words and phrases of the poet into other language; the change made is always—or almost always—a change for the worse.

2. Passages from good prose writers are sometimes given out to paraphrase, but most often passages from poetical writers. The reason of this is that poetry is in general much more highly compressed than prose, and hence the meaning is sometimes obscure, for want of a little more expansion. The following lines by Sir Henry Wotton, the Provost of Eton College, are a good example of much thought compressed within a little space :—

THE HAPPY LIFE.

1. How happy is he born and taught
   That serveth not another's will—
   Whose armour is his honest thought,
   And simple truth his utmost skill !

2. Whose passions not his masters are,
   Whose soul is still prepared for death—
   Not tied unto the worldly care
   Of public fame or private breath !

3. Who envies none that chance doth raise,
   Or vice; who never understood
   How deepest wounds are given by praise;
   Nor rules of state, but rules of good;

4. Who hath his life from humours freed,
   Whose conscience is his strong retreat;
   Whose state can neither flatterers feed,
   Nor ruin make accusers great ;

5. Who God doth late and early pray
   More of His grace than gifts to lend ;
   And entertains the harmless day
   With a well-chosen book or friend :—

6. This man is freed from servile bands
   Of hope to rise, or fear to fall—
   Lord of himself, though not of lands ;
   And, having nothing, yet hath all.

3. Let us try now to paraphrase these lines—that is, to develop the thought by the aid of more words. But, though we are obliged to use more words, we must do our utmost to find and to employ the most fitting. We must not merely throw down a mass of words and phrases, and leave the reader to make his own selection and to grope among them for the meaning.

1. How happy, by birth as well as by education, is the man who is not obliged to be a slave to the will of another—whose only armour is his honesty and simple goodness, whose best and utmost skill lies in plain straightforwardness.

2. How happy is the man who is not the slave of his own passions, whose soul is always prepared for death, who is not tied to the world or the world's opinion by anxiety about his public reputation or the tattle of individuals.

M

3. Happy, too, because he envies no man who has been raised to rank by accident or by vicious means ; because he never understood the sneer that stabs while it seems to praise ; because he cares nothing for rules of expediency or of policy, but thinks only of what is good and right.

4. Who has freed himself from obedience to humours and to whims, whose conscience is his sure stronghold ; whose rank is not exalted enough to draw flatterers, or to tempt accusers to build their own greatness upon his fall.

5. Who, night and morning, asks God for grace, and not for gifts ; and fills his day with the study of a good book or conversation with a thoughtful friend.

6. This man is freed from the slavery of hope and fear—the hope of rising, the fear of falling—lord, not of lands, but of himself; and though without wealth or possessions, yet having all that the heart of man need desire.

THE GRAMMAR OF VERSE, OR PROSODY.

1. **Verse** is the form of poetry ; and **Prosody** is the part of Grammar which deals with the laws and nature of verse.

(i) **Verse** comes from the Latin **versa**, turned. *Oratio versa* was " turned speech "—that is, when the line came to an end, the reader or writer or printer had to begin a new line. It is opposed to **oratio prorsa**, which means "straight-on speech"—whence our word **prose**. A line in prose *may* be of any length ; a line in verse *must* be of the length which the poet gives to it.

(ii) It is of importance for us to become acquainted with the laws of verse. First, because it enables us to enjoy poetry more. Secondly, it enables us to read poetry better—and to avoid putting an emphasis on a syllable, merely because it is accented. Thirdly, it shows us how to write verse ; and the writing of verse is very good practice in composition —as it compels us to choose the right phrase, and makes us draw upon our store of words to substitute and to improve here or there.

2. Verse differs from prose in two things : (i) in the **regular recurrence of accents**; and (ii) in the **proportion of un- accented to accented syllables.**

(i) Thus, in the line

In an'swer nought' could An'gus speak',

the accent occurs **regularly** in every second syllable.

(ii) But, in the line

> Mer'rily, mer'rily, shall' we live now',

the accent not only comes first, but there are two unaccented syllables for every one that is accented (except in the last foot).

3. Every English word of more than one syllable has an accent on one of its syllables.

(i) *Begin', commend', attack'* have the accent on the last syllable.

(ii) *Hap'py, la'dy, wel'come* have the accent on the first syllable.

4. English verse is made up of lines; each line of verse contains a **fixed number of accents**; each accent has a **fixed number of unaccented syllables** attached to it.

(i) Let us take these lines from 'Marmion' (canto v.) :—

> Who loves' | not more' | the night' | of June'
> Than dull' | Decem' | ber's gloom' | of noon'?

Each line here contains **four** accents ; the accented syllable comes **last** ; each accented syllable has **one** unaccented attached to it.

(ii) Now let us compare these lines from T. Hood's "Bridge of Sighs" :

> Touch' her not | scorn'fully,
> Think' of her | mourn'fully.

Each line here contains **two** accents ; the accented syllable comes **first** ; and each accented syllable has **two** unaccented syllables attached to it.

5. One **accented** syllable + one or two **unaccented**, taken together, is called a **foot**.   A foot is the **unit** of metre.
Let x stand for an unaccented, and a for an accented syllable.

6. One accented **preceded** by one unaccented syllable is called an **Iambus**.   Its formula is **x a.**—One accented syllable **followed** by one unaccented is called a **Trochee**.   Its formula is **a x.**

(i) The following are iambuses : *Perhaps' ; condemn' ; compel' ; without' ; career'.*

(ii) The following are trochees : *Gen'tle ; riv'er; la'dy ; ra'ven ; tum'ble.*

(iii) The following verse is made up of four iambuses—that is, it is iambic verse :—

> 'Twere long', | and need' | less, here' | to tell'
> How to my hand these papers fell.

(iv) The following verse is made up of four trochees—that is, it is trochaic :—

> In' his | cham'ber, | weak' and | dy'ing
> Was the Norman baron lying.

(v) Iam' | bics march' | from short' | to long'.

(vi) Tro'chee | trips' from | long' to | short' — | .

7. One accented syllable **preceded by two** unaccented is called an **Anapæst**. Its formula is **xxa.**—One accented syllable **followed by two** unaccented is called a **Dactyl**. Its formula is **axx**.

(i) The following are anapæsts : *Serenade' ; disappear' ; comprehend' ; intercede'.*

(ii) The following are dactyls : *Hap'pily; mer'rily; sim'ilar; bil'lowy.*

(iii) The following lines are in anapæstic verse :—

> I am mon' | arch of all' | I survey',
> My right there is none to dispute.

(iv) With a leap' | and a bound' | the swift an' | apæsts throng' | .

(v) The following are in dactylic verse :—

> Can'non to | right' of them |
> Can'non to | left' of them |.

(*a*) The word *dactyl* comes from the Greek *daktŭlos*, a finger. For a finger has **one** long and **two** short joints.

(*b*) The word *anapæst* comes from two Greek words : *paio*, I strike, and *ana*, back ; because it is the *reverse* of a dactyl.

8. The Anapæst belongs to the same kind or **system of** verse as the Iambus ; because the accented syllable in each comes **last**. —The Dactyl belongs to the same kind or **system** of verse as the Trochee ; because the accented syllable in each comes **first**.

(i) Hence anapæsts and iambuses may be mixed (as in "My right' | there is none' | to dispute' | "); and so may dactyls and trochees (as in " Hark' to the | sum'mons | ").

(ii) But we very seldom see a trochee introduced into an iambic line ; or an iambus into a trochaic.

9. An accented syllable with **one** unaccented syllable **on each** side of it is called an **Amphibrach**. Its formula is **xax**.

The word *amphibrach* comes from two Greek words : *amphi*, on both sides ; and *brachus*, short. (Compare *amphibious*.)

(i) The following are amphibrachs : *Despair'ing; almight'y; tremend'-ous; deceit'ful.*

(ii) The following is an amphibrachic line :—

> There came' to | the beach' a | poor ex'ile | of E'rin |.

10. A verse made up of iambuses is called **Iambic Verse** ; of trochees, **Trochaic** ; of anapæsts, **Anapæstic** ; and of dactyls, **Dactylic.**

11. A verse of three feet is called **Trimeter** ; of four feet, **Tetrameter** ; of five feet, **Pentameter** ; and of six feet, **Hexameter.**

(i) We find the prefixes of these words in *Triangle ; Tetrarch* (a ruler over a *fourth* part); *Pentateuch* (the *five* books of Moses); and *Hexagon* (a figure with *six* corners or angles).

12. By much the most usual kind of verse in English is **Iambic Verse.**

(i) **Iambic Tetrameter (4 x a)** is the metre of most of Scott's poems ; of Coventry Patmore's "Angel in the House"; of Gay's Fables, and many other poems of the eighteenth century.

(ii) **Iambic Pentameter (5 x a)** is the most common line in English verse. There are probably more than a thousand iambic pentameter lines for one that there exists of any other kind. Iambic Pentameter is the verse of Chaucer, of Shakespeare, of Milton, of Dryden, of Pope, and of almost all our greater English poets.

13. Rhymed Iambic Pentameter is called **Heroic Verse** ; unrhymed, it is called **Blank Verse.**

(i) Any unrhymed verse may be called **blank**—such as the verse employed by Longfellow in his "Hiawatha"—but the term is usually restricted to the unrhymed iambic pentameter.

(ii) Blank verse is the noblest of all verse. It *seems* the easiest to write ; it *is* the most difficult. It is the verse of Shakespeare and Milton, and of most of our great dramatists.

14. Iambic Trimeter consists of three iambuses ; and its formula is 3 x a.

> The king' | was on' | his throne'; |
> His sa' | traps thronged' | the hall'; |
> A thou' | sand bright' | lamps shone' |
> On that' | high fes' | tival'. |

There is very little of this kind of verse in English.

15. Iambic Tetrameter consists of four iambuses; and its formula is 4 x a.

> The fire,' | with well' | dried logs' | supplied,' |
> Went roar' | ing up' | the chim' | ney wide'; |
> The huge' | hall-ta' | ble's oak' | en face' |
> Scrubbed till' | it shone,' | the day' | to grace.' |

There is a good deal of this verse in English; and most of it is by Scott.

16. Iambic Tetrameter with Iambic Trimeter in alternate lines—the second and fourth rhyming—is called **Ballad Metre**. When used, as it often is, in hymns, it is called **Service Metre**.

> They set him high upon a cart; = 4 x a
> The hangman rode below; = 3 x a
> They drew his hands behind his back, = 4 x a
> And bared his noble brow. = 3 x a

This is the metre of Macaulay's 'Lays of Ancient Rome,' of Scott's 'Lay of the Last Minstrel,' and many other poems. Scott mixes frequently, but at quite irregular intervals, the iambic trimeter with the iambic tetrameter; and this he called the "light-horse gallop of verse."

> Front, flank, and rear, the squadrons sweep = 4 x a
> To break the Scottish circle deep, = 4 x a
> That fought' | around' | their king.' = 3 x a

17. Iambic Pentameter consists of five iambuses; and its formula is 5 x a.

(i) The following is rhymed iambic pentameter :—

> True wit' | is na' | ture to' | advan' | tage dressed,' | = 5 x a
> What oft' | was thought,' | but ne'er' | so well' | expressed.' | = 5 x a

(ii) The following is unrhymed iambic pentameter :—

> You all' | do know' | this man' | tle; I' | remem' | ber = 5 x a
> The first' | time ev' | er Cæs' | ar put' | it on'. | = 5 x a

The first extract is from Pope's "Essay on Criticism"; the second from Shakespeare's "Julius Cæsar."

18. Iambic Hexameter consists of six iambuses; and its formula is 6 x a.

(i) The following is from Drayton's "Polyolbion" :—

> Upon the Midlands now the industrious muse doth fall, |=6xa.
> That shire which we the heart of England well may call.|=6xa

The objection to this kind of verse is its intolerable monotony. It pretends to be hexameter; but it is indeed-simply two tri-meter verses printed in one long line. The monotony comes from the fact that the pause is always in the middle of the line. There is very little of this kind of verse in English. The line of 6xa is also called an **Alexandrine**, and is used to close the long stanza employed by Spenser.

19. Trochaic Tetrameter consists of four trochees; and its formula is 4ax.

(i) The following is rhymed trochaic tetrameter :—

> When the heathen trumpet's clang – | = 4ax
> Round beleaguered Chester rang, – | = 4ax
> Veilèd nun and friar gray – | = 4ax
> Marched from Bangor's fair abbaye – | = 4ax

It will be noticed that each line has a syllable wanting to make up the four complete feet. But the missing syllable is only an **unaccented** syllable; and the line contains four accents. (The above extract is from "The Monks of Bangor's March," by Scott.)

(ii) The following is unrhymed trochaic tetrameter :—

> Then the | little | Hia | watha | = 4ax
> Learned of | ev'ry | bird the | language, |=4ax
> Learned their | names and | all their | secrets, |=4ax
> How they | built their | nests in | summer, |=4ax
> Where they | hid them | selves in | winter, |=4ax
> Talked with | them when | e'er he | met them, |=4ax
> Called them | "Hia | watha's | Chickens." |=4ax

It will be observed that, in the above lines from Longfellow's "Hiawatha," each trochee is complete; and this is the case throughout the whole of this poem. "Hiawatha" is the only long poem in the language that is written in unrhymed trochees.

20. Trochaic Octometer consists of eight trochees; and its formula is 8ax.

(i) The chief example of it that we have is Tennyson's poem of "Locksley Hall" :—

Com'rades, | leave' me | here' a | lit'tle, | while' as | yet' 'tis | ear'ly | morn'– | = 8 a x
Leave' me | here', and, | when' you | want' me, | sound' up | on' the | bu'gle | horn'– | = 8 a x

(ii) There is a syllable wanting in each line of "Locksley Hall"; but it is only an unaccented syllable. Each line consists of eight accents.

21. Anapæstic Tetrameter consists of four anapæsts; and its formula is $4 \times x \times a$.

(i) There is very little anapæstic verse in English; and what little there exists is written in tetrameter.

(ii) The following lines, from "Macgregors' Gathering," by Scott, is in anapæstic verse :—

The moon's' | on the lake', | and the mist's' | on the brae', | = 4 x x a
And the clan' | has a name' | that is name' | less by day'. | = 4 x x a

(iii) It will be observed that the first line begins with an iambus. This is admissible; because an iambus and an anapæst, both having the accented syllable **last**, belong to the same system.

22. Dactylic Dimeter consists of two dactyls; and its formula is $2 a x x$.

(i) A well-known example is Tennyson's "Charge of the Light Brigade."

Can'non to | right' of them, | 2 a x x
Can'non to | left' of them, | 2 a x x
Can'non be | hind' them, – | 2 a x x
Vol'leyed and | thun'dered. – | 2 a x x

(ii) It will be observed that the last two lines want a syllable to make up the two dactyls. Such a line is said to be $= 2 a x x - (\text{minus})$.

(iii) Or we may say that the last foot is a trochee; for a trochee and a dactyl can go together in one line, both belonging to the same system —both having their accented syllable **first**.

23. Dactylic Tetrameter consists of four dactyls; and its formula is $4 a x x$.

(i) Bishop Heber's hymn is one of the best examples :—

Bright'est and | best' of the | sons' of the | morn'ing.

(ii) The last foot here again is a trochee.

(iii) There is very little of this kind of verse in English poetry.

24. Amphibrachic Tetrameter consists of four amphibrachs; and its formula is $4 x a x$.

(i) Campbell's well-known poem is a good example :—

There came' to | the beach' a | poor ex'ile | of E'rin.

(ii). There are very few examples in English of this kind of verse.

25. The following lines by Coleridge give both examples and descriptions of the most important metres explained in the preceding paragraphs. It must be observed that Coleridge uses the term *long* for *accented;* and *short* for *unaccented* syllables:—

Tro'chee | trips' from | long' to | short'— |
From long to long in solemn sort,
Slow spon | dee[1] stalks ‖ strong' foot, yet | ill' able
E'ver to | come' up with | dac'tyl tri | syl'lable | .
Iam' | bics march' | from sho'rt | to long' | ;
With a leap' | and a bound' | the swift an' | apæsts throng' | ;
One syl'la | ble long' with | one short' at | each side— |
Amphi'brach | ys hastes' with | a state'ly | stride.

26. A verse with a syllable **over** and above the number of feet of which it consists is called **Hypermetrical.**

(i) Thus, Coleridge has, in his "Ancient Mariner"—

Day af | ter day, | day af | ter day, |
We stuck : | nor breath | nor mo | tion, (*hyper*)
As id | le as | a paint | ed ship |
Upon | a paint | ed o | cean. (*hyper*)

Here the syllables *tion* and *cean* are **over** from the iambic trimeter verse, and the line is therefore said to be hypermetrical.

27. A verse with a syllable **wanting** to the number of feet of which it consists is said to be **defective.**

(i) Thus, in Scott's "Monks of Bangor"—

Slaugh'tered | down' by | heath'en | blade'- | 4ax-
Ban'gor's | peace'ful | monks' are | laid'. - | 4ax-

we find a syllable wanting to each line. But that syllable is an unaccented one ; and the verse consists of four trochees *minus* one syllable, or 4ax-.

(ii) **Caution !**—Some persons confuse the defective with the hypermetrical line. Thus, in the verses—

Shall' I | wast'ing | in' de | spair', - |
Die' be | cause a | wom'an's | fair' ?- |

the syllable *spair* is not hypermetrical. An unaccented syllable is wanting to it ; and the lines are 4ax defective or minus.

---

[1] A *spondee* consists of two long or accented syllables. It is a foot not employed in English ; but it exists in the two words *amen* and *farewell.*

RHYME.

28. Rhyme has been defined by Milton as the "jingling sound of like endings." It may also be defined as a **correspondence in sound** at the ends of lines in poetry.

(i) *Rhyme* is properly spelled **rime**. The word originally meant *number;* and the Old English word for *arithmetic* was **rime-craft.** It received its present set of letters from a confusion with the Greek word *rhythm*, which means a *flowing*.

(ii) Professor Skeat says "it is one of the worst-spelt words in the language." "It is," he says, "impossible to find an instance of the spelling *rhyme* before 1550." Shakespeare generally wrote *rime*.

29. No rhyme can be good unless it satisfies **four conditions.** These are :—

1. The rhyming syllable must be **accented.** Thus *ring* rhymes with *sing;* but not with *think'ing.*

2. The vowel **sound** must be the same—to the ear, that is ; though not necessarily to the eye. Thus *lose* and *close* are not good rhymes.

3. The final consonant must be the same. (*Mix* and *tricks* are good rhymes ; because *x* = *ks*.)

4. The preceding consonant must be different.

Beat and *feet; jump* and *pump* are good rhymes.

30. The English language is very poor in rhymes, when compared with Italian or German. Accordingly, **half-rhymes** are admissible, and are frequently employed.

The following rhymes may be used :—

| Sun. | Love. | Allow. | Ever. | Taste. |
| Gone. | Move. | Bestow. | River. | Past. |

THE CÆSURA.

31. The **rhythm** or musical flow of verse-depends on the varied succession of phrases of different lengths. But, most of all, it is upon the **Cæsura,** and the position of the Cæsura, that musical flow depends.

The word *cæsura* is a Latin word, and means a *cutting.*

32. The Cæsura in a line is the **rest** or halt or break or pause for the voice in reading aloud. It is found in short as well as in long lines.

(i) The following is an example from the short lines of ' Marmion' (vi. 332) :—

    1½ More pleased that ‖ in a barbarous age
    2½ He gave rude Scotland ‖ Virgil's page,
    1 Than that ‖ beneath his rule he held
    2 The bishopric ‖ of fair Dunkeld.

It will be seen from this that Sir Walter Scott takes care to vary the position of the cæsura in each line—sometimes having it after 1½ feet, sometimes after 2 ; and so on.

(ii) The following is an example from the long lines of the " Lycidas " of Milton :—

    2 Now, Lycidas, ‖ the shepherds weep no more ;
    1 Henceforth ‖ thou art the genius of the shore
    3 In thy large recompense, ‖ and shalt be good
    2½ To all that wander ‖ in that perilous flood.

Milton, too, is careful to vary the position of his cæsura ; and most of the music and much of the beauty of his blank verse depend upon the fact that the cæsura appears now at the beginning, now at the middle, now at the end of his lines ; and never in the same place in two consecutive verses.

(iii) Of all the great writers of English verse, Pope is the one who places the cæsura worst — worst, because it is almost always in the same place. Let us take an example from his "Rape of the Lock" (canto i.) :—

    2 The busy sylphs   ‖ surround their darling care,
    2 These set the head, ‖ and these divide the hair ;
    2 Some fold the sleeve, ‖ whilst others plait the gown ;
    2 And Betty's praised ‖ for labours not her own.

And so he goes on for thousands upon thousands of verses. The symbol of Pope's cæsura is a straight line ; the symbol of Milton's is " the line of beauty "—a line of perpetually varying and harmonious curves.

THE STANZA.

33. A **Stanza** is a **group** of **rhymed lines.**

The word comes from an old Italian word, *stantia*, an abode.

34. Two rhymed lines are called a **couplet;** and this may be looked upon as the shortest kind of stanza.

(i) The most usual couplet in English consists of two rhymed iambic pentameter lines. This is called the "**heroic couplet.**"

35. A stanza of **three** rhymed lines is called a **triplet.**

(i) A very good example is to be found in Tennyson's poem of "The Two Voices," which consists entirely of triplets :—

> " Whatever crazy sorrow saith,
> No life that breathes with human breath
> Has ever truly longed for death."

36. A stanza of **four** rhymed lines—of which the first (sometimes) rhymes with the third, and the second (always) with the fourth—is called a **quatrain.**

(i) The ordinary ballad metre consists of quatrains—that is, four lines, two of iambic tetrameter, and two of iambic trimeter.

(ii) A quatrain of iambic pentameters is called **Elegiac Verse.** The best known example is Gray's "Elegy in a Country Churchyard."

37. A stanza of **six** lines is called a **sextant.**

(i) There are many kinds. One is used in Hood's "Dream of Eugene Aram," which is written in 4xa and 3xa; the second, fourth, and sixth lines rhyming.

(ii) Another in Whittier's "Barclay of Ury," which has the first and second lines, the third and sixth, the fourth and fifth, rhyming with each other.

(iii) Another in Lowell's "Yussouf," which has the first and third lines, the second and fourth, and the fifth and sixth rhyming.

38. A stanza of **eight** lines is called an **octave,** or **ottava rima.**

(Pronounced *ottahra reema.*)

39. A stanza of **nine** lines is called the **Spenserian stanza,** because Edmund Spenser employed it in his "Faeric Queene."

(i) The first eight lines of this stanza are in 5 x a; the last line, in 6 x a.

(ii) The rhymes run thus : a b a b ; b c b c c.

40. A short poem of **fourteen** iambic pentameter lines—with the rhymes arranged in a peculiar way—is called a **sonnet.**

(i) This is a form which has been imported into England from Italy, where it was cultivated by many poets—the greatest among these being Dante and Petrarch, both of them poets of the thirteenth century. The best English sonnet-writers are Milton, Wordsworth, and Mrs Browning.

(ii) The sonnet consists of two parts—an **octave** (of eight lines), and a **sestette** (of six). The rhymes in the octave are often varied, being sometimes a b b a, a c c a : those in the sestette are sometimes a b c, a b c ; or a b a b c c.

(iii) Shakespeare's "Sonnets" are not formed on the Italian model, and can hardly be called sonnets at all. They are really short poems of three quatrains, ending in each case with a rhymed couplet.

(iv) The following is Wordsworth's sonnet on "THE SONNET" :—

OCTAVE.	"Scorn not the Sonnet; critic, you have frowned	a
	Mindless of its just honours : with this key	b
	Shakspeare unlocked his heart; the melody	b
	Of this small lute gave ease to Petrarch's wound ;	a
	A thousand times this pipe did Tasso sound ;	a
	With it Camöens soothed an exile's grief ;	c
	The sonnet glittered a gay myrtle leaf	c
	Amid the cypress with which Dante crowned	a
SESTETTE.	His visionary brow ; a glow-worm lamp	d
	It cheered mild Spenser, called from fairyland	c
	To struggle through dark ways; and when a damp	d
	Fell round the path of Milton, in his hand	e
	The thing became a trumpet, whence he blew	f
	Soul-animating strains—alas, too few!"	f

PART III.

THE HISTORY OF THE ENGLISH LANGUAGE

1. Tongue, Speech, Language.—We speak of the "English tongue" or of the "French language"; and we say of two nations that they "do not understand each other's speech." The existence of these three words—**speech, tongue, language** —proves to us that a language is something **spoken**,—that it is a number of **sounds**; and that the writing or printing of it upon paper is a quite secondary matter. Language, rightly considered, then, is an **organised set of sounds.** These sounds convey a meaning from the mind of the speaker to the mind of the hearer, and thus serve to connect man with man.

2. Written Language.—It took many hundreds of years— perhaps thousands—before human beings were able to invent a mode of writing upon paper—that is, of representing **sounds** by **signs.** These signs are called **letters**; and the whole set of them goes by the name of the **Alphabet**—from the two first letters of the Greek alphabet, which are called *alpha, beta.* There are languages that have never been put upon paper at all, such as many of the African languages, many in the South Sea Islands, and other parts of the globe. But in all cases, every language that we know anything about—English, Latin, French, German—existed for hundreds of years before any one thought of writing it down on paper.

3. A Language Grows.—A language is an **organism** or **organic existence.** Now every organism lives; and, if it lives, it grows; and, if it grows, it also dies. Our language grows; it is growing still; and it has been growing for many

N

hundreds of years. As it grows it loses something, and it gains something else; it alters its appearance; changes take place in this part of it and in that part,—until at length its appearance in age is something almost entirely different from what it was in its early youth. If we had the photograph of a man of forty, and the photograph of the same person when he was a child of one, we should find, on comparing them, that it was almost impossible to point to the smallest trace of likeness in the features of the two photographs. And yet the two pictures represent the same person. And so it is with the English language. The oldest English, which is usually called Anglo-Saxon, is as different from our modern English as if they were two distinct languages; and yet they are not two languages, but really and fundamentally one and the same. Modern English differs from the oldest English as a giant oak does from a small oak sapling, or a broad stalwart man of forty does from a feeble infant of a few months old.

4. The English Language.—The English language is the speech spoken by the Anglo-Saxon race in England, in most parts of Scotland, in the larger part of Ireland, in the United States, in Canada, in Australia and New Zealand, in South Africa, and in many other parts of the world. In the middle of the **fifth** century it was spoken by a few thousand men who had lately landed in England from the Continent: it is now spoken by more than one hundred millions of people. In the course of the next sixty years, it will probably be the speech of two hundred millions.

5. English on the Continent.—In the middle of the fifth century it was spoken in the north-west corner of Europe— between the mouths of the Rhine, the Weser, and the Elbe; and in Schleswig there is a small district which is called **Angeln** to this day. But it was not then called **English**; it was more probably called **Teutish**, or **Teutsch**, or **Deutsch**—all words connected with a generic word which covers many families and languages—**Teutonic**. It was a rough guttural speech of one or two thousand words; and it was brought over to this country by the **Jutes, Angles,** and **Saxons** in the year 449. These men left their home on the Continent to find here farms to till and houses to live in; and they drove the inhabitants of the island—the **Britons**—ever farther and farther west, until they at length left them in peace in the more mountainous parts of the island—in the southern and western corners, in Cornwall and in Wales.

6. **The British Language.**—What language did the Teutonic conquerors, who wrested the lands from the poor Britons, find spoken in this island when they first set foot on it? Not a Teutonic speech at all. They found a language not one word of which they could understand. The island itself was then called **Britain**; and the tongue spoken in it belonged to the Keltic group of languages. Languages belonging to the Keltic group are still spoken in Wales, in Brittany (in France), in the Highlands of Scotland, in the west of Ireland, and in the Isle of Man. A few words—very few—from the speech of the Britons, have come into our own English language; and what these are we shall see by-and-by.

7. **The Family to which English belongs.**—Our English tongue belongs to the **Aryan** or **Indo-European Family** of languages. That is to say, the main part or substance of it can be traced back to the race which inhabited the high table-lands that lie to the back of the western end of the great range of the Himalaya, or "Abode of Snow." This Aryan race grew and increased, and spread to the south and west; and from it have sprung languages which are now spoken in India, in Persia, in Greece and Italy, in France and Germany, in Scandinavia, and in Russia. From this Aryan family we are sprung; out of the oldest Aryan speech our own language has grown.

8. **The Group to which English belongs.** — The Indo-European family of languages consists of several groups. One of these is called the **Teutonic Group,** because it is spoken by the **Teuts** (or the **Teutonic race**), who are found in Germany, in England and Scotland, in Holland, in parts of Belgium, in Denmark, in Norway and Sweden, in Iceland, and the Faroe Islands. The Teutonic group consists of three branches— **High German, Low German,** and **Scandinavian.** High

German is the name given to the kind of German spoken in
Upper Germany—that is, in the table-land which lies south of
the river Main, and which rises gradually till it runs into the
Alps. **New High German** is the German of books—the
literary language—the German that is taught and learned in
schools. **Low German** is the name given to the German
dialects spoken in the lowlands—in the German part of the
Great Plain of Europe, and round the mouths of those German
rivers that flow into the Baltic and the North Sea. **Scandinavian** is the name given to the languages spoken in
Denmark and in the great Scandinavian Peninsula. Of these
three languages, Danish and Norwegian are practically the same
—their literary or book-language is one ; while Swedish is very
different. Icelandic is the oldest and purest form of Scandinavian. The following is a table of the

GROUP OF TEUTONIC LANGUAGES.

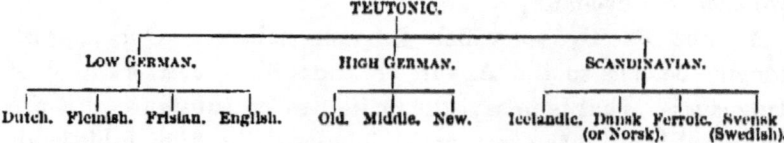

It will be observed, on looking at the above table, that High
German is subdivided according to time, but that the other
groups are subdivided according to space.

9. English a Low-German Speech.—Our English tongue is
the **lowest of all Low-German dialects.** Low German is the
German spoken in the lowlands of Germany. As we descend
the rivers, we come to the lowest level of all—the level of the
sea. Our English speech, once a mere dialect, came down to
that, crossed the German Ocean, and settled in Britain, to which
it gave in time the name of Angla-land or England. The Low
German spoken in the Netherlands is called **Dutch;** the Low
German spoken in Friesland—a prosperous province of Holland
—is called **Frisian;** and the Low German spoken in Great
Britain is called **English.** These three languages are extremely
like one another; but the Continental language that is likest

the English is the Dutch or Hollandish dialect called *Frisian*. We even possess a couplet, every word of which is both English and Frisian. It runs thus—

> Good butter and good cheese
> Is good English and good Fries.

10. Dutch and Welsh—a Contrast.—When the Teuton conquerors came to this country, they called the Britons foreigners, just as the Greeks called all other peoples besides themselves *barbarians*. By this they did not at first mean that they were uncivilised, but only that they were *not* Greeks. Now, the Teutonic or Saxon or English name for foreigners was **Wealhas**, a word afterwards contracted into **Welsh.** To this day the modern Teuts or Teutons (or *Germans*, as *we* call them) call all Frenchmen and Italians *Welshmen ;* and, when a German peasant crosses the border into France, he says : " I am going into Welshland."

11. The Spread of English over Britain.—The Jutes, who came from Juteland or Jylland—now called Jutland—settled in Kent and in the Isle of Wight. The Saxons settled in the south and western parts of England, and gave their names to those kingdoms—now counties—whose names came to end in **sex.** There was the kingdom of the East Saxons, or **Essex;** the kingdom of the West Saxons, or **Wessex;** the kingdom of the Middle Saxons, or **Middlesex;** and the kingdom of the South Saxons, or **Sussex.** The Angles settled chiefly on the east coast. The kingdom of **East Anglia** was divided into the regions of the **North Folk** and the **South Folk,** words which are still perpetuated in the names *Norfolk* and *Suffolk.* These three sets of Teutons all spoke different dialects of the same Teutonic speech ; and these dialects, with their differences, peculiarities, and odd habits, took root in English soil, and lived an independent life, apart from each other, uninfluenced by each other, for several hundreds of years. But, in the slow course of time, they joined together to make up our beautiful English language—a language which, however, still bears in itself the traces of dialectic forms, and is in no respect of one kind or of one fibre all through.

CHAPTER I.

1. **Dead and Living Languages.**—A language is said to be **dead** when it is no longer spoken. Such a language we know only in books. Thus, **Latin** is a dead language, because no nation anywhere now speaks it. A dead language can undergo no change; it remains, and must remain, as we find it written in books. But a living language is always changing, just like a tree or the human body. The human body has its periods or stages. There is the period of infancy, the period of boyhood, the period of manhood, and the period of old age. In the same way, a language has its periods.

2. **No Sudden Changes—a Caution.**—We divide the English language into periods, and then mark, with some approach to accuracy, certain distinct changes in the habits of our language, in the inflexions of its words, in the kind of words it preferred, or in the way it liked to put its words together. But we must be carefully on our guard against fancying that, at any given time or in any given year, the English people threw aside one set of habits as regards language, and adopted another set. It is not so, nor can it be so. The changes in language are as gentle, gradual, and imperceptible as the changes in the growth of a tree or in the skin of the human body. We renew our skin slowly and gradually; but we are never conscious of the process, nor can we say at any given time that we have got a completely new skin.

3. The Periods of English.—Bearing this caution in mind, we can go on to look at the chief periods in our English language. These are five in number; and they are as follows:—

I. Ancient English or Anglo-Saxon, .	449-1100
II. Early English, ...	1100-1250
III. Middle English, ...	1250-1485
IV. Tudor English, ...	1485-1603
V. Modern English, . . .	1603-1900

These periods merge very slowly, or are shaded off, so to speak, into each other in the most gradual way. If we take the English of 1250 and compare it with that of 900, we shall find a great difference; but if we compare it with the English of 1100 the difference is not so marked. The difference between the English of the nineteenth and the English of the fourteenth century is very great, but the difference between the English of the fourteenth and that of the thirteenth century is very small.

4. Ancient English or Anglo-Saxon, 450-1100.—This form of English differed from modern English in having a much larger number of inflexions. The noun had five cases, and there were several declensions, just as in Latin; adjectives were declined, and had three genders; some pronouns had a dual as well as a plural number; and the verb had a much larger number of inflexions than it has now. The vocabulary of the language contained very few foreign elements. The poetry of the language employed head-rhyme or alliteration, and not end-rhyme, as we do now. The works of the poet **Caedmon** and the great prose-writer **King Alfred** belong to this Anglo-Saxon period.

5. Early English, 1100-1250.—The coming of the Normans in 1066 made many changes in the land, many changes in the Church and in the State, and it also introduced many changes into the language. The inflexions of our speech began to drop off, because they were used less and less; and though we never adopted new *inflexions* from French or from any other language, new French *words* began to creep in. In some parts of the country English had ceased to be written in books; the language existed as a spoken language only; and hence accuracy in the use of words and the inflexions of words could not be ensured. Two notable books—written, not printed, for there was no printing in this island till the year 1474—belong to this period. These are the **Ormulum**, by **Orm** or **Ormin**, and the **Brut**, by a monk called **Layamon** or **Laweman**. The latter tells the story of Brutus, who was believed to have been the son of Æneas of Troy; to have escaped after the downfall of that city; to have sailed through the Mediterranean, ever farther and farther to the west; to have landed in Britain, settled here, and given the country its name.

6. **Middle English, 1250-1485.**—Most of the inflexions of nouns and adjectives have in this period—between the middle of the thirteenth and the end of the fifteenth century—completely disappeared. The inflexions of verbs are also greatly reduced in number. The **strong**[1] mode of inflexion has ceased to be employed for verbs that are new-comers, and the **weak** mode has been adopted in its place. During the earlier part of this period, even country-people tried to speak French, and in this and other modes many French words found their way into English. A writer of the thirteenth century, John de Trevisa, says that country-people "fondeth [that is, try] with great bysynes for to speke Freynsch for to be more y-told of." The country-people did not succeed very well, as the ordinary proverb shows: "Jack would be a gentleman if he could speak French." Boys at school were expected to turn their Latin into French, and in the courts of law French only was allowed to be spoken. But in 1362 Edward III. gave his assent to an Act of Parliament allowing English to be used instead of Norman-French. "The yer of oure Lord," says John de Trevisa, "a thousond thre hondred foure score and fyve of the secunde Kyng Richard after the conquest, in al the gramer scoles of Engelond children leveth Freynsch, and construeth and turneth an Englysch." To the first half of this period belong a **Metrical Chronicle**, attributed to **Robert of Gloucester**; **Langtoft's** Metrical Chronicle, translated by **Robert de Brunne**; the **Agenbite of Inwit**, by Dan Michel of Northgate in Kent; and a few others. But to the second

[1] See p. 43.

half belong the rich and varied productions of **Geoffrey Chaucer,** our first great poet and always one of our greatest writers; the alliterative poems of **William Langley** or **Langlande**; the more learned poems of **John Gower**; and the translation of the **Bible** and theological works of the reformer John **Wyclif.**

7. **Tudor English, 1485-1603.**—Before the end of the sixteenth century almost all our inflexions had disappeared. The great dramatist Ben Jonson (1574-1637) laments the loss of the plural ending en for verbs, because *wenten* and *hopen* were much more musical and more useful in verse than *went* or *hope;* but its recovery was already past praying for. This period is remarkable for the introduction of an enormous number of Latin words, and this was due to the new interest taken in the literature of the Romans—an interest produced by what is called the **Revival of Letters.** But the most striking, as it is also the most important fact relating to this period, is the appearance of a group of dramatic writers, the greatest the world has ever seen. Chief among these was **William Shakespeare.** Of pure poetry perhaps the greatest writer was **Edmund Spenser.** The greatest prose-writer was **Richard Hooker,** and the pithiest **Francis Bacon.**

8. **Modern English, 1603-1900.**—The grammar of the language was fixed before this period, most of the accidence having entirely vanished. The vocabulary of the language, however, has gone on increasing, and is still increasing; for the English language, like the English people, is always ready to offer hospitality to all peaceful foreigners—words or human beings—that will land and settle within her coasts. And the tendency at the present time is not only to give a hearty welcome to new-comers from other lands, but to call back old words and old phrases that had been allowed to drop out of existence. Tennyson has been one of the chief agents in this happy restoration.

CHAPTER II.

THE HISTORY OF THE VOCABULARY OF THE ENGLISH LANGUAGE.

1. The English Nation.—The English people have for many centuries been the greatest travellers in the world. It was an Englishman—Francis Drake—who first went round the globe; and the English have colonised more foreign lands in every part of the world than any other people that ever existed. The English in this way have been influenced by the world without. But they have also been subjected to manifold influences from within — they have been exposed to greater political changes, and profounder though quieter political revolutions, than any other nation. In 1066 they were conquered by the Norman - French; and for several centuries they had French kings. Seeing and talking with many different peoples, they learned to adopt foreign words with ease, and to give them a home among the native-born words of the language. Trade is always a kindly and useful influence; and the trade of Great Britain has for many centuries been larger than that of any other nation. It has spread into every part of the world; it gives and receives from all tribes and nations, from every speech and tongue.

2. The English Element in English.—When the English came to this island in the fifth century, the number of words in the language they spoke was probably not over **two thousand.** Now, however, we possess a vocabulary of perhaps more than **one hundred thousand words.** And so eager and willing have we been to welcome foreign words, that it may be said with truth that: **The majority of words in the English Tongue are not English.** In fact, if we take the Latin language by itself, there are in our language more **Latin** words than **English.** But the grammar is distinctly English, and not Latin at all.

3. **The Spoken Language and the Written Language—a Caution.**—We must not forget what has been said about a language,—that it is not a printed thing—not a set of black marks upon paper, but that it is in truest truth a **tongue** or a **speech.** Hence we must be careful to distinguish between the **spoken** language and the **written** or **printed** language ; between the language of the **ear** and the language of the **eye** ; between the language of the **mouth** and the language of the **dictionary** ; between the **moving** vocabulary of the market and the street, and the **fixed** vocabulary that has been catalogued and imprisoned in our dictionaries. If we can only keep this in view, we shall find that, though there are more Latin words in our vocabulary than English, the English words we possess are **used** in speaking a hundred times, or even a thousand times, oftener than the Latin words. It is the genuine English words that have life and movement ; it is they that fly about in houses, in streets, and in markets ; it is they that express with greatest force our truest and most usual sentiments—our inmost thoughts and our deepest feelings. Latin words are found often enough in books ; but, when an English man or woman is deeply moved, he speaks pure English and nothing else. Words are the coin of human intercourse ; and it is the native coin of pure English with the native stamp that is in daily circulation.

4. **A Diagram of English.**—If we were to try to represent to the eye the proportions of the different elements in our vocabulary, as it is found in the dictionary, the diagram would take something like the following form :—

DIAGRAM OF THE ENGLISH LANGUAGE.

ENGLISH WORDS.
LATIN WORDS (including Norman-French, which are also Latin).

GREEK WORDS.	Italian, Spanish, Portuguese, Dutch, Hebrew, Arabic, Hindustani, Persian, Malay, American, etc. etc.

5. The Foreign Elements in our English Vocabulary.— The different peoples and the different circumstances with which we have come in contact, have had many results—one among others, that of presenting us with contributions to our vocabulary. We found Kelts here; and hence we have a number of Keltic words in our vocabulary. The Romans held this island for several hundred years; and when they had to go in the year 410, they left behind them six Latin words, which we have inherited. In the seventh century, Augustine and his missionary monks from Rome brought over to us a larger number of Latin words; and the Church which they founded introduced ever more and more words from Rome. The Danes began to come over to this island in the eighth century; we had for some time a Danish dynasty seated on the throne of England: and hence we possess many Danish words. The Norman-French invasion in the eleventh century brought us many hundreds of Latin words; for French is in reality a branch of the Latin tongue. The Revival of Learning in the sixteenth century gave us several thousands of Latin words. And wherever our sailors and merchants have gone, they have brought back with them foreign words as well as foreign things —Arabic words from Arabia and Africa, Hindustani words from India, Persian words from Persia, Chinese words from China, and even Malay words from the peninsula of Malacca. Let us look a little more closely at these foreign elements.

6. The Keltic Element in English.—This element is of

three kinds : (i) Those words which we received direct from the ancient Britons whom we found in the island ; (ii) those which the Norman-French brought with them from Gaul ; (iii) those which have lately come into the language from the Highlands of Scotland, or from Ireland, or from the writings of Sir Walter Scott.

7. **The First Keltic Element.**—This first contribution contains the following words : *Breeches, clout, crock, cradle, darn, dainty, mop, pillow ; barrow* (a funeral mound), *glen, havoc, kiln, mattock, pool.* It is worthy of note that the first eight in the list are the names of domestic—some even of kitchen —things and utensils. It may, perhaps, be permitted us to conjecture that in many cases the Saxon invader married a British wife, who spoke her own language, taught her children to speak their mother tongue, and whose words took firm root in the kitchen of the new English household. The names of most rivers, mountains, lakes, and hills are, of course, Keltic ; for these names would not be likely to be changed by the English new-comers. There are two names for rivers which are found—in one form or another—in every part of Great Britain. These are the names **Avon** and **Ex.** The word **Avon** means simply *water.* We can conceive the children on a farm near a river speaking of it simply as "the water"; and hence we find fourteen Avons in this island. **Ex** also means *water;* and there are perhaps more than twenty streams in Great Britain with this name. The word appears as **Ex** in **Exeter** (the older and fuller form being *Exanceaster*—the camp on the Exe) ; as **Ax** in **Axminster**; as **Ox** in **Oxford**; as **Ux** in **Uxbridge**; and as **Ouse** in Yorkshire and other eastern counties. In Wales and Scotland, the hidden **k** changes its place and comes at the end. Thus in Wales we find **Usk**; and in Scotland, **Esk**. There are at least eight Esks in the kingdom of Scotland alone. The commonest Keltic name for a mountain is **Pen** or **Ben** (in Wales it is *Pen ;* in Scotland the flatter form *Ben* is used). We find this word in England also under the form of **Pennine** ; and, in Italy, as **Apennine**.

8. **The Second Keltic Element.**—The Normans came from

Scandinavia early in the tenth century, and wrested the valley of the Seine out of the hands of Charles the Simple, the then king of the French. The language spoken by the people of France was a broken-down form of spoken Latin, which is now called French; but in this language they had retained many Gaulish words out of the old Gaulish language. Such are the words : *Bag, bargain, barter; barrel, basin, basket, bucket; bonnet, button, ribbon; car, cart; dagger, gown; mitten, motley; rogue; varlet, vassal, wicket.* The above words were brought over to Britain by the Normans; and they gradually took an acknowledged place among the words of our own language, and have held that place ever since.

9. The Third Keltic Element.—This consists of comparatively few words—such as *clan; claymore* (a sword); *philabeg* (a kind of kilt), *kilt* itself, *brogue* (a kind of shoe), *plaid; pibroch* (bagpipe war-music), *slogan* (a war-cry); and *whisky.* Ireland has given us *shamrock, gag, log, clog,* and *brogue*—in the sense of a mode of speech.

10. The Scandinavian Element in English.—Towards the end of the eighth century—in the year 787—the Teutons of the North, called Northmen, Normans, or Norsemen—but more commonly known as Danes—made their appearance on the eastern coast of Great Britain, and attacked the peaceful towns and quiet settlements of the English. These attacks became so frequent, and their occurrence was so much dreaded, that a prayer was inserted against them in a Litany of the time— "From the incursions of the Northmen, good Lord, deliver us!" In spite of the resistance of the English, the Danes had, before the end of the ninth century, succeeded in obtaining a permanent footing in England; and, in the eleventh century, a Danish dynasty sat upon the English throne from the year 1016 to 1042. From the time of King Alfred, the Danes of the Danelagh were a settled part of the population of England; and hence we find, especially on the east coast, a large number of Danish names still in use.

11. Character of the Scandinavian Element.—The Northmen, as we have said, were Teutons ; and they spoke a dialect of the great Teutonic (or German) language. The sounds of the Danish dialect—or language, as it must now be called—are harder than those of the German. We find a **k** instead of a **ch**; a **p** preferred to an **f**. The same is the case in Scotland, where the hard form **kirk** is preferred to the softer **church**. Where the Germans say **Dorf**—our English word **Thorpe**, a village—the Danes say **Drup**.

12. Scandinavian Words (i).—The words contributed to our language by the Scandinavians are of two kinds : (i) Names of places ; and (ii) ordinary words. (i) The most striking instance of a Danish place-name is the noun **by,** a town. Mr Isaac Taylor [1] tells us that there are in the east of England more than six hundred names of towns ending in **by.** Almost all of these are found in the Danelagh, within the limits of the great highway made by the Romans to the north-west, and well-known as **Watling Street.** We find, for example, **Whitby,** or the town on the *white* cliffs ; **Grimsby,** or the town of Grim, a great sea-rover, who obtained for his countrymen the right that all ships from the Baltic should come into the port of Grimsby free of duty ; **Tenby,** that is Daneby ; **by-law,** a law for a special town ; and a vast number of others. The following Danish words also exist in our times—either as separate and individual words, or in composition—**beck,** a stream ; **fell,** a hill or table-land ; **firth or fiord,** an arm of the sea—the same as the Danish fiord ; **force,** a waterfall ; **garth,** a yard or enclosure ; **holm,** an island in a river ; **kirk,** a church ; **oe,** an island ; **thorpe,** a village ; **thwaite,** a forest clearing ; and **vik** or **wick,** a station for ships, or a creek.

13. Scandinavian Words (ii).—The most useful and the most frequently employed word that we have received from the Danes is the word **are.** The pure English word for this is **beoth** or **sindon.** The Danes gave us also the habit of using **to** before an infinitive. Their word for **to** was **at** ; and at still survives and is in use in Lincolnshire. We find also the following Danish words in our language : **blunt, bole** (of a tree), **bound** (on a journey—properly **boun**), **busk** (to dress), **cake,**

[1] Words and Places, p. 158.

call, crop (to cut), curl, cut, **dairy**, **daze**, **din**, **droop**, **fellow**,
flit, **for**, **froward**, **hustings**, **ill**, **irk**, **kid**, **kindle**, **loft**, **odd**,
plough, **root**, **scold**, **sky**, **tarn** (a small mountain lake), **weak**,
and **ugly**.   It is in Northumberland, Durham, Yorkshire, Lin-
coln, Norfolk, and even in the western counties of Cumberland and Lancashire, that we find the largest admixture of
Scandinavian words.

14. Influence of the Scandinavian Element.—The introduction of the Danes and the Danish language into England
had the result, in the east, of unsettling the inflexions of our
language, and thus of preparing the way for their complete dis-
appearance.   The declensions of nouns became unsettled;
nouns that used to make their plural in **a** or in u took the
more striking plural suffix **as** that belonged to a quite different declension.   The same things happened to adjectives,
verbs, and other parts of language.   The causes of this are not
far to seek.   Spoken language can never be so accurate as written language; the mass of the English and Danes never cared
or could care much for grammar; and both parties to a conversation would of course hold firmly to the **root** of the word,
which was intelligible to both of them, and let the inflexions
slide, or take care of themselves.   The more the English and
Danes mixed with each other, the oftener they met at church,
at games, and in the market-place, the more rapidly would this
process of stripping go on,—the smaller care would both peoples
take of the grammatical inflexions which they had brought with
them into this country.

15. The Latin Element in English.—So far as the number of
words—the vocabulary—of the language is concerned, the Latin
contribution is by far the most important element in our language.   Latin was the language of the Romans; and the Romans
at one time were masters of the whole known world.   No wonder, then, that they influenced so many peoples, and that their
language found its way—east and west, and south and north—
into almost all the countries of Europe.   There are, as we have
seen, more Latin than English words in our own language; and
it is therefore necessary to make ourselves acquainted with the

character and the uses of the Latin element—an element so important—in English.[1] Not only have the Romans made contributions of large **numbers** of words to the English language, but they have added to it a quite new **quality**, and given to its genius new **powers** of expression. So true is this, that we may say—without any sense of unfairness, or any feeling of exaggeration—that, until the Latin element was thoroughly mixed, united with, and transfused into the original English, the writings of Shakespeare were impossible, the poetry of the sixteenth and seventeenth centuries could not have come into existence. This is true of Shakespeare ; and it is still more true of Milton. His most powerful poetical thoughts are written in lines, the most telling words in which are almost always Latin. This may be illustrated by the following lines from " Lycidas " :—

> "It was that *fatal* and *perfidious* bark,
> Built in the *eclipse*, and rigged with curses dark,
> That sunk so low that *sacred* head of thine !"

16. The Latin Contributions and their Dates.—The first contribution of Latin words was made by the Romans—not, however, to the English, but to the Britons. The Romans held this island from A.D. **43** to A.D. **410**. They left behind them—when they were obliged to go—a small contribution of six words—six only, but all of them important. The second contribution—to a large extent ecclesiastical—was made by Augustine and his missionary monks from Rome, and their visit took place in the year **596**. The third contribution was made through the medium of the Norman-French, who seized and subdued this island in the year **1066** and following years. The fourth contribution came to us by the aid of the Revival of Learning—rather a process than an event, the dates of which are vague, but which may be said to have taken place in the sixteenth and seventeenth centuries. The Latin left for us by the Romans is called **Latin of the First Period**; that brought over by the missionaries from Rome, **Latin of the**

---

[1] In the last half of this sentence, all the essential words—*necessary, acquainted, character, uses, element, important,* are Latin (except *character,* which is Greek).

Second Period; that given us by the Norman-French, **Latin of the Third Period**; and that which came to us from the Revival of Learning, **Latin of the Fourth Period.** The first consists of a few names handed down to us through the Britons; the second, of a number of words—mostly relating to ecclesiastical affairs—brought into the spoken language by the monks; the third, of a large vocabulary, that came to us by **mouth** and **ear**; and the fourth, of a very large treasure of words, which we received by means of **books** and the **eye.** Let us now look more closely and carefully at them, each in its turn.

17. **Latin of the First Period.**—(i) The Romans held Britain for nearly four hundred years; and they succeeded in teaching the wealthier classes among the Southern Britons to speak Latin.. They also built towns in the island, made splendid roads, formed camps at important points, framed good laws, and administered the affairs of the island with considerable justice and uprightness. But, never having come directly into contact with the Angles or Saxons themselves, they could not in any way influence their language by oral communication— by speaking to them. What they left behind them was only six words, most of which became merely the prefixes or the suffixes of the names of places. These six words were **Castra,** a camp; **Strata** (*via*), a paved road; **Colonia,** a settlement (generally of soldiers); **Fossa,** a trench; **Portus,** a harbour; and **Vallum,** a rampart.

18. **Latin of the First Period** (ii).—(*a*) The treatment of the Latin word **castra** in this island has been both singular and significant. It has existed in this country for nearly nineteen hundred years; and it has always taken the colouring of the locality into whose soil it struck root. In the north and east of England it is sounded hard, and takes the form of **caster,** as in **Lancaster, Doncaster, Tadcaster,** and others. In the midland counties, it takes the softer form of **cester,** as in **Leicester, Towcester**; and in the extreme west and south, it takes the still softer form of **chester,** as in **Chester, Manchester, Winchester,** and others. It is worthy of notice that there are in Scotland no words ending in *caster*. Though

the Romans had camps in Scotland, they do not seem to have been so important as to become the centres of towns. (*b*) The word **strata** has also taken different forms in different parts of England.   While **castra** has always been a suffix, **strata** shows itself constantly as a prefix.   When the Romans came to this island, the country was impassable by man.   There were no roads worthy of the name,—what paths there were being merely foot-paths or bridle-tracks.   One of the first things the Romans did was to drive a strongly built military road from **Richborough**, near Dover, to the river Dee, on which they formed a standing camp **(Castra stativa)** which to this day bears the name of **Chester**.   This great road became the high-way of all travellers from north to south, — was known as "The Street," and was called by the Saxons **Watling Street**. But this word **street** also became a much-used prefix, and took the different forms of **strat, strad, stret**, and **streat**.   All towns with such names are to be found on this or some other great Roman road.   Thus we have **Stratford-on-Avon, Strat-ton, Stradbroke, Stretton, Stretford** (near Manchester), and **Streatham** (near London).—Over the other words we need not dwell so long.   **Colonia** we find in **Colne, Lincoln**, and others; **fossa** in **Fossway, Fosbrooke**, and **Fosbridge** ; **portus**, in **Portsmouth** and **Bridport**; and **vallum** in the words **wall, bailey**, and **bailiff**.   The Normans called the two courts in front of their castles the inner and outer baileys ; and the officer in charge of them was called the bailiff.

19. **Latin Element of the Second Period** (i).—The story of Pope Gregory and the Roman mission to England is widely known.   Gregory, when a young man, was crossing the Roman forum one morning, and, when passing the side where the slave-mart was held, observed, as he walked, some beautiful boys, with fair hair, blue eyes, and clear bright complexion. He asked a bystander of what nation the boys were.   The answer was, that they were Angles.   "No, not Angles," he replied ; " they are angels."   On learning further that they were heathens, he registered a silent vow that he would, if Providence gave him an opportunity, deliver them from the

darkness of heathendom, and bring them and their relatives into the light and liberty of the Gospel. Time passed by; and in the long course of time Gregory became Pope. In his unlooked-for greatness, he did not forget his vow. In the year 596 he sent over to Kent a missionary, called Augustine, along with forty monks. They were well received by the King of Kent, allowed to settle in Canterbury, and to build a small cathedral there.

20. Latin Element of the Second Period (ii).—This mission, the churches that grew out of it, the Christian customs that in time took root in the country, and the trade that followed in its track, brought into the language a number of Latin words, most of them the names of church offices, services, and observances. Thus we find, in our oldest English, the words, **postol** from *apostolus*, a person sent; **biscop,** from *episcopus*, an overseer; **calc,** from *calix*, a cup; **clerc,** from *clericus*, an ordained member of the church; **munec,** from *mondchus*, a solitary person or monk; **preost,** from *presbyter*, an elder; **aelmesse,** from *eleēmosūnē*, alms; **predician,** from *prædicare*, to preach; **regol,** from *regula*, a rule. (*Apostle, bishop, clerk, monk, priest,* and *alms* come to us really from Greek words—but through the Latin tongue.)

21. Latin Element of the Second Period (iii).—The intro-duction of the Roman form of Christianity brought with it increased communication with Rome and with the Continent generally; widened the experience of Englishmen; gave a stimulus to commerce; and introduced into this island new things and products, and along with the things and products new names. To this period belongs the introduction of the words: **Butter, cheese; cedar, fig, pear, peach; lettuce, lily; pepper, pease; camel, lion, elephant; oyster, trout; pound, ounce; candle, table; marble; mint.**

22. Latin of the Third Period (i).—The Latin element of the Third Period is in reality the French that was brought over to this island by the Normans in 1066, and is generally called **Norman-French.** It differed from the French of Paris both in spelling and in pronunciation. For example, Norman-

French wrote **people** for **peuple**; **léal** for **loyal**; **réal** for **royal**; **réalm** for **royaume**; and so on. But both of these dialects (and every dialect of French) are simply forms of Latin —not of the Latin written and printed in books, but of the Latin spoken in the camp, the fields, the streets, the village, and the cottage. The Romans conquered Gaul, where a Keltic tongue was spoken; and the Gauls gradually adopted Latin as their mother tongue, and—with the exception of the Brétons of Brittany—left off their Keltic speech almost entirely. In adopting the Latin tongue, they had—as in similar cases—taken firm hold of the root of the word, but changed the pronunciation of it, and had, at the same time, compressed very much or entirely dropped many of the Latin inflexions. The French people, an intermixture of Gauls and other tribes (some of them, like the Franks, German), ceased, in fact, to speak their own language, and learned the Latin tongue. The Norsemen, led by Duke Rolf or Rollo or Rou, marched south in large numbers; and, in the year 912, wrested from King Charles the Simple the fair valley of the Seine, settled in it, and gave to it the name of Normandy. These Norsemen, now Normans, were Teutons, and spoke a Teutonic dialect; but, when they settled in France, they learned in course of time to speak French. The kind of French they spoke is called Norman-French, and it was this kind of French that they brought over with them in 1066. But Norman-French had made its appearance in England before the famous year of '66; for Edward the Confessor, who succeeded to the English throne in 1042, had been educated at the Norman Court; and he not only spoke the language himself, but insisted on its being spoken by the nobles who lived with him in his Court.

23. **Latin of the Third Period** (ii). **Chief Dates.**—The Normans, having utterly beaten down the resistance of the English, seized the land and all the political power of this country, and filled all kinds of offices—both spiritual and temporal—with their Norman brethren. Norman-French became the language of the Court and the nobility, the language of Parliament and the law courts, of the universities and the schools, of the Church

and of literature.   The English people held fast to their own
tongue ; but they picked up many French words in the markets
and other places "where men most do congregate."   But
French, being the language of the upper and ruling classes, was
here and there learned by the English or Saxon country-people
who had the ambition to be in the fashion, and were eager "to
speke Frensch, for to be more y-told of,"—to be more highly
considered than their neighbours.   It took about three hundred
years for French words and phrases to soak thoroughly into
English ; and it was not until England was saturated with
French words and French rhythms that the great poet Chaucer
appeared to produce poetic narratives that were read with
delight both by Norman baron and by Saxon yeoman.   In the
course of these three hundred years this intermixture of French
with English had been slowly and silently going on.   Let us
look at a few of the chief land-marks in the long process.   In
1042 Edward the Confessor introduces Norman-French into his
Court.   In **1066** Duke William introduces Norman-French into
the whole country, and even into parts of Scotland.   The oldest
English, or Anglo-Saxon, ceases to be written, anywhere in the
island, in public documents, in the year **1154**.   In **1204** we
lost Normandy, a loss that had the effect of bringing the English and the Normans closer together.   Robert of Gloucester
writes his chronicle in **1272**, and uses a large number of French
words.   But, as early as the reign of Henry the Third, in the
year **1258**, the reformed and reforming Government of the day
issued a proclamation in English, as well as in French and Latin.
In **1303**, Robert of Brunn introduces a large number of French
words.   The French wars in Edward the Third's reign brought
about a still closer union of the Norman and the Saxon elements
of the nation.   But, about the middle of the fourteenth century
a reaction set in, and it seemed as if the genius of the English
language refused to take in any more French words.   The
English silent stubbornness seemed to have prevailed, and
Englishmen had made up their minds to be English in speech,
as they were English to the backbone in everything else.
Norman-French had, in fact, become provincial, and was spoken.

only here and there. Before the great Plague — commonly spoken of as "The Black Death"—of **1349**, both high and low seemed to be alike bent on learning French, but the reaction may be said to date from this year. The culminating point of this reaction may perhaps be seen in an Act of Parliament passed in **1362** by Edward III., by which both French and Latin had to give place to English in our courts of law. The poems of Chaucer are the literary result — "the bright consummate flower" of the union of two great powers—the brilliance of the French language on the one hand and the homely truth and steadfastness of English on the other. Chaucer was born in 1340, and died in **1400;** so that we may say that he and his poems—though not the causes—are the signs and symbols of the great influence that French obtained and held over our mother tongue. But although we accepted so many *words* from our Norman-French visitors and immigrants, we accepted from them no *habit* of speech whatever. We accepted from them no phrase or idiom : the build and nature of the English language remained the same—unaffected by foreign manners or by foreign habits. It is true that Chaucer has the ridiculous phrase, "I n'am but dead" (for "I am quite dead"[1])—which is a literal translation of the well-known French idiom, "Je ne suis que." But, though our tongue has always been and is impervious to foreign idiom, it is probably owing to the great influx of French words which took place chiefly in the thirteenth century that many people have acquired a habit of using a long French or Latin word when an English word would do quite as well—or, indeed, a great deal better. Thus some people are found to call a *good house*, a *desirable mansion;* and, instead of the quiet old English proverb, "Buy once, buy twice," we have the roundabout Latinisms, "A single commission will ensure a repetition of orders." An American writer, speaking of the foreign ambassadors who had been attacked by Japanese soldiers in Yeddo, says that "they concluded to occupy a location more salubrious." This is only a foreign language, instead of the simple and homely English : "They made up their minds to settle in a healthier spot."

---

[1] Or, as an Irishman would say, "I am kilt entirely."

24. Latin of the Third Period (iii). **Norman Words** (*a*).—
The Norman-French words were of several different kinds.
There were words connected with war, with feudalism, and
with the chase. There were new law terms, and words connected with the State, and the new institutions introduced by
the Normans. There were new words brought in by the Norman churchmen. New titles unknown to the English were
also introduced. A better kind of cooking, a higher and less
homely style of living, was brought into this country by the
Normans ; and, along with these, new and unheard-of words.

25. Norman Words (*b*).—The following are some of the
Norman - French terms connected with war : **Arms, armour;
assault, battle ; captain, chivalry ; joust, lance ; standard,
trumpet ; mail, vizor.** The English word for **armour** was
harness; but the Normans degraded that word into the armour
of a horse. **Battle** comes from the Fr. *battre*, to beat : the
corresponding English word is **fight**. **Captain** comes from
the Latin *caput*, a head. **Mail** comes from the Latin *macula*,
the mesh of a net ; and the first coats of mail were made of rings
or a kind of metal network. **Vizor** comes from the Fr. *viser*,
to look. It was the barred part of the helmet which a man
could see through.

26. Norman Words (*c*).—Feudalism may be described as the
holding of land on condition of giving or providing service in
war. Thus a knight held land of his baron, under promise to
serve him so many days ; a baron of his king, on condition
that he brought so many men into the field for such and such
a time at the call of his Overlord. William the Conqueror
made the feudal system universal in every part of England,
and compelled every English baron to swear homage to himself personally. Words relating to feudalism are, among
others : **Homage, fealty ; esquire, vassal ; herald, scutcheon,** and others. **Homage** is the declaration of obedience for
life of one man to another—that the inferior is the *man* (Fr.
homme ; L. *homo*) of the superior. **Fealty** is the Norman-French
form of the word *fidelity.* An **esquire** is a **scutiger** (L.), or
shield-bearer ; for he carried the shield of the knight, when

they were travelling and no fighting was going on. A **vassal** was a "little young man,"—in Low-Latin **vassallus**, a diminutive of *vassus*, from the Keltic word *gwâs*, a man. (The form *vassaletus* is also found, which gives us our *varlet* and *valet*.) **Scutcheon** comes from the Lat. *scutum*, a shield. Then scutcheon or escutcheon came to mean *coat-of-arms*—or the marks and signs on his shield by which the name and family of a man were known, when he himself was covered from head to foot in iron mail.

27. **Norman Words** (*d*).—The terms connected with the chase are : **Brace, couple ; chase, course ; covert, copse, forest ; leveret, mews ; quarry, venison.** A few remarks about some of these may be interesting. **Brace** comes from the Old French *brace*, an arm (Mod. French *bras*) ; from the Latin *brachium*. The root-idea seems to be that which encloses or holds up. Thus *bracing* air is that which *strings* up the nerves and muscles ; and a *brace* of birds was two birds tied together with a string.—The word **forest** contains in itself a good deal of unwritten Norman history. It comes from the Latin adverb *foras*, out of doors. Hence, in Italy, a stranger or foreigner is still called a *forestiere*. A forest in Norman-French was not necessarily a breadth of land covered with trees ; it was simply land *out of* the jurisdiction of the common law. Hence, when William the Conqueror created the New Forest, he merely took the land *out of* the rule and charge of the common law, and put it under his own regal power and personal care. In land of this kind—much of which was kept for hunting in—trees were afterwards planted, partly to shelter large game, and partly to employ ground otherwise useless in growing timber.—**Mews** is a very odd word. It comes from the Latin verb *mutare*, to change. When the falcons employed in hunting were changing their feathers, or *moulting* (the word *moult* is the same as *mews* in a different dress), the French shut them in a cage, which they called **mue**—from *mutare*. Then the stables for horses were put in the same place ; and hence a row of stables has come to be called a **mews**.—**Quarry** is quite as strange. The word *quarry*, which means a mine of stones,

comes from the Latin *quadrāre*, to make square. But the hunting term *quarry* is of a quite different origin. That comes from the Latin *cor* (the heart), which the Old French altered into **quer**. When a wild beast was run down and killed, the heart and entrails were thrown to the dogs as their share of the hunt. Hence Milton says of the eagle, " He scents his quarry from afar."—The word **venison** comes to us, through French, from the Lat. *venāri*, to hunt ; and hence it means *hunted flesh*. The same word gives us *venery*—the term that was used in the fourteenth century, by Chaucer among others, for hunting.

28. Norman Words (*e*).—The Normans introduced into England their own system of law, their own law officers ; and hence, into the English language, came Norman-French law terms. The following are a few : **Assize, attorney ; chancellor, court ; judge, justice ; plaintiff, sue ; summons, trespass.** A few remarks about some of these may be useful. The **chancellor** (*cancellarius*) was the legal authority who sat behind lattice- work, which was called in Latin *cancelli*. This word means, primarily, *little crabs ;* and it is a diminutive from *cancer*, a crab. It was so called because the lattice-work looked like crabs' claws crossed. Our word *cancel* comes from the same root : it means to make cross lines through anything we wish deleted.—**Court** comes from the Latin *cors* or *cohors*, a sheep- pen. It afterwards came to mean an enclosure, and also a body of Roman soldiers.—The proper English word for a *judge* is **deemster** or **demster** (which appears as the proper name *Dempster*) ; and this is still the name for a judge in the Isle of Man. The French word comes from two Latin words, *dico*, I utter, and *jus*, right. The word **jus** is seen in the other French term which we have received from the Normans— **justice.**—**Sue** comes from the Old Fr. *suir*, which appears in Modern Fr. as *suivre*. It is derived from the Lat. word *sequor*, I follow (which gives our *sequel*) ; and we have compounds of it in *ensue, issue*, and *pursue*.—The **tres** in **trespass** is a French form of the Latin *trans*, beyond or across. *Trespass*, therefore, means to cross the bounds of right.

29. Norman Words (*f*).—Some of the church terms intro-

duced by the Norman-French are : **Altar, Bible**; **baptism,
ceremony**; **friar**; **tonsure**; **penance, relic.**—The Normans
gave us the words **title** and **dignity** themselves, and also
the following titles: **Duke, marquis**; **count, viscount**;
peer; **mayor,** and others.   A **duke** is a *leader ;* from the
Latin *dux* (= *duc-s*).   A **marquis** is a lord who has to ride
the *marches* or borders between one county, or between one
country, and another.   A marquis was also called a **Lord-
Marcher.**   The word **count** never took root in this island,
because its place was already occupied by the Danish name
earl ; but we preserve it in the names **countess** and **viscount**
—the latter of which means a person *in the place of* (L. *vice*)
a count.   **Peer** comes from the Latin *par,* an equal.   The
House of Peers is the House of Lords—that is, of those who
are, at least when in the House, *equal* in rank and *equal* in
power of voting.   It is a fundamental doctrine in English
law that every man "is to be tried by his *peers.*"—It is worthy
of note that, in general, the French names for different kinds
of food designated the **cooked** meats; while the names for
the **living** animals that furnish them are **English.**   Thus
we have *beef* and *ox ; mutton* and *sheep ; veal* and *calf ; pork*
and *pig.*   There is a remarkable passage in Sir Walter Scott's
'Ivanhoe,' which illustrates this fact with great force and picturesqueness :—

" ' Gurth, I advise thee to call off Fangs, and leave the herd to
their destiny, which, whether they meet with bands of travelling
soldiers, or of outlaws, or of wandering pilgrims, can be little
else than to be converted into Normans before morning, to thy
no small ease and comfort.'

" ' The swine turned Normans to my comfort ! ' quoth Gurth;
' expound that to me, Wamba, for my brain is too dull, and my
mind too vexed, to read riddles.'

" ' Why, how call you those grunting brutes running about on
their four legs ? ' demanded Wamba.

" ' Swine, fool, swine,' said the herd; ' every fool knows
that.'

" ' And swine is good Saxon,' said the jester; ' but how call you the sow when she is flayed, and drawn, and quartered, and hung up by the heels, like a traitor?'

"'Pork,' answered the swine-herd.

"'I am very glad every fool knows that too,' said Wamba; 'and pork, I think, is good Norman-French: and so when the brute lives, and is in the charge of a Saxon slave, she goes by her Saxon name; but becomes a Norman, and is called pork, when she is carried to the castle-hall to feast among the nobles; what dost thou think of this, friend Gurth, ha?'

"'It is but too true doctrine, friend Wamba, however it got into thy fool's pate.'

"'Nay, I can tell you more,' said Wamba, in the same tone; 'there is old Alderman Ox continues to hold his Saxon epithet, while he is under the charge of serfs and bondsmen such as thou, but becomes Beef, a fiery French gallant, when he arrives before the worshipful jaws that are destined to consume him. Myhneer Calf, too, becomes Monsieur de Veau in the like manner; he is Saxon when he requires tendance, and takes a Norman name when he becomes matter of enjoyment.'"

30. General Character of the Norman-French Contributions. —The Norman-French contributions to our language gave us a number of **general names** or **class-names**; while the names for **individual** things are, in general, of purely English origin. The words **animal** and **beast**, for example, are French (or Latin); but the words **fox, hound, whale, snake, wasp,** and **fly** are purely English.—The words **family, relation, parent, ancestor,** are French; but the names **father, mother, son, daughter, gossip,** are English.—The words **title** and **dignity** are French; but the words **king** and **queen, lord** and **lady, knight** and **sheriff,** are English.—Perhaps the most remarkable instance of this is to be found in the abstract terms employed for the offices and functions of State. Of these, the English language possesses only one—the word **kingdom.** Norman-French, on the other hand, has given us the words **realm, court, state, constitution, people, treaty, audience, navy, army,** and others—amounting in all to nearly forty. When, however, we come to terms denoting labour and work—such as agriculture and seafaring, we find the proportions entirely reversed. The English language, in such cases, contributes almost everything ; the French nearly nothing. In agriculture, while **plough, rake, harrow, flail,** and many others are English words, not a single term for an agricultural process or implement has been given us by the warlike Norman-French.—While the words **ship** and **boat; hull** and **fleet; oar** and **sail,** are all English, the Normans have presented us with only the single word **prow.** It is as if all the Norman conqueror had to do was to take his stand at the prow, gazing upon the land he was going to seize, while the Low-German sailors worked for him at oar and sail.—Again, while the names of the various parts of the body —**eye, nose, cheek, tongue, hand, foot,** and more than eighty others—are all English, we have received only about ten similar words from the French—such as **spirit** and **corpse; perspiration; face** and **stature.** Speaking broadly, we may say that all words that express **general notions,** or generalisations, are French or Latin ; while words that express **specific** actions or concrete existences are pure English. Mr Spalding observes— " We use a foreign term naturalised when we speak of ' colour ' universally ; but we fall back on our home stores if we have to tell what the colour is, calling it ' red ' or ' yellow,' ' white ' or ' black,' ' green ' or ' brown.' We are Romans when we speak in a *general* way of ' moving '; but we are Teutons if we ' leap ' or ' spring,' if we ' slip,' ' slide,' or ' fall,' if we ' walk,' ' run,' ' swim,' or ' ride,' if we ' creep ' or ' crawl ' or ' fly.' "

31. **Gains to English from Norman-French.**—The gains from the Norman-French contribution are large, and are also of very great importance. Mr Lowell says, that the Norman element came in as quickening leaven to the rather heavy and lumpy Saxon dough. It stirred the whole mass, gave new life to the language, a much higher and wider scope to the thoughts, much greater power and copiousness to the expression of our thoughts, and a finer and brighter rhythm to our English sentences. " To Chaucer," he says, in 'My Study Windows,' " French must have been almost as truly a mother tongue as English. In him we see the first result of the Norman yeast

upon the home-baked Saxon loaf. The flour had been honest, the paste well kneaded, but the inspiring leaven was wanting till the Norman brought it over. Chaucer works still in the solid material of his race, but with what airy lightness has he not infused it? Without ceasing to be English, he has escaped from being insular." Let us look at some of these gains a little more in detail.

32. Norman-French Synonyms.—We must not consider a **synonym** as a word that means exactly *the same thing* as the word of which it is a synonym; because then there would be neither room nor use for such a word in the language. A synonym is a word of the same meaning as another, but with a slightly different shade of meaning,—or it is used under different circumstances and in a different connection, or it puts the same idea under a new angle. **Begin** and **commence, will** and **testament,** are exact equivalents—are complete synonyms; but there are very few more of this kind in our language. The moment the genius of a language gets hold of two words of the same meaning, it sets them to do different kinds of work,—to express different parts or shades of that meaning. Thus **limb** and **member, luck** and **fortune,** have the same meaning; but we cannot speak of a *limb* of the Royal Society, or of the *luck* of the Rothschilds, who made their *fortune* by hard work and steady attention to business. We have, by the aid of the Norman-French contributions, **flower** as well as **bloom; branch** and **bough; purchase** and **buy; amiable** and **friendly; cordial** and **hearty; country** and **land; gentle** and **mild; desire** and **wish; labour** and **work; miserable** and **wretched.** These pairs of words enable poets and other writers to use the right word in the right place. And we, preferring our Saxon or good old English words to any French or Latin importations, prefer to speak of **a hearty welcome** instead of **a cordial reception;** of **a loving wife** instead of **an amiable consort;** of **a wretched man** instead of **a miserable individual.**

33. Bilingualism.—How did these Norman-French words find their way into the language? What was the road by which they came? What was the process that enabled them to find a place in and to strike deep root into our English soil? Did the learned men—the monks and the clergy—make a selection of words, write them in their books, and teach them to the English people? Nothing of the sort. The process was a much ruder one—but at the same time one much more practical, more effectual, and more lasting in its results. The two peoples—the Normans and the English—found that they had to live together. They met at church, in the market-place, in the drilling field, at the archery butts, in the courtyards of castles; and, on the battle-fields of France, the Saxon bowman showed that he could fight as well, as bravely, and even to better purpose than his lord —the Norman baron. At all these places, under all these circumstances, the Norman and the Englishman were obliged to speak with each other. Now arose a striking phenomenon. Every man, as Professor Earle puts it, turned himself as it were into a walking phrase-book or dictionary. When a Norman had to use a French word, he tried to put the English word for it alongside of the French word; when an Englishman used an English word, he joined with it the French equivalent. Then the language soon began to swarm with "yokes of words"; our words went in couples; and the habit then begun has continued down even to the present day. And thus it is that we possess such couples as **will and testament; act and deed; use and wont; aid and abet.** Chaucer's poems are full of these pairs. He joins together **hunting and venery** (though both words mean exactly the same thing); **nature and kind; cheere and face; pray and beseech; mirth and jollity.** Later on, the Prayer-Book, which was written in the years 1540 to 1559, keeps up the habit: and we find the pairs **acknowledge and confess; assemble and meet together; dissemble and cloak; humble and lowly.** To the more English part of the congregation the simple Saxon words would come home with kindly association; to others, the words *confess, assemble, dissemble,* and *humble* would speak with greater force and clearness. —Such is the phenomenon called by Professor Earle **bilingualism.** "It is, in fact," he says, "a putting of colloquial formulæ to do the duty of a French-English and English-French vocabulary." Even Hooker, who wrote at the end of the sixteenth century, seems to have been obliged to use these pairs; and we find in his writings the couples " cecity and blindness," "nocive and hurtful," "sense and meaning."

34. Losses of English from the Incoming of Norman-French. —(i) Before the coming of the Normans, the English language was in the habit of forming compounds with ease and effect. But, after the introduction of the Norman-French language, that power seems gradually to have disappeared; and ready-made French or Latin words usurped the place of the home-grown English compound. Thus **despair** pushed out **wanhope; suspicion** dethroned **wantrust; bidding - sale** was expelled by **auction; learning-knight** by **disciple; rime-craft** by the Greek word **arithmetic; gold-hoard** by **treasure; book-hoard** by **library; earth - tilth** by **agriculture; wonstead** by **residence;** and so with a large number of others.—Many English words, moreover, had their meanings depreciated and almost degraded; and the words themselves lost their ancient rank and dignity. Thus the Norman conquerors put their foot—literally and metaphorically—on the Saxon **chair,**[1] which thus became a **stool,** or a **footstool. Thatch,** which is a doublet of the word **deck,** was the name for any kind of roof; but the coming of the Norman-French lowered it to indicate a *roof of straw.* **Whine** was used for the weeping or crying of human beings; but it is now restricted to the cry of a dog. **Hide** was the generic term for the skin of any animal; it is now limited in modern English to the skin of a beast.—The most damaging result upon our language was that it entirely **stopped the growth of English words.** We could, for example, make out of the word **burn**—the derivatives **brunt, brand, brandy, brown, brimstone,** and others; but this power died out with the coming in of the Norman - French language. After that, instead of growing our own words, we

---

[1] *Chair* is the Norman-French form of the French *chaise.* The Germans still call a chair a *stuhl;* and among the English, *stool* was the universal name till the twelfth century.

adopted them ready-made.—Professor Craik compares the English and Latin languages to two banks; and says that, when the Normans came over, the account at the English bank was closed, and we drew only upon the Latin bank. But the case is worse than this. English lost its power of growth and expansion from the centre; from this time, it could only add to its bulk by borrowing and conveying from without—by the external accretion of foreign words.

35. Losses of English from the Incoming of Norman-French. —(ii) The arrestment of growth in the purely English part of our language, owing to the irruption of Norman-French, and also to the ease with which we could take a ready-made word from Latin or from Greek, killed off an old power which we once possessed, and which was not without its own use and expressiveness. This was the power of making compound words. The Greeks in ancient times had, and the Germans in modern times have, this power in a high degree. Thus a Greek comic poet has a word of fourteen syllables, which may be thus translated—

" Meanly-rising-early-and-hurrying-to-the-tribunal-to-denounce-another-
for-an-infraction-of-the-law-concerning-the-exportation-of-figs."[1]

And the Germans have a compound like " the-all-to-nothing-crushing philosopher." The Germans also say *iron-path* for *railway*, *handshoe* for *glove*, and *finger-hat* for *thimble*. We also possessed this power at one time, and employed it both in proper and in common names. Thus we had and have the names *Brakespear*, *Shakestaff*, *Shakespear*, *Golightly*, *Dolittle*, *Standfast*; and the common nouns *want-wit*, *find-fault*, *mumble-news* (for *tale-bearer*), *pinch-penny* (for *miser*), *slugabed*. In older times we had *three-foot-stool*, *three-man-beetle*[2]; *stone-cold*, *heaven-bright*, *honey-sweet*, *snail-slow*, *nut-brown*, *lily-livered* (for *cowardly*); *brand-fire-new*; *earth-wandering*, *wind-dried*, *thunder-blasted*, *death-doomed*, and many others. But such words as *forbears* or *fore-elders* have been pushed out by *ances-*

---

[1] In two words, a *fig-shower* or *sycophant*.
[2] A club for beating clothes, that could be handled only by three men.

tors ; forewit by *caution* or *prudence ;* and *inwit* by *conscience*. Mr Barnes, the Dorsetshire poet, would like to see these and similar compounds restored, and thinks that we might well return to the old clear well-springs of "English undefiled," and make our own compounds out of our own words.   He even carries his desires into the region of English grammar, and, for *degrees of comparison*, proposes the phrase *pitches of suchness*.   Thus, instead of the Latin word *omnibus*, he would have *folk-wain ;* for the Greek *botany*, he would substitute *wort-lore ;* for *auction*, he would give us *bode-sale ; globule* he would replace with *ballkin ;* the Greek word *horizon* must give way to the pure English *sky-edge ;* and, instead of *quadrangle*, he would have us all write and say *four-winkle*.

36. Losses of English from the Incoming of Norman-French.—(iii) When once a way was made for the entrance of French words into our English language, the immigrations were rapid and numerous.   Hence there were many changes both in the grammar and in the vocabulary of English from the year 1100, the year in which we may suppose those English-men who were living at the date of the battle of Hastings had died out.   These changes were more or less rapid, according to circumstances.   But perhaps the most rapid and remarkable change took place in the lifetime of William Caxton, the great printer, who was born in 1410.   In his preface to his translation of the 'Æneid' of Virgil, which he published in 1490, when he was eighty years of age, he says that he cannot understand old books that were written when he was a boy—that "the olde Englysshe is more lyke to dutche than englysshe," and that "our langage now vsed varyeth ferre from that whiche was vsed and spoken when I was borne.   For we Englysshemen ben borne ynder the domynacyon of the mone [moon], which is neuer stedfaste, but euer wauerynge, wexynge one season, and waneth and dycreaseth another season."   This as regards time.—But he has the same complaint to make as regards place.   "Comyn englysshe that is spoken in one shyre varyeth from another." And he tells an odd story in illustration of this fact.   He tells about certain merchants who were in a ship " in Tamyse " (on the

Thames), who were bound for Zealand, but were wind-stayed at the Foreland, and took it into their heads to go on shore there. One of the merchants, whose name was Sheffelde, a mercer, entered a house, "and axed for mete, and specyally he axyd after eggys." But the "goode-wyf" replied that she "coude speke no frenshe." The merchant, who was a steady English-man, lost his temper, "for he also coude speke no frenshe, but wolde have hadde eggys; and she understode hym not." Fortu-nately, a friend happened to join him in the house, and he acted as interpreter. The friend said that "he wolde have eyren; then the goode wyf sayde that she understod hym wel." And then the simple-minded but much-perplexed Caxton goes on to say: "Loo! what sholde a man in thyse dayes now wryte, eggüs or eyren?" Such were the difficulties that beset printers and writers in the close of the fifteenth century.

37. Latin of the Fourth Period.—(i) This contribution differs very essentially in character from the last. The Norman-French contribution was a gift from a people to a people—from living beings to living beings; this new contribution was rather a con-veyance of words from books to books, and it never influenced —in any great degree—the **spoken language** of the English people. The ear and the mouth carried the Norman-French words into our language; the eye, the pen, and the printing-press were the instruments that brought in the Latin words of the Fourth Period. The Norman-French words that came in took and kept their place in the spoken language of the masses of the people; the Latin words that we received in the sixteenth and seventeenth centuries kept their place in the written or printed language of books, of scholars, and of literary men. These new Latin words came in with the **Revival of Learning,** which is also called the **Renascence.**

The Turks attacked and took Constantinople in the year **1453;** and the great Greek and Latin scholars who lived in that city hurriedly packed up their priceless manuscripts and books, and fled to all parts of Italy, Germany, France, and even into England. The loss of the East became the gain of the West. These scholars became teachers; they taught the Greek

and Roman classics to eager and earnest learners; and thus a
new impulse was given to the study of the great masterpieces of
human thought and literary style.   And so it came to pass in
course of time that every one who wished to become an educated man studied the literature of Greece and Rome.   Even
women took to the study.   Lady Jane Grey was a good Greek
and Latin scholar; and so was Queen Elizabeth.   From this
time began an enormous importation of Latin words into our
language.   Being imported by the eye and the pen, they suffered
little or no change; the spirit of the people did not influence
them in the least—neither the organs of speech nor the ear
affected either the pronunciation or the spelling of them.   If we
look down the columns of any English dictionary, we shall find
these later Latin words in hundreds.   *Opinionem* became
opinion; *factionem*, **faction**; *orationem*, **oration**; *pungentem*
passed over in the form of **pungent** (though we had *poignant*
already from the French); *pauperem* came in as **pauper**; and
separatum became **separate**.

38. **Latin of the Fourth Period**. — (ii) This went on to
such an extent in the sixteenth and the beginning of the
seventeenth century, that one writer says of those who spoke
and wrote this Latinised English, "If some of their mothers
were alive, they were not able to tell what they say."   And
Sir Thomas Browne (1605 - 1682) remarks : "If elegancy
(= the use of Latin words) still proceedeth, and English
pens maintain that stream we have of late observed to flow
from many, we shall, within a few years, be fain to learn Latin
to understand English, and a work will prove of equal facility
in either."   Mr Alexander Gill, an eminent schoolmaster, and
the then head-master of St Paul's School, where, among his
other pupils, he taught John Milton, wrote a book in 1619 on
the English language; and, among other remarks, he says : "O
harsh lips! I now hear all around me such words as *common,
vices, envy, malice;* even *virtue, study, justice, pity, mercy, com-
passion, profit, commodity, colour, grace, favour, acceptance.*
But whither, I pray, in all the world, have you banished those
words which our forefathers used for these new-fangled ones?

Are our words to be executed like our citizens?"   And he calls this fashion of using Latin words "the new mauge in our speaking and writing."   But the fashion went on growing; and even uneducated people thought it a clever thing to use a Latin instead of a good English word.   Samuel Rowlánds, a writer in the seventeenth century, ridicules this affectation in a few lines of verse.   He pretends that he was out walking on the highroad, and met a countryman who wanted to know what o'clock it was, and whether he was on the right way to the town or village he was making for.   The writer saw at once that he was a simple bumpkin; and, when he heard that he had lost his way, he turned up his nose at the poor fellow, and ordered him to be off at once.   Here are the lines :—

> " As on the way I itinerated,
> A rural person I obviated,
> Interrogating time's transitation,
> And of the passage demonstration.
> My apprehension did ingenious scan
> That he was merely a simplician ;
> So, when I saw he was extravagánt,
> Unto the óbscure vulgar consonánt,
> I bade him vanish most promiscuously,
> And not contaminate my company."

39. Latin of the Fourth Period.—(iii) What happened in the case of the Norman-French contribution, happened also in this. The language became saturated with these new Latin words, until it became satiated, then, as it were, disgusted, and would take no more.   Hundreds of

> " Long-tailed words in *osity* and *ation* "

crowded into the English language; but many of them were doomed to speedy expulsion.   Thus words like *discerptibility*, *supervacaneousness, septentrionality, ludibundness* (love of sport), came in in crowds.   The verb *intenerate* tried to turn out *soften ;* and *deturpate* to take the place of *defile*.   But good writers, like Bacon and Raleigh, took care to avoid the use of such terms, and to employ only those Latin words which gave them the power to indicate a new idea—a new meaning or a new shade of meaning.   And when we come to the eighteenth century, we find that a writer like Addison would have shuddered at the very mention of such "inkhorn terms."

40. Eye-Latin and Ear-Latin.—(i) One slight influence produced by this spread of devotion to classical Latin—to the Latin of Cicero and Livy, of Horace and Virgil—was to alter the spelling of French words.   We had already received—through the ear—the French words *assaute, aventure, defaut, dette, vitaille,* and others.   But when our scholars became accustomed to the book-form of these words in Latin books, they gradually altered them—for the eye and ear—into *assault, adventure, default, debt,* and *victuals.*   They went further.   A large number of Latin words that already existed in the language in their Norman-French form (for we must not forget that French is Latin "with the ends bitten off"—changed by being spoken peculiarly and heard imperfectly) were reintroduced in their original Latin form.   Thus we had **caitiff** from the Normans; but we reintroduced it in the shape of **captive,** which comes almost unaltered from the Latin *captivum.*   **Feat** we had from the Normans; but the Latin *factum,* which provided the word, presented us with a second form of it in the word **fact.**   Such words might be called **Ear-Latin** and **Eye-Latin; Mouth-Latin** and **Book-Latin; Spoken Latin** and **Written Latin;** or Latin at second-hand and Latin at first-hand.

41. Eye-Latin and Ear-Latin.—(ii) This coming in of the same word by two different doors—by the Eye and by the Ear—has given rise to the phenomenon of **Doublets.**   The following is a list of **Latin Doublets;** and it will be noticed that Latin [1] stands for Latin at first-hand—from books; and Latin [2] for Latin at second-hand—through the Norman-French.

LATIN DOUBLETS OR DUPLICATES.

LATIN.	LATIN [1].	LATIN [2].
Antecessorem	Antecessor	Ancestor.
Benedictionem	Benediction	Benison.
Cadentia (Low Lat. noun)	Cadence	Chance.
Captivum	Captive	Caitiff.

Conceptionem	Conception	Conceit.
Consuetudinem	Consuetude	{ Custom. Costume.
Cophinum	Coffin	Coffer.
Corpus (a body)	Corpse	Corps.
Debitum (something owed)	Debit	- Debt.
Defectum (something wanting)	Defect	Defeat.
Dilatāre	Dilate	Delay.
Exemplum	Example	Sample.
Fabrīca (a workshop)	Fabric	Forge.
Factionem	Faction	Fashion.
Factum	Fact	Feat.
Fidelitatem	Fidelity	Fealty.
Fragilem	Fragile	Frail.
Gentīlis (belonging to a *gens* or family)	Gentile	Gentle.
Historia	History	Story.
Hospitale	Hospital	Hotel.
Lectionem	Lection	Lesson.
Legalem	Legal	Loyal.
Magister	Master	Mr.
Majorem (greater)	Major	Mayor.
Maledictionem	Malediction	Malison.
Moneta	Mint	Money.
Nutrimentum	Nutriment	Nourishment.
Orationem	Oration	Orison (a prayer).
Paganum (a dweller in a *pagus* or country district)	Pagan	Payne (a proper name).
Particulam (a little part)	Particle	Parcel.
Pauperem	Pauper	Poor.
Penitentiam	Penitence	Penance.
Persecutum	Persecute	Pursue.
Potionem (a draught)	Potion	Poison.
Pungentem	Pungent	Poignant.
Quietum	Quiet	Coy.
Radius	Radius	Ray.
Regālem	Regal	Royal.
Respectum	Respect	Respite.
Securum	Secure	Sure.
Seniorem	Senior	Sir.
Separatum	Separate	Sever.
Species	Species	Spice.
Statum	State	Estate.
Tractum	Tract	Trait.
Traditionem	Tradition	Treason.
Zelosum	Zealous	Jealous.

42. Remarks on the above Table.—The word **benison**, a blessing, may be contrasted with its opposite, **malison**, a curse. —**Cadence** is the falling of sounds; **chance** the befalling of events.—A **caitiff** was at first a *captive*—then a person who made no proper defence, but *allowed* himself to be taken captive. —A **corps** is a *body* of troops.—The word **sample** is found, in older English, in the form of **ensample.**—A **feat** of arms is a deed or **fact** of arms, *par excellence.*—To understand how **fragile** became **frail**, we must pronounce the **g** hard, and notice how the hard guttural falls easily away—as in our own native words *flail* and *hail*, which formerly contained a hard **g.**—A **major** is a *greater* captain; a **mayor** is a *greater* magistrate.—A **magister** means a *bigger man*—as opposed to a **minister** (from *minus*), a smaller man.—**Moneta** was the name given to a stamped coin, because these coins were first struck in the temple of Juno Moneta, Juno the Adviser or the Warner. (From the same root—**mon**—come *monition, admonition; monitor; admonish.*) —Shakespeare uses the word **orison** freely for *prayer*, as in the address of Hamlet to Ophelia, where he says, "Nymph, in thy orisons, be all my sins remembered!"—**Poor** comes to us from an Old French word *poure;* the newer French is *pauvre.*—To understand the vanishing of the **g** sound in *poignant*, we must remember that the Romans sounded it always hard.—**Sever** we get through *separate*, because **p** and **v** are both labials, and therefore easily interchangeable.—**Treason**—with its **s** instead of ti—may be compared with **benison, malison, orison, poison,** and **reason.**

43. Conclusions from the above Table.—If we examine the table on page 231 with care, we shall come to several undeniable conclusions.   (i) First, the words which come to us direct from Latin are found more in books than in everyday speech. (ii) Secondly, they are longer.   The reason is that the words that have come through French have been worn down by the careless pronunciation of many generations—by that desire for ease in the pronouncing of words which characterises all languages, and have at last been compelled to take that form which was least difficult to pronounce.   (iii) Thirdly, the two sets of words have, in each case, either (a) very different meanings, or (b) different shades of meaning. There is no likeness of meaning in *cadence* and *chance*, except the common meaning of *fall* which belongs to the root from which they both spring. And the different shades of meaning between **history** and **story**, between **regal** and **royal**, between **persecute** and **pursue**, are also quite plainly marked, and are of the greatest use in composition.

44. Latin Triplets.—Still more remarkable is the fact that there are in our language words that have made three appearances—one through Latin, one through Norman-French, and one through ordinary French. These seem to live quietly side by side in the language; and no one asks by what claim they are here. They are useful : that is enough. These triplets are— **regal, royal,** and **real**; **legal, loyal,** and **leal**; **fidelity, faithfulness,**[1] and **fealty.** The adjective **real** we no longer possess in the sense of *royal*, but Chaucer uses it; and it still exists in the noun **real-m.** **Leal** is most used in Scotland, where it has a settled abode in the well-known phrase "the land o' the leal."

45. Greek Doublets.—The same double introduction, which we noticed in the case of Latin words, takes place in regard to Greek words. It seems to have been forgotten that our English forms of them had been already given us by St Augustine and the Church, and a newer form of each was reintroduced. The following are a few examples :—

GREEK.	OLDER FORM.	LATER FORM.
Adamanta[2] (the untameable)	Diamond	Adamant.
Balsamon	Balm	Balsam.
Blasphōmein (to speak ill of)	Blame	Blaspheme.
Cheirourgon[2] (a worker with the hand)	Chirurgeon	Surgeon.

[1] The word *faith* is a true French word with an English ending—the ending th. Hence it is a hybrid. The old French word was *fei*—from the Latin *fidem ;* and the ending th was added to make it look more like *truth, wealth, health,* and other purely English words.

[2] The accusative or objective case is given in all these words.

Dactŭlon (a finger)	Date (the fruit)	Dactyl.
Phantasia	Fancy	Phantasy.
Phantasma (an appearance)	Phantom	Phantasm.
Presbuteron (an elder)	Priest	Presbyter.
Paralysis	Palsy	Paralysis.
Scandŭlon	Slander	Scandal.

It may be remarked of the word *fancy*, that, in Shakespeare's time, it meant *love* or *imagination*—

> "Tell me, where is *fancy* bred,
> Or in the heart, or in the head ?"

It is now restricted to mean a lighter and less serious kind of imagination. Thus we say that Milton's 'Paradise Lost' is a work of imagination; but that Moore's 'Lalla Rookh' is a product of the poet's fancy.

46. Characteristics of the Two Elements of English.—If we keep our attention fixed on the two chief elements in our language—the English element and the Latin element—the Teutonic and the Romance—we shall find some striking qualities manifest themselves. We have already said that whole sentences can be made containing only English words, while it is impossible to do this with Latin or other foreign words. Let us take two passages — one from a daily newspaper, and the other from Shakespeare :—

(i) "We find the *functions* of such an *official defined* in the *Act*. He is to be a *legally qualified medical practitioner* of skill and *experience*, to *inspect* and *report periodically* on the *sanitary condition* of town or *district*; to *ascertain* the *existence* of *diseases*, more *especially epidemics increasing* the *rates* of *mortality*, and to *point* out the *existence* of any *nuisances* or other *local causes*, which are likely to *originate* and *maintain* such *diseases*, and *injuriously affect* the health of the *inhabitants* of such town or *district*; to take *cognisance* of the *existence* of any *contagious disease*, and to *point* out the most *efficacious means* for the *ventilation* of *chapels*, *schools*, *registered lodging*-houses, and other *public* buildings."

In this passage, all the words in italics are either Latin or Greek. But, if the purely English words were left out, the sentence would fall into ruins—would become a mere rubbish-heap of words. It is the small particles that give life and motion to each sentence. They are the joints and hinges on which the whole sentence moves.—Let us now look at a passage from Shakespeare. It is from the speech of Macbeth, after he has made up his mind to murder Duncan :—

> (ii) " Go bid thy *mistress*, when my drink is ready,
> She strike upon the bell. Get thee to bed !—
> Is this a dagger which I see before me,
> The handle toward my hand ? Come ! let me clutch thee !
> —I have thee not ; and yet I see thee still."

In this passage there is only one Latin (or French) word—the word *mistress*. If Shakespeare had used the word **lady**, the passage would have been entirely English.—The passage from the newspaper deals with large **generalisations**; that from Shakespeare with individual **acts** and **feelings**—with things that come **home** " to the business and bosom " of man as man. Every master of the English language understands well the art of mingling the two elements—so as to obtain a fine effect; and none better than writers like Shakespeare, Milton, Gray, and Tennyson. Shakespeare makes Antony say of Cleopatra :—

> " Age cannot wither her ; nor *custom* stale
> Her infinite *variety*."

Here the French (or Latin) words *custom* and *variety* form a vivid contrast to the English verb *stale*, throw up its meaning and colour, and give it greater prominence.—Milton makes Eve say :—

> " I thither went
> With *inexperienc'd* thought, and laid me down
> On the green bank, to look into the *clear*
> Smooth *lake*, that to me seem'd another sky."

Here the words *inexperienced* and *clear* give variety to the sameness of the English words.—Gray, in the Elegy, has this verse:—

> " The breezy call of *incense*-breathing morn,
> The swallow twittering from the straw-built shed,
> The cock's shrill *clarion* or the *echoing* horn,
> No more shall rouse them from their lowly bed."

Here *incense, clarion,* and *echoing* give a vivid colouring to the
plainer hues of the homely English phrases.—Tennyson, in the
Lotos-Eaters, vi., writes :—

> " Dear is the *memory* of our wedded lives,
> And dear the last *embraces* of our wives
> And their warm tears : but all hath *suffer'd change ;*
> For *surely* now our household hearths are cold :
> Our sons *inherit* us : our looks are *strange :*
> And we should come like ghosts to *trouble joy.*"

Most powerful is the introduction of the French words *suffered
change, inherit, strange,* and *trouble joy ;* for they give with
painful force the contrast of the present state of desolation with
the homely rest and happiness of the old abode, the love of the
loving wives, the faithfulness of the stalwart sons.

47. English and other Doublets.—We have already seen
how, by the presentation of the same word at two different
doors—the door of Latin and the door of French—we are in
possession of a considerable number of doublets. But this
phenomenon is not limited to Latin and French—is not solely
due to the contributions we receive from these languages. We
find it also **within** English itself; and causes of the most
different description bring about the same results. For various
reasons, the English language is very rich in doublets. It
possesses nearly five hundred pairs of such words. The language
is all the richer for having them, as it is thereby enabled to
give fuller and clearer expression to the different shades and
delicate varieties of meaning in the mind.

48. The sources of doublets are various. But five different
causes seem chiefly to have operated in producing them. They
are due to differences of **pronunciation;** to differences in **spelling;** to **contractions** for convenience in daily speech; to
differences in **dialects;** and to the fact that many of them come
from **different languages.** Let us look at a few examples of
each. At bottom, however, all these differences will be found
to resolve themselves into **differences of pronunciation.** They
are either differences in the pronunciation of the same word by

different tribes, or by men in different counties, who speak different dialects; or by men of different nations.

49. Differences in Pronunciation.—From this source we have **parson** and **person** (the parson being the *person* or representative of the Church); **sop** and **soup**; **task** and **tax** (the sk has here become **ks**); **thread** and **thrid**; **ticket** and **etiquette**; **sauce** and **souse** (to steep in brine); **squall** and **squeal**.

50. Differences in Spelling.—**To** and **too** are the same word —one being used as a preposition, the other as an adverb; **of** and **off, from** and **fro,** are only different spellings, which represent different functions or uses of the same word; **onion** and **union** are the same word. An union[1] comes from the Latin **unus,** one, and it meant a large single pearl—a unique jewel; the word was then applied to the plant, the head of which is of a pearl-shape.

51. Contractions.—Contraction has been a pretty fruitful source of doublets in English. A long word has a syllable or two cut off; or two or three are compressed into one. Thus **example** has become **sample; alone** appears also as **lone; amend** has been shortened into **mend; defend** has been cut down into **fend** (as in **fender); manœuvre** has been contracted into **manure** (both meaning originally *to work with the hand*); **madam** becomes **'m** in **yes 'm**[2]; and **presbyter** has been squeezed down into **priest.**[3] Other examples of contraction are: **capital** and **cattle; chirurgeon** (a worker with the hand) and **surgeon; cholera** and **choler** (from **chŏlos,** the Greek word for *bile*); **disport** and **sport; estate** and **state; esquire** and **squire; Egyptian** and

---

[1] In Hamlet v. 2. 283, Shakespeare makes the King say—

> "The King shall drink to Hamlet's better breath;
> And in the cup an union shall he throw."

[2] Professor Max Müller gives this as the most remarkable instance of cutting down. The Latin *mea domina* became in French *madame;* in English *ma'am;* and, in the language of servants, *'m.*

[3] Milton says, in one of his sonnets—

> "New Presbyter is but old Priest writ large."

From the etymological point of view, the truth is just the other way about. *Priest* is old *Presbyter* writ small.

gipsy; emmet and ant; gammon and game; grandfather
and gaffer; grandmother and gammer; iota (the Greek
letter i) and jot; maximum and maxim; mobile and mob;
mosquito and musket; papa and pope; periwig and wig;
poesy and posy; procurator and proctor; shallop and
sloop; unity and unit. It is quite evident that the above
pairs of words, although in reality one, have very different
meanings and uses.

52. Difference of English Dialects. — Another source of
doublets is to be found in the dialects of the English language.
Almost every county in England has its own dialect; but three
main dialects stand out with great prominence in our older
literature, and these are the **Northern,** the **Midland,** and the
Southern. The grammar of these dialects[1] was different; their
pronunciation of words was different—and this has given rise to
a splitting of one word into two. In the North, we find a hard
c, as in the *caster* of **Lancaster**; in the Midlands, a soft c, as
in **Leicester**; in the South, a ch, as in **Winchester.** We shall
find similar differences of hardness and softness in ordinary
words. Thus we find **kirk** and **church; canker** and **cancer;
canal** and **channel; deck** and **thatch; drill** and **thrill; fan**
and **van** (in a winnowing-machine); **fitch** and **vetch; hale** and
whole; mash and **mess; naught, nought,** and **not; pike,
peak,** and **beak; poke** and **pouch; quid** (a piece of tobacco for
chewing) and **cud** (which means the thing *chewed*); **reave**
and **rob; ridge** and **rig; scabby** and **shabby; scar** and
share; screech and **shriek; shirt** and **skirt; shuffle** and
scuffle; spray and **sprig; wain** and **waggon**—and other pairs.
All of these are but different modes of pronouncing the same
word in different parts of England; but the genius of the
language has taken advantage of these different **ways of pronouncing** to make different **words** out of them, and to give
them different functions, meanings, and uses.

[1] See p. 242.

CHAPTER III.

1. The Oldest English Synthetic.—The oldest English, or Anglo-Saxon, that was brought over here in the fifth century, was a language that showed the relations of words to each other by adding different endings to words, or by **synthesis.** These endings are called **inflexions.** Latin and Greek are highly inflected languages; French and German have many more inflexions than modern English; and ancient English (or Anglo-Saxon) also possessed a large number of inflexions.

2. Modern English Analytic.—When, instead of inflexions, a language employs small particles—such as prepositions, auxiliary verbs, and suchlike words—to express the relations of words to each other, such a language is called **analytic** or **non-inflexional.** When we say, as we used to say in the oldest English, "God is ealra cyninga cyning," we speak a synthetic language. But when we say, "God is king *of* all kings," then we employ an analytic or uninflected language.

3. Short View of the History of English Grammar.—From the time when the English language came over to this island, it has grown steadily in the number of its words. On the other hand, it has lost just as steadily in the number of its inflexions. Put in a broad and somewhat rough fashion, it may be said that—

(i) **Up to the year 1100—one generation after the Battle of Senlac —the English language was a** SYNTHETIC **Language.**

(ii) From the year 1100 or thereabouts, English has been losing its inflexions, and gradually becoming more and more an ANALYTIC Language.

4. Causes of this Change.—Even before the coming of the Danes and the Normans, the English people had shown a tendency to get rid of some of their inflexions. A similar tendency can be observed at the present time among the Germans of the Rhine Province, who often drop an n at the end of a word, and show in other respects a carelessness about grammar. But, when a foreign people comes among natives, such a tendency is naturally encouraged, and often greatly increased. The natives discover that these inflexions are not so very important, if only they can get their meaning rightly conveyed to the foreigners. Both parties, accordingly, come to see that the **root** of the word is the most important element; they stick to that, and they come to neglect the mere inflexions. Moreover, the accent in English words always struck the root; and hence this part of the word always fell on the ear with the greater force, and carried the greater weight. When the Danes —who spoke a cognate language—began to settle in England, the tendency to drop inflexions increased; but when the Normans—who spoke an entirely different language—came, the tendency increased enormously, and the inflexions of Anglo-Saxon began to "fall as the leaves fall" in the dry wind of a frosty October. Let us try to trace some of these changes and losses.

5. Grammar of the First Period, 450-1100.—The English of this period is called the **Oldest English** or **Anglo-Saxon.** The gender of nouns was arbitrary, or—it may be—poetical; it did not, as in modern English it does, follow the sex. Thus **nama,** a name, was masculine; **tunge,** a tongue, feminine; and **eáge,** an eye, neuter. Like *nama,* the proper names of men ended in *a*; and we find such names as Isa, Offa, Penda, as the names of kings. Nouns at this period had five cases, with inflexions for each; now we possess but one inflexion—that for the possessive. —Even the definite article was inflected.—The infinitive of verbs ended in **an;** and the sign *to*—which we received from the

Danes—was not in use, except for the dative of the infinitive. This dative infinitive is still preserved in such phrases as "a house to let;" "bread to eat;" "water to drink."—The present participle ended in **ende** (in the North **ande**). This present participle may be said still to exist—in spoken, but not in written speech; for some people regularly say *walkin, goin*, for *walking* and *going*.—The plural of the present indicative ended in **ath** for all three persons. In the perfect tense, the plural ending was **on**.—There was no future tense; the work of the future was done by the present tense. Fragments of this usage still survive in the language, as when we say, "He goes up to town next week." — Prepositions governed various cases; and not always the objective (or accusative), as they do now.

6. Grammar of the Second Period, 1100-1250.—The English of this period is called **Early English**. Even before the coming of the Normans, the inflexions of our language had—as we have seen—begun to drop off, and it was slowly on the way to becoming an analytic language. The same changes—the same simplification of grammar, has taken place in nearly every Low German language. But the coming of the Normans hastened these changes, for it made the inflexional endings of words of much less practical importance to the English themselves.—Great changes took place in the pronunciation also. The hard **c or k** was softened into **ch**; and the hard guttural **g** was refined into a **y** or even into a silent **w**.—A remarkable addition was made to the language. The Oldest English or Anglo-Saxon had no indefinite article. They said *ofer stán* for *on a rock*. But, as the French have made the article **un** out of the Latin **unus,** so the English pared down the northern **ane** (= **one**) into the article **an or a**. The Anglo-Saxon definite article was **se, seo, þaet**; and in the grammar of this Second Period it became **þe, þeo, þe**.—The French plural in **es** took the place of the English plural in **en**. But *housen* and *shoon* existed for many centuries after the Norman coming; and Mr Barnes, the Dorsetshire poet, still deplores the ugly sound of *nests* and *fists,* and would like to be able to say and to write *nesten* and *fisten.*—The dative plural, which ended in **um**, becomes an **e** or an **en**. The **um,**

however, still exists in the form of **om** in **seldom** (=at few times) and **whilom** (=in old times).—The gender of nouns falls into confusion, and begins to show a tendency to follow the sex. —Adjectives show a tendency to drop several of their inflexions, and to become as serviceable and accommodating as they are now—when they are the same with all numbers, genders, and cases.—The **an** of the infinitive becomes **en,** and sometimes even the n is dropped.—**Shall** and **will** begin to be used as tense-auxiliaries for the future tense.

7. **Grammar of the Third Period, 1250-1350.**—The English of this period is often called **Middle English.**—The definite article still preserves a few inflexions.—Nouns that were once masculine or feminine· become neuter, for the sake of convenience.—The possessive in **es** becomes general.—Adjectives make their plural in **e.**—The infinitive now takes **to** before it—except after a few verbs, like *bid, see, hear,* etc.—The present participle in **inge** makes its appearance about the year 1300.

8. **Grammar of the Fourth Period, 1350-1485.**—This may be called **Later Middle English.** An old writer of the fourteenth century points out that, in his time—and before it—the English language was " a-deled a thre," divided into three ; that is, that there were three main dialects, the **Northern,** the **Midland,** and the **Southern.** There were many differences in the grammar of these dialects ; but the chief of these differences is found in the plural of the present indicative of the verb. This part of the verb formed its plurals in the following manner :—

NORTHERN.	MIDLAND.	SOUTHERN.
We hopës	We hopen	We hopeth.
You hopës	You hopen	You hopeth.
They hopës	They hopen	They hopeth.[1]

In time the Midland dialect conquered ; and the East Midland form of it became predominant all over England. As early as the beginning of the thirteenth century, this dialect had thrown off most of the old inflexions, and had become almost as flexion-

---

[1] This plural we still find in the famous Winchester motto, " Manners maketh man."

less as the English of the present day. Let us note a few of the more prominent changes.—The first personal pronoun **Ic** or **Ich** loses the guttural, and becomes **I**.—The pronouns **him, them,** and **whom,** which are true datives, are used either as datives or as objectives.—The imperative plural ends in **eth.** "Riseth up," Chaucer makes one of his characters say, "and stondeth by me!"—The useful and almost ubiquitous letter **e** comes in as a substitute for **a, u,** and even **an.** Thus **nama** becomes **name, sunu** (son) becomes **sune,** and **withutan** changes into **withute.**—The dative of adjectives is used as an adverb. Thus we find **softë, brightë** employed like our **softly, brightly.** —The n in the infinitive has fallen away; but the **ë** is sounded as a separate syllable. Thus we find **brekë, smitë** for *breken* and *smiten.*

9. General View.—In the time of King Alfred, the West-Saxon speech—the Wessex dialect—took precedence of the rest, and became the literary dialect of England. But it had not, and could not have, any influence on the spoken language of other parts of England, for the simple reason that very few persons were able to travel, and it took days—and even weeks—for a man to go from Devonshire to Yorkshire. In course of time the Midland dialect—that spoken between the Humber and the Thames — became the predominant dialect of England; and the East Midland variety of this dialect became the parent of modern standard English. This predominance was probably due to the fact that it, soonest of all, got rid of its inflexions, and became most easy, pleasant, and convenient to use. And this disuse of inflexions was itself probably due to the early Danish settlements in the east, to the larger number of Normans in that part of England, to the larger number of thriving towns, and to the greater and more active communication between the eastern seaports and the Continent. The inflexions were first confused, then weakened, then forgotten, finally lost. The result was an extreme simplification, which still benefits all learners of the English language. Instead of spending a great deal of time on the learning of a large number of inflexions, which are to them arbitrary and meaningless, foreigners have only to fix their attention on the words and phrases themselves, that is, on the very pith and marrow of the language—indeed, on the language itself.   Hence the great German grammarian Grimm, and others, predict that English will spread itself all over the world, and become the universal language of the future.   In addition to this almost complete sweeping away of all inflexions,—which made Dr Johnson say, "Sir, the English language has no grammar at all,"—there were other remarkable and useful results which accrued from the coming in of the Norman-French and other foreign elements.

10. Monosyllables.—The stripping off of the inflexions of our language cut a large number of words down to the root. Hundreds, if not thousands, of our verbs were dissyllables, but, by the gradual loss of the ending **en** (which was in Anglo-Saxon **an**), they became monosyllables.   Thus **bindan, drincan, findan,** became **bind, drink, find;** and this happened with hosts of other verbs.   Again, the expulsion of the guttural, which the Normans never could or would take to, had the effect of compressing many words of two syllables into one.   Thus **haegel, twaegen,** and **faegen,** became **hail, twain,** and **fain.**— In these and other ways it has come to pass that the present English is to a very large extent of a monosyllabic character.   So much is this the case, that whole books have been written for children in monosyllables.   It must be confessed that the monosyllabic style is often dull, but it is always serious and homely. We can find in our translation of the Bible whole verses that are made up of words of only one syllable.   Many of the most powerful passages in Shakespeare, too, are written in monosyllables.   The same may be said of hundreds of our proverbs—such as, "Cats hide their claws"; "Fair words please fools"; "He that has most time has none to lose."   Great poets, like Tennyson and Matthew Arnold, understand well the fine effect to be produced from the mingling of short and long words—of the homely English with the more ornate Romance language.   In the following verse from Matthew Arnold the words are all monosyllables, with the exception of *tired* and *contention* (which is Latin) :—

"Let the long contention cease ;
   Geese are swans, and swans are geese ;
   Let them have it how they will,
   Thou art tired.   Best be still !"

In Tennyson's "Lord of Burleigh," when the sorrowful husband comes to look upon his dead wife, the verse runs almost entirely in monosyllables :—

"And he came to look upon her,
   And he looked at her, and said :
'Bring the dress, and put it on her,
   That she wore when she was wed.' "

An American writer has well indicated the force of the English monosyllable in the following sonnet :—

"Think not that strength lies in the big, *round* word,
   Or that the *brief* and *plain* must needs be weak.
To whom can this be true who once has heard
   The cry for help, the tongue that all men speak,
When want, or fear, or woe, is in the throat,
   So that each word gasped out is like a shriek
Pressed from the sore heart, or a *strange*, wild *note*
   Sung by some *fay* or fiend !   There is a strength,
Which dies if stretched too far, or spun too fine,
   Which has more height than breadth, more depth than length ;
Let but this *force* of thought and speech be mine,
   And he that will may take the sleek fat *phrase*,
Which glows but burns not, though it beam and shine ;
   Light, but no heat,—a flash, but not a blaze."

It will be observed that this sonnet consists entirely of monosyllables, and yet that the style of it shows considerable power and vigour.   The words printed in italics are all derived from Latin, with the exception of the word *phrase*, which is Greek.

11. **Change in the Order of Words.**—The syntax—or order of words—of the oldest English was very different from that of Norman-French.   The syntax of an Old English sentence was clumsy and involved ; it kept the attention long on the strain ; it was rumbling, rambling, and unpleasant to the ear.   It kept the attention on the strain, because the verb in a subordinate clause was held back, and not revealed till we had come to the

end of the clause. Thus the Anglo-Saxon wrote (though in different form and spelling)—

"When Darius saw, that he overcome be would."

The newer English, under French influence, wrote—

"When Darius saw that he was going to be overcome."

This change has made an English sentence lighter and more easy to understand, for the reader or hearer is not kept waiting for the verb; but each word comes just when it is expected, and therefore in its "natural" place. The Old English sentence —which is very like the German sentence of the present day— has been compared to a heavy cart without springs, while the newer English sentence is like a modern well-hung English carriage. Norman-French, then, gave us a brighter, lighter, freer rhythm, and therefore a sentence more easy to understand and to employ, more supple, and better adapted to everyday use.

12. The Expulsion of Gutturals.—(i) Not only did the Normans help us to an easier and pleasanter kind of sentence, they aided us in getting rid of the numerous throat-sounds that infested our language. It is a remarkable fact that there is not now in the French language a single guttural. There is not an h in the whole language. The French *write* an h in several of their words, but they never sound it. Its use is merely to serve as a fence between two vowels—to keep two vowels separate, as in *la haine*, hatred. No doubt the Normans could utter throat-sounds well enough when they dwelt in Scandinavia; but, after they had lived in France for several generations, they acquired a great dislike to all such sounds. No doubt, too, many, from long disuse, were unable to give utterance to a guttural. This dislike they communicated to the English; and hence, in the present day, there are many people—especially in the south of England—who cannot sound a guttural at all. The muscles in the throat that help to produce these sounds have become atrophied —have lost their power for want of practice. The purely English part of the population, for many centuries after the Norman invasion, could sound gutturals quite easily—just as the Scotch and the Germans do now; but it gradually became the fashion in England to leave them out.

13. The Expulsion of Gutturals.—(ii) In some cases the guttural disappeared entirely; in others, it was changed into or represented by other sounds. The **ge** at the beginning of the passive (or past) participles of many verbs disappeared entirely. Thus **gebróht, gebóht, geworht,** became **brought, bought,** and **wrought.** The **g** at the beginning of many words also dropped off. Thus **Gyppenswich** became **Ipswich; gif** became **if; genoh, enough.**—The guttural at the end of words—hard **g** or **c**—also disappeared. Thus **halig** became **holy; eordhlic, earthly; gastlic, ghastly** or **ghostly.** The same is the case in **dough, through, plough,** etc.—the guttural appearing to the eye but not to the ear.—Again, the guttural was changed into quite different sounds—into labials, into sibilants, into other sounds also. The following are a few examples :—

(*a*) The guttural has been softened, through Norman-French influence, into a **sibilant.** Thus **rigg, egg,** and **brigg** have become **ridge, edge,** and **bridge.**

(*b*) The guttural has become a **labial**—f—as in **cough, enough, trough, laugh, draught,** etc.

(*c*) The guttural has become an additional syllable, and is represented by a **vowel-sound.** Thus **sorg** and **mearh** have become **sorrow** and **marrow.**

(*d*) In some words it has disappeared both to eye and ear. Thus **makëd** has become **made.** `

14. The Story of the GH.—How is it, then, that we have in so many words the two strongest gutturals in the language—g and h—not only separately, in so many of our words, but combined? The story is an odd one. Our Old English or Saxon scribes wrote—not **light, might,** and **night,** but **liht, miht,** and **niht.** When, however, they found that the Norman-French gentlemen would not sound the **h,** and say—as is still said in Scotland —*licht,* &c., they redoubled the guttural, strengthened the **h** with a hard **g,** and again presented the dose to the Norman. But, if the Norman could not sound the **h** alone, still less could he sound the double guttural; and he very coolly let both alone

—ignored both.   The Saxon scribe doubled the signs for his
guttural, just as a farmer might put up a strong wooden fence in
front of a hedge ; but the Norman cleared both with perfect
ease and indifference.   And so it came to pass that we have the
symbol **gh** in more than seventy of our words, and that in most of
these we do not sound it at all   The **gh** remains in our language,
like a moss-grown boulder, brought down into the fertile valley
in a glacial period, when gutturals were both spoken and written,
and men believed in the truthfulness of letters—but now passed
by in silence and noticed by no one.

  15. The Letters that represent Gutturals. — The English
guttural has been quite Protean in the written or printed forms
it takes.   It appears as an **i**, as a **y**, as a **w**, as a **ch**, as a **dge**,
as a **j**, and — in its more native forms — as a **g**, a **k**, or a
gh.   The following words give all these forms : hail, day, fowl,
teach, edge, ajar, drag, truck, and trough.   Now *hail* was
hagol, day was *daeg, fowl* was *fugol, teach* was *taecan, edge* was
egg, ajar was *achar*.   In **seek, beseech, sought**—which are
all different forms of the same word—we see the guttural appearing in three different forms—as a hard **k**, as a soft **ch**, as an un-
noticed **gh**.   In **think** and **thought, drink** and **draught, sly**
and **sleight, dry** and **drought, slay** and **slaughter**, it takes
two different forms.   In **dig, ditch**, and **dike**—which are all
the same word in different shapes—it again takes three forms.
In **fly, flew**, and **flight**, it appears as a **y**, a **w**, and a **gh**.   But,
indeed, the manners of a guttural, its ways of appearing and
disappearing, are almost beyond counting.

  16. Grammatical Result of the Loss of Inflexions.—When
we look at a Latin or French or German word, we know whether
it is a verb or a noun or a preposition by its mere appearance
—by its face or by its dress, so to speak.   But the loss of
inflexions which has taken place in the English language has
resulted in depriving us of this advantage—if advantage it is.
Instead of **looking** at the **face** of a word in English, we are
obliged to **think** of its **function**,—that is, of what it does.   We
have, for example, a large number of words that are both nouns
and verbs—we may use them as the one or as the other ; and,

till we have used them, we cannot tell whether they are the one or the other. Thus, when we speak of "a **cut** on the finger," **cut** is a noun, because it is a name; but when we say, "Harry **cut** his finger," then **cut** is a verb, because it tells something about Harry. Words like **bud, cane, cut, comb, cap, dust, fall, fish, heap, mind, name, pen, plaster, punt, run, rush, stone,** and many others, can be used either as nouns or as verbs. Again, **fast, quick,** and **hard** may be used either as **adverbs** or as **adjectives**; and **back** may be employed as an **adverb,** as a **noun,** and even as an **adjective.** Shakespeare is very daring in the use of this licence. He makes one of his characters say, "But me no buts!" In this sentence, the first *but* is a **verb** in the imperative mood; the second is a **noun** in the objective case. Shakespeare uses also such verbs as *to glad, to mad,* such phrases as *a seldom pleasure,* and *the fairest she.* Dr Abbott says, "In Elizabethan English, almost any part of speech can be used as any other part of speech. An adverb can be used as a verb, 'they *askance* their eyes'; as a noun, 'the *backward* and abysm of time'; or as an adjective, 'a seldom pleasure.' Any noun, adjective, or neuter verb can be used as an active verb. You can 'happy' your friend, 'malice' or 'fool' your enemy, or 'fall' an axe upon his neck." Even in modern English, almost any noun can be used as a verb. Thus we can say, "to *paper* a room"; "to *water* the horses"; "to *black-ball* a candidate"; to "*iron* a shirt" or "a prisoner"; "to *toe* the line." On the other hand, verbs may be used as nouns; for we can speak of a *work,* of a beautiful *print,* of a long *walk,* and so on.

CHAPTER IV.

SPECIMENS OF ENGLISH OF DIFFERENT PERIODS.

1. Vocabulary and Grammar.—The oldest English or Anglo-Saxon differs from modern English both in vocabulary and in grammar—in the words it uses and in the inflexions it employs. The difference is often startling. And yet, if we look closely at the words and their dress, we shall most often find that the words which look so strange are the very words with which we are most familiar—words that we are in the habit of using every day; and that it is their dress alone that is strange and anti-quated. The effect is the same as if we were to dress a modern man in the clothes worn a thousand years ago : the chances are that we should not be able to recognise even our dearest friend.

2. A Specimen from Anglo-Saxon.—Let us take as an example a verse from the Anglo-Saxon version of one of the Gospels. The well-known verse, Luke ii. 40, runs thus in our oldest English version :—

Sóplíce daet cild weox, and waes gestrangod, wisdómes full ; and Godes gyfu waes on him.

Now this looks like an extract from a foreign language ; but it is not : it is our own veritable mother-tongue. Every word is pure ordinary English ; it is the dress—the spelling and the inflexions—that is quaint and old-fashioned. This will be plain from a literal translation :—

Soothly that child waxed, and was strengthened, wisdoms full (= full of wisdom) ; and God's gift was on him.

3. A Comparison.—This will become plainer if we compare the English of the Gospels as it was written in different periods of our language.   The alteration in the meanings of words, the changes in the application of them, the variation in the use of phrases, the falling away of the inflexions—all these things become plain to the eye and to the mind as soon as we thoughtfully compare the different versions.   The following are extracts from the Anglo-Saxon version (995), the version of Wycliffe (1389) and of Tyndale (1526), of the passage in Luke ii. 44, 45 :—

ANGLO-SAXON.	WYCLIFFE.	TYNDALE.
Wéndon daet he on heora geféro wǽere, dá comon hig ánes daeges faer, and hine sóhton betweox his magas and his cúdan.	Forsothe thei gessinge him to be in the felowschipe, camen the wey of á day, and souȝten him among his cosyns and knowen.	For they supposed he had bene in the company, they cam a days iorney, and sought hym amonge their kynsfolke and acquayntaunce.
Đa hig hyne ne fúndon, hig gewendon to Hierusalem, hine sécende.	And thei not fyndinge, wenten aȝen to Jerusalem, sckynge him.	And founde hym not, they went backe agayne to Hierusalem, and sought hym.

The literal translation of the Anglo-Saxon version is as follows :—

(They) weened that he on their companionship were (=was), when came they one day's faring, and him sought betwixt his relations and his couth (folk=acquaintances).

When they him not found, they turned to Jerusalem, him seeking.

4. The Lord's Prayer.—The same plan of comparison may be applied to the different versions of the Lord's Prayer that have come down to us ; and it will be seen from this comparison that the greatest changes have taken place in the grammar, and especially in that part of the grammar which contains the inflexions.

THE LORD'S PRAYER.

1130.	1250.	1380.	1526.
REIGN OF STEPHEN.	REIGN OF HENRY III.	WYCLIFFE'S VERSION.	TYNDALE'S VERSION.
Fader ure, þe art on heofone.	Fadir ur, that es in heuene,	Our Fadir, that art in hevenys,	Our Father, which art in heaven ;
Sy gebletsod name þin,	Halud thi nam to nevene ;	Halewid be thi name ;	Halowed be thy name ;
Cume þin rike.	Thou do as thi rich rike ;	Thi kingdom come to ;	Let thy kingdom come ;
Si þin wil swa swa on heofone and on corþan.	Thi will on erd be wrought, eek as it is wrought in heuen ay.	Be thi wil done in erthe, as in hevene.	Thy will be fulfilled as well in earth as it is in heven.
Breod ure degwamlich geof us to daeg.	Ur ilk day brede give us to day.	Give to us this day oure breed ovir othir *substaunce*,	Geve us this day ur dayly bred,
And forgeof us ageltes ura swa swa we forgeofen agiltendum urum.	Forgive thou all us dettes urs, als we forgive till ur detturs.	And forgive to us our *dettis*, as we forgiven to oure *dettouris*.	And forgeve us oure dettes as we forgeve ur detters.
And ne led us on costunge.	And ledde us in na fandung.	And lede us not into *temptacioun* ;	And leade us not into temptation,
Ac alys us fram yfele. Swa beo hit.	But sculd us fra ivel thing. Amen.	But *delyvere* us from yvel. Amen.	But delyver us from evyll. For thyne is the kyngdom, and the power, and the glorye, for ever. Amen.

It will be observed that Wycliffe's version contains five Romance terms — *substaunce, dettis, dettouris, temptacioun,* and *delyvere.*

5. Oldest English and Early English.—The following is a short passage from the Anglo-Saxon Chronicle, under date 1137 : first, in the Anglo-Saxon form ; second, in Early English, or — as it has sometimes been called—Broken Saxon ;

third, in modern English. The breaking-down of the grammar becomes still more strikingly evident from this close
juxtaposition.

(i)	Hí	swencton	þá	wreccan	menn
(ii)	Hí	swencten	the	wrecce	men
(iii)	They	swinked (harassed)	the	wretched	men

(i)	þaes landes	mid	castel-weorcum.
(ii)	Of-the-land	mid	castel-weorces.
(iii)	Of the land	with	castle-works.

(i)	Đa	þá	castelas	waeron	gemacod,
(ii)	Tha	the	castles	waren	maked,
(iii)	When	the	castles	were	made,

(i)	þá	fyldon	hí	hí	mid	yfelum	mannum.
(ii)	thá	fylden	hi	hi	mid	yvele	men.
(iii)	then	filled	they	them	with	evil	men.

6. Comparisons of Words and Inflexions.—Let us take a
few of the most prominent words in our language, and observe
the changes that have fallen upon them since they made their
appearance in our island in the fifth century. These changes
will be best seen by displaying them in columns :—

ANGLO-SAXON.	EARLY ENGLISH.	MIDDLE ENGLISH.	MODERN ENGLISH.
heom.	to heom.	to hem.	to them.
seó.	heó.	ho, scho.	she.
sweostrum.	to the swestres.	to the swistren.	to the sisters.
geboren.	gebore.	iboré.	born.
lufigende.	lufigend.	lovand.	loving.
weoxon.	woxen.	wexide.	waxed.

7. Conclusions from the above Comparisons.—We can now
draw several conclusions from the comparisons we have made
of the passages given from different periods of the language.
These conclusions relate chiefly to verbs and nouns ; and they

may become useful as a KEY to enable us to judge to what
period in the history of our language a passage presented to us
must belong.   If we find such and such marks, the language is
Anglo-Saxon ; if other marks, it is Early English ; and so on.

I.—MARKS OF ANGLO-SAXON.	II.—MARKS OF EARLY ENGLISH (1100-1250).	III.—MARKS OF MIDDLE ENGLISH (1250-1485).
VERBS.	**VERBS.**	**VERBS.**
Infinitive in **an.**	Infin. in **en** or **e.**	Infin. with **to** (the **en** was dropped about 1400).
Pres. part. in **ende.**	Pres. part. in **ind.**	
Past part. with **ge.**	**ge** of past part. turned into **i** or **y.**	Pres. part. in **inge.**
3d plural pres. in **ath.**	3d plural in **en.**	3d plural in **en.**
3d plural past in **on.**		Imperative in **eth.**
Plural of imperatives in **ath.**		Plurals in **es** (separate syllable).
NOUNS.	**NOUNS.**	**NOUNS.**
Plurals in **an, as,** or **a.**	Plural in **es.**	Possessives in **es** (separate syllable).
Dative plural in **um.**	Dative plural in **es.**	

8. The English of the Thirteenth Century.—In this century
there was a great breaking-down and stripping-off of inflexions.
This is seen in the **Ormulum** of Orm, a canon of the Order of
St Augustine, whose English is nearly as flexionless as that of
Chaucer, although about a century and a half before him.   Orm
has also the peculiarity of always doubling a consonant after a
short vowel.   Thus, in his introduction, he says :—

> " Þiss boc iss nemmnedd Orrmulum
> Forr þi þatt Orrm itt wrohhte."

That is, "This book is named Ormulum, for the (reason) that
Orm wrought it."   The absence of inflexions is probably due
to the fact that the book is written in the East-Midland dialect.
But, in a song called "The Story of Genesis and Exodus,"
written about 1250, we find a greater number of inflexions.
Thus we read :—

> " Hunger wex in lond Chanaan ;
> And his x sunes Jacob for-ðan

> Sente in to Egypt to bringen coren ;
> He bilefe at hom ðe was gungest boren."

That is, "Hunger waxed (increased) in the land of Canaan ; and Jacob for that (reason) sent his ten sons into Egypt to bring corn : he remained at home that was youngest born."

9. The English of the Fourteenth Century. — The four greatest writers of the fourteenth century are — in verse, **Chaucer** and **Langlande**; and in prose, **Mandeville** and **Wycliffe.** The inflexions continue to drop off; and, in Chaucer at least, a larger number of French words appear. Chaucer also writes in an elaborate verse-measure that forms a striking contrast to the homely rhythms of Langlande. Thus, in the "Man of Lawes Tale," we have the verse :—

> " O queenës, lyvynge in prosperitéc,
> Duchessës, and ladyës everichonc,
> Haveth som routhe on hir adversitée ;
> An emperourës doughter stant allone ;
> She hath no wight to whom to make hir moue.
> O blood roial ! that stondest in this dredë
> Fer ben thy frendës at thy gretë nedö !"

Here, with the exception of the imperative in *Haveth som routhe* (= have some pity), *stant*, and *ben* (= *are*), the grammar of Chaucer is very near the grammar of to-day. How different this is from the simple English of Langlande ! He is speaking of the great storm of wind that blew on January 15, 1362 :—

> " Piries and Plomtres   weore passchet to þe grounde,
> In ensaumple to Men   þat we scholde do þe bettre,
> Beches and brode okes   weore blowen to þe eorþe."

Here it is the spelling of Langlande's English that differs most from modern English, and not the grammar.—Much the same may be said of the style of Wycliffe (1324-1384) and of Mandeville (1300-1372). In Wycliffe's version of the Gospel of Mark, v. 26, he speaks of a woman "that hadde suffride many thingis of ful many lechis (doctors), and spendid alle hir thingis ; and no-thing profitide." Sir John Mandeville's English keeps many old inflexions and spellings ; but is, in other respects, modern enough. Speaking of Mahomet, he says : " And ȝee

schulle understonds that Machamete was born in Arabye, that
was first a pore knave that kept cameles, that wenten with
marchantes for marchandise." *Knave* for boy, and *wenten* for
went are the two chief differences—the one in the use of words,
the other in grammar—that distinguish this piece of Mandeville's English from our modern speech.

10. **The English of the Sixteenth Century.**—This, which is
also called Tudor-English, differs as regards grammar hardly at
all from the English of the nineteenth century. This becomes
plain from a passage from one of Latimer's sermons (1490-1555),
"a book which gives a faithful picture of the manners, thoughts,
and events of the period." "My father," he writes, "was a
yeoman, and had no lands of his own, only he had a farm of
three or four pound a year at the uttermost, and hereupon he
tilled so much as kept half a dozen men. He had walk for a
hundred sheep; and my mother milked thirty kine." In this
passage, it is only the old-fashionedness, homeliness, and quaint-
ness of the English—not its grammar—that makes us feel that
it was not written in our own times. When Ridley, the fellow-
martyr of Latimer, stood at the stake, he said, "I commit our
cause to Almighty God, which shall indifferently judge all."
Here he used *indifferently* in the sense of *impartially*—that is,
in the sense of *making no difference between parties;* and this
is one among a very large number of instances of Latin words,
when they had not been long in our language, still retaining the
older Latin meaning.

11. **The English of the Bible (i).**—The version of the Bible
which we at present use was made in 1611; and we might
therefore suppose that it is written in seventeenth-century English. But this is not the case. The translators were com-
manded by James I. to "follow the Bishops' Bible"; and the
Bishops' Bible was itself founded on the "Great Bible," which
was published in 1539. But the Great Bible is itself only a
revision of Tyndale's, part of which appeared as early as 1526.
When we are reading the Bible, therefore, we are reading English of the sixteenth century, and, to a large extent, of the early
part of that century. It is true that successive generations of

printers have, of their own accord, altered the spelling, and even, to a slight extent, modified the grammar.   Thus we have *fetched* for the older *fet*, *more* for *moe*, *sown* for *sowen*, *brittle* for *brickle* (which gives the connection with *break*), *jaws* for *chaws*, *sixth* for *sixt*, and so on.   But we still find such participles as *shined* and *understanded;* and such phrases as "they can skill to hew timber" (1 Kings v. 6), "abjects" for *abject persons*, "three days agone" for *ago*, the "captivated Hebrews" for "the captive Hebrews," and others.

12. The English of the Bible (ii).—We have, again, old words retained, or used in the older meaning.   Thus we find, in Psalm v. 6, the phrase "them that speak leasing," which reminds us of King Alfred's expression about "leasum spellum" (lying stories).   *Trow* and *ween* are often found; the "champaign over against Gilgal" (Deut. xi. 30) means the *plain;* and a publican in the New Testament is a tax-gatherer, who sent to the Roman Treasury or Publicum the taxes he had collected from the Jews.   An "ill-favoured person" is an ill-looking person; and "bravery" (Isa. iii. 18) is used in the sense of finery in dress.—Some of the oldest grammar, too, remains, as in Esther viii. 8, "Write ye, as it liketh you," where the *you* is a dative.   Again, in Ezek. xxx. 2, we find "Howl ye, Woe worth the day!" where the imperative *worth* governs *day* in the dative case.   This idiom is still found in modern verse, as in the well-known lines in the first canto of the "Lady of the Lake":—

> "Woe worth the chase, woe worth the day
> That cost thy life, my gallant grey!"

CHAPTER V.

MODERN ENGLISH.

1. Grammar Fixed.—From the date of 1485—that is, from the beginning of the reign of Henry VII.—the changes in the grammar or constitution of our language are so extremely small, that they are hardly noticeable. Any Englishman of ordinary education can read a book belonging to the latter part of the fifteenth or to the sixteenth century without difficulty. Since that time the grammar of our language has hardly changed at all, though we have altered and enlarged our vocabulary, and have adopted thousands of new words. The introduction of Printing, the Revival of Learning, the Translation of the Bible, the growth and spread of the power to read and write—these and other influences tended to fix the language and to keep it as it is to-day. It is true that we have dropped a few old-fashioned endings, like the **n** or **en** in *silvern* and *golden;* but, so far as form or grammar is concerned, the English of the sixteenth and the English of the nineteenth centuries are substantially the same.

2. New Words.—But, while the grammar of English has remained the same, the vocabulary of English has been growing, and growing rapidly, not merely with each century, but with each generation. The discovery of the New World in 1492 gave an impetus to maritime enterprise in England, which it never lost, brought us into connection with the Spaniards, and hence contributed to our language several Spanish words. In the sixteenth and seventeenth centuries, Italian literature was largely read; Wyatt and Surrey show its influence in their poems; and Italian words began to come in in considerable numbers. Commerce, too, has done much for us in this way; and along with the article imported, we have in general introduced also the name it bore in its own native country. In later times, Science has been making rapid strides—has been bringing to light new discoveries and new inventions almost every week; and along with these new discoveries, the language has been enriched with new names and new terms. Let us look a little more closely at the character of these foreign contributions to the vocabulary of our tongue.

3. **Spanish Words.**—The words we have received from the Spanish language are not numerous, but they are important. In addition to the ill-fated word **armada,** we have the Spanish for *Mr,* which is **Don** (from Lat. *dominus,* a lord), with its feminine **Duenna.** They gave us also **alligator,** which is our English way of writing *el lagarto,* the lizard. They also presented us with a large number of words that end in o—such as **buffalo, cargo, desperado, guano, indigo, mosquito, mulatto, negro, potato, tornado,** and others. The following is a tolerably full list:—

Alligator.	Cork.	Galleon (a ship).	Mulatto.
Armada.	Creole.	Grandee.	Negro.
Barricade.	Desperado.	Grenade.	Octoroon.
Battledore.	Don.	Guerilla.	Quadroon.
Bravado.	Duenna.	Indigo.	Renegade.
Buffalo.	Eldorado.	Jennet.	Savannah.
Cargo.	Embargo.	Matador.	Sherry (= Xeres).
Cigar.	Filibuster.	Merino.	Tornado.
Cochineal.	Flotilla.	Mosquito.	Vanilla.

4. **Italian Words.**—Italian literature has been read and cultivated in England since the time of Chaucer — since the fourteenth century; and the arts and artists of Italy have for many centuries exerted a great deal of influence on those of England. Hence it is that we owe to the Italian language a large number of words. These relate to poetry, such as **canto, sonnet, stanza**; to music, as **pianoforte, opera, oratorio, soprano, alto, contralto**; to architecture and sculpture, as

portico, piazza, cupola, torso; and to painting, as **studio, fresco** (an open-air painting), and others. The following is a complete list :—

Alarm.	Charlatan.	Incognito.	Proviso.
Alert.	Citadel.	Influenza.	Quarto.
Alto.	Colonnade.	Lagoon.	Regatta.
Arcade.	Concert.	Lava.	Ruffian.
Balcony.	Contralto.	Lazaretto.	Serenade.
Balustrade.	Conversazione.	Macaroni.	Sonnet.
Bandit.	Cornice.	Madonna.	Soprano.
Bankrupt.	Corridor.	Madrigal.	Stanza.
Bravo.	Cupola.	Malaria.	Stiletto.
Brigade.	Curvet.	Manifesto.	Stucco.
Brigand.	Dilettante.	Motto.	Studio.
Broccoli.	Ditto.	Moustache.	Tenor.
Burlesque.	Doge.	Niche.	Terra-cotta.
Bust.	Domino.	Opera.	Tirade.
Cameo.	Extravaganza.	Oratorio.	Torso.
Canteen.	Fiasco.	Palette.	Trombone.
Canto.	Folio.	Pantaloon.	Umbrella.
Caprice.	Fresco.	Parapet.	Vermilion.
Caricature.	Gazette.	Pedant.	Vertu.
Carnival.	Gondola.	Pianoforte.	Virtuoso.
Cartoon.	Granite.	Piazza.	Vista.
Cascade.	Grotto.	Pistol.	Volcano.
Cavalcade.	Guitar.	Portico.	Zany.

5. Dutch Words.—We have had for many centuries commercial dealings with the Dutch; and as they, like ourselves, are a great seafaring people, they have given us a number of words relating to the management of ships. In the fourteenth century, the southern part of the German Ocean was the most frequented sea in the world; and the chances of plunder were so great that ships of war had to keep cruising up and down to protect the trading vessels that sailed between England and the Low Countries. The following are the words which we owe to the Netherlands :—

Ballast.	Luff.	Sloop.	Trigger.
Boom.	Reef.	Smack.	Wear (said of a
Boor.	Schiedam (gin).	Smuggle.	ship).
Burgomaster.	Skates.	Stiver.	Yacht.
Hoy.	Skipper.	Taffrail.	Yawl.

6. French Words. — Besides the large additions to our language made by the Norman-French, we have from time to time imported direct from France a number of French words, without change in the spelling, and with little change in the pronunciation. The French have been for centuries the most polished nation in Europe; from France the changing fashions in dress spread over all the countries of the Continent; French literature has been much read in England since the time of Charles II.; and for a long time all diplomatic correspondence between foreign countries and England was carried on in French. Words relating to manners and customs are common, such as **soirée, etiquette, séance, élite**; and we have also the names of things which were invented in France, such as **mitrailleuse, carte-de-visite, coup d'état,** and others. Some of these words are, in spelling, exactly like English; and advantage of this has been taken in a well-known epigram :—

> The French have taste in all they do,
> Which we are quite without;
> For Nature, which to them gave goût,[1]
> To us gave only gout.

The following is a list of French words which have been imported in comparatively recent times :—

Aide-de-camp.	Carte-de-visite.	Etiquette.	Personnel.
Belle.	Coup-d'état.	Façade.	Précis.
Bivouac.	Débris.	Goût.	Programme.
Blonde.	Début.	Naïve.	Protégé.
Bouquet.	Déjeûner.	Naïveté.	Recherché.
Brochure.	Depot.	Nonchalance.	Séance.
Brunette.	Éclat.	Outré.	Soirée.
Brusque.	Ennui.	Penchant.	Trousseau.

The Scotch have always had a closer connection with the French nation than England; and hence we find in the Scottish dialect of English a number of French words that are not used in South Britain at all. A leg of mutton is called in Scotland a **gigot**; the dish on which it is laid is an **ashet** (from *assiette*); a cup for tea or for wine is a **tassie** (from *tasse*); the gate of a town is

---

[1] *Goût* (goo) from Latin *gustus*, taste.

called the **port**; and a stubborn person is **dour** (Fr. *dur*, from Lat. *durus*); while a gentle and amiable person is **douce** (Fr. *douce*, Lat. *dulcis*).

7. German Words.—It must not be forgotten that English is a Low-German dialect, while the German of books is New High-German. We have never borrowed directly from High-German, because we have never needed to borrow. Those modern German words that have come into our language in recent times are chiefly the names of minerals, with a few striking exceptions, such as **loafer,** which came to us from the German immigrants to the United States, and **plunder,** which seems to have been brought from Germany by English soldiers who had served under Gustavus Adolphus. The following are the German words which we have received in recent times :—

Cobalt.	Landgrave.	Meerschaum.	Poodle.
Felspar.	Loafer.	Nickel.	Quartz.
Hornblende.	Margrave.	Plunder.	Zinc.

8. Hebrew Words.—These, with very few exceptions, have come to us from the translation of the Bible, which is now in use in our homes and churches. **Abbot** and **abbey** come from the Hebrew word **abba,** father; and such words as **cabal** and **Talmud,** though not found in the Old Testament, have been contributed by Jewish literature. The following is a tolerably complete list :—

Abbey.	Cinnamon.	Leviathan.	Sabbath.
Abbot.	Hallelujah.	Manna.	Sadducees.
Amen.	Hosannah.	Paschal.	Satan.
Behemoth.	Jehovah.	Pharisee.	Seraph.
Cabal.	Jubilee.	Pharisaical.	Shibboleth.
Cherub.	Gehenna.	Rabbi.	Talmud.

9. Other Foreign Words.—The English have always been the greatest travellers in the world; and our sailors always the most daring, intelligent, and enterprising. There is hardly a port or a country in the world into which an English ship has not penetrated; and our commerce has now been maintained for centuries with every people on the face of the globe. We exchange goods with almost every nation and tribe under the sun. When we import articles or produce from abroad, we in general import the native name along with the thing. Hence it is that we have **guano, maize,** and **tomato** from the two Americas; **coffee, cotton,** and **tamarind** from Arabia; **tea, congou,** and **nankeen** from China; **calico, chintz,** and **rupee** from Hindostan; **bamboo, gamboge,** and **sago** from the Malay Peninsula; **lemon, musk,** and **orange** from Persia; **boomerang** and **kangaroo** from Australia; **chibouk, ottoman,** and **tulip** from Turkey. The following are lists of these foreign words; and they are worth examining with the greatest minuteness :—

AFRICAN DIALECTS.

Baobab.	Gnu.	Karoo.	Quagga.
Canary.	Gorilla.	Kraal.	Zebra.
Chimpanzee.	Guinea.	Oasis.	

AMERICAN TONGUES.

Alpaca.	Condor.	Maize.	Racoon.
Buccaneer.	Guano.	Manioc.	Skunk.
Cacique.	Hammock.	Moccasin.	Squaw.
Cannibal.	Jaguar.	Mustang.	Tapioca.
Canoe.	Jalap.	Opossum.	Tobacco.
Caoutchouc.	Jerked (beef).	Pampas.	Tomahawk.
Cayman.	Llama.	Pemmican.	Tomato.
Chocolate.	Mahogany.	Potato.	Wigwam.

ARABIC.

(The word *al* means *the.* Thus al*cohol* = *the spirit.*)

Admiral (Milton	Azure.	Harem.	Salaam.
writes *am-*	Caliph.	Hookah.	Senna.
miral.	Carat.	Koran (or Al-	Sherbet.
Alcohol.	Chemistry.	coran).	Shrub (the
Alcove.	Cipher.	Lute.	drink).
Alembic.	Civet.	Magazine.	Simoom.
Algebra.	Coffee.	Mattress.	Sirocco.
Alkali.	Cotton.	Minaret.	Sofa.
Amber.	Crimson.	Mohair.	Sultan.
Arrack.	Dragoman.	Monsoon.	Syrup.
Arsenal.	Elixir.	Mosque.	Talisman. ·
Artichoke.	Emir.	Mufti.	Tamarind.
Assassin.	Fakir.	Nabob.	Tariff.
Assegai.	Felucca.	Nadir.	Vizier.
Attar.	Gazelle.	Naphtha.	Zenith.
Azimuth.	Giraffe.	Saffron.	Zero.

CHINESE.

Bohea.	Hyson.	Nankeen.	Souchong.
China.	Joss.	Pekoe.	Tea.
Congou.	Junk.	Silk.	Typhoon.

HINDU.

Avatar.	Cowrie.	Pagoda.	Ryot.
Banyan.	Durbar.	Palanquin.	Sepoy.
Brahmin.	Jungle.	Pariah.	Shampoo.
Bungalow.	Lac (of rupees).	Punch.	Sugar.
Calico.	Loot.	Pundit.	Suttee.
Chintz.	Mulligatawny.	Rajah.	Thug.
Coolie.	Musk.	Rupee.	Toddy.

HUNGARIAN.

Hussar.	Sabre.	Shako.	Tokay.

MALAY.

Amuck.	Cassowary.	Gong.	Orang-outang.
Bamboo.	Cockatoo.	Gutta-percha.	Rattan.
Bantam.	Dugong.	Mandarin.	Sago.
Caddy.	Gamboge.	Mango.	Upas.

PERSIAN.

Awning.	Dervish.	Jasmine.	Pasha.
Bazaar.	Divan.	Lac (a gum).	Rook.
Bashaw.	Firman.	Lemon.	Saraband.
Caravan.	Hazard.	Lilac.	Sash.
Check.	Horde.	Lime (the fruit).	Scimitar.
Checkmate.	Houri.	Musk.	Shawl.
Chess.	Jar.	Orange.	Taffeta.
Curry.	Jackal.	Paradise.	Turban.

POLYNESIAN DIALECTS.

Boomerang.	Kangaroo.	Taboo.	Tattoo.

PORTUGUESE.

Albatross.	Cocoa-nut.	Lasso.	Molasses.
Caste.	Commodore.	Marmalade.	Palaver.
Cobra.	Fetish.	Moidore.	Port (= Oporto).

RUSSIAN.

Czar.	Knout.	Rouble.	Ukase.
Drosky.	Morse.	Steppe.	Verst.

TARTAR.
Khan.

TURKISH.

Bey.	Chouse.	Kiosk.	Tulip.
Caftan.	Dey.	Odalisque.	Yashmak.
Chibouk.	Janissary.	Ottoman.	Yataghan.

10. Scientific Terms.—A very large number of discoveries in science have been made in this century; and a large number of inventions have introduced these discoveries to the people, and made them useful in daily life. Thus we have *telegraph* and *telegram; photograph; telephone* and even *photophone.* The word *dynamite* is also modern; and the unhappy employment of it has made it too widely known. Then passing fashions have given us such words as *athlete* and *æsthete.* In general, it may be said that, when we wish to give a name to a new thing—a new discovery, invention, or fashion—we have recourse not to our own stores of English, but to the vocabularies of the Latin and Greek languages.

LANDMARKS IN THE HISTORY OF THE ENGLISH LANGUAGE.

A.D.

1. **The Beowulf,** an old English epic, "written on the mainland" **450**

2. **Christianity** introduced by St Augustine (and with it many Latin and a few Greek words) **597**

3. **Caedmon**—'Paraphrase of the Scriptures,'—first English poem **670**

4. **Baeda**—"The Venerable Bede"—translated into English part of St John's Gospel **735**

5. **King Alfred** translated several Latin works into English, among others, Bede's 'Ecclesiastical History of the English Nation' . . . . . (851) **901**

6. **Aelfric,** Archbishop of York, turned into English most of the historical books of the Old Testament . . . **1000**

7. **The Norman Conquest,** which introduced Norman French words **1066**

8. **Anglo-Saxon Chronicle,** said to have been begun by King Alfred, and brought to a close in **1160**

9. **Orm** or **Orrmin's Ormulum,** a poem written in the East Midland dialect, about **1200**

10. **Normandy** lost under King John. Norman-English now have their only home in England, and use our English speech more and more **1204**

11. **Layamon** translates the 'Brut' from the French of Robert Wace. This is the first English book (written in *Southern English*) after the stoppage of the Anglo-Saxon Chronicle . **1205**

12. **The Ancren Riwle** ("Rules for Anchorites") written in the Dorsetshire dialect. "It is the forerunner of a wondrous change in our speech." "It swarms with French words" **1220**

13. **First Royal Proclamation** in English, issued by Henry III. . **1258**

14. **Robert of Gloucester's** Chronicle (swarms with foreign terms) **1300**

15. **Robert Manning,** "Robert of Brunn," compiles the 'Handlyng Synne.' "It contains a most copious proportion of French words" 1303

16. **Ayenbite of Inwit** (="Remorse of Conscience") . . 1340

17. **The Great Plague.** After this it becomes less and less the fashion to speak French 1349

18. **Sir John Mandeville,** first writer of the newer English Prose— in his 'Travels,' which contained a large admixture of French words. "His English is the speech spoken at Court in the latter days of King Edward III." 1356

19. **English** becomes the language of the Law Courts . . 1362

20. **Wickliffe's** Bible 1380

21. **Geoffrey Chaucer,** the first great English poet, author of the 'Canterbury Tales'; born in 1340, died . . . 1400

22. **William Caxton,** the first English printer, brings out (in the Low Countries) the first English book ever printed, the 'Recuyell of the Historyes of Troye,'—"not written with pen and ink, as other books are, to the end that every man may have them at once" 1471

23. **First English Book** printed in England (by Caxton) the 'Game and Playe of the Chesse' 1474

24. **Lord Berners'** translation of Froissart's Chronicle . . 1523

25. **William Tyndale,** by his translation of the Bible "fixed our tongue once for all." "His New Testament has become the standard of our tongue: the first ten verses of the Fourth Gospel are a good sample of his manly Teutonic pith" **1526-30**

26. **Edmund Spenser** publishes his 'Faerie Queene.' "Now began the golden age of England's literature; and this age was to last for about fourscore years" 1590

27. **Our English Bible,** based chiefly on Tyndale's translation. "Those who revised the English Bible in 1611 were bidden to keep as near as they could to the old versions, such as Tyndale's" 1611

28. **William Shakespeare** carried the use of the English language to the greatest height of which it was capable. He employed 15,000 words. "The last act of 'Othello' is a rare specimen of Shakespeare's diction: of every five nouns, verbs, and adverbs, four are Teutonic" . . . **(Born 1564) 1616**

29. **John Milton,** "the most learned of English poets," publishes his 'Paradise Lost,'—"a poem in which Latin words are introduced with great skill" 1667

30. **The Prayer-Book** revised and issued in its final form. "*Are* was substituted for *be* in forty-three places. This was a great victory of the North over the South " . . **1661**

31. **John Bunyan** writes his ' Pilgrim's Progress '—a book full of pithy English idiom. "The common folk had the wit at once to see the worth of Bunyan's masterpiece, and the learned long afterwards followed in the wake of the common folk " . . . . . **(Born 1628) 1688**

32. **Sir Thomas Browne,** the author of ' Urn-Burial' and other works written in a highly Latinised diction, such as the ' Religio Medici,' written **1642**

33. **Dr Samuel Johnson** was the chief supporter of the use of "long-tailed words in osity and ation," such as his novel called ' Rasselas,' published **1759**

34. **Tennyson,** Poet-Laureate, a writer of the best English—"a countryman of Robert Manning's, and a careful student of old Malory, has done much for the revival of pure English among us " . . . . . **(Born 1809)**

PART IV.

OUTLINE OF THE HISTORY OF ENGLISH LITERATURE

CHAPTER I.

1. **Literature.**—The history of English Literature is, in its external aspect, an account of the best books in prose and in verse that have been written by English men and English women; and this account begins with a poem brought over from the Continent by our countrymen in the fifth century, and comes down to the time in which we live. It covers, therefore, a period of nearly fourteen hundred years.

2. **The Distribution of Literature.**—We must not suppose that literature has always existed in the form of printed books. Literature is a living thing—a living outcome of the living mind; and there are many ways in which it has been distributed to other human beings. The oldest way is, of course, by one person repeating a poem or other literary composition he has made to another; and thus literature is stored away, not upon book-shelves, but in the memory of living men. Homer's poems are said to have been preserved in this way to the Greeks for five hundred years. Father chanted them to son; the sons to their sons; and so on from generation to generation. The next way of distributing literature is by the aid of signs called letters made upon leaves, flattened reeds, parchment, or the inner bark of trees. The next is by the help of writing upon paper. The last is by the aid of type upon paper. This has existed in England for more than four hundred years—since the year **1474**; and thus it is that our libraries contain many hundreds of thousands of valuable books.

For the same reason is it, most probably, that as our power of retaining the substance and multiplying the copies of books has grown stronger, our living memories have grown weaker. This defect can be remedied only by education—that is, by training the memories of the young. While we possess so many printed books, it must not be forgotten that many valuable works exist still in manuscript—written either upon paper or on parchment.

    3. **Verse, the earliest form of Literature.**—It is a remarkable fact that the earliest kind of composition in all languages is in the form of **Verse**. The oldest books, too, are those which are written in verse. Thus Homer's poems are the oldest literary work of Greece; the Sagas are the oldest productions of Scandinavian literature; and the Beowulf is the oldest piece of literature produced by the Anglo-Saxon race. It is also from the strong creative power and the lively inventions of poets that we are even now supplied with new thoughts and new language—that the most vivid words and phrases come into the language; just as it is the ranges of high mountains that send down to the plains the ever fresh soil that gives to them their unending fertility. And thus it happens that our present English speech is full of words and phrases that have found their way into the most ordinary conversation from the writings of our great poets—and especially from the writings of our greatest poet, Shakespeare. The fact that the life of prose depends for its supplies on the creative minds of poets has been well expressed by an American writer :—

> " I looked upon a plain of green,
>   Which some one called the Land of Prose,
> Where many living things were seen
>   In movement or repose.
>
> I looked upon a stately hill
>   That well was named the Mount of Song,
> Where golden shadows dwelt at will,
>   The woods and streams among.
>
> But most this fact my wonder bred
>   (Though known by all the nobly wise),
> It was the mountain stream that fed
>   That fair green plain's amenities."

4. Our oldest English Poetry.—The verse written by our old English writers was very different in form from the verse that appears now from the hands of Tennyson, or Browning, or Matthew Arnold. The old English or Anglo-Saxon writers used a kind of rhyme called **head-rhyme** or **alliteration**; while, from the fourteenth century downwards, our poets have always employed **end-rhyme** in their verses.

> "*L*ightly down *l*eaping he *l*oosened his helmet."

Such was the rough old English form. At least three words in each long line were alliterative—two in the first half, and one in the second. Metaphorical phrases were common, such as *war-adder* for arrow, *war-shirts* for armour, *whale's-path* or *swan-road* for the sea, *wave-horse* for a ship, *tree-wright* for carpenter. Different statements of the same fact, different phrases for the same thing—what are called **parallelisms** in Hebrew poetry—as in the line—

> "Then saw they the sea head-lands—the windy walls,"

were also in common use among our oldest English poets.

5. Beowulf.—The **Beowulf** is the oldest poem in the English language. It is our "old English epic"; and, like much of our ancient verse, it is a war poem. The author of it is unknown. It was probably composed in the fifth century —not in England, but on the Continent—and brought over to this island—not on paper or on parchment—but in the memories of the old Jutish or Saxon vikings or warriors. It was not written down at all, even in England, till the end of the ninth century, and then, probably, by a monk of Northumbria. It tells among other things the story of how Beowulf sailed from Sweden to the help of Hrothgar, a king in Jutland, whose life was made miserable by a monster—half man, half fiend—named Grendel. For about twelve years this monster had been in the habit of creeping up to the banqueting-hall of King Hrothgar, seizing upon his thanes, carrying them off, and devouring them. Beowulf attacks and overcomes the dragon, which is mortally wounded, and flees away to die. The

S

poem belongs both to the German and to the English literature; for it is written in a Continental English, which is somewhat different from the English of our own island. But its literary shape is, as has been said, due to a Christian writer of Northumbria; and therefore its written or printed form—as it exists at present—is not German, but English. Parts of this poem were often chanted at the feasts of warriors, where all sang in turn as they sat after dinner over their cups of mead round the massive oaken table. The poem consists of 3184 lines, the rhymes of which are solely alliterative.

6. **The First Native English Poem.**—The Beowulf came to us from the Continent; the first native English poem was produced in Yorkshire. On the dark wind-swept cliff which rises above the little land-locked harbour of **Whitby**, stand the ruins of an ancient and once famous abbey. The head of this religious house was the Abbess Hild or Hilda: and there was a secular priest in it,—a very shy retiring man, who looked after the cattle of the monks, and whose name was **Caedmon**. To this man came the gift of song, but somewhat late in life. And it came in this wise. One night, after a feast, singing began, and each of those seated at the table was to sing in his turn. Caedmon was very nervous—felt he could not sing. Fear overcame his heart, and he stole quietly away from the table before the turn could come to him. He crept off to the cowshed, lay down on the straw and fell asleep. He dreamed a dream; and, in his dream, there came to him a voice: "Caedmon, sing me a song!" But Caedmon answered: "I cannot sing; it was for this cause that I had to leave the feast." "But you must and shall sing!" "What must I sing, then?" he replied. "Sing the beginning of created things!" said the vision; and forthwith Caedmon sang some lines in his sleep, about God and the creation of the world. When he awoke, he remembered some of the lines that had come to him in sleep, and, being brought before Hilda, he recited them to her. The Abbess thought that this wonderful gift, which had come to him so suddenly, must have come from God, received him into the monastery, made him a monk, and

had him taught sacred history. " All this Caedmon, by re-membering, and, like a clean animal, ruminating, turned into sweetest verse." His poetical works consist of a metrical para-phrase of the Old and the New Testament. It was written about the year 670; and he died in 680. It was read and re-read in manuscript for many centuries, but it was not printed in a book until the year 1655.

7. **The War-Poetry of England.**—There were many poems about battles, written both in Northumbria and in the south of England; but it was only in the south that these war-songs were committed to writing; and of these written songs there are only two that survive up to the present day. These are the **Song of Brunanburg,** and the **Song of the Fight at Maldon.** The first belongs to the date 938; the second to 991. The Song of Brunanburg was inscribed in the SAXON CHRONICLE—a current narrative of events, written chiefly by monks, from the ninth century to the end of the reign of Stephen. The song tells the story of the fight of King Athelstan with Anlaf the Dane. It tells how five young kings and seven earls of Anlaf's host fell on the field of battle, and lay there "quieted by swords," while their fellow-Northmen fled, and left their friends and comrades to "the screamers of war—the black raven, the eagle, the greedy battle-hawk, and the grey wolf in the wood." The Song of the Fight at Maldon tells us of the heroic deeds and death of **Byrhtnoth,** an ealdorman of North-umbria, in battle against the Danes at Maldon, in Essex. The speeches of the chiefs are given; the single combats between heroes described; and, as in Homer, the names and genealogies of the foremost men are brought into the verse.

8. **The First English Prose.**—The first writer of English prose was **Baeda,** or, as he is generally called, the **Venerable Bede.** He was born in the year 672 at Monkwearmouth, a small town at the mouth of the river Wear, and was, like Caedmon, a native of the kingdom of Northumbria. He spent most of his life at the famous monastery of Jarrow-on-Tyne. He spent his life in writing. His works, which were written in Latin, rose to the number of forty-five; his chief

work being an **Ecclesiastical History**.　But though Latin
was the tongue in which he wrote his books, he wrote one book
in English; and·he may therefore be fairly considered the first
writer of English prose.　This book was a **Translation of the
Gospel of St John**—a work which he laboured at until the
very moment of his death.　His disciple Cuthbert tells the
story of his last hours.　"Write quickly!" said Baeda to his
scribe, for he felt that his end could not be far off.　When the
last day came, all his scholars stood around his bed.　"There
is still one chapter wanting, Master," said the scribe; "it is
hard for thee to think and to speak."　"It must be done," said
Baeda; "take thy pen and write quickly."　So through the long
day they wrote—scribe succeeding scribe; and when the shades
of evening were coming on, the young writer looked up from
his task and said, "There is yet one sentence to write, dear
Master."　"Write it quickly!"　Presently the writer, looking
up with joy, said, "It is finished!"　"Thou sayest truth,"
replied the weary old man; "it is finished: all is finished."
Quietly he sank back upon his pillow, and, with a psalm of
praise upon his lips, gently yielded up to God his latest breath.
It is a great pity that this translation — the first piece of
prose in our language—is utterly lost.　No MS. of it is at
present known to be in existence.

9. The Father of English Prose.—For several centuries, up
to the year 866, the valleys and shores of Northumbria were
the homes of learning and literature.　But a change was not
long in coming.　Horde after horde of Danes swept down upon
the coasts, ravaged the monasteries, burnt the books—after
stripping the beautiful bindings of the gold, silver, and precious
stones which decorated them—killed or drove away the monks,
and made life, property, and thought insecure all along that once
peaceful and industrious coast.　Literature, then, was forced
to desert the monasteries of Northumbria, and to seek for a
home in the south—in Wessex, the kingdom over which Alfred
the Great reigned for more than thirty years.　The capital of
Wessex was Winchester; and an able writer says: " As

Whitby is the cradle of English poetry, so is Winchester of English prose." King Alfred founded colleges, invited to England men of learning from abroad, and presided over a school for the sons of his nobles in his own Court. He himself wrote many books, or rather, he translated the most famous Latin books of his time into English. He translated into the English of Wessex, for example, the 'Ecclesiastical History' of Baeda; the 'History of Orosius,' into which he inserted geographical chapters of his own; and the 'Consolations of Philosophy,' by the famous Roman writer, Boëthius. In these books he gave to his people, in their own tongue, the best existing works on history, geography, and philosophy.

10. **The Anglo-Saxon Chronicle.**—The greatest prose-work of the oldest English, or purely Saxon, literature, is a work—not by one person, but by several authors. It is the historical work which is known as **The Saxon Chronicle.** It seems to have been begun about the middle of the ninth century; and it was continued, with breaks now and then, down to 1154—the year of the death of Stephen and the accession of Henry II. It was written by a series of successive writers, all of whom were monks; but Alfred himself is said to have contributed to it a narrative of his own wars with the Danes. The Chronicle is found in seven separate forms, each named after the monastery in which it was written. It was the newspaper, the annals, and the history of the nation. "It is the first history of any Teutonic people in their own language; it is the earliest and most venerable monument of English prose." This Chronicle possesses for us a twofold value. It is a valuable storehouse of historical facts; and it is also a storehouse of specimens of the different states of the English language—as regards both words and grammar — from the eighth down to the twelfth century.

11. **Layamon's Brut.**—Layamon was a native of Worcestershire, and a priest of Ernley on the Severn. He translated, about the year 1205, a poem called **Brut,** from the French of a monkish writer named Master Wace. Wace's work itself is

little more than a translation of parts of a famous "Chronicle
or History of the Britons," written in Latin by Geoffrey of
Monmouth, who was Bishop of St Asaph in 1152.   But
Geoffrey himself professed only to have translated from a chronicle in the British or Celtic tongue, called the "Chronicle of the
Kings of Britain," which was found in Brittany—long the home
of most of the stories, traditions, and fables about the old British Kings and their great deeds.   Layamon's poem called the
"Brut" is a metrical chronicle of Britain from the landing of
Brutus to the death of King Cadwallader, about the end of the
seventh century.   Brutus was supposed to be a great-grandson
of Æneas, who sailed west and west till he came to Great
Britain, where he settled with his followers.—This metrical
chronicle is written in the dialect of the West of England ; and
it shows everywhere a breaking down of the grammatical forms
of the oldest English, as we find it in the Anglo-Saxon Chronicle.   In fact, between the landing of the Normans and the
fourteenth century, two things may be noted : first, that during
this time—that is, for three centuries—the inflections of the
oldest English are gradually and surely stripped off; and, secondly, that there is little or no original English literature given
to the country, but that by far the greater part consists chiefly
of translations from French or from Latin.

12. **Orm's Ormulum.**—Less than half a century after Layamon's Brut appeared a poem called the **Ormulum**, by a monk
of the name of Orm or Ormin.   It was probably written
about the year 1215.   Orm was a monk of the order of St
Augustine, and his book consists of a series of religious poems.
It is the oldest, purest, and most valuable specimen of thirteenth-
century English, and it is also remarkable for its peculiar
spelling.   It is written in the purest English, and not five
French words are to be found in the whole poem of twenty
thousand short lines.   Orm, in his spelling, doubles every consonant that has a short vowel before it ; and he writes *þann* for
þan, but *þan* for *þane*.   The following is a specimen of his
poem :—

Icc hafe wennd inntill Ennglissh	I have wended (turned) into English
Goddspelless hallghe lare,	Gospel's holy lore,
Affterr thatt little witt tatt me	After the little wit that me
Min Drihhtin hafethth lenedd.	My Lord hath lent.

Other famous writers of English between this time and the appearance of Chaucer were **Robert of Gloucester** and **Robert of Brunne,** both of whom wrote Chronicles of England in verse.

CHAPTER II.

THE FOURTEENTH CENTURY.

1. The opening of the fourteenth century saw the death of the great and able king, Edward I., the "Hammer of the Scots," the "Keeper of his word." The century itself—a most eventful period—witnessed the feeble and disastrous reign of Edward II.; the long and prosperous rule—for fifty years—of Edward III.; the troubled times of Richard II., who exhibited almost a repetition of the faults of Edward II.; and the appearance of a new and powerful dynasty—the House of Lancaster—in the person of the able and ambitious Henry IV. This century saw also many striking events, and many still more striking changes. It beheld the welding of the Saxon and the Norman elements into one—chiefly through the French wars; the final triumph of the English language over French in 1362; the frequent coming of the Black Death; the victories of Crecy and Poitiers; it learned the universal use of the mariner's compass; it witnessed two kings—of France and of Scotland—prisoners in London; great changes in the condition of labourers; the invention of gunpowder in 1340; the rise of English commerce under Edward III.; and everywhere in England the rising up of new powers and new ideas.

2. The first prose-writer in this century is **Sir John Mandeville** (who has been called the "Father of English Prose"). King Alfred has also been called by this name; but as the English written by Alfred was very different from that written

by Mandeville,—the latter containing a large admixture of French and of Latin words, both writers are deserving of the epithet. The most influential prose-writer was **John Wyclif**, who was, in fact, the first English Reformer of the Church. In poetry, two writers stand opposite each other in striking contrast—**Geoffrey Chaucer** and **William Langlande**, the first writing in courtly "King's English" in end-rhyme, and with the fullest inspirations from the literatures of France and Italy, the latter writing in head-rhyme, and—though using more French words than Chaucer—with a style that was always homely, plain, and pedestrian. **John Gower**, in Kent, and **John Barbour**, in Scotland, are also noteworthy poets in this century. The English language reached a high state of polish, power, and freedom in this period; and the sweetness and music of Chaucer's verse are still unsurpassed by modern poets. The sentences of the prose-writers of this century are long, clumsy, and somewhat helpless; but the sweet homely English rhythm exists in many of them, and was continued, through Wyclif's version, down into our translation of the Bible in 1611.

3. SIR JOHN MANDEVILLE, (1300-1372), "the first prose-writer in formed English," was born at St Albans, in Hertfordshire, in the year 1300. He was a physician; but, in the year 1322, he set out on a journey to the East; was away from home for more than thirty years, and died at Liège, in Belgium, in 1372. He wrote his travels first in Latin, next in French, and then turned them into English, "that every man of my nation may understand it." The book is a kind of guide-book to the Holy Land; but the writer himself went much further east—reached Cathay or China, in fact. He introduced a large number of French words into our speech, such as *cause, contrary, discover, quantity,* and many hundred others. His works were much admired, read, and copied; indeed, hundreds of manuscript copies of his book were made. There are nineteen still in the British Museum. The book was not printed till the year 1499—that is, twenty-five years after printing was introduced into this country. Many of the Old English inflexions still survive in his style. Thus he says: "Machamete was born in Arabye, that was a pore knave (boy) that kepte cameles that wenten with marchantes for marchandise."

4. JOHN WYCLIF (his name is spelled in about forty different ways)—**1324-1384**—was born at Hipswell, near Richmond, in Yorkshire, in the year 1324, and died at the vicarage of Lutterworth, in Leicestershire, in 1384. His fame rests on two bases—his efforts as a reformer of the abuses of the Church, and his complete translation of the **Bible**. This work was finished in 1383, just one year before his death. But the translation was not done by himself alone; the larger part of the Old Testament version seems to have been made by Nicholas de Hereford. Though often copied in manuscript, it was not printed for several centuries. Wyclif's New Testament was printed in 1731, and the Old Testament not until the year 1850. But the words and the style of his translation, which was read and re-read by hundreds of thoughtful men, were of real and permanent service in fixing the language in the form in which we now find it.

5. JOHN GOWER (**1325-1408**) was a country gentleman of Kent. As Mandeville wrote his travels in three languages, so did Gower his poems. Almost all educated persons in the fourteenth century could read and write with tolerable and with almost equal ease, English, French, and Latin. His three poems are the **Speculum Meditantis** ("The Mirror of the Thoughtful Man"), in French; the **Vox Clamantis** ("Voice of One Crying"), in Latin; and **Confessio Amantis** ("The Lover's Confession"), in English. No manuscript of the first work is known to exist. He was buried in St Saviour's, Southwark, where his effigy is still to be seen—his head resting on his three works. Chaucer called him "the moral Gower"; and his books are very dull, heavy, and difficult to read.

6. WILLIAM LANGLANDE (**1332-1400**), a poet who used the old English head-rhyme, as Chaucer used the foreign end-rhyme, was born at Cleobury-Mortimer in Shropshire, in the year 1332. The date of his death is doubtful. His poem is called the **Vision of Piers the Plowman**; and it is the last long poem in our literature that was written in Old English alliterative rhyme. From this period, if rhyme is employed at all, it is the end-rhyme, which we borrowed from the French and Italians. The poem has an appendix called **Do-well, Do-bet, Do-best** — the three stages in the growth of a Christian. Langlande's writings remained in manuscript until the reign of Edward VI.; they were printed then, and went through three editions in one year. The English used in the **Vision** is the Midland dialect—much the same as that used by Chaucer; only, oddly enough, Langlande admits into his English a

larger amount of French words than Chaucer. The poem is a distinct landmark in the history of our speech. The following is a specimen of the lines. There are three alliterative words in each line, with a pause near the middle—

> " A voice *l*oud in that *l*ight · to *L*ucifer criĕd,
> ' *P*rinces of this *p*alace · *p*rest[1] undo the gatĕs,
> For here cometh with *c*rown · the *k*ing of all glory!'"

7. GEOFFREY CHAUCER (1340-1400), the "father of English poetry," and the greatest narrative poet of this country, was born in London in or about the year 1340. He lived in the reigns of Edward III., Richard II., and one year in the reign of Henry IV. His father was a vintner. The name *Chaucer* is a Norman name, and is found on the roll of Battle Abbey. He is said to have studied both at Oxford and Cambridge; served as page in the household of Prince Lionel, Duke of Clarence, the third son of Edward III.; served also in the army, and was taken prisoner in one of the French campaigns. In 1367, he was appointed gentleman-in-waiting (*valettus*) to Edward III., who sent him on several embassies. In 1374 he married a lady of the Queen's chamber; and by this marriage he became connected with John of Gaunt, who afterwards married a sister of this lady. While on an embassy to Italy, he is reported to have met the great poet Petrarch, who told him the story of the Patient Griselda. In 1381, he was made Comptroller of Customs in the great port of London— an office which he held till the year 1386. In that year he was elected knight of the shire—that is, member of Parliament for the county of Kent. In 1389, he was appointed Clerk of the King's Works at Westminster and Windsor. From 1381 to 1389 was probably the best and most productive period of his life; for it was in this period that he wrote the **House of Fame**, the **Legend of Good Women**, and the best of the **Canterbury Tales**. From 1390 to 1400 was spent in writing the other **Canterbury Tales**, ballads, and some moral poems. He died at Westminster in the year 1400, and was the first writer who was buried in the Poets' Corner of the Abbey. We see from his life—and it was fortunate for his poetry—that Chaucer had the most varied experience as student, courtier, soldier, ambassador, official, and member of Parliament; and was able to mix freely and on equal terms with all sorts and conditions of men, from the king to the poorest hind in the fields. He was a stout man, with a small bright face, soft eyes,

---

[1] Quickly.

dazed by long and hard reading, and with the English passion for flowers, green fields, and all the sights and sounds of nature.

8. **Chaucer's Works.**—Chaucer's greatest work is the **Canterbury Tales.** It is a collection of stories written in heroic metre— that is, in the rhymed couplet of five iambic feet. The finest part of the Canterbury Tales is the **Prologue** ; the noblest story is probably the **Knightes Tale.** It is worthy of note that, in 1362, when Chaucer was a very young man, the session of the House of Commons was first opened with a speech in English ; and in the same year an Act of Parliament was passed, substituting the use of English for French in courts of law, in schools, and in public offices. English had thus triumphed over French in all parts of the country, while it had at the same time become saturated with French words. In the year 1383 the Bible was translated into English by Wyclif. Thus Chaucer, whose writings were called by Spenser "the well of English undefiled," wrote at a time when our English was freshest and newest. The grammar of his works shows English with a large number of inflexions still remaining. The Canterbury Tales are a series of stories supposed to be told by a number of pilgrims who are on their way to the shrine of St Thomas (Becket) at Canterbury. The pilgrims, thirty-two in number, are fully described—their dress, look, manners, and character in the Prologue. It had been agreed, when they met at the Tabard Inn in Southwark, that each pilgrim should tell four stories—two going and two returning—as they rode along the grassy lanes, then the only roads, to the old cathedral city. But only four-and-twenty stories exist.

9. **Chaucer's Style.**—Chaucer expresses, in the truest and liveliest way, "the true and lively of everything which is set before him ;" and he first gave to English poetry that force, vigour, life, and colour which raised it above the level of mere rhymed prose. All the best poems and histories in Latin, French, and Italian were well known to Chaucer ; and he borrows from them with the greatest freedom. He handles, with masterly power, all the characters and events in his Tales ; and he is hence, beyond doubt, the greatest narrative poet that England ever produced. In the Prologue, his masterpiece, Dryden says, "we have our forefathers and great-grand-dames all before us, as they were in Chaucer's days." His dramatic power, too, is nearly as great as his narrative power ; and Mr Marsh affirms that he was "a dramatist before that which is technically known as the existing drama had been invented." That is to say, he could set men and women talking as they would and did talk in real life, but with more point, spirit, *verve*, and picturesqueness. As regards the matter of his poems, it may be sufficient to say that

Dryden calls him "a perpetual fountain of good sense;" and that Hazlitt makes this remark : "Chaucer was the most practical of all the great poets,—the most a man of business and of the world. His poetry reads like history." Tennyson speaks of him thus in his " Dream of Fair Women ":—

> " Dan Chaucer, the first warbler, whose sweet breath
>   Preluded those melodious bursts that fill
> The spacious times of great Elizabeth,
>   With sounds that echo still."

10. JOHN BARBOUR (1316-1396).—The earliest Scottish poet of any importance in the fourteenth century is John Barbour, who rose to be Archdeacon of Aberdeen. Barbour was of Norman blood, and wrote Northern English, or, as it is sometimes called, Scotch. He studied both at Oxford and at the University of Paris. His chief work is a poem called **The Bruce.** The English of this poem does not differ very greatly from the English of Chaucer. Barbour has *fechtand* for *fighting; pressit* for *pressed; theretill* for *thereto;* but these differences do not make the reading of his poem very diffi- cult. As a Norman he was proud of the doings of Robert de Bruce, another Norman ; and Barbour must often have heard stories of him in his boyhood, as he was only thirteen when Bruce died.

CHAPTER III.

THE FIFTEENTH CENTURY.

1. The fifteenth century, a remarkable period in many ways, saw three royal dynasties established in England—the Houses of Lancaster, York, and Tudor. Five successful French campaigns of Henry V., and the battle of Agincourt; and, on the other side, the loss of all our large possessions in France, with the exception of Calais, under the rule of the weak Henry VI., were among the chief events of the fifteenth century. The Wars of the Roses did not contribute anything to the prosperity of the century, nor could so unsettled and quarrelsome a time encourage the cultivation of literature. For this among other reasons, we find no great compositions in prose or verse; but a considerable activity in the making and distribution of ballads. The best of these are **Sir Patrick Spens, Edom o' Gordon, The Nut-Brown Mayde,** and some of those written about **Robin Hood** and his exploits. The ballad was everywhere popular; and minstrels sang them in every city and village through the length and breadth of England. The famous ballad of **Chevy Chase** is generally placed after the year 1460, though it did not take its present form till the seventeenth century. It tells the story of the Battle of Otterburn, which was fought in 1388. This century was also witness to the short struggle of Richard III., followed by the rise of the House of Tudor. And, in 1498, just at its close, the wonderful apparition of a new world—of **The New World**—

rose on the horizon of the English mind, for England then first heard of the discovery of America. But, as regards thinking and writing, the fifteenth century is the most barren in our literature. It is the most barren in the **production** of original literature; but, on the other hand, it is, compared with all the centuries that preceded it, the most fertile in the dissemination and **distribution** of the literature that already existed. For England saw, in the memorable year of **1474,** the establishment of the first printing-press in the Almonry at Westminster, by **William Caxton.** The first book printed by him in this country was called 'The Game and Playe of the Chesse.' When Edward IV. and his friends visited Caxton's house and looked at his printing-press, they spoke of it as a pretty toy; they could not foresee that it was destined to be a more powerful engine of good government and the spread of thought and education than the Crown, Parliaments, and courts of law all put together. The two greatest names in literature in the fifteenth century are those of **James I.** (of Scotland) and **William Caxton** himself. Two followers of Chaucer, **Occleve** and **Lydgate** are also generally mentioned. Put shortly, one might say that the chief poetical productions of this century were its **ballads;** and the chief prose productions, **translations** from Latin or from foreign works.

2. JAMES I. OF SCOTLAND **(1394-1437),** though a Scotchman, owed his education to England. He was born in 1394. Whilst on his way to France when a boy of eleven, he was captured, in time of peace, by the order of Henry IV., and kept prisoner in England for about eighteen years. It was no great misfortune, for he received from Henry the best education that England could then give in language, literature, music, and all knightly accomplishments. He married Lady Jane Beaufort, the grand-daughter of John of Gaunt, the friend and patron of Chaucer. His best and longest poem is **The Kings Quair** (that is, Book), a poem which was inspired by the subject of it, Lady Jane Beaufort herself. The poem is written in a stanza of seven lines (called **Rime Royal**); and the style is a close copy of the style of Chaucer. After reigning thirteen years in Scotland, King James was murdered at Perth, in the year 1437. A Norman by blood, he is the best poet of the fifteenth century.

3. WILLIAM CAXTON **(1422-1492)** is the name of greatest importance and significance in the history of our literature in the fifteenth
century.   He was born in Kent in the year 1422.   He was not merely
a printer, he was also a literary man; and, when he devoted himself
to printing, he took to it as an art, and not as a mere mechanical
device.   Caxton in early life was a mercer in the city of London ;
and in the course of his business, which was a thriving one, he had
to make frequent journeys to the Low Countries.   Here he saw the
printing - press for the first time, with the new separate types,
was enchanted with it, and fired by the wonderful future it opened.
It had been introduced into Holland about the year 1450.   Caxton's
press was set up in the Almonry at Westminster, at the sign of the
Red Pole.   It produced in all sixty-four books, nearly all of them in
English, some of them written by Caxton himself.   One of the most
important of them was Sir Thomas Malory's **History of King
Arthur,** the storehouse from which Tennyson drew the stories
which form the groundwork of his *Idylls of the King*.

CHAPTER IV.

THE SIXTEENTH CENTURY.

1. The Wars of the Roses ended in 1485, with the victory of Bosworth Field. A new dynasty—the House of Tudor—sat upon the throne of England; and with it a new reign of peace and order existed in the country, for the power of the king was paramount, and the power of the nobles had been gradually destroyed in the numerous battles of the fifteenth century. Like the fifteenth, this century also is famous for its ballads, the authors of which are not known, but which seem to have been composed "by the people for the people." They were sung everywhere, at fairs and feasts, in town and country, at going to and coming home from work; and many of them were set to popular dance-tunes.

> "When Tom came home from labour,
> And Cis from milking rose,
> Merrily went the tabor,
> And merrily went their toes."

The ballads of **King Lear** and **The Babes in the Wood** are perhaps to be referred to this period.

2. The first half of the sixteenth century saw the beginning of a new era in poetry; and the last half saw the full meridian splendour of this new era. The beginning of this era was marked by the appearance of **Sir Thomas Wyatt** (1503-1542), and of the **Earl of Surrey** (1517-1547). These two eminent

T

writers have been called the "twin-stars of the dawn," the
"founders of English lyrical poetry"; and it is worthy of
especial note, that it is to Wyatt that we owe the introduction
of the **Sonnet** into our literature, and to Surrey that is due the
introduction of **Blank Verse.** The most important prose-
writers of the first half of the century were **Sir Thomas More,**
the great lawyer and statesman, and **William Tyndale,** who
translated the New Testament into English. In the latter half
of the century, the great poets are **Spenser** and **Shakespeare**;
the great prose-writers, **Richard Hooker** and **Francis Bacon.**

3. SIR THOMAS MORE'S **(1480-1535)** chief work in English is the
Life and Reign of Edward V. It is written in a plain, strong,
nervous English style. Hallam calls it "the first example of good
English—pure and perspicuous, well chosen, without vulgarisms, and
without pedantry." His **Utopia** (a description of the country of
Nowhere) was written in Latin.

4. WILLIAM TYNDALE **(1484-1536)**—a man of the greatest significance, both in the history of religion, and in the history of our language and literature—was a native of Gloucestershire, and was
educated at Magdalen Hall, Oxford. His opinions on religion and
the rule of the Catholic Church, compelled him to leave England,
and drove him to the Continent in the year 1523. He lived in
Hamburg for some time. With the German and Swiss reformers
he held that the Bible should be in the hands of every grown-up
person, and not in the exclusive keeping of the Church. He accordingly set to work to translate the Scriptures into his native
tongue. Two editions of his version of the **New Testament** were
printed in 1525-34. He next translated the five books of Moses, and
the book of Jonah. In 1535 he was, after many escapes and adventures, finally tracked and hunted down by an emissary of the
Pope's faction, and thrown into prison at the castle of Vilvoorde,
near Brussels. In 1536 he was brought to Antwerp, tried, con-
demned, led to the stake, strangled, and burned.

5. **The Work of William Tyndale.** — Tyndale's translation
has, since the time of its appearance, formed the basis of all the
after versions of the Bible. It is written in the purest and simplest
English; and very few of the words used in his translation have
grown obsolete in our modern speech. Tyndale's work is indeed,

one of the most striking landmarks in the history of our language. Mr Marsh says of it : "Tyndale's translation of the New Testament is the most important philological monument of the first half of the sixteenth century,—perhaps I should say, of the whole period between Chaucer and Shakespeare. . . . The best features of the translation of 1611 are derived from the version of Tyndale." It may be said without exaggeration that, in the United Kingdom, America, and the colonies, about one hundred millions of people now speak the English of Tyndale's Bible; nor is there any book that has exerted so great an influence on English rhythm, English style, the selection of words, and the build of sentences in our English prose.

6. EDMUND SPENSER (1552-1599), "The Poet's Poet," and one of the greatest poetical writers of his own or of any age, was born at East Smithfield, near the Tower of London, in the year 1552, about nine years before the birth of Bacon, and in the reign of Edward VI. He was educated at Merchant Taylors' School in London, and at Pembroke Hall, Cambridge. In 1579, we find him settled in his native city, where his best friend was the gallant Sir Philip Sidney, who introduced him to his uncle, the Earl of Leicester, then at the height of his power and influence with Queen Elizabeth. In the same year was published his first poetical work, **The Shepheard's Calendar**—a set of twelve pastoral poems. In 1580, he went to Ireland as Secretary to Lord Grey de Wilton, the Viceroy of that country. For some years he resided at Kilcolman Castle, in county Cork, on an estate which had been granted him out of the forfeited lands of the Earl of Desmond. Sir Walter Raleigh had obtained a similar but larger grant, and was Spenser's near neighbour. In 1590 Spenser brought out the first three books of **The Faerie Queene**. The second three books of his great poem appeared in 1596. Towards the end of 1598, a rebellion broke out in Ireland; it spread into Munster; Spenser's house was attacked and set on fire ; in the fighting and confusion his only son perished; and Spenser escaped with the greatest difficulty. In deep distress of body and mind, he made his way to London, where he died—at an inn in King Street, Westminster, at the age of forty-six, in the beginning of the year 1599. He was buried in the Abbey, not far from the grave of Chaucer.

7. **Spenser's Style.**—His greatest work is **The Faerie Queene** ; but that in which he shows the most striking command of language is his **Hymn of Heavenly Love**. **The Faerie Queene** is written in a nine-lined stanza, which has since been called the *Spenserian*

Stanza. The first eight lines are of the usual length of five iambic feet; the last line contains six feet, and is therefore an Alexandrine. Each stanza contains only three rhymes, which are disposed in this order: *a b a b b c b c c.*—The music of the stanza is long-drawn out, beautiful, involved, and even luxuriant.—The story of the poem is an allegory, like the 'Pilgrim's Progress'; and in it Spenser undertook, he says, "to represent all the moral virtues, assigning to every virtue a knight to be the patron and defender of the same."[1] Only six books were completed; and these relate the adventures of the knights who stand for *Holiness, Temperance, Chastity, Friendship, Justice,* and *Courtesy.* The **Faerie Queene** herself is called **Gloriana,** who represents *Glory* in his "general intention," and Queen Elizabeth in his "particular intention."

8. **Character of the Faerie Queene.**—This poem is the greatest of the sixteenth century. Spenser has not only been the delight of nearly ten generations; he was the study of Shakespeare, the poetical master of Cowley and of Milton, and, in some sense, of Dryden and Pope. Keats, when a boy, was never tired of reading him. "There is something," says Pope, "in Spenser that pleases one as strongly in old age as it did in one's youth." Professor Craik says: "Without calling Spenser the greatest of all poets, we may still say that his poetry is the most poetical of all poetry." The outburst of national feeling after the defeat of the Armada in 1588; the new lands opened up by our adventurous Devonshire sailors; the strong and lively loyalty of the nation to the queen; the great statesmen and writers of the period; the high daring shown by England against Spain—all these animated and inspired the glowing genius of Spenser. His rhythm is singularly sweet and beautiful. Hazlitt says: "His versification is at once the most smooth and the most sounding in the language. It is a labyrinth of sweet sounds." Nothing can exceed the wealth of Spenser's phrasing and expression; there seems to be no limit to its flow. He is very fond of the Old-English practice of alliteration or head-rhyme—"hunting the letter," as it was called. Thus he has—

> " In woods, in waves, in wars, she wont to dwell.
> Gay without good is good heart's greatest loathing."

9. WILLIAM SHAKESPEARE (**1564-1616**), the greatest dramatist that England ever produced, was born at Stratford-on-Avon, in Warwickshire, on the 23d of April—St George's Day—of the year 1564. His father, John Shakespeare, was a wool dealer and grower.

----

[1] This use of the phrase "the same" is antiquated English.

William was educated at the grammar-school of the town, where he learned "small Latin and less Greek"; and this slender stock was his only scholastic outfit for life. At the early age of eighteen he married Anne Hathaway, a yeoman's daughter. In 1586, at the age of twenty-two, he quitted his native town, and went to London.

10. **Shakespeare's Life and Character.**—He was employed in some menial capacity at the Blackfriars Theatre, but gradually rose to be actor and also adapter of plays. He was connected with the theatre for about five-and-twenty years; and so diligent and so successful was he, that he was able to purchase shares both in his own theatre and in the Globe. As an actor, he was only second-rate: the two parts he is known to have played are those of the *Ghost* in **Hamlet**, and *Adam* in **As You Like It.** In 1597, at the early age of thirty-three, he was able to purchase New Place, in Stratford, and to rebuild the house. In 1612, at the age of forty-eight, he left London altogether, and retired for the rest of his life to New Place, where he died in the year 1616. His old father and mother spent the last years of their lives with him, and died under his roof. Shakespeare had three children — two girls and a boy. The boy, Hamnet, died at the age of twelve. Shakespeare himself was beloved by every one who knew him; and "gentle Shakespeare" was the phrase most often upon the lips of his friends. A placid face, with a sweet, mild expression; a high, broad, noble, "two-storey" forehead; bright eyes; a most speaking mouth — though it seldom opened; an open, frank manner, a kindly, handsome look,—such seems to have been the external character of the man Shakespeare.

11. **Shakespeare's Works.**—He has written thirty-seven plays and many poems. The best of his rhymed poems are his Sonnets, in which he chronicles many of the various moods of his mind. The plays consist of tragedies, historical plays, and comedies. The greatest of his tragedies are probably **Hamlet** and **King Lear**; the best of his historical plays, **Richard III.** and **Julius Cæsar**; and his finest comedies, **Midsummer Night's Dream** and **As You Like It.** He wrote in the reign of Elizabeth as well as in that of James; but his greatest works belong to the latter period.

12. **Shakespeare's Style.**—Every one knows that Shakespeare is great; but how is the young learner to discover the best way of forming an adequate idea of his greatness? In the first place, Shakespeare has very many sides; and, in the second place, he is great on every one of them. Coleridge says: "In all points, from the most important to the most minute, the judgment of Shakespeare

is commensurate with his genius—nay, his genius reveals itself in
his judgment, as in its most exalted form." He has been called
"mellifluous Shakespeare;" "honey-tongued Shakespeare;" "silver-
tongued Shakespeare;" "the thousand-souled Shakespeare;" "the
myriad-minded;" and by many other epithets. He seems to have
been master of all human experience; to have known the human
heart in all its phases; to have been acquainted with all sorts and
conditions of men—high and low, rich and poor; and to have studied
the history of past ages, and of other countries. He also shows a
greater and more highly skilled mastery over language than any
other writer that ever lived. The vocabulary employed by Shakespeare amounts in number of words to twenty-one thousand. The
vocabulary of Milton numbers only seven thousand words. But it
is not sufficient to say that Shakespeare's power of thought, of feeling, and of expression required three times the number of words
to express itself; we must also say that Shakespeare's power of expression shows infinitely greater skill, subtlety, and cunning than
is to be found in the works of Milton. Shakespeare had also a marvellous power of making new phrases, most of which have become
part and parcel of our language. Such phrases as *every inch a king;
witch the world; the time is out of joint*, and hundreds more, show
that modern Englishmen not only speak Shakespeare, but think
Shakespeare. His knowledge of human nature has enabled him to
throw into English literature a larger number of genuine "characters" that will always live in the thoughts of men, than any other
author that ever wrote. And he has not drawn his characters from
England alone and from his own time—but from Greece and Rome,
from other countries, too, and also from all ages. He has written in
a greater variety of styles than any other writer. "Shakespeare,"
says Professor Craik, "has invented twenty styles." The knowledge, too, that he shows on every kind of human endeavour is as
accurate as it is varied. Lawyers say that he was a great lawyer;
theologians, that he was an able divine, and unequalled in his knowledge of the Bible; printers, that he must have been a printer; and
seamen, that he knew every branch of the sailor's craft.

13. **Shakespeare's contemporaries.**—But we are not to suppose
that Shakespeare stood alone in the end of the sixteenth and the beginning of the seventeenth century as a great poet; and that everything
else was flat and low around him. This never is and never can be
the case. Great genius is the possession, not of one man, but of
several in a great age; and we do not find a great writer standing
alone and unsupported, just as we do not find a high mountain rising

from a low plain. The largest group of the highest mountains in the world, the Himalayas, rise from the highest table-land in the world; and peaks nearly as high as the highest—Mount Everest—are seen cleaving the blue sky in the neighbourhood of Mount Everest itself. And so we find Shakespeare surrounded by dramatists in some respects nearly as great as himself; for the same great forces welling up within the heart of England that made *him* created also the others. **Marlowe**, the teacher of Shakespeare, **Peele**, and **Greene**, preceded him; **Ben Jonson**, **Beaumont** and **Fletcher**, **Massinger** and **Ford**, **Webster**, **Chapman**, and many others, were his contemporaries, lived with him, talked with him; and no doubt each of these men influenced the work of the others. But the works of these men belong chiefly to the seventeenth century. We must not, however, forget that the reign of Queen Elizabeth—called in literature the **Elizabethan Period**—was the greatest that England ever saw, —greatest in poetry and in prose, greatest in thought and in action, and perhaps also greatest in external events.

14. CHRISTOPHER MARLOWE (**1564-1593**), the first great English dramatist, was born at Canterbury in the year 1564, two months before the birth of Shakespeare himself. He studied at Corpus Christi College, Cambridge, and took the degree of Master of Arts in 1587. After leaving the university, he came up to London and wrote for the stage. He seems to have led a wild and reckless life, and was stabbed in a tavern brawl on the 1st of June 1593. "As he may be said to have invented and made the verse of the drama, so he created the English drama." His chief plays are **Dr Faustus** and **Edward the Second**. His style is one of the greatest vigour and power: it is often coarse, but it is always strong. Ben Jonson spoke of "Marlowe's mighty line"; and Lord Jeffrey says of him: "In felicity of thought and strength of expression, he is second only to Shakespeare himself."

15. BEN JONSON (**1574-1637**), the greatest dramatist of England after Shakespeare, was born in Westminster in the year 1574, just nine years after Shakespeare's birth. He received his education at Westminster School. It is said that, after leaving school, he was obliged to assist his stepfather as a bricklayer; that he did not like the work; and that he ran off to the Low Countries, and there enlisted as a soldier. On his return to London, he began to write for

the stage. Jonson was a friend and companion of Shakespeare's ;
and at the Mermaid, in Fleet Street, they had, in presence of men
like Raleigh, Marlowe, Greene, Peele, and other distinguished
Englishmen, many "wit-combats" together. Jonson's greatest
plays are **Volpone** or the Fox, and the **Alchemist** — both
comedies. In 1616 he was created Poet-Laureate. For many
years he was in receipt of a pension from James I. and from Charles
I. ; but so careless and profuse were his habits, that he died in
poverty in the year 1637. He was buried in an upright position in
Westminster Abbey ; and the stone over his grave still bears the
inscription, "O rare Ben Jonson !" He has been called a "robust,
surly, and observing dramatist."

16. RICHARD HOOKER (1553-1600), one of the greatest of Elizabethan prose-writers, was born at Heavitree, a village near the city
of Exeter, in the year 1553. By the kind aid of Jewel, Bishop of
Salisbury, he was sent to Oxford, where he distinguished himself
as a hard-working student, and especially for his knowledge of
Hebrew. In 1581 he entered the Church. In the same year he
made an imprudent marriage with an ignorant, coarse, vulgar, and
domineering woman. He was appointed Master of the Temple in
1585; but, by his own request, he was removed from that office,
and chose the quieter living of Boscombe, near Salisbury. Here
he wrote the first four books of his famous work, **The Laws
of Ecclesiastical Polity**, which were published in the year 1594.
In 1595 he was translated to the living of Bishopsborne, near Canterbury. His death took place in the year 1600. The complete
work, which consisted of eight books, was not published till 1662.

17. **Hooker's Style.**—His writings are said to "mark an era in
English prose." His sentences are generally very long, very elaborate, but full of "an extraordinary musical richness of language."
The order is often more like that of a Latin than of an English
sentence ; and he is fond of Latin inversions. Thus he writes :
"That which by wisdom he saw to be requisite for that people, was
by as great wisdom compassed." The following sentences give us a
good example of his sweet and musical rhythm. "Of law there can
be no less acknowledged, than that her seat is the bosom of God, her
voice the harmony of the world. All things in heaven and earth do
her homage ; the very least as feeling her care, and the greatest as
not exempted from her power: both angels and men, and creatures
of what condition soever, though each in different sort and manner,
yet all, with uniform consent, admiring her as the mother of their
peace and joy."

18. SIR PHILIP SIDNEY (**1554-1586**), a noble knight, a states-man, and one of the best prose-writers of the Elizabethan age, was born at Penshurst, in Kent, in the year 1554. He was educated at Shrewsbury School, and then at•Christ Church, Oxford. At the age of seventeen he went abroad for three years' travel on the Con-tinent; and, while in Paris, witnessed, from the windows of the English Embassy, the horrible Massacre of St Bartholomew in the year 1572. At the early age of twenty-two he was sent as am-bassador to the Emperor of Germany; and while on that embassy, he met William of Orange—"William the Silent"—who pronounced him one of the ripest statesmen in Europe. This was said of a young man "who seems to have been the type of what was noblest in the youth of England during times that could produce a statesman." In 1580 he wrote the **Arcadia**, a romance, and dedicated it to his sister, the Countess of Pembroke. The year after, he produced his **Apologie for Poetrie.** His policy as a statesman was to side with Protestant rulers, and to break the power of the strongest Catholic kingdom on the Continent—the power of Spain. In 1585 the Queen sent him to the Netherlands as governor of the important fortress of Flushing. He was mortally wounded in a skirmish at Zutphen; and as he was being carried off the field, handed to a private the cup of cold water that had been brought to quench his raging thirst. He died of his wounds on the 17th of October 1586. One of his friends wrote of him :—

"Death, courage, honour, make thy soul to live !—
Thy soul in heaven, thy name in tongues of men ! "

19. **Sidney's Poetry.**—In addition to the **Arcadia** and the **Apologie for Poetrie,** Sidney wrote a number of beautiful poems. The best of these are a series of sonnets called **Astrophel** and **Stella,** of which his latest critic says : " As a series of sonnets, the **Astrophel** and **Stella** poems are second only to Shakespeare's ; as a series of love-poems, they are perhaps unsurpassed." Spenser wrote an elegy upon Sidney himself, under the title of **Astrophel.** Sidney's prose is among the best of the sixteenth century. " He reads more modern than any other author of that century." He does not use "ink-horn terms," or cram his sentences with Latin or French or Italian words ; but both his words and his idioms are of pure English. He is fond of using personifications. Such phrases as, "About the time that the candles began to inherit the sun's office;" "Seeing the day begin to disclose her comfortable beauties," are not uncommon. The rhythm of his sentences is always melodious, and each of them has a very pleasant close.

CHAPTER V.

THE SEVENTEENTH CENTURY.

1. **The First Half.**—Under the wise and able rule of Queen Elizabeth, this country had enjoyed a long term of peace. The Spanish Armada had been defeated in 1588; the Spanish power had gradually waned before the growing might of England; and it could be said with perfect truth, in the words of Shakespeare :—

> "In her days every man doth eat in safety
> Under his own vine what he plants, and sing
> The merry songs of peace to all his neighbours."

The country was at peace; and every peaceful art and pursuit prospered. As one sign of the great prosperity and outstretching enterprise of commerce, we should note the foundation of the East India Company on the last day of the year 1600. The reign of James I. (1603-1625) was also peaceful; and the country made steady progress in industries, in commerce, and in the arts and sciences. The two greatest prose-writers of the first half of the seventeenth century were **Raleigh** and **Bacon**; the two greatest poets were **Shakespeare** and **Ben Jonson**.

2. SIR WALTER RALEIGH **(1552-1618).**—**Walter Raleigh,** soldier, statesman, coloniser, historian, and poet, was born in Devonshire, in the year 1552. He was sent to Oriel College, Oxford; but he left at the early age of seventeen to fight on the side of the Protestants in France. From that time his life is one long series of schemes, plots,

adventures, and misfortunes—culminating in his execution at Westminster in the year 1618. He spent "the evening of a tempestuous
life" in the Tower, where he lay for thirteen years; and during this
imprisonment he wrote his greatest work, the **History of the
World,** which was never finished. His life and adventures belong to the sixteenth; his works to the seventeenth century.
Raleigh was probably the most dazzling figure of his time; and is
"in a singular degree the representative of the vigorous versatility
of the Elizabethan period." Spenser, whose neighbour he was for
some time in Ireland, thought highly of his poetry, calls him "the
summer's nightingale," and says of him—

> "Yet æmuling[1] my song, he took in hand
> My pipe, before that æmulëd of many,
> And played thereon (for well that skill he conn'd),
> Himself as skilful in that art as any."

Raleigh is the author of the celebrated verses, "Go, soul, the body's
guest;" "Give me my scallop-shell of quiet;" and of the lines which
were written and left in his Bible on the night before he was
beheaded :—

> "Even such is time, that takes in trust
> Our youth, our joys, our all we have,
> And pays us but with age and dust;
> Who, in the dark and silent grave,
> When we have wandered all our ways,
> Shuts up the story of our days:
> But from this earth, this grave, this dust,
> The Lord shall raise me up, I trust!"

Raleigh's prose has been described as "some of the most flowing
and modern-looking prose of the period;" and there can be no
doubt that, if he had given himself entirely to literature, he would
have been one of the greatest poets and prose-writers of his time.
His style is calm, noble, and melodious. The following is the last
sentence of the **History of the World** :—

> "O eloquent, just, and mighty Death! whom none could advise, thou hast
> persuaded; what none hath dared, thou hast done; and whom all the world
> hath flattered, thou only hast cast out of the world and despised; thou hast
> drawn together all the far-stretched greatness, all the pride, cruelty, and am-
> bition of man, and covered it all over with these two narrow words *Hic jacet.*"

3. FRANCIS BACON **(1561-1626)**, one of the greatest of English
thinkers, and one of our best prose-writers, was born at York House,

---

[1] Emulating.

in the Strand, London, in the year 1561. He was a grave and precocious child; and Queen Elizabeth, who knew him and liked him, used to pat him and call him her "young Lord Keeper"—his father being Lord Keeper of the Seals in her reign. At the early age of twelve he was sent to Trinity College, Cambridge, and remained there for three years. In 1582 he was called to the bar; in 1593 he was M.P. for Middlesex. But his greatest rise in fortune did not take place till the reign of James I.; when, in the year 1618, he had risen to be Lord High Chancellor of England. The title which he took on this occasion—for the Lord High Chancellor is chairman of the House of Lords—was **Baron Verulam**; and a few years after he was created **Viscount St Albans**. His eloquence was famous in England; and Ben Jonson said of him: "The fear of every man that heard him was lest he should make an end." In the year 1621 he was accused of taking bribes, and of giving unjust decisions as a judge. He had not really been unconscientious, but he had been careless; was obliged to plead guilty; and he was sentenced to pay a fine of £40,000, and to be imprisoned in the Tower during the king's pleasure. The fine was remitted; Bacon was set free in two days; a pension was allowed him; but he never afterwards held office of any kind. He died on Easter-day of the year 1626, of a chill which he caught while experimenting on the preservative properties of snow.

4. His chief prose-works in English—for he wrote many in Latin— are the **Essays**, and the **Advancement of Learning**. His **Essays** make one of the wisest books ever written; and a great number of English thinkers owe to them the best of what they have had to say. They are written in a clear, forcible, pithy, and picturesque style, with short sentences, and a good many illustrations, drawn from history, politics, and science. It is true that the style is sometimes stiff, and even rigid; but the stiffness is the stiffness of a richly embroidered cloth, into which threads of gold and silver have been worked. Bacon kept what he called a **Promus** or Commonplace-Book; and in this he entered striking thoughts, sentences, and phrases that he met with in the course of his reading, or that occurred to him during the day. He calls these sentences "salt-pits, that you may extract salt out of, and sprinkle as you will." The following are a few examples:—

"That that is Forced is not Forcible."

"No Man loveth his Fetters though they be of Gold."

"Clear and Round Dealing is the Honour of Man's Nature."

"The Arch-flatterer, with whom all the petty Flatterers have intelligence, is a Man's Self."

"If Things be not tossed upon the Arguments of Counsell, they will be tossed upon the Waves of Fortune."

The following are a few striking sentences from his **Essays** :—

"Virtue is like a rich stone, best plain set."

"A man's nature runs either to herbs or weeds ; therefore, let him seasonably water the one, and destroy the other."

"A crowd is not company, and faces are but a gallery of pictures, and talk but a tinkling cymbal, when there is no love."

No man could say wiser things in pithier words ; and we may well say of his thoughts, in the words of Tennyson, that they are—

> "Jewels, five words long,
> That on the stretched forefinger of all time
> Sparkle for ever."

5. WILLIAM SHAKESPEARE **(1564-1616)** has been already treated of in the chapter on the sixteenth century. But it may be noted here that his first two periods—as they are called—fall within the sixteenth, and his last two periods within the seventeenth century. His **first period** lies between 1591 and 1596; and to it are ascribed his early poems, his play of **Richard II.**, and some other historical plays. His **second period**, which stretches from 1596 to 1601 holds the Sonnets, the **Merchant of Venice**, the **Merry Wives of Windsor**, and a few historical dramas. But his third and fourth periods were richer in production, and in greater productions. The **third period**, which belongs to the years 1601 to 1608, produced the play of **Julius Cæsar**, the great tragedies of **Hamlet, Othello, Lear, Macbeth**, and some others. To the **fourth period**, which lies between 1608 and 1613, belong the calmer and wiser dramas, —**Winter's Tale, The Tempest**, and **Henry VIII.** Three years after—in 1616—he died.

6. **The Second Half.**—The second half of the great and unique seventeenth century was of a character very different indeed from that of the first half. The Englishmen born into it had to face a new world ! New thoughts in religion, new forces in politics, new powers in social matters had been slowly, steadily, and irresistibly rising into supremacy ever since the Scottish King James came to take his seat upon the throne of England in 1603. These new forces had, in fact, become so

strong that they led a king to the scaffold, and handed over the
government of England to a section of Republicans. Charles
I. was executed in 1649; and, though his son came back
to the throne in 1660, the face, the manners, the thoughts of
England and of Englishmen had undergone a complete internal
and external change. The Puritan party was everywhere the
ruling party; and its views and convictions, in religion, in
politics, and in literature, held unquestioned sway in almost
every part of England. In the Puritan party, the strongest
section was formed by the Independents—the "root and branch
men"—as they were called; and the greatest man among the
Independents was Oliver Cromwell, in whose government **John
Milton** was Foreign Secretary. Milton was certainly by far
the greatest and most powerful writer, both in prose and in
verse, on the side of the Puritan party. The ablest verse-writer
on the Royalist or Court side was **Samuel Butler,** the unrivalled
satirist— the Hogarth of language,—the author of **Hudibras.**
The greatest prose-writer on the Royalist and Church side was
Jeremy Taylor, Bishop of Down, in Ireland, and the author
of **Holy Living, Holy Dying,** and many other works written
with a wonderful eloquence. The greatest philosophical writer
was **Thomas Hobbes,** the author of the **Leviathan.** The most
powerful writer for the people was **John Bunyan,** the immortal
author of **The Pilgrim's Progress.** When, however, we come
to the reigns of Charles II. and James II., and the new influences
which their rule and presence imparted, we find the greatest poet
to be **John Dryden,** and the most important prose-writer, **John
Locke.**

7. **The Poetry of the Second Half.**—The poetry of the second
half of the seventeenth century was not an outgrowth or lineal
descendant of the poetry of the first half. No trace of the
strong Elizabethan poetical emotion remained; no writer of this
half-century can claim kinship with the great authors of the
Elizabethan period. The three most remarkable poets in the
latter half of this century are **John Milton, Samuel Butler,**
and **John Dryden.** But Milton's culture was derived chiefly
from the great Greek and Latin writers; and his poems show

few or no signs of belonging to any age or generation in particular of English literature. Butler's poem, the **Hudibras,** is the only one of its kind; and if its author owes anything to other writers, it is to France and not to England that we must look for its sources. Dryden, again, shows no sign of being related to Shakespeare or the dramatic writers of the early part of the century; he is separated from them by a great gulf; he owes most, when he owes anything, to the French school of poetry.

8. JOHN MILTON (1608-1674), the second greatest name in English poetry, and the greatest of all our epic poets, was born in Bread Street, Cheapside, London, in the year 1608—five years after the accession of James I. to the throne, and eight years before the death of Shakespeare. He was educated at St Paul's School, and then at Christ's College, Cambridge. He was so handsome—with a delicate complexion, clear blue eyes, and light-brown hair flowing down his shoulders—that he was known as the "Lady of Christ's." He was destined for the Church; but, being early seized with a strong desire to compose a great poetical work which should bring honour to his country and to the English tongue, he gave up all idea of becoming a clergyman. Filled with his secret purpose, he retired to Horton, in Buckinghamshire, where his father had bought a small country seat. Between the years 1632 and 1638 he studied all the best Greek and Latin authors, mathematics, and science; and he also wrote **L'Allegro** and **Il Penseroso, Comus, Lycidas,** and some shorter poems. These were preludes, or exercises, towards the great poetical work which it was the mission of his life to produce. In 1638-39 he took a journey to the Continent. Most of his time was spent in Italy; and, when in Florence, he paid a visit to Galileo in prison. It had been his intention to go on to Greece; but the troubled state of politics at home brought him back sooner than he wished. The next ten years of his life were engaged in teaching and in writing his prose works. His ideas on teaching are to be found in his **Tractate on Education.** The most eloquent of his prose-works is his **Areopagitica, a Speech for the Liberty of Unlicensed Printing (1644)**—a plea for the freedom of the press, for relieving all writings from the criticism of censors. In 1649—the year of the execution of Charles I.—Milton was appointed Latin or Foreign Secretary to the Government of Oliver Cromwell; and for the next ten years his time was taken up with official work, and with writing prose-volumes in defence of the action of the

Republic. In 1660 the Restoration took place; and Milton was at length free, in his fifty-third year, to carry out his long-cherished scheme of writing a great Epic poem. He chose the subject of the fall and the restoration of man. **Paradise Lost** was completed in 1665; but, owing to the Plague and the Fire of London, it was not published till the year 1667. Milton's young Quaker friend, Ellwood, said to him one day: "Thou hast said much of Paradise Lost, what hast thou to say of Paradise Found?" **Paradise Regained** was the result—a work which was written in 1666, and appeared, along with **Samson Agonistes,** in the year 1671. Milton died in the year 1674—about the middle of the reign of Charles II. He had been three times married.

9. **L'Allegro** (or "The Cheerful Man") is a companion poem to **Il Penseroso** (or "The Meditative Man"). The poems present two contrasted views of the life of the student. They are written in an irregular kind of octosyllabic verse. The **Comus**—mostly in blank verse—is a lyrical drama; and Milton's work was accompanied by a musical composition by the then famous musician Henry Lawes. **Lycidas**—a poem in irregular rhymed verse—is a threnody on the death of Milton's young friend, Edward King, who was drowned in sailing from Chester to Dublin. This poem has been called "the touchstone of taste;" the man who cannot admire it has no feeling for true poetry. The **Paradise Lost** is the story of how Satan was allowed to plot against the happiness of man; and how Adam and Eve fell through his designs. The style is the noblest in the English language; the music of the rhythm is lofty, involved, sustained, and sublime. "In reading 'Paradise Lost,'" says Mr Lowell, "one has a feeling of spaciousness such as no other poet gives." **Paradise Regained** is, in fact, the story of the Temptation, and of Christ's triumph over the wiles of Satan. Wordsworth says: "'Paradise Regained' is most perfect in execution of any written by Milton;" and Coleridge remarks that "it is in its kind the most perfect poem extant, though its kind may be inferior in interest." **Samson Agonistes** ("Samson in Struggle") is a drama, in highly irregular unrhymed verse, in which the poet sets forth his own unhappy fate—

"Eyeless, in Gaza, at the mill with slaves."

It is, indeed, an autobiographical poem—it is the story of the last years of the poet's life.

10. SAMUEL BUTLER **(1612-1680),** the wittiest of English poets, was born at Strensham, in Worcestershire, in the year 1612, four years

after the birth of Milton, and four years before the death of Shake-speare. He was educated at the grammar-school of Worcester, and afterwards at Cambridge—but only for a short time. At the Resto-ration he was made secretary to the Earl of Carbery, who was then President of the Principality of Wales, and steward of Ludlow Castle. The first part of his long poem called **Hudibras** appeared in 1662; the second part in 1663; the third in 1678. Two years after, Butler died in the greatest poverty in London. He was buried in St Paul's, Covent Garden; but a monument was erected to him in Westminster Abbey. Upon this fact Wesley wrote the following epigram :—

> " While Butler, needy wretch, was yet alive,
> No generous patron would a dinner give ;
> See him, when starved to death, and turned to dust,
> Presented with a monumental bust.
> The poet's fate is here in emblem shown,—
> He asked for bread, and he received a stone."

11. The **Hudibras** is a burlesque poem,—a long lampoon, a laboured caricature,—in mockery of the weaker side of the great Puritan party. It is an imaginary account of the adventures of a Puritan knight and his squire in the Civil Wars. It is choke-full of all kinds of learning, of the most pungent remarks—a very hoard of sentences and saws, " of vigorous locutions and picturesque phrases, of strong, sound sense, and robust English." It has been more quoted from than almost any book in our language. Charles II. was never tired of reading it and quoting from it—

> " He never ate, nor drank, nor slept,
> But Hudibras still near him kept "—

says Butler himself.

The following are some of his best known lines :—

> " And, like a lobster boil'd, the morn
> From black to red began to turn."

> " For loyalty is still the same,
> Whether it win or lose the game:
> True as the dial to the sun,
> Altho' it be not shin'd upon."

> " He that complies against his will,
> Is of his own opinion still."

12. JOHN DRYDEN (1631-1700), the greatest of our poets in the second rank, was born at Aldwincle, in Northamptonshire, in the

year 1631. He was descended from Puritan ancestors on both
sides of his house. He was educated at Westminster School, and
at Trinity College, Cambridge. London became his settled abode in
the year 1657. At the Restoration, in 1660, he became an ardent
Royalist ; and, in the year 1663, he married the daughter of a Royalist
nobleman, the Earl of Berkshire. It was not a happy marriage; the
lady, on the one hand, had a violent temper, and, on the other, did
not care a straw for the literary pursuits of her husband. In 1666 he
wrote his first long poem, the **Annus Mirabilis** ("The Wonderful
Year"), in which he paints the war with Holland, and the Fire of
London ; and from this date his life is "one long literary labour."
In 1670, he received the double appointment of Historiographer-
Royal and Poet-Laureate. Up to the year 1681, his work lay chiefly
in writing plays for the theatre; and these plays were written in
rhymed verse, in imitation of the French plays ; for, from the date
of the Restoration, French influence was paramount both in literature
and in fashion. But in this year he published the first part of
Absalom and Achitophel—one of the most powerful satires in the
language. In the year 1683 he was appointed Collector of Customs
in the port of London—a post which Chaucer had held before him.
(It is worthy of note that Dryden "translated" the Tales of Chaucer
into modern English.) At the accession of James II., in 1685, Dryden
became a Roman Catholic ; most certainly neither for gain nor out
of gratitude, but from conviction. In 1687, appeared his poem of
The Hind and the Panther, in which he defends his new creed.
He had, a few years before, brought out another poem called **Religio
Laici** ("A Layman's Faith "), which was a defence of the Church of
England and of her position in religion. In **The Hind and the
Panther,** the Hind represents the Roman Catholic Church, "a milk-
white hind, unspotted and unchanged," the Panther the Church of
England ; and the two beasts reply to each other in all the arguments used by controversialists on these two sides. When the
Revolution of 1688 took place, and James II. had to flee the kingdom, Dryden lost both his offices and the pension he had from
the Crown. Nothing daunted, he set to work once more. Again
he wrote for the stage; but the last years of his life were spent
chiefly in translation. He translated passages from Homer, Ovid,
and from some Italian writers; but his most important work was
the translation of the whole of Virgil's Æneid. To the last he
retained his fire and vigour, action and rush of verse ; and some of
his greatest lyric poems belong to his later years. His ode called
Alexander's Feast was written at the age of sixty-six ; and it was
written at one sitting. At the age of sixty-nine he was meditating a

translation of the whole of Homer—both the Iliad and the Odyssey. He died at his house in London, on May-day of 1700, and was buried with great pomp and splendour in Poets' Corner in Westminster Abbey.

13. His best satire is the **Absalom and Achitophel;** his best specimen of reasoning in verse is **The Hind and the Panther.** His best ode is his **Ode to the Memory of Mrs Anne Killigrew.** Dryden's style is distinguished by its power, sweep, vigour, and "long majestic march." No one has handled the heroic couplet— and it was this form of verse that he chiefly used—with more vigour than Dryden; Pope was more correct, more sparkling, more finished, but he had not Dryden's magnificent march or sweeping impulsiveness. "The fire and spirit of the 'Annus Mirabilis,'" says his latest critic, "are nothing short of amazing, when the difficulties which beset the author are remembered. The glorious dash of the performance is his own." His prose, though full of faults, is also very vigorous. It has "something of the lightning zigzag vigour and splendour of his verse." He always writes clear, homely, and pure English,—full of force and point.

Many of his most pithy lines are often quoted:—

"Men are but children of a larger growth."

" Errors, like straws, upon the surface flow ;
He that would search for pearls must dive below."

"The greatest argument for love is love."

"The secret pleasure of the generous act,
Is the great mind's great bribe."

The great American critic and poet, Mr Lowell, compares him to "an ostrich, to be classed with flying things, and capable, what with leap and flap together, of leaving the earth for a longer or a shorter space, but loving the open plain, where wing and foot help each other to something that is both flight and run at once."

14. JEREMY TAYLOR (**1613-1667**), the greatest master of ornate and musical English prose in his own day, was born at Cambridge in the year 1613—just three years before Shakespeare died. His father was a barber. After attending the free grammar-school of Cambridge, he proceeded to the University. He took holy orders and removed to London. When he was lecturing one day at St Paul's, Archbishop Laud was so taken by his "youthful beauty, pleasant air," fresh eloquence, and exuberant style, that he had him created

a Fellow of All Souls' College, Oxford. When the Civil War broke out, he was taken prisoner by the Parliamentary forces; and, indeed, suffered imprisonment more than once. After the Restoration, he was presented with a bishopric in Ireland, where he died in 1667.

15. Perhaps his best works are his **Holy Living** and **Holy Dying**. His style is rich, even to luxury, full of the most imaginative illustrations, and often overloaded with ornament. He has been called "the Shakespeare of English prose," "the Spenser of divinity," and by other appellations. The latter title is a very happy description; for he has the same wealth of style, phrase, and description that Spenser has, and the same boundless delight in setting forth his thoughts in a thousand different ways. The following is a specimen of his writing. He is speaking of a shipwreck :—

"These are the thoughts of mortals, this is the end and sum of all their designs. A dark night and an ill guide, a boisterous sea and a broken cable, a hard rock and a rough wind, dash in pieces the fortune of a whole family; and they that shall weep loudest for the accident are not yet entered into the storm, and yet have suffered shipwreck."

His writings contain many pithy statements. The following are a few of them :—

"No man is poor that does not think himself so."

"He that spends his time in sport and calls it recreation, is like him whose garment is all made of fringe, and his meat nothing but sauce.

"A good man is as much in awe of himself as of a whole assembly."

16. THOMAS HOBBES **(1588-1679)**, a great philosopher, was born at Malmesbury in the year 1588. He is hence called "the philosopher of Malmesbury." He lived during the reigns of four English sovereigns—Elizabeth, James I., Charles I., and Charles II.; and he was twenty-eight years of age when Shakespeare died. He is in many respects the type of the hard-working, long-lived, persistent Englishman. He was for many years tutor in the Devonshire family—to the first Earl of Devonshire, and to the third Earl of Devonshire—and lived for several years at the family seat of Chatsworth. In his youth he was acquainted with Bacon and Ben Jonson; in his middle age he knew Galileo in Italy; and as he lived to the age of ninety-two, he might have conversed with John Locke or with Daniel Defoe. His greatest work is the **Leviathan**; or, **The Matter, Form, and Power of a Commonwealth**. His style is clear, manly, and vigorous. He tried to write poetry too. At

the advanced age of eighty-five, he wrote a translation of the whole of Homer's Iliad and Odyssey into rhymed English verse, using the same quatrain and the same measure that Dryden employed in his 'Annus Mirabilis.' Two lines are still remembered of this translation: speaking of a child and his mother, he says—

> " And like a star upon her bosom lay
> His beautiful and shining golden head."

17. JOHN BUNYAN (1628-1688), one of the most popular of our prose-writers, was born at Elstow, in Bedfordshire, in the year 1628—just three years before the birth of Dryden. He served, when a young man, with the Parliamentary forces, and was present at the siege of Leicester. At the Restoration, he was apprehended for preaching, in disobedience to the Conventicle Act, "was had home to prison, and there lay complete twelve years." Here he supported himself and his family by making tagged laces and other small-wares; and here, too, he wrote the immortal **Pilgrim's Progress.** After his release, he became pastor of the Baptist congregation at Bedford. He had a great power of bringing persons who had quarrelled together again; and he was so popular among those who knew him, that he was generally spoken of as "Bishop Bunyan." On a journey, undertaken to reconcile an estranged father and a rebellious son, he caught a severe cold, and died of fever in London, in the year 1698. Every one has read, or will read, the **Pilgrim's Progress;** and it may be said, without exaggeration, that to him who has not read the book, a large part of English life and history is dumb and unintelligible. Bunyan has been called the " Spenser of the people," and "the greatest master of allegory that ever lived." His power of imagination is something wonderful; and his simple, homely, and vigorous style makes everything so real, that we seem to be reading a narrative of everyday events and conversations. His vocabulary is not, as Macaulay said, "the vocabulary of the common people;" rather should we say that his English is the English of the Bible and of the best religious writers. His style is, almost everywhere, simple, homely, earnest, and vernacular—without being vulgar. Bunyan's books have, along with Shakespeare and Tyndale's works, been among the chief supports of an idiomatic, nervous, and simple English.

18. JOHN LOCKE (1632-1704), a great English philosopher, was born at Wrington, near Bristol, in the year 1632. He was educated

at Oxford; but he took little interest in the Greek and Latin classics, his chief studies lying in medicine and the physical sciences. He became attached to the famous Lord Shaftesbury, under whom he filled several public offices—among others, that of Commissioner of Trade. When Shaftesbury was obliged to flee to Holland, Locke followed him, and spent several years in exile in that country. All his life a very delicate man, he yet, by dint of great care and thought-fulness, contrived to live to the age of seventy-two. His two most famous works are **Some Thoughts concerning Education,** and the celebrated **Essay on the Human Understanding.** The latter, which is his great work, occupied his time and thoughts for eighteen years. In both these books, Locke exhibits the very genius of common-sense. The purpose of education is, in his opinion, not to make learned men, but to maintain "a sound mind in a sound body;" and he begins the education of the future man even from his cradle. In his philosophical writings, he is always simple; but, as he is loose and vacillating in his use of terms, this simplicity is often purchased at the expense of exactness and self-consistency.

CHAPTER VI.

1. **The Age of Prose.**—The eighteenth century was an age of prose in two senses. In the first place, it was a prosaic age ; and, in the second place, better prose than poetry was produced by its writers. One remarkable fact may also be noted about the chief prose-writers of this century—and that is, that they were, most of them, not merely able writers, not merely distinguished literary men, but also men of affairs—men well versed in the world and in matters of the highest practical moment, while some were also statesmen holding high office. Thus, in the first half of the century, we find Addison, Swift, and Defoe either holding office or influencing and guiding those who held office ; while, in the latter half, we have men like Burke, Hume, and Gibbon, of whom the same, or nearly the same, can be said. The poets, on the contrary, of this eighteenth century, are all of them—with the very slightest exceptions—men who devoted most of their lives to poetry, and had little or nothing to do with practical matters. It may also be noted here that the character of the eighteenth century becomes more and more prosaic as it goes on—less and less under the influence of the spirit of poetry, until, about the close, a great reaction makes itself felt in the persons of Cowper, Chatterton, and Burns, of Crabbe and Wordsworth.

2. **The First Half.**—The great prose-writers of the first half of the eighteenth century are **Addison** and **Steele, Swift** and

Defoe. All of these men had some more or less close connection with the rise of journalism in England; and one of
them, Defoe, was indeed the founder of the modern newspaper.
By far the most powerful intellect of these four was Swift.
The greatest poets of the first half of the eighteenth century
were **Pope, Thomson, Collins,** and **Gray.** Pope towers above
all of them by a head and shoulders, because he was much
more fertile than any, and because he worked so hard and so
untiringly at the labour of the file—at the task of polishing and
improving his verses. But the vein of poetry in the three
others—and more especially in Collins—was much more pure
and genuine than it was in Pope at any time of his life—at any
period of his writing. Let us look at each of these writers a
little more closely.

3. DANIEL DEFOE **(1661-1731)**, one of the most fertile writers
that England ever saw, and one who has been the delight of
many generations of readers, was born in the city of London in the
year 1661. He was educated to be a Dissenting minister; but he
turned from that profession to the pursuit of trade. He attempted
several trades,—was a hosier, a hatter, a printer; and he is said also
to have been a brick and tile maker. In 1692 he failed in business;
but, in no long time after, he paid every one of his creditors to the
uttermost farthing. Through all his labours and misfortunes he was
always a hard and careful reader,—an omnivorous reader, too, for
he was in the habit of reading almost every book that came in his
way. He made his first reputation by writing political pamphlets.
One of his pamphlets brought him into high favour with King
William; another had the effect of placing him in the pillory and
lodging him in prison. But while in Newgate, he did not idle away
his time or "languish"; he set to work, wrote hard, and started a
newspaper, **The Review,** — the earliest genuine newspaper England had seen up to his time. This paper he brought out two or
three times a-week; and every word of it he wrote himself. He
continued to carry it on single-handed for eight years. In 1706,
he was made a member of the Commission for bringing about the
union between England and Scotland; and his great knowledge of
commerce and commercial affairs were of singular value to this Commission. In 1715 he had a dangerous illness, brought on by political
excitement; and, on his recovery, he gave up most of his political

writing, and took to the composition of stories and romances. Although now a man of fifty-four, he wrote with the vigour and ease of a young man of thirty. His greatest imaginative work was written in 1719—when he was nearly sixty—**The Life and Strange Surprising Adventures of Robinson Crusoe, of York, Mariner, . . . written by Himself.** Within six years he had produced twelve works of a similar kind. He is said to have written in all two hundred and fifty books in the course of his lifetime. He died in 1731.

4. His best known—and it is also his greatest—work is **Robinson Crusoe**; and this book, which every one has read, may be compared with 'Gulliver's Travels,' for the purpose of observing how imaginative effects are produced by different means and in different ways. Another vigorous work of imagination by Defoe is the **Journal of the Plague,** which appeared in 1722. There are three chief things to be noted regarding Defoe and his writings. These are: first, that Defoe possessed an unparalleled knowledge—a knowledge wider than even Shakespeare's—of the circumstances and details of human life among all sorts, ranks, and conditions of men; secondly, that he gains his wonderful realistic effects by the freest and most copious use of this detailed knowledge in his works of imagination; and thirdly, that he possessed a vocabulary of the most wonderful wealth. His style is strong, homely, and vigorous, but the sentences are long, loose, clumsy, and sometimes ungrammatical. Like Sir Walter Scott, he was too eager to produce large and broad effects to take time to balance his clauses or to polish his sentences. Like Sir Walter Scott, again, he possesses in the highest degree the art of *particularising.*

5. Jonathan Swift (**1667-1745**), the greatest prose-writer, in his own kind, of the eighteenth century, and the opposite in most respects — especially in style — of Addison, was born in Dublin in the year 1667. Though born in Ireland, he was of purely English descent—his father belonging to a Yorkshire family, and his mother being a Leicestershire lady. His father died before he was born; and he was educated by the kindness of an uncle. After being at a private school at Kilkenny, he was sent to Trinity College, Dublin, where he was plucked for his degree at his first examination, and, on a second trial, only obtained his B.A. "by special favour." He next came to England, and for eleven years acted as private secretary to Sir William Temple, a retired statesman and ambassador, who lived at Moor Park, near Richmond-on-

Thames. In 1692 he paid a visit to Oxford, and there obtained the degree of M.A. In 1700 he went to Ireland with Lord Berkeley as his chaplain, and while in that country was presented with several livings. He at first attached himself to the Whig party, but stung by this party's neglect of his labours and merits, he joined the Tories, who raised him to the Deanery of St Patrick's Cathedral in Dublin. But, though nominally resident in Dublin, he spent a large part of his time in London. Here he knew and met everybody who was worth knowing, and for some time he was the most imposing figure, and wielded the greatest influence in all the best social, political, and literary circles of the capital. In 1714, on the death of Queen Anne, Swift's hopes of further advancement died out; and he returned to his Deanery, settled in Dublin, and "commenced Irishman for life." A man of strong passions, he usually spent his birthday in reading that chapter of the Book of Job which contains the verse, "Let the day perish in which I was born." He died insane in 1745, and left his fortune to found a lunatic asylum in Dublin. One day, when taking a walk with a friend, he saw a blasted elm, and, pointing to it, he said : "I shall be like that tree, and die first at the top." For the last three years of his life he never spoke one word.

6. Swift has written verse ; but it is his prose-works that give him his high and unrivalled place in English literature. His most powerful work, published in 1704, is the **Tale of a Tub**—a satire on the disputes between the Roman Catholic, Anglican, and Presbyterian Churches. His best known prose-work is the **Gulliver's Travels,** which appeared in 1726. This work is also a satire; but it is a satire on men and women,—on humanity. "The power of Swift's prose," it has been said by an able critic, "was the terror of his own, and remains the wonder of after times." His style is strong, simple, straightforward; he uses the plainest words and the homeliest English, and every blow tells. Swift's style—as every genuine style does—reflects the author's character. He was an ardent lover and a good hater. Sir Walter Scott describes him as "tall, strong, and well made, dark in complexion, but with bright blue eyes (Pope said they were "as azure as the heavens"), black and bushy eyebrows, aquiline nose, and features which expressed the stern, haughty, and dauntless turn of his mind." He grew savage under the slightest contradiction ; and dukes and great lords were obliged to pay court to him. His prose was as trenchant and powerful as were his manners : it has been compared to "cold steel." His own definition of a good style is " proper words in proper places."

7. JOSEPH ADDISON **(1672-1719)**, the most elegant prose-writer—
as Pope was the mose polished verse-writer—of the eighteenth century, was born at Milston, in Wiltshire, in the year 1672.   He was
educated at Charterhouse School, in London, where one of his friends
and companions was the celebrated Dick Steele—afterwards Sir
Richard Steele.   He then went to Oxford, where he made a name for
himself by his beautiful compositions in Latin verse.   In 1695 he
addressed a poem to King William ; and this poem brought him into
notice with the Government of the day.   Not long after, he received
a pension of £300 a-year, to enable him to travel ; and he spent some
time in France and Italy.   The chief result of this tour was a poem
entitled **A Letter from Italy** to Lord Halifax.   In 1704, when
Lord Godolphin was in search of a poet who should celebrate in an
adequate style the striking victory of Blenheim, Addison was introduced to him by Lord Halifax.   His poem called **The Campaign**
was the result ; and one simile in it took and held the attention
of all English readers, and of "the town."   A violent storm had
passed over England ; and Addison compared the calm genius of
Marlborough, who was as cool and serene amid shot and shell as in
a drawing-room or at the dinner-table, to the Angel of the Storm.
The lines are these :—

> "So when an Angel by divine command
>   With rising tempests shakes a guilty land,
>   Such as of late o'er pale Britannia passed,
>   Calm and serene he drives the furious blast ;
>   And, pleased the Almighty's orders to perform,
>   Rides in the whirlwind, and directs the storm."

For this poem Addison was rewarded with the post of Commissioner
of Appeals.   He rose, successively, to be Under Secretary of State ;
Secretary for Ireland ; and, finally, Secretary of State for England—
an office which would correspond to that of our present Home
Secretary.   He married the Countess of Warwick, to whose son he
had been tutor ; but it was not a happy marriage.   Pope says of him
in regard to it, that—

> " He married discord in a noble wife."

He died at Holland House, Kensington, London, in the year 1719, at
the age of forty-seven.
      8.   But it is not at all as a poet, but as a prose-writer, that Addison
is famous in the history of literature.   While he was in Ireland,
his friend Steele started **The Tatler**, in 1709 ; and Addison sent
numerous contributions to this little paper.   In 1711, Steele began
a still more famous paper, which he called **The Spectator** ; and

Addison's writings in this morning journal made its reputation. His contributions are distinguishable by being signed with some one of the letters of the name *Clio*—the Muse of History. A third paper, **The Guardian,** appeared a few years after ; and Addison's contributions to it are designated by a hand (☞) at the foot of each. In addition to his numerous prose-writings, Addison brought out the tragedy of **Cato** in 1713. It was very successful ; but it is now neither read nor acted. Some of his hymns, however, are beautiful, and are well known. Such are the hymn beginning, "The spacious firmament on high ; " and his version of the 23d Psalm, "The Lord my pasture shall prepare."

9. Addison's prose style is inimitable, easy, graceful, full of humour —full of good humour, delicate, with a sweet and kindly rhythm, and always musical to the ear. He is the most graceful of social satirists ; and his genial creation of the character of **Sir Roger de Coverley** will live for ever. While his work in verse is never more than second-rate, his writings in prose are always first-rate. Dr Johnson said of his prose : "Whoever wishes to attain an English style—familiar but not coarse, and elegant but not ostentatious, —must give his days and nights to the study of Addison." Lord Lytton also remarks : "His style has that nameless urbanity in which we recognise the perfection of manner ; courteous, but not courtier-like ; so dignified, yet so kindly ; so easy, yet high-bred. It is the most perfect form of English." His style, however, must be acknowledged to want force—to be easy rather than vigorous ; and it has not the splendid march of Jeremy Taylor, or the noble power of Savage Landor.

10. RICHARD STEELE (1671-1729), commonly called "Dick Steele," the friend and colleague of Addison, was born in Dublin, but of English parents, in the year 1671. The two friends were educated at Charterhouse and at Oxford together ; and they remained friends, with some slight breaks and breezes, to the close of life. Steele was a writer of plays, essays, and pamphlets—for one of which he was expelled from the House of Commons ; but his chief fame was earned in connection with the Society Journals, which he founded. He started many—such as **Town-Talk, The Tea-Table, Chit-Chat;** but only the **Tatler** and the **Spectator** rose to success and to fame. The strongest quality in his writings is his pathos : the source of tears is always at his command ; and, although himself of a gay and even rollicking temperament, he seems to have preferred this vein. The literary skill of Addison—his happy art in

the choosing of words—did not fall to the lot of Steele; but he is more hearty and more human in his description of character. He died in 1729, ten years after the departure of his friend Addison.

11. ALEXANDER POPE (1688-1744), the greatest poet of the eighteenth century, was born in Lombard Street, London, in the year of the Revolution, 1688. His father was a wholesale linendraper, who, having amassed a fortune, retired to Binfield, on the borders of Windsor Forest. In the heart of this beautiful country young Pope's youth was spent. On the death of his father, Pope left Windsor and took up his residence at Twickenham, on the banks of the Thames, where he remained till his death in 1744. His parents being Roman Catholics, it was impossible for young Pope to go either to a public school or to one of the universities; and hence he was educated privately. At the early age of eight, he met with a translation of Homer in verse; and this volume became his companion night and day. At the age of ten, he turned some of the events described in Homer into a play. The poems of Spenser, the poets' poet, were his next favourites; but the writer who made the deepest and most lasting impression upon his mind was Dryden. Little Pope began to write verse very early. He says of himself—

> "As yet a child, nor yet a fool to fame,
> I lisped in numbers, for the numbers came."

His **Ode to Solitude** was written at the age of twelve; his **Pastorals** when he was fifteen. His **Essay on Criticism,** which was composed in his twentieth year, though not published till 1711, established his reputation as a writer of neat, clear, sparkling, and elegant verse. The **Rape of the Lock** raised his reputation still higher. Macaulay pronounced it his best poem. De Quincey declared it to be "the most exquisite monument of playful fancy that universal literature offers." Another critic has called it the "perfection of the mock-heroic." Pope's most successful poem—if we measure it by the fame and the money it brought him—was his translation of the **Iliad** of Homer. A great scholar said of this translation that it was "a very pretty poem, but not Homer." The fact is that Pope did not translate directly from the Greek, but from a French or a Latin version which he kept beside him. Whatever its faults, and however great its deficiency as a representation of the powerful and deep simplicity of the original Greek, no one can deny the charm and finish of its versification, or the rapidity, facility, and melody of the flow of the verse. These qualities make this work unique in English poetry.

12. After finishing the **Iliad**, Pope undertook a translation of the **Odyssey** of Homer. This was not so successful; nor was it so well done. In fact, Pope translated only half of it himself; the other half was written by two scholars called Broome and Fenton. His next great poem was the **Dunciad**,—a satire upon those petty writers, carping critics, and hired defamers who had tried to write down the reputation of Pope's Homeric work. "The composition of the 'Dunciad' revealed to Pope where his true strength lay, in blending personalities with moral reflections."

13. Pope's greatest works were written between 1730 and 1740; and they consist of the **Moral Essays**, the **Essay on Man**, and the **Epistles and Satires**. These poems are full of the finest thoughts, expressed in the most perfect form. Mr Ruskin quotes the couplet—

> " Never elated, while one man's oppressed;
> Never dejected, whilst another's blessed,"—

as " the most complete, concise, and lofty expression of moral temper existing in English words." The poem of Pope which shows his best and most striking qualities in their most characteristic form, is probably the **Epistle to Dr Arbuthnot or Prologue to the Satires**. In this poem occur the celebrated lines about Addison— which make a perfect portrait, although it is far from being a true likeness.

His pithy lines and couplets have obtained a permanent place in literature. Thus we have :—

> " True wit is nature to advantage dressed,
> What oft was thought, but ne'er so well expressed."

> " Good-nature and good-sense must ever join.
> To err is human, to forgive divine."

> " All seems infected that the infected spy,
> As all looks yellow to the jaundic'd eye."

> " Fear not the anger of the wise to raise ;
> Those best can bear reproof who merit praise."

The greatest conciseness is visible in his epigrams and in his compliments :—

> " A vile encomium doubly ridicules:
> There's nothing blackens like the ink of fools."

> " And not a vanity is given in vain."

> " Would ye be blest? despise low joys, low gains,
> Disdain whatever Cornbury disdains,
> Be virtuous, and be happy for your pains."

14. Pope is the foremost literary figure of his age and century; and he is also the head of a school. He brought to perfection a style of writing verse which was followed by hundreds of clever writers. Cowper says of him :—

> " But Pope—his musical finesse was such,
> So nice his ear, so delicate his touch,—
> Made poetry a mere mechanic art,
> And every warbler has his tune by heart."

Pope was not the poet of nature or of humanity; he was the poet of "the town," and of the Court. He was greatly influenced by the neatness and polish of French verse ; and, from his boyhood, his great ambition was to be "a correct poet." He worked and worked, polished and polished, until each idea had received at his hands its very neatest and most epigrammatic expression. In the art of condensed, compact, pointed, and yet harmonious and flowing verse, Pope has no equal. But, as a vehicle for poetry—for the love and sympathy with nature and man which every true poet must feel, Pope's verse is artificial ; and its style of expression has now died out. It was one of the chief missions of Wordsworth to drive the Popian second-hand vocabulary out of existence.

15. JAMES THOMSON (1700-1748), the poet of The Seasons, was born at Ednam in Roxburghshire, Scotland, in the year 1700. He was educated at the grammar-school of Jedburgh, and then at the University of Edinburgh. It was intended that he should enter the ministry of the Church of Scotland ; but, before his college course was finished, he had given up this idea: poetry proved for him too strong a magnet. While yet a young man, he had written his poem of Winter ; and, with that in his pocket, he resolved to try his fortune in London. While walking about the streets, looking at the shops, and gazing at the new wonders of the vast metropolis, his pocket was picked of his pocket-handkerchief and his letters of introduction ; and he found himself alone in London — thrown entirely on his own resources. A publisher was, however, in time found for Winter ; and the poem slowly rose into appreciation and popularity. This was in 1726. Next year, Summer ; two years after, Spring appeared ; while Autumn, in 1730, completed the Seasons. The Castle of Indolence—a poem in the Spenserian stanza—appeared· in 1748. In the same year he was appointed Surveyor-General of the Leeward Islands, though he never visited the scene of his duty, but had his work done by deputy. He died at Kew in the year 1748.

16. Thomson's place as a poet is high in the second rank. His **Seasons** have always been popular; and, when Coleridge found a well-thumbed and thickly dog's-eared copy lying on the window-sill of a country inn, he exclaimed "This is true fame!" His **Castle of Indolence** is, however, a finer piece of poetical work than any of his other writings. The first canto is the best. But the **Seasons** have been much more widely read; and a modern critic says: "No poet has given the special pleasure which poetry is capable of giving to so large a number of persons in so large a measure as Thomson." Thomson is very unequal in his style. Sometimes he rises to a great height of inspired expression; at other times he sinks to a dull dead level of pedestrian prose. His power of describing scenery is often very remarkable. Professor Craik says: "There is no other poet who surrounds us with so much of the truth of nature;" and he calls the **Castle of Indolence** "one of the gems of the language."

17. THOMAS GRAY **(1716-1771)**, the greatest elegiac poet of the century, was born in London in 1716. His father was a "money-scrivener," as it was called; in other words, he was a stock-broker. His mother's brother was an assistant-master at Eton; and at Eton, under the care of this uncle, Gray was brought up. One of his schoolfellows was the famous Horace Walpole. After leaving school, Gray proceeded to Cambridge; but, instead of reading mathematics, he studied classical literature, history, and modern languages, and never took his degree. After some years spent at Cambridge, he entered himself of the Inner Temple; but he never gave much time to the study of law. His father died in 1741; and Gray, soon after, gave up the law and went to live entirely at Cambridge. The first published of his poems was the **Ode on a Distant Prospect of Eton College.** The **Elegy written in a Country Churchyard** was handed about in manuscript before its publication in 1750; and it made his reputation at once. In 1755 the **Progress of Poesy** was published; and the ode entitled **The Bard** was begun. In 1768 he was appointed Professor of Modern History at Cambridge; but, though he studied hard, he never lectured. He died at Cambridge, at the age of fifty-four, in the year 1771. Gray was never married. He was said by those who knew him to be the most learned man of his time in Europe. Literature, history, and several sciences—all were thoroughly known to him. He had read everything in the world that was best worth reading; while his knowledge of botany, zoology, and entomology was both wide and exact.

18. Gray's **Elegy** took him seven years to write ; it contains thirty-two stanzas ; and Mr Palgrave says "they are perhaps the noblest stanzas in the language." General Wolfe, when sailing down to attack Quebec, recited the Elegy to his officers, and declared, " Now, gentlemen, I would rather be the author of that poem than take Quebec." Lord Byron called the Elegy "the corner-stone of Gray's poetry." Gray ranks with Milton as the most finished workman in English verse ; and certainly he spared no pains. Gray said himself that "the style he aimed at was extreme conciseness of expression, yet pure, perspicuous, and musical ; " and this style, at which he aimed, he succeeded fully in achieving. One of the finest stanzas in the whole Elegy is the last, which the writer omitted in all the later editions :—

> " There scattered oft, the earliest of the year,
>   By hands unseen, are showers of violets found ;
> The red-breast loves to build and warble there,
>   And little footsteps lightly print the ground."

19. WILLIAM COLLINS **(1721-1759)**, one of the truest lyrical poets of the century, was born at Chichester on Christmas-day, 1721. He was educated at Winchester School ; afterwards at Queen's, and also at Magdalen College, Oxford. Before he left school he had written a set of poems called **Persian Eclogues.** He left the university with a reputation for ability and for indolence ; went to London "with many projects in his head and little money in his pocket;" and there found a kind and fast friend in Dr Johnson. His **Odes** appeared in 1747. The volume fell still-born from the press : not a single copy was sold ; no one bought, read, or noticed it. In a fit of furious despair, the unhappy author called in the whole edition and burnt every copy with his own hands. And yet it was, with the single exception of the songs of Burns, the truest poetry that had appeared in the whole of the eighteenth century. A great critic says: "In the little book there was hardly a single false note : there was, above all things, a purity of music, a clarity of style, to which I know of no parallel in English verse from the death of Andrew Marvell to the birth of William Blake." Soon after this great disappointment he went to live at Richmond, where he formed a friendship with Thomson and other poets. In 1749 he wrote the **Ode on the Death of Thomson,** beginning—

> "In yonder grave a Druid lies "—

one of the finest of his poems. Not long after, he was attacked by a

X

disease of the brain, from which he suffered, at intervals, during the remainder of his short life. He died at Chichester in 1759, at the age of thirty-eight.

20. Collins's best poem is the **Ode to Evening**; his most elaborate, the **Ode on the Passions**; and his best known, the **Ode** beginning—

> " How sleep the brave, who sink to rest
> By all their country's wishes blessed ! "

His latest and best critic says of his poems : " His range of flight was perhaps the narrowest, but assuredly the highest, of his generation. He could not be taught singing like a finch, but he struck straight upward for the sun like a lark. . . . The direct sincerity and purity of their positive and straightforward inspiration will always keep his poems fresh and sweet in the senses of all men. He was a solitary song-bird among many more or less excellent pipers and pianists. He could put more spirit of colour into a single stroke, more breath of music into a single note, than could all the rest of his generation into all the labours of their lives."

CHAPTER VII.

THE SECOND HALF OF THE EIGHTEENTH CENTURY.

1. **Prose - Writers.**—The four greatest prose-writers of the latter half of the eighteenth century are **Johnson, Goldsmith, Burke,** and **Gibbon.** Dr Johnson was the most prominent literary figure in London at this period ; and filled in his own time much the same position that Carlyle lately held in literary circles. He wrote on many subjects—but chiefly on literature and morals; and hence he was called "The Great Moralist." Goldsmith stands out clearly as the writer of the most pleasant and easy prose ; his pen was ready for any subject; and it has been said of him with perfect truth, that he touched nothing that he did not adorn. Burke was the most eloquent writer of his time, and by far the greatest political thinker that England has ever produced. He is known by an essay he wrote when a very young man—on "The Sublime and Beautiful"; but it is to his speeches and political writings that we must look for his noblest thoughts and most eloquent language. Gibbon is one of the greatest historians and most powerful writers the world has ever seen.

2. SAMUEL JOHNSON **(1709-1784),** the great essayist and lexicographer, was born at Lichfield in the year 1709. His father was a bookseller ; and it was in his father's shop that Johnson acquired his habit of omnivorous reading, or rather devouring of books. The mistress of the dame's school, to which he first went, declared him

to be the best scholar she ever had. After a few years at the free grammar-school of Lichfield, and one year at Stourbridge, he went to Pembroke College, Oxford, at the age of nineteen. Here he did not confine himself to the studies of the place, but indulged in a wide range of miscellaneous reading. He was too poor to take a degree, and accordingly left Oxford without graduating. After acting for some time as a bookseller's hack, he married a Mrs Porter of Birmingham—a widow with £800. With this money he opened a boarding-school, or "academy" as he called it; but he had never more than three scholars—the most famous of whom was the celebrated player, David Garrick. In 1737 he went up to London, and for the next quarter of a century struggled for a living by the aid of his pen. During the first ten years of his London life he wrote chiefly for the 'Gentleman's Magazine.' In 1738 his **London**—a poem in heroic metre—appeared. In 1747 he began his famous **Dictionary**; it was completed in 1755; and the University of Oxford conferred on him the honorary degree of M.A. In 1749 he wrote another poem—also in heroic metre—the 'Vanity of Human Wishes.' In 1750 he had begun the periodical that raised his fame to its full height—a periodical to which he gave the name of **The Rambler**. It appeared twice a-week; and Dr Johnson wrote every article in it for two years. In 1759 he published the short novel called **Rasselas**: it was written to defray the expenses of his mother's funeral; and he wrote it "in the evenings of a week." The year 1762 saw him with a pension from the Government of £300 a-year; and henceforth he was free from heavy hack-work and literary drudgery, and could give himself up to the largest enjoyment of that for which he cared most—social conversation. He was the best talker of his time; and he knew everybody worth knowing —Burke, Goldsmith, Gibbon, the great painter Sir Joshua Reynolds, and many other able men. In 1764 he founded the "Literary Club," which still exists and meets in London. Oddly enough, although a prolific writer, it is to another person—to Mr James Boswell, who first met him in 1763—that he owes his greatest and most lasting fame. A much larger number of persons read **Boswell's Life of Johnson**—one of the most entertaining books in all literature— than Johnson's own works. Between the years 1779 and 1781 appeared his last and ablest work, **The Lives of the Poets**, which were written as prefaces to a collective edition of the English Poets, published by several London booksellers. He died in 1784.

3. Johnson's earlier style was full of Latin words; his later style is more purely English than most of the journalistic writing of the present day. His Rambler is full of "long-tailed words in *osity* and

ation;" but his 'Lives of the Poets' is written in manly, vigorous, and idiomatic English.   In verse, he occupies a place between Pope and Goldsmith, and is one of the masters in the "didactic school" of English poetry.   His rhythm and periods are swelling and sonorous; and here and there he equals Pope in the terseness and condensation of his language.   The following is a fair specimen :—

> " Of all the griefs that harass the distressed,
>   Sure the most bitter is a scornful jest ;
>   Fate never wounds more deep the generous heart,
>   Than when a blockhead's insult points the dart."

4. OLIVER GOLDSMITH (1728-1774), poet, essayist, historian, and dramatist, was born at Pallas, in the county of Longford, Ireland, in the year 1728.   His father was an Irish clergyman, careless, good-hearted, and the original of the famous Dr Primrose, in **The Vicar of Wakefield.**   He was also the original of the "village preacher" in **The Deserted Village.**

> " A man he was to all the country dear,
>   And passing rich with forty pounds a-year."

Oliver was educated at Trinity College, Dublin ; but he left it with no fixed aim.   He thought of law, and set off for London, but spent all his money in Dublin.   He thought of medicine, and resided two years in Edinburgh.   He started for Leyden, in Holland, to continue what he called his medical studies ; but he had a thirst to see the world—and so, with a guinea in his pocket, one shirt, and a flute, he set out on his travels through the continent of Europe.   At length, on the 1st of February 1756, he landed at Dover, after an absence of two years, without a farthing in his pocket.   London reached, he tried many ways of making a living, as assistant to an apothecary, physician, reader for the press, usher in a school, writer in journals.   His first work was 'An Inquiry into the State of Polite Learning in Europe,' in 1759 ; but it appeared without his name.   From that date he wrote books of all kinds, poems, and plays.   He died in his chambers in Brick Court, Temple, London, in 1774.

5. Goldsmith's best poems are **The Traveller** and **The Deserted Village,**—both written in the Popian couplet.   His best play is **She Stoops to Conquer.**   His best prose work is **The Vicar of Wakefield,** "the first genuine novel of domestic life."   He also wrote histories of England, of Rome, of Animated Nature.   All this was done as professional, nay, almost as hack work ; but

always in a very pleasant, lively, and readable style. Ease, grace, charm, naturalness, pleasant rhythm, purity of diction—these were the chief characteristics of his writings. "Almost to all things could he turn his hand"—poem, essay, play, story, history, natural science. Even when satirical, he was good-natured ; and his **Retaliation** is the friendliest and pleasantest of satires. In his poetry, his words seem artless, but are indeed delicately chosen with that consummate art which conceals and effaces itself : where he seems most simple and easy, there he has taken most pains and given most labour.

6. Edmund Burke **(1730-1797)** was born at Dublin in the year 1730. He was educated at Trinity College, Dublin ; and in 1747 was entered of the Middle Temple, with the purpose of reading for the Bar. In 1766 he was so fortunate as to enter Parliament as member for Wendover, in Buckinghamshire ; and he sat in the House of Commons for nearly thirty years. While in Parliament, he worked hard to obtain justice for the colonists of North America, and to avert the separation of them from the mother country ; and also to secure good government for India. At the close of his life, it was his intention to take his seat in the House of Peers as Earl Beaconsfield—the title afterwards assumed by Mr Disraeli ; but the death of his son, and only child—for whom the honour was really meant and wished—quite broke his heart, and he never carried out his purpose. He died at Beaconsfield in the year 1797. The lines of Goldsmith on Burke, in his poem of " Retaliation," are well known :—

> " Here lies our good Edmund, whose genius was such
> We scarcely can praise it or blame it too much ;
> Who, born for the universe, narrowed his mind,
> And to party gave up what was meant for mankind ;
> Who, too deep for his hearers, still went on refining,
> And thought of convincing while they thought of dining."

7. Burke's most famous writings are **Thoughts on the Cause of the present Discontents,** published in 1773 ; **Reflections on the French Revolution** (1790) ; and the **Letters on a Regicide Peace** (1797). His " Thoughts " is perhaps the best of his works in point of style ; his " Reflections," are full of passages of the highest and most noble eloquence. Burke has been described by a great critic as " the supreme writer of the century ; " and Macaulay says, that " in richness of imagination, he is superior to every orator ancient and modern." In the power of expressing thought in the strongest, fullest, and most vivid manner, he must be classed with Shakespeare

and Bacon—and with these writers when at their best. He indulges in repetitions; but the repetitions are never monotonous; they serve to place the subject in every possible point of view, and to enable us to see all sides of it. He possessed an enormous vocabulary, and had the fullest power over it; "never was a man under whose hands language was more plastic and ductile." He is very fond of metaphor, and is described by an able critic as "the greatest master of metaphor that the world has ever seen."

8. EDWARD GIBBON (1737-1794), the second great prose-writer of the second half of the eighteenth century, was born at Putney, London, in 1737. His father was a wealthy landowner. Young Gibbon was a very sickly child—the only survivor of a delicate family of seven; he was left to pass his time as he pleased, and for the most part to educate himself. But he had the run of several good libraries; and he was an eager and never satiated reader. He was sent to Oxford at the early age of fifteen; and so full was his knowledge in some directions, and so defective in others, that he went there, he tells us himself, "with a stock of knowledge that might have puzzled a doctor, and a degree of ignorance of which a schoolboy would have been ashamed." He was very fond of disputation while at Oxford; and the Dons of the University were astonished to see the pathetic "thin little figure, with a large head, disputing and arguing with the greatest ability." In the course of his reading, he lighted on some French and English books that convinced him for the time of the truth of the Roman Catholic faith; he openly professed his change of belief; and this obliged him to leave the University. His father sent him to Lausanne, and placed him under the care of a Swiss clergyman there, whose arguments were at length successful in bringing him back to a belief in Protestantism. On his return to England in 1758, he lived in his father's house in Hampshire; read largely, as usual; but also joined the Hampshire militia as captain of a company, and the exercises and manœuvres of his regiment gave him an insight into military matters which was afterwards useful to him when he came to write history. He published his first work in 1761. It was an essay on the study of literature, and was written in French. In 1770 his father died; he came into a fortune, entered Parliament, where he sat for eight years, but never spoke; and, in 1776, he began his history of the **Decline and Fall of the Roman Empire**. This, by far the greatest of his works, was not completed till 1787, and was published in 1788, on his fifty-first birthday. His

account of the completion of the work—it was finished at Lausanne, where he had lived for six years—is full of beauty: "It was on the day, or rather night, of June 27, 1787, between the hours of eleven and twelve, that I wrote the last lines of the last page in a summer-house in my garden. After laying down my pen, I took several turns in a covered walk of acacias, which commands a prospect of the country, the lake, and the mountains. The air was temperate, the sky was serene. The silver orb of the moon was reflected from the waters, and all nature was silent. I will not describe the first emotion of joy on the recovery of my freedom, and perhaps the establishment of my fame. But my pride was soon humbled, and a sober melancholy was spread over my mind by the idea that I had taken an everlasting leave of an old and agreeable companion, and that, whatever might be the future fate of my history, the life of the historian must be short and precarious." Gibbon died in 1794, about one year before the birth of another great historian, Grote, the author of the ‘History of Greece.’

9. Gibbon’s book is one of the great historical works of the world. It covers a space of about thirteen centuries, from the reign of Trajan (98), to the fall of the Eastern Empire in 1453; and the amount of reading and study required to write it, must have been almost beyond the power of our conceiving. The skill in arranging and disposing the enormous mass of matter in his history is also unparalleled. His style is said by a critic to be "copious, splendid, elegantly rounded, distinguished by supreme artificial skill." It is remarkable for the proportion of Latin words employed. While some parts of our translation of the Bible contain as much as 96 per cent of pure English words, Gibbon has only 58 per cent: the rest, or 42 per cent, are words of Latin origin. In fact, of all our great English writers, Gibbon stands lowest in his use of pure English words; and the two writers who come nearest him in this respect are Johnson and Swift. The great Greek scholar, Professor Porson, said of Gibbon’s style, that "there could not be a better exercise for a schoolboy than to turn a page of it into English."

10. **Poets.**—The chief poets of the latter half of the eighteenth century belong to a new world, and show very little trace in their writings of eighteenth-century culture, ideas, or prejudices. Most of the best poets who were born in this half of the eighteenth century and began to write in it—such as Crabbe and Wordsworth—are true denizens, in the character of their minds and feelings, of the nineteenth. The greatest poets of the

period are **Cowper, Crabbe,** and **Burns**; and along with these may be mentioned as little inferior, **Chatterton** and **Blake,** two of the most original poets that have appeared in any literature.

11. WILLIAM COWPER (**1731-1800**), one of the truest, purest, and sweetest of English poets, was born at Great Berkhampstead, in Hertfordshire, in 1731. His father, Dr Cowper, who was a nephew of Lord Chancellor Cowper, was rector of the parish, and chaplain to George II. Young Cowper was educated at Westminster School; and "the great proconsul of India," Warren Hastings, was one of his schoolfellows. After leaving Westminster, he was entered of the Middle Temple, and was also articled to a solicitor. At the age of thirty-one he was appointed one of the Clerks to the House of Lords; but he was so terribly nervous and timid, that he threw up the appointment. He was next appointed Clerk of the Journals—a post which even the shyest man might hold; but, when he found that he would have to appear at the bar of the House of Lords, he went home and attempted to commit suicide. When at school, he had been terribly and persistently bullied; and, about this time, his mind had been somewhat affected by a disappointment in love. The form of his insanity was melancholia; and he had several long and severe attacks of the same disease in the after-course of his life. He had to be placed in the keeping of a physician; and it was only after fifteen months' seclusion that he was able to face the world. Giving up all idea of professional or of public life, he went to live at Huntingdon with the Unwins; and, after the death of Mr Unwin, he removed with Mrs Unwin to Olney, in Buckinghamshire. Here, in 1773, another attack of melancholia came upon him. In 1779, Cowper joined with Mr Newton, the curate of the parish, in publishing the **Olney Hymns,** of which he wrote sixty-eight. But it was not till he was past fifty years of age that he betook himself seriously to the writing of poetry. His first volume, which contained **Table-Talk, Conversation, Retirement,** and other poems in heroic metre, appeared in 1782. His second volume, which included **The Task** and **John Gilpin,** was published in 1785. His translation of the **Iliad** and **Odyssey** of Homer—a translation into blank verse, which he wrote at the regular rate of forty lines a-day—was published in 1791. Mrs Unwin now had a shock of paralysis; Cowper himself was again seized with mental illness; and from 1791 till his death in 1800, his condition was one of extreme misery, depression, and despair. He thought himself an outcast from the mercy of God. " I seem to

myself," he wrote to a friend, "to be scrambling always in the dark, among rocks and precipices, without a guide, but with an enemy ever at my heels, prepared to push me headlong." The cloud never lifted; gloom and dejection enshrouded all his later years; a pension of £300 a-year from George III. brought him no pleasure; and he died insane, at East Dereham, in Norfolk, in the year 1800. In the poem of **The Castaway** he compares himself to a drowning sailor :—

> " No voice divine the storm allayed,
>   No light propitious shone,
> When, far from all effectual aid,
>   We perished—each alone—
> But I beneath a rougher sea,
> And whelmed in blacker gulfs than he."

12. His greatest work is **The Task**; and the best poem in it is probably "The Winter Evening." His best-known poem is **John Gilpin**, which, like "The Task," he wrote at the request of his friend, Lady Austen. His most powerful poem is **The Castaway**. He always writes in clear, crisp, pleasant, and manly English. He himself says, in a letter to a friend : " Perspicuity is always more than half the battle. . . A meaning that does not stare you in the face is as bad as no meaning ;" and this direction he himself always carried out. Cowper's poems mark a new era in poetry ; his style is new, and his ideas are new. He is no follower of Pope ; Southey compared Pope and Cowper as " formal gardens in comparison with woodland scenery." He is always original, always true— true to his own feeling, and true to the object he is describing. " My descriptions," he writes of " The Task," " are all from nature ; not one of them second-handed. My delineations of the heart are from my own experience." Everywhere in his poems we find a genuine love of nature ; humour and pathos in his description of persons ; and a purity and honesty of style that have never been surpassed. Many of his well-put lines have passed into our common stock of everyday quotations. Such are—

> " God made the country, and man made the town."

> " Variety's the very spice of life
> That gives it all its flavour."

> " The heart
> May give a useful lesson to the head,
> And Learning wiser grow without his books."

> " Beware of desperate steps. The darkest day,
> Live till to-morrow, will have passed away."

13. GEORGE CRABBE **(1754-1832)**, the poet of the poor, was born at Aldborough, in Suffolk, on Christmas Eve of the year 1754.   He stands thus midway between Goldsmith and Wordsworth—midway between the old and the new school of poetry.   His father was salt-master — or collector of salt duties—at the little seaport. After being taught a little at several schools, it was agreed that George should be made a surgeon.   He was accordingly apprenticed ; but he was fonder of writing verses than of attending cases.   His memory for poetry was astonishing ; he had begun to write verses at the age of fourteen ; and he filled the drawers of the surgery with his poetical attempts.   After a time he set up for himself in practice at Aldborough ; but most of his patients were poor people and poor relations, who paid him neither for his physic nor his advice.   In 1779 he resolved "to go to London and venture all."   Accordingly, he took a berth on board of a sailing-packet, carrying with him a little money and a number of manuscript poems.   But nothing succeeded with him ; he was reduced to his last eightpence.   In this strait, he wrote to the great statesman, Edmund Burke ; and, while the answer was coming, he 'walked all night up and down Westminster Bridge.   Burke took him in to his own house and found a publisher for his poems.

14. In 1781 **The Library** appeared ; and in the same year Crabbe entered the Church.   In 1783 he published **The Village**— a poem which Dr Johnson revised for him.   This work won for him an established reputation ; but, for twenty-four years after, Crabbe gave himself up entirely to the care of his parish, and published only one poem—**The Newspaper**.   In 1807 appeared **The Parish Register**; in 1810, **The Borough**; in 1812, **Tales in Verse**; and, in 1819, his last poetical work, **Tales of the Hall.**   From this time, till his death in 1832—thirteen years after—he produced no other poem.   Personally, he was one of the noblest and kindest of men ; he was known as "the gentleman with the sour name and the sweet countenance ; " and he spent most of his income on the wants of others.

15. Crabbe's poetical work forms a prominent landmark in English literature.   His style is the style of the eighteenth century —with a strong admixture of his own ; his way of thinking, and the objects he selects for description, belong to the nineteenth.   While Pope depicted "the town," politics, and abstract moralities, Crabbe describes the country and the country poor, social matters, real life— the lowest and poorest life, and more especially, the intense misery of the village population of his time in the eastern counties—

"the wild amphibious race
With sullen woe displayed in every face."

He does not paint the lot of the poor with the rose-coloured tints used by Goldsmith; he boldly denies the existence of such a village as Auburn; he groups such places with Eden, and says—

"Auburn and Eden can be found no more;"

he shows the gloomy, hard, despairing side of English country life. He has been called a "Pope in worsted stockings," and "the Hogarth of song." Byron describes him as

"Nature's sternest painter, yet the best."

Now and then his style is flat, and even coarse; but there is everywhere a genuine power of strong and bold painting. He is also an excellent master of easy dialogue.

All of his poems are written in the Popian couplet of two ten-syllabled lines.

16. ROBERT BURNS (1759-1796), the greatest poet of Scotland, was born in Ayrshire, two miles from the town of Ayr, in 1759. The only education he received from his father was the schooling of a few months; but the family were fond of reading, and Robert was the most enthusiastic reader of them all. Every spare moment he could find—and they were not many—he gave to reading; he sat at meals "with a book in one hand and a spoon in the other;" and in this way he read most of the great English poets and prose-writers. This was an excellent education—one a great deal better than most people receive; and some of our greatest men have had no better. But, up to the age of sixteen, he had to toil on his father's farm from early morning till late at night. In the intervals of his work he contrived, by dint of thrift and industry, to learn French, mathematics, and a little Latin. On the death of his father, he took a small farm, but did not succeed. He was on the point of embarking for Jamaica, where a post had been found for him, when the news of the successful sale of a small volume of his poems reached him; and he at once changed his mind, and gave up all idea of emigrating. His friends obtained for him a post as exciseman, in which his duty was to gauge the quantity and quality of ardent spirits—a post full of dangers to a man of his excitable and emotional temperament. He went a great deal into what was called society, formed the acquaintance of many boon companions, acquired habits of intemperance that he could not shake off, and died at Dumfries in 1796, in his thirty-seventh year.

17. His best poems are lyrical, and he is himself one of the fore-

most lyrical poets in the world. His songs have probably been more sung, and in more parts of the globe, than the songs of any other writer that ever lived. They are of every kind—songs of love, war, mirth, sorrow, labour, and social gatherings. Professor Craik says: "One characteristic that belongs to whatever Burns has written is that, of its kind and in its own way, it is a perfect production. His poetry is, throughout, real emotion melodiously uttered, instinct with passion, but not less so with power of thought,—full of light as well as of fire." Most of his poems are written in the North-English, or Lowland - Scottish, dialect. The most elevated of his poems is **The Vision,** in which he relates how the Scottish Muse found him at the plough, and crowned him with a wreath of holly. One of his longest, as well as finest poems, is **The Cottar's Saturday Night,** which is written in the Spenserian stanza. Perhaps his most pathetic poem is that entitled **To Mary in Heaven.** It is of a singular eloquence, elevation, and sweetness. The first verse runs thus—

> " Thou lingering star, with lessening ray,.
>   That lov'st to greet the early morn,
> Again thou usher'st in the day
>   My Mary from my soul was torn.
> O Mary! dear departed shade!
>   Where is thy place of blissful rest?
> See'st thou thy lover lowly laid?
>   Hear'st thou the groans that rend his breast?"

He is, as his latest critic says, " the poet of homely human nature ; " and his genius shows the beautiful elements in this homeliness; and that what is homely need not therefore be dull and prosaic.

18. THOMAS CHATTERTON and WILLIAM BLAKE are two minor poets, of whom little is known and less said, but whose work is of the most poetical and genuine kind.—Chatterton was born at Bristol in the year 1752. He was the son of a schoolmaster, who died before he was born. He was educated at Colston's Blue-Coat School in Bristol ; and, while at school, read his way steadily through every book in three circulating libraries. He began to write verses at the age of fifteen, and in two years had produced a large number of poems —some of them of the highest value. In 1770, he came up to London, with something under five pounds in his pocket, and his mind made up to try his fortune as a literary man, resolved, though he was only a boy of seventeen, to live by literature or to die. Accordingly, he set to work and wrote every kind of production—poems,

essays, stories, political articles, songs for public singers; and all the time he was half starving. A loaf of bread lasted him a week; and it was "bought stale to make it last longer." He had made a friend of the Lord Mayor, Beckford; but before he had time to hold out a hand to the struggling boy, Beckford died. The struggle became harder and harder—more and more hopeless; his neighbours offered a little help—a small coin or a meal—he rejected all; and at length, on the evening of the 24th August 1770, he went up to his garret, locked himself in, tore up all his manuscripts, took poison, and died. He was only seventeen.

19. Wordsworth and Coleridge spoke with awe of his genius; Keats dedicated one of his poems to his memory; and Coleridge copied some of his rhythms. One of his best poems is the **Minstrel's Roundelay**—

> " O sing unto my roundelay,
>   O drop the briny tear with me,
> Dance no more on holy-day,
>   Like a running river be.
>   My love is dead,
>   Gone to his death-bed
>   All under the willow-tree.

> " Black his hair as the winter night,
>   White his skin as the summer snow,
> Red his face as the morning light,
>   Cold he lies in the grave below.
>   My love is dead,
>   Gone to his death-bed
>   All under the willow-tree."

20. WILLIAM BLAKE (1757-1827), one of the most original poets that ever lived, was born in London in the year 1757. He was brought up as an engraver; worked steadily at his business, and did a great deal of beautiful work in that capacity. He in fact illustrated his own poems—each page being set in a fantastic design of his own invention, which he himself engraved. He was also his own printer and publisher. The first volume of his poems was published in 1783; the **Songs of Innocence,** probably his best, appeared in 1787. He died in Fountain Court, Strand, London, in the year 1827.

21. His latest critic says of Blake: " His detachment from the ordinary currents of practical thought left to his mind an unspoiled and delightful simplicity which has perhaps never been matched in English poetry." Simplicity—the perfect simplicity of a child—

beautiful simplicity—simple and childlike beauty,—such is the chief note of the poetry of Blake. "Where he is successful, his work has the fresh perfume and perfect grace of a flower."   The most remarkable point about Blake is that, while living in an age when the poetry of Pope—and that alone — was everywhere paramount, his poems show not the smallest trace of Pope's influence, but are absolutely original.   His work, in fact, seems to be the first bright streak of the golden dawn that heralded the approach of the full and splendid daylight of the poetry of Wordsworth and Coleridge, of Shelley and Byron.   His best-known poems are those from the 'Songs of Innocence'—such as **Piping down the valleys wild; The Lamb; The Tiger,** and others. Perhaps the most remarkable element in Blake's poetry is the sweetness and naturalness of the rhythm. It seems careless, but it is always beautiful; it grows, it is not made; it is like a wild field-flower thrown up by Nature in a pleasant green field.   Such are the rhythms in the poem entitled **Night:—**

> " The sun descending in the west,
>   The evening star does shine ;
>   The birds are silent in their nest,
>   And I must seek for mine.
>   The moon, like a flower
>   In heaven's high bower,
>   With silent delight
>   Sits and smiles on the night.

> " Farewell, green fields and happy grove,
>   Where flocks have ta'en delight ;
>   Where lambs have nibbled, silent move
>   The feet of angels bright :
>   Unseen they pour blessing,
>   And joy without ceasing,
>   On each bud and blossom,
>   On each sleeping bosom."

CHAPTER VIII.

THE FIRST HALF OF THE NINETEENTH CENTURY.

1. New Ideas.—The end of the eighteenth and the beginning of the nineteenth century are alike remarkable for the new powers, new ideas, and new life thrown into society. The coming up of a high flood-tide of new forces seems to coincide with the beginning of the French Revolution in 1789, when the overthrow of the Bastille marked the downfall of the old ways of thinking and acting, and announced to the world of Europe and America that the old *régime*—the ancient mode of governing—was over. Wordsworth, then a lad of nineteen, was excited by the event almost beyond the bounds of self-control. He says in his "Excursion"—

> "Bliss was it in that dawn to be alive,
> But to be young was very Heaven!"

It was, indeed, the dawn of a new day for the peoples of Europe. The ideas of freedom and equality—of respect for man as man—were thrown into popular form by France; they became living powers in Europe; and in England they animated and inspired the best minds of the time—Burns, Coleridge, Wordsworth, Shelley, and Byron. Along with this high tide of hope and emotion, there was such an outburst of talent and genius in every kind of human endeavour in England, as was never seen before except in the Elizabethan period. Great events produced great powers; and great powers in their turn brought about great events. The war with America, the long struggle with Napoleon, the new political ideas, great victories by sea and land,—all these were to be found in the beginning of the nineteenth century. The English race produced great men in numbers—almost, it might be said, in groups. We had great leaders, like Nelson and Wellington; brilliant generals, like Sir Charles Napier and Sir John Moore; great statesmen, like Fox and Pitt, like Washington and Franklin; great engineers, like Stephenson and Brunel; and great poets, like Wordsworth and Byron. And as regards literature, an able critic remarks: "We have recovered in this century the Elizabethan magic and passion, a more than Elizabethan sense of the beauty and complexity of nature, the Elizabethan music of language."

2. **Great Poets.**—The greatest poets of the first half of the nineteenth century may be best arranged in groups. There were **Wordsworth, Coleridge,** and **Southey**—commonly, but unnecessarily, described as the Lake Poets. In their poetic thought and expression they had little in common; and the fact that two of them lived most of their lives in the Lake country, is not a sufficient justification for the use of the term. There were **Scott** and **Campbell**—both of them Scotchmen. There were **Byron** and **Shelley**—both Englishmen, both brought up at the great public schools and the universities, but both carried away by the influence of the new revolutionary ideas. Lastly, there were **Moore,** an Irishman, and young **Keats,** the splendid promise of whose youth went out in an early death. Let us learn a little more about each, and in the order of the dates of their birth.

3. WILLIAM WORDSWORTH (**1770-1850**) was born at Cockermouth, a town in Cumberland, which stands at the confluence of the Cocker and the Derwent. His father, John Wordsworth, was law agent to Sir James Lowther, who afterwards became Earl of Lonsdale. William was a boy of a stiff, moody, and violent temper; and as his mother died when he was a very little boy, and his father when he was fourteen, he grew up with very little care from his

Y

parents and guardians. He was sent to school at Hawkshead, in the Vale of Esthwaite, in Lancashire ; and, at the age of seventeen, proceeded to St John's College, Cambridge. After taking his degree of B.A. in 1791, he resided for a year in France. He took sides with one of the parties in the Reign of Terror, and left the country only in time to save his head. He was designed by his uncles for the Church ; but a friend, Raisley Calvert, dying, left him £900; and he now resolved to live a plain and frugal life, to join no profession, but to give himself wholly up to the writing of poetry. In 1798, he published, along with his friend, S. T. Coleridge, the **Lyrical Ballads.** The only work of Coleridge's in this volume was the "Ancient Mariner." In 1802 he married Mary Hutchinson, of whom he speaks in the well-known lines—

> " Her eyes as stars of Twilight fair,
> Like Twilight's, too, her dusky hair ;
> But all things else about her drawn
> From May-time and the cheerful dawn."

He obtained the post of Distributor of Stamps for the county of Westmoreland; and, after the death of Southey, he was created **Poet-Laureate** by the Queen.—He settled with his wife in the Lake country ; and, in 1813, took up his abode at Rydal Mount, where he lived till his death in 1850. He died on the 23d of April —the death-day of Shakespeare.

4. His longest works are the **Excursion** and the **Prelude**—both being parts of a longer and greater work which he intended to write on the growth of his own mind. His best poems are his shorter pieces, such as the poems on **Lucy, The Cuckoo**, the **Ode to Duty**, the **Intimations of Immortality**, and several of his **Sonnets.** He says of his own poetry that his purpose in writing it was "to console the afflicted; to add sunshine to daylight by making the happy happier; to teach the young and the gracious of every age to see, to think, and feel, and therefore to become more actively and securely virtuous." His poetical work is the noble landmark of a great transition—both in thought and in style. He drew aside poetry from questions and interests of mere society and the town to the scenes of Nature and the deepest feelings of man as man. In style, he refused to employ the old artificial vocabulary which Pope and his followers revelled in ; he used the simplest words he could find ; and, when he hits the mark in his simplest form of expression, his style is as forcible as it is true. He says of his own verse—

> " The moving accident is not my trade,
>   To freeze the blood I have no ready arts ;
>   'Tis my delight, alone, in summer shade,
>   To pipe a simple song for *thinking hearts.*"

If one were asked what four lines of his poetry best convey the feeling of the whole, the reply must be that these are to be found in his " Song at the Feast of Brougham Castle,"—lines written about " the good Lord Clifford."

> " Love had he found in huts where poor men lie,
>   His daily teachers had been woods and rills,—
>   The silence that is in the starry sky,
>   The sleep that is among the lonely hills."

5. WALTER SCOTT (1771-1832), poet and novelist, the son of a Scotch attorney (called in **Edinburgh** a W.S. or Writer to H.M.'s Signet), was born there in the year 1771. He was educated at the High School, and then at the College—now called the University —of Edinburgh. In 1792 he was called to the Scottish Bar, or became an "advocate." During his boyhood, he had had several illnesses, one of which left him lame for life. Through those long periods of sickness and of convalescence, he read Percy's 'Reliques of Ancient Poetry,' and almost all the romances, old plays, and epic poems that have been published in the English language. This gave his mind and imagination a set which they never lost all through life.

6. His first publications were translations of German poems. In the year 1805, however, an original poem, the **Lay of the Last Minstrel,** appeared ; and Scott became at one bound the foremost poet of the day. **Marmion,** the **Lady of the Lake,** and other poems, followed with great rapidity. But, in 1814, Scott took it into his head that his poetical vein was worked out ; the star of Byron was rising upon the literary horizon ; and he now gave himself up to novel-writing. His first novel, **Waverley,** appeared anonymously in 1814. **Guy Mannering, Old Mortality, Rob Roy,** and others, quickly followed ; and, though the secret of the authorship was well kept both by printer and publisher, Walter Scott was generally believed to be the writer of these works, and he was frequently spoken of as "the Great Unknown." He was made a baronet by George IV. in 1820.

7. His expenses in building Abbotsford, and his desire to acquire land, induced him to go into partnership with Ballantyne, his printer, and with Constable, his publisher. Both firms failed in the dark

year of 1826 ; and Scott found himself unexpectedly liable for the
large sum of £147,000. Such a load of debt would have utterly
crushed most men ; but Scott stood clear and undaunted in front of
it. "Gentlemen," he said to his creditors, "time and I against any
two. Let me take this good ally into my company, and I believe
I shall be able to pay you every farthing." He left his beautiful
country house at Abbotsford; he gave up all his country pleasures ;
he surrendered all his property to his creditors ; he took a small house
in Edinburgh ; and, in the short space of five years, he had paid off
£130,000. But the task was too terrible ; the pace had been too hard ;
and he was struck down by paralysis. But even this disaster did not
daunt him. Again he went to work, and again he had a paralytic
stroke. At last, however, he was obliged to give up ; the Government of the day placed a royal frigate at his disposal ; he went to
Italy ; but his health had utterly broken down, he felt he could get
no good from the air of the south, and he turned his face towards
home to die. He breathed his last breath at Abbotsford, in sight of
his beloved Tweed, with his family around him, on the 21st of September 1832.

8. His poetry is the poetry of action. In imaginative power he
ranks below no other poet, except Homer and Shakespeare. He
delighted in war, in its movement, its pageantry, and its events ;
and, though lame, he was quartermaster of a volunteer corps of
cavalry. On one occasion he rode to muster one hundred miles in
twenty-four hours, composing verses by the way. Much of " Marmion "
was composed on horseback. " I had many a grand gallop," he says,
" when I was thinking of ' Marmion.' " His two chief powers in verse
are his narrative and his pictorial power. His boyhood was passed
in the Borderland of Scotland—" a district in which every field has
its battle and every rivulet its song ; " and he was at home in every
part of the Highlands and the Lowlands, the Islands and the Borders,
of his native country. But, both in his novels and his poems, he was
a painter of action rather than of character.

9. His prose works are now much more read than his poems ; but
both are full of life, power, literary skill, knowledge of men and
women, and strong sympathy with all past ages. He wrote so fast
that his sentences are often loose and ungrammatical; but they are
never unidiomatic or stiff. The rush of a strong and large life goes
through them, and carries the reader along, forgetful of all minor
blemishes. His best novels are **Old Mortality** and **Kenilworth** ;
his greatest romance is **Ivanhoe**.

10. SAMUEL TAYLOR COLERIDGE (1772-1834), a true poet, and

a writer of noble prose, was born at Ottery St Mary, in Devonshire, in 1772. His father, who was vicar of the parish, and master of the grammar - school, died when the boy was only nine years of age. He was educated at Christ's Hospital, in London, where his most famous schoolfellow was Charles Lamb; and from there he went to Jesus College, Cambridge. In 1793 he had fallen into debt at College; and, in despair, left Cambridge, and enlisted in the 15th Light Dragoons, under the name of Silas Tomkins Comberbatch. He was quickly discovered, and his discharge soon obtained. While on a visit to his friend Robert Southey, at Bristol, the plan of emigrating to the banks of the Susquehanna, in Pennsylvania, was entered on; but, when all the friends and fellow-emigrants were ready to start, it was discovered that no one of them had any money.—Coleridge finally became a literary man and journalist. His real power, however, lay in poetry; but by poetry he could not make a living. His first volume of poems was published at Bristol, in the year 1796; but it was not till 1798 that the **Rime of the Ancient Mariner** appeared in the 'Lyrical Ballads.' His next greatest poem, **Christabel,** though written in 1797, was not published till the year 1816. His other best poems are **Love; Dejection—an Ode;** and some of his shorter pieces. His best poetry was written about the close of the century: "Coleridge," said Wordsworth, "was in blossom from 1796 to 1800."—As a critic and prose-writer, he is one of the greatest men of his time. His best works in prose are **The Friend** and the **Aids to Reflection.** He died at Highgate, near London, in the year 1834.

11. His style, both in prose and in verse, marks the beginning of the modern era. His prose style is noble, elaborate, eloquent, and full of subtle and involved thought; his style in verse is always musical, and abounds in rhythms of the most startling and novel—yet always genuine—kind. **Christabel** is the poem that is most full of these fine musical rhythms.

12. ROBERT SOUTHEY (**1774-1843**), poet, reviewer, historian, but, above all, man of letters, — the friend of Coleridge and Wordsworth,—was born at Bristol in 1774. He was educated at Westminster School and at Balliol College, Oxford. After his marriage with Miss Edith Fricker—a sister of Sara, the wife of Coleridge—he settled at Greta Hall, near Keswick, in 1803; and resided there until his death in 1843. In 1813 he was created **Poet-Laureate** by George III.—He was the most indefatigable of writers. He wrote poetry before breakfast; history between breakfast and

dinner; reviews between dinner and supper; and, even when taking a constitutional, he had always a book in his hand, and walked along the road reading. He began to write and to publish at the age of nineteen; he never ceased writing till the year 1837, when his brain softened from the effects of perpetual labour.

13. Southey wrote a great deal of verse, but much more prose. His prose works amount to more than one hundred volumes; but his poetry, such as it is, will probably live longer than his prose. His best-known poems are **Joan of Arc**, written when he was nineteen; **Thalaba the Destroyer**, a poem in irregular and unrhymed verse; **The Curse of Kehama**, in verse rhymed, but irregular; and **Roderick, the last of the Goths**, written in blank verse. He will, however, always be best remembered by his shorter pieces, such as **The Holly Tree, Stanzas written in My Library**, and others.—His most famous prose work is the **Life of Nelson**. His prose style is always firm, clear, compact, and sensible.

14. THOMAS CAMPBELL **(1777-1844)**, a noble poet and brilliant reviewer, was born in Glasgow in the year 1777. He was educated at the High School and the University of Glasgow. At the age of twenty-two, he published his **Pleasures of Hope**, which at once gave him a place high among the poets of the day. In 1803 he removed to London, and followed literature as his profession; and, in 1806, he received a pension of £200 a-year from the Government, which enabled him to devote the whole of his time to his favourite study of poetry. His best long poem is the **Gertrude of Wyoming**, a tale written in the Spenserian stanza, which he handles with great ease and power. But he is best known, and will be longest remembered, for his short lyrics — which glow with passionate and fiery eloquence—such as **The Battle of the Baltic, Ye Mariners of England, Hohenlinden**, and others. He was twice Lord Rector of the University of Glasgow. He died at Boulogne in 1844, and was buried in Poets' Corner, Westminster Abbey.

15. THOMAS MOORE **(1779-1852)**, poet, biographer, and historian —but most of all poet—was born in Dublin in the year 1779. He began to print verses at the age of thirteen, and may be said, like Pope, to have "lisped in numbers, for the numbers came." He came to London in 1799, and was quickly received into fashionable society. In 1803 he was made Admiralty Registrar

at Bermuda ; but he soon gave up the post, leaving a deputy in his place, who, some years after, embezzled the Government funds, and brought financial ruin upon Moore. The poet's friends offered to help him out of his money difficulties ; but he most honourably declined all such help, and, like Sir W. Scott, resolved to clear off all claims against him by the aid of his pen alone. For the next twenty years of his life he laboured incessantly; and volumes of poetry, history, and biography came steadily from his pen. His best poems are his **Irish Melodies**, some fifteen or sixteen of which are perfect and imperishable ; and it is as a writer of songs that Moore will live in the literature of this country. He boasted, and with truth, that it was he who awakened for this century the long-silent harp of his native land—

> " Dear Harp of my Country ! in darkness I found thee,
>   The cold chain of silence had hung o'er thee long,
> When proudly, my own Island Harp, I unbound thee,
>   And gave all thy chords to light, freedom, and song."

His best long poem is **Lalla Rookh**.—His prose works are little read nowadays. The chief among them are his **Life of Sheridan**, and his **Life of Lord Byron**.—He died at Sloperton, in Wiltshire, in 1852, two years after the death of Wordsworth.

16. GEORGE GORDON, LORD BYRON **(1788-1824)**, a great English poet, was born in London in the year 1788. He was the only child of a reckless and unprincipled father and a passionate mother. He was educated at Harrow School, and afterwards at Trinity College, Cambridge. His first volume—**Hours of Idleness**—was published in 1807, before he was nineteen. A critique of this juvenile work which appeared in the ' Edinburgh Review ' stung him to passion ; and he produced a very vigorous poetical reply in **English Bards and Scotch Reviewers**. After the publication of this book, Byron travelled in Germany, Spain, Greece, and Turkey for two years ; and the first two cantos of the poem entitled **Childe Harold's Pilgrimage** were the outcome of these travels. This poem at once placed him at the head of English poets ; "he woke one morning," he said, "and found himself famous." He was married in the year 1815, but left his wife in the following year ; left his native country also, never to return. First of all he settled at Geneva, where he made the acquaintance of the poet Shelley, and where he wrote, among other poems, the third canto of **Childe Harold** and the **Prisoner of Chillon**. In 1817 he removed to Venice, where he

composed the fourth canto of **Childe Harold** and the **Lament of Tasso**; his next resting-place was Ravenna, where he wrote several plays. Pisa saw him next ; and at this place he spent a great deal of his time in close intimacy with Shelley. In 1821 the Greek nation rose in revolt against the cruelties and oppression of the Turkish rule ; and Byron's sympathies were strongly enlisted on the side of the Greeks. He helped the struggling little country with contributions of money; and, in 1823, sailed from Geneva to take a personal share in the war of liberation. He died, however, of fever, at Missolonghi, on the 19th of April 1824, at the age of thirty-six.

17. His best-known work is **Childe Harold**, which is written in the Spenserian stanza. His plays, the best of which are **Manfred** and **Sardanapālus**, are written in blank verse.—His style is remarkable for its strength and elasticity, for its immensely powerful sweep, tireless energy, and brilliant illustrations.

18. PERCY BYSSHE SHELLEY (1792-1822),—who has, like Spenser, been called "the poet's poet,"—was born at Field Place, near Horsham, in Sussex, in the year 1792. He was educated at Eton, and then at University College, Oxford. A shy, diffident, retiring boy, with sweet, gentle looks and manners—like those of a girl—but with a spirit of the greatest fearlessness and the noblest independence, he took little share in the sports and pursuits of his schoolfellows. Obliged to leave Oxford, in consequence of having written a tract of which the authorities did not approve, he married at the very early age of nineteen. The young lady whom he married died in 1816 ; and he soon after married Mary, daughter of William Godwin, the eminent author of ' Political Justice.' In 1818 he left England for Italy,—like his friend, Lord Byron, for ever. It was at Naples, Leghorn, and Pisa that he chiefly resided. In 1822 he bought a little boat—"a perfect plaything for the summer," he calls it; and he used often to make short voyages in it, and wrote many of his poems on these occasions. When Leigh Hunt was lying ill at Leghorn, Shelley and his friend Williams resolved on a coasting trip to that city. They reached Leghorn in safety ; but, on the return journey, the boat sank in a sudden squall. Captain Roberts was watching the vessel with his glass from the top of the Leghorn lighthouse, as it crossed the Bay of Spezzia : a black cloud arose; a storm came down; the vessels sailing with Shelley's boat were wrapped in darkness ; the cloud passed ; the sun shone out, and all was clear again ; the larger vessels rode on ; but Shelley's boat had disappeared. The poet's body was cast on

shore, but the quarantine laws of Italy required that everything thrown up on the coast should be burned : no representations could alter the law ; and Shelley's ashes were placed in a box and buried in the Protestant cemetery at Rome.

19. Shelley's best long poem is the **Adonaïs,** an elegy on the death of John Keats. It is written in the Spenserian stanza. But this true poet will be best remembered by his short lyrical poems, such as **The Cloud, Ode to a Skylark, Ode to the West Wind, Stanzas written in Dejection,** and others. — Shelley has been called " the poet's poet," because his style is so thoroughly transfused by pure imagination. He has also been called " the master-singer of our modern race and age ; for his thoughts, his words, and his deeds all sang together." He is probably the greatest lyric poet of this century.

20. JOHN KEATS **(1795 - 1821),** one of our truest poets, was born in Moorfields, London, in the year 1795. He was educated at a private school at Enfield. His desire for the pleasures of the intellect and the imagination showed itself very early at school ; and he spent many a half-holiday in writing translations from the Roman and the French poets. On leaving school, he was apprenticed to a surgeon at Edmonton—the scene of one of John Gilpin's adventures ; but, in 1817, he gave up the practice of surgery, devoted himself entirely to poetry, and brought out his first volume. In 1818 appeared his **Endymion.** The 'Quarterly Review' handled it without mercy. Keats's health gave way ; the seeds of consumption were in his frame ; and he was ordered to Italy in 1820, as the last chance of saving his life. But it was too late. The air of Italy could not restore him. He settled at Rome with his friend Severn ; but, in spite of all the care, thought, devotion, and watching of his friend, he died in 1821, at the age of twenty-five. He was buried in the Protestant cemetery at Rome ; and the inscription on his tomb, composed by himself, is, " *Here lies one whose name was writ in water.*"

21. His greatest poem is **Hyperion,** written, in blank verse, on the overthrow of the " early gods " of Greece. But he will most probably be best remembered by his marvellous odes, such as the **Ode to a Nightingale, Ode on a Grecian Urn, To Autumn,** and others. His style is clear, sensuous, and beautiful ; and he has added to our literature lines that will always live. Such are the following :—

" A thing of beauty is a joy for ever."

" Silent, upon a peak in Darien."

" Then felt I like some watcher of the skies
  When a new planet swims into his ken."

" Perhaps the self-same song that found a path
  Through the sad heart of Ruth, when, sick for home,
  She stood in tears amid the alien corn."

22. **Prose-Writers.**—We have now to consider the greatest
prose-writers of the first half of the nineteenth century.   First
comes **Walter Scott,** one of the greatest novelists that ever
lived, and who won the name of "The Wizard of the North"
from the marvellous power he possessed of enchaining the
attention and fascinating the minds of his readers.   Two other
great writers of prose were **Charles Lamb** and **Walter Savage
Landor,** each in styles essentially different.   **Jane Austen,**
a young English lady, has become a classic in prose, because her
work is true and perfect within its own sphere.   **De Quincey**
is perhaps the writer of the most ornate and elaborate English
prose of this period.   **Thomas Carlyle,** a great Scotsman, with
a style of overwhelming power, but of occasional grotesqueness,
like a great prophet and teacher of the nation, compelled statesmen and philanthropists to think, while he also gained for himself a high place in the rank of historians.   **Macaulay,** also of
Scottish descent, was one of the greatest essayists and ablest
writers on history that Great Britain has produced.   A short
survey of each of these great men may be useful.   Scott has
been already treated of.

23. CHARLES LAMB **(1775 - 1834),** a perfect English essayist,
was born in the Inner Temple, in London, in the year 1775.
His father was clerk to a barrister of that Inn of Court.   Charles
was educated at Christ's Hospital, where his most famous schoolfellow was S. T. Coleridge.   Brought up in the very heart of
London, he had always a strong feeling for the greatness of the
metropolis of the world.   "I often shed tears," he said, "in the
motley Strand, for fulness of joy at so much life."   He was, indeed,
a thorough Cockney and lover of London, as were also Chaucer,

Spenser, Milton, and Lamb's friend Leigh Hunt. Entering the India House as a clerk in the year 1792, he remained there thirty-three years; and it was one of his odd sayings that, if any one wanted to see his "works," he would find them on the shelves of the India House.—He is greatest as a writer of prose; and his prose is, in its way, unequalled for sweetness, grace, humour, and quaint terms, among the writings of this century. His best prose work is the **Essays of Elia,** which show on every page the most whimsical and humorous subtleties, a quick play of intellect, and a deep sympathy with the sorrows and the joys of men. Very little verse came from his pen. "Charles Lamb's nosegay of verse," says Professor Dowden, "may be held by the small hand of a maiden, and there is not in it one flaunting flower." Perhaps the best of his poems are the short pieces entitled **Hester** and **The Old Familiar Faces.**—He retired from the India House, on a pension, in 1825, and died at Edmonton, near London, in 1834. His character was as sweet and refined as his style; Wordsworth spoke of him as "Lamb the frolic and the gentle;" and these and other fine qualities endeared him to a large circle of friends.

24. WALTER SAVAGE LANDOR **(1775-1864),** the greatest prose-writer in his own style of the nineteenth century, was born at Ipsley Court, in Warwickshire, on the 30th of January 1775—the anniversary of the execution of Charles I. He was educated at Rugby School and at Oxford; but his fierce and insubordinate temper—which remained with him, and injured him all his life—procured his expulsion from both of these places. As heir to a large estate, he resolved to give himself up entirely to literature; and he accordingly declined to adopt any profession. Living an almost purely intellectual life, he wrote a great deal of prose and some poetry; and his first volume of poems appeared before the close of the eighteenth century. His life, which began in the reign of George III., stretched through the reigns of George IV. and William IV., into the twenty-seventh year of Queen Victoria; and, in the course of this long life, he had manifold experiences, many loves and hates, friendships and acquaintanceships, with persons of every sort and rank. He joined the Spanish army to fight Napo-leon, and presented the Spanish Government with large sums of money. He spent about thirty years of his life in Florence, where he wrote many of his works. He died at Florence in the year 1864. His greatest prose work is the **Imaginary Conversations;** his best poem is **Count Julian;** and the character of Count Julian has been

ranked by De Quincey with the Satan of Milton. Some of his smaller poetic pieces are perfect; and there is one, **Rose Aylmer,** written about a dear young friend, that Lamb was never tired of repeating :—

> " Ah ! what avails the sceptred race !
>   Ah ! what the form divine !
> What every virtue, every grace !
>   Rose Aylmer, all were thine !
>
> " Rose Aylmer, whom these wakeful eyes
>   Shall weep, but never see !
> A night of memories and sighs
>   I consecrate to thee."

25. JANE AUSTEN (**1775-1817**), the most delicate and faithful painter of English social life, was born at Steventon, in Hampshire, in 1775—in the same year as Landor and Lamb. She wrote a small number of novels, most of which are almost perfect in their minute and true painting of character. Sir Walter Scott, Macaulay, and other great writers, are among her fervent admirers. Scott says of her writing : " The big bow-wow strain I can do myself, like any now going ; but the exquisite touch which renders ordinary commonplace things and characters interesting, from the truth of the description and the sentiment, is denied to me." She works out her characters by making them reveal themselves in their talk, and by an infinite series of minute touches. Her two best novels are **Emma** and **Pride and Prejudice.** The interest of them depends on the truth of the painting ; and many thoughtful persons read through the whole of her novels every year.

26. THOMAS DE QUINCEY (**1785-1859**), one of our most brilliant essayists, was born at Greenhays, Manchester, in the year 1785. He was educated at the Manchester grammar - school and at Worcester College, Oxford. While at Oxford he took little share in the regular studies of his college, but read enormous numbers of Greek, Latin, and English books, as his taste or whim suggested. He knew no one ; he hardly knew his own tutor. "For the first two years of my residence in Oxford," he says, "I compute that I did not utter one hundred words." After leaving Oxford, he lived for about twenty years in the Lake country ; and there he became acquainted with Wordsworth, Hartley Coleridge (the son of S. T. Coleridge), and John Wilson (afterwards known as

Professor Wilson, and also as the "Christopher North" of ' Black-wood's Magazine '). Suffering from repeated attacks of neuralgia, he gradually formed the habit of taking laudanum ; and by the time he had reached the age of thirty, he drank about 8000 drops a-day. This unfortunate habit injured his powers of work and weakened his will. In spite of it, however, he wrote many hundreds of essays and articles in reviews and magazines. In the latter part of his life, he lived either near or in Edinburgh, and was always employed in dream-ing (the opium increased his power both of dreaming and of mus-ing), or in studying or writing. He died in Edinburgh in the year 1859.—Many of his essays were written under the signature of "The English Opium-Eater." Probably his best works are **The Confes-sions of an Opium-Eater** and **The Vision of Sudden Death.** The chief characteristics of his style are majestic rhythm and elabo-rate eloquence. Some of his sentences are almost as long and as sus-tained as those of Jeremy Taylor ; while, in many passages of reasoning that glows and brightens with strong passion and emotion, he is not inferior to Burke. He possessed an enormous vocabulary —in wealth of words and phrases he surpasses both Macaulay and Carlyle ; and he makes a very large—perhaps even an excessive—use of Latin words. He is also very fond of using metaphors, personifi-cations, and other figures of speech. It may be said without exaggera-tion that, next to Carlyle's, De Quincey's style is the most stimulating and inspiriting that a young reader can find among modern writers.

27. THOMAS CARLYLE (1795-1881), a great thinker, essayist, and historian, was born at Ecclefechan, in Dumfriesshire, in the year 1795. He was educated at the burgh school of Annan, and afterwards at the University of Edinburgh. Classics and the higher mathematics were his favourite studies ; and he was more especially fond of astronomy. He was a teacher for some years after leaving the University. For a few years after this he was engaged in minor literary work; and translating from the German occupied a good deal of his time. In 1826 he married Jane Welsh, a woman of abilities only inferior to his own. His first original work was **Sartor Resartus** ("The Tailor Repatched"), which appeared in 1834, and excited a great deal of attention—a book which has proved to many the electric spark which first woke into life their powers of thought and reflection. From 1837 to 1840 he gave courses of lec-tures in London ; and these lectures were listened to by the best and most thoughtful of the London people. The most striking series afterwards appeared in the form of a book, under the title of **Heroes**

and **Hero-Worship.** Perhaps his most remarkable book—a book that is unique in all English literature—is **The French Revolution,** which appeared in 1837. In the year 1845, his **Cromwell's Letters and Speeches** were published, and drew after them a large number of eager readers. In 1865 he completed the hardest piece of work he had ever undertaken, his **History of Frederick II., commonly called the Great.** This work is so highly regarded in Germany as a truthful and painstaking history that officers in the Prussian army are obliged to study it, as containing the best account of the great battles of the Continent, the fields on which they were fought, and the strategy that went to win them. One of the crowning external honours of Carlyle's life was his appointment as Lord Rector of the University of Edinburgh in 1866; but at the very time that he was delivering his famous and remarkable Installation Address, his wife lay dying in London. This stroke brought terrible sorrow on the old man; he never ceased to mourn for his loss, and to recall the virtues and the beauties of character in his dead wife; "the light of his life," he said, "was quite gone out;" and he wrote very little after her death. He himself died in London on the 5th of February 1881.

28. **Carlyle's Style.**—Carlyle was an author by profession, a teacher of and prophet to his countrymen by his mission, and a student of history by the deep interest he took in the life of man. He was always more or less severe in his judgments—he has been called "The Censor of the Age,"—because of the high ideal which he set up for his own conduct and the conduct of others.—He shows in his historic writings a splendour of imagery and a power of dramatic grouping second only to Shakespeare's. In command of words he is second to no modern English writer. His style has been highly praised and also energetically blamed. It is rugged, gnarled, disjointed, full of irregular force—shot across by sudden lurid lights of imagination — full of the most striking and indeed astonishing epithets, and inspired by a certain grim Titanic force. His sentences are often clumsily built. He himself said of them: "Perhaps not more than nine-tenths stand straight on their legs; the remainder are in quite angular attitudes; a few even sprawl out helplessly on all sides, quite broken-backed and dismembered." There is no modern writer who possesses so large a profusion of figurative language. His works are also full of the pithiest and most memorable sayings, such as the following :—

" Genius is an immense capacity for taking pains."

" Do the duty which lies nearest thee ! Thy second duty will already have become clearer."

"History is a mighty drama, enacted upon the theatre of time, with suns for lamps, and eternity for a background."

"All true work is sacred. In all true work, were it but true hand-labour, there is something of divineness. Labour, wide as the earth, has its summit in heaven."

'Remember now and always that Life is no idle dream, but a solemn reality based upon Eternity, and encompassed by Eternity. Find out your task: stand to it: the night cometh when no man can work."

29. THOMAS BABINGTON MACAULAY (1800-1859), the most popular of modern historians,—an essayist, poet, statesman, and orator, —was born at Rothley Temple, in Leicestershire, in the year 1800. His father was one of the greatest advocates for the abolition of slavery; and received, after his death, the honour of a monument in Westminster Abbey. Young Macaulay was educated privately, and then at Trinity College, Cambridge. He studied classics with great diligence and success, but detested mathematics—a dislike the consequences of which he afterwards deeply regretted. In 1824 he was elected Fellow of his college. His first literary work was done for Knight's 'Quarterly Magazine'; but the earliest piece of writing that brought him into notice was his famous essay on **Milton**, written for the 'Edinburgh Review' in 1825. Several years of his life were spent in India, as Member of the Supreme Council; and, on his return, he entered Parliament, where he sat as M.P. for Edinburgh. Several offices were filled by him, among others that of Paymaster-General of the Forces, with a seat in the Cabinet of Lord John Russell. In 1842 appeared his **Lays of Ancient Rome,** poems which have found a very large number of readers. His greatest work is his **History of England from the Accession of James II.** To enable himself to write this history he read hundreds of books, Acts of Parliament, thousands of pamphlets, tracts, broadsheets, ballads, and other flying fragments of literature; and he never seems to have forgotten anything he ever read. In 1849 he was elected Lord Rector of the University of Glasgow; and in 1857 was raised to the peerage with the title of Baron Macaulay of Rothley—the first literary man who was ever called to the House of Lords. He died at Holly Lodge, Kensington, in the year 1859.

30. **Macaulay's Style.**—One of the most remarkable qualities in his style is the copiousness of expression, and the remarkable power of putting the same statement in a large number of different ways. This enormous command of expression corresponded with the extraordinary power of his memory. At the age of eight he could repeat

the whole of Scott's poem of "Marmion." He was fond, at this early age, of big words and learned English; and once, when he was asked by a lady if his toothache was better, he replied, "Madam, the agony is abated!" He knew the whole of Homer and of Milton by heart; and it was said with perfect truth that, if Milton's poetical works could have been lost, Macaulay would have restored every line with complete exactness. Sydney Smith said of him: "There are no limits to his knowledge, on small subjects as on great; he is like a book in breeches." His style has been called "abrupt, pointed, and oratorical." He is fond of the arts of surprise—of antithesis—and of epigram. Sentences like these are of frequent occurrence:—

"Cranmer could vindicate himself from the charge of being a heretic only by arguments which made him out to be a murderer."

"The Puritan hated bear-baiting, not because it gave pain to the bear, but because it gave pleasure to the spectators."

Besides these elements of epigram and antithesis, there is a vast wealth of illustration, brought from the stores of a memory which never seemed to forget anything. He studied every sentence with the greatest care and minuteness, and would often rewrite paragraphs and even whole chapters, until he was satisfied with the variety and clearness of the expression. "He could not rest," it was said, "until the punctuation was correct to a comma; until every paragraph concluded with a telling sentence, and every sentence flowed like clear running water." But, above all things, he strove to make his style perfectly lucid and immediately intelligible. He is fond of countless details; but he so masters and marshals these details that each only serves to throw more light upon the main statement. His prose may be described as pictorial prose. The character of his mind was, like Burke's, combative and oratorical; and he writes with the greatest vigour and animation when he is attacking a policy or an opinion.

CHAPTER IX.

1. Science.—The second half of the nineteenth century is distinguished by the enormous advance made in science, and in the application of science to the industries and occupations of the people. Chemistry and electricity have more especially made enormous strides. Within the last twenty years, chemistry has remade itself into a new science; and electricity has taken a very large part of the labour of mankind upon itself. It carries our messages round the world—under the deepest seas, over the highest mountains, to every continent, and to every great city; it lights up our streets and public halls; it drives our engines and propels our trains. But the powers of imagination, the great literary powers of poetry, and of eloquent prose, —especially in the domain of fiction,—have not decreased because science has grown. They have rather shown stronger developments. We must, at the same time, remember that a great deal of the literary work published by the writers who lived, or are still living, in the latter half of this century, was written in the former half. Thus, Longfellow was a man of forty-three, and Tennyson was forty-one, in the year 1850; and both had by that time done a great deal of their best work. The same is true of the prose-writers, Thackeray, Dickens, and Ruskin.

2. Poets and Prose-Writers.—The six greatest poets of the latter half of this century are **Longfellow**, a distinguished American poet, **Tennyson, Mrs Browning, Robert Brown-**

z

ing, **William Morris**, and **Matthew Arnold**. Of these, Mrs
Browning and Longfellow are dead—Mrs Browning having died
in 1861, and Longfellow in 1882.—The four greatest writers of
prose are **Thackeray, Dickens, George Eliot**, and **Ruskin.**
Of these, only Ruskin is alive.

3. HENRY WADSWORTH LONGFELLOW (1807 - 1882), the most
popular of American poets, and as popular in Great Britain as he
is in the United States, was born at Portland, Maine, in the year
1807.   He was educated at Bowdoin College, and took his degree
there in the year 1825.   His profession was to have been the law ;
but, from the first, the whole bent of his talents and character was
literary.   At the extraordinary age of eighteen the professorship of
modern languages in his own college was offered to him ; it was
eagerly accepted, and in order to qualify himself for his duties, he
spent the next four years in Germany, France, Spain, and Italy.
His first important prose work was **Outre-Mer,** or a **Pilgrimage
beyond the Sea.**   In 1837 he was offered the Chair of Modern
Languages and Literature in Harvard University, and he again paid
a visit to Europe—this time giving his thoughts and study chiefly to
Germany, Denmark, and Scandinavia.   In 1839 he published the
prose romance called **Hyperion.**   But it was not as a prose-writer
that Longfellow gained the secure place he has in the hearts of the
English-speaking peoples ; it was as a poet.   His first volume of
poems was called **Voices of the Night,** and appeared in 1841 ;
Evangeline was published in 1848; and **Hiawatha,** on which his
poetical reputation is perhaps most firmly based, in 1855.   Many
other volumes of poetry—both original and translations—have also
come from his pen ; but these are the best.   The University of Oxford created him Doctor of Civil Law in 1869.   He died at Harvard
in the year 1882.   A man of singularly mild and gentle character, of
sweet and charming manners, his own lines may be applied to him
with perfect appropriateness—

> " His gracious presence upon earth
> Was as a fire upon a hearth ;
> As pleasant songs, at morning sung,
> The words that dropped from his sweet tongue
> Strengthened our hearts, or—heard at night—
> Made all our slumbers soft and light."

4. **Longfellow's Style.**—In one of his prose works, Longfellow
himself says, " In character, in manners, in style, in all things, the

supreme excellence is simplicity." This simplicity he steadily aimed at, and in almost all his writings reached ; and the result is the sweet lucidity which is manifest in his best poems. His verse has been characterised as "simple, musical, sincere, sympathetic, clear as crystal, and pure as snow." He has written in a great variety of measures — in more, perhaps, than have been employed by Tennyson himself. His "Evangeline" is written in a kind of dactylic hexameter, which does not always scan, but which is almost always musical and impressive—

> " Fair was she and young, when in hope began the long journey;
> Faded was she and old, when in disappointment it ended."

The " Hiawatha," again, is written in a trochaic measure—each verse containing four trochees—

> " ' Farewell !' said he, " Minnehaha,
> Farewell, O my laughing water !
> All my heart is buried with you,
> All' my | thou'ghts go | on'ward | wi'th you !' "

He is always careful and painstaking with his rhythm and with the cadence of his verse. It may be said with truth that Longfellow has taught more people to love poetry than any other English writer, however great.

5. ALFRED TENNYSON, a great English poet, who has written beautiful poetry for more than fifty years, was born at Somersby, in Lincolnshire, in the year 1809. He is the youngest of three brothers, all of whom are poets. He was educated at Cambridge, and some of his poems have shown, in a striking light, the forgotten beauty of the fens and flats of Cambridge and Lincolnshire. In 1829 he obtained the Chancellor's medal for a poem on " Timbuctoo." In 1830 he published his first volume, with the title of **Poems chiefly Lyrical**—a volume which contained, among other beautiful verses, the " Recollections of the Arabian Nights " and " The Dying Swan." In 1833 he issued another volume, called simply **Poems**; and this contained the exquisite poems entitled " The Miller's Daughter" and " The Lotos-Eaters." **The Princess**, a poem as remarkable for its striking thoughts as for its perfection of language, appeared in 1847. The **In Memoriam**, a long series of short poems in memory of his dear friend, Arthur Henry Hallam, the son of Hallam the historian, was published in the year 1850. When Wordsworth died in 1850, Tennyson was appointed to the office of Poet-Laureate. This office, from the time when Dryden was forced to resign it in 1689, to the

time when Southey accepted it in 1813, had always been held by
third or fourth rate writers; in the present day it is held by the man
who has done the largest amount of the best poetical work. **The
Idylls of the King** appeared in 1859. This series of poems—perhaps his greatest—contains the stories of "Arthur and the Knights
of the Round Table." Many other volumes of poems have been given
by him to the world. In his old age he has taken to the writing of
ballads and dramas. His ballad of **The Revenge** is one of the
noblest and most vigorous poems that England has ever seen. The
dramas of **Harold, Queen Mary,** and **Becket,** are perhaps his
best; and the last was written when the poet had reached the age
of seventy-four. In the year 1882 he was created Baron Tennyson,
and called to the House of Peers.

6. **Tennyson's Style.**—Tennyson has been to the last two generations of Englishmen the national teacher of poetry. He has tried
many new measures; he has ventured on many new rhythms; and
he has succeeded in them all. He is at home equally in the slowest,
most tranquil, and most meditative of rhythms, and in the rapidest
and most impulsive. Let us look at the following lines as an
example of the first. The poem is written on a woman who is
dying of a lingering disease—

> " Fair is her cottage in its place,
>   Where yon broad water sweetly slowly glides:
> It sees itself from thatch to base
>   Dream in the sliding tides.

> " And fairer she: but, ah! how soon to die!
>   Her quiet dream of life this hour may cease:
> Her peaceful being slowly passes by
>   To some more perfect peace."

The very next poem, " The Sailor Boy," in the same volume, is—
though written in exactly the same measure—driven on with the
most rapid march and vigorous rhythm—

> " He rose at dawn and, fired with hope,
>   Shot o'er the seething harbour-bar,
> And reached the ship and caught the rope
>   And whistled to the morning-star."

And this is a striking and prominent characteristic of all Tennyson's
poetry. Everywhere the sound is made to be "an echo to the sense";
the style is in perfect keeping with the matter. In the "Lotos-
Eaters," we have the sense of complete indolence and deep repose
in—

> " A land of streams ! Some, like a downward smoke,
> Slow-dropping veils of thinnest lawn, did go."

In the " Boädicea," we have the rush and the shock of battle, the closing of legions, the hurtle of arms and the clash of armed men—

> " Phantom sound of blows descending, moan of an͏̄ enemy massacred,
> Phantom wail of women and children, multitudinous agonies."

Many of Tennyson's sweetest and most pathetic lines have gone right into the heart of the nation, such as—

> " But oh for the touch of a vanished hand,
> And the sound of a voice that is still ! "

All his language is highly polished, ornate, rich—sometimes Spenserian in luxuriant imagery and sweet music, sometimes even Homeric in massiveness and severe simplicity. Thus, in the " Morte d'Arthur," he speaks of the knight walking to the lake as—

> " Clothed with his breath, and looking as he walked,
> Larger than human on the frozen hills."

Many of his pithy lines have taken root in the memory of the English people, such as these—

> " 'Tis better to have loved and lost,
> Than never to have loved at all."

> " For words, like Nature, half reveal,
> And half conceal, the soul within."

> " Kind hearts are more than coronets,
> And simple faith than Norman blood."

7. ELIZABETH BARRETT BARRETT, afterwards MRS BROWNING, the greatest poetess of this century, was born in London in the year 1809. She wrote verses " at the age of eight—and earlier," she says ; and her first volume of poems was published when she was seventeen. When still a girl, she broke a blood-vessel upon the lungs, was ordered to a warmer climate than that of London ; and her brother, whom she loved very dearly, took her down to Torquay. There a terrible tragedy was enacted before her eyes. One day the weather and the water looked very tempting ; her brother took a sailing-boat for a short cruise in Torbay ; the boat went down in front of the house, and in view of his sister ; the body was never recovered. This sad event completely destroyed her already weak health ; she returned to London, and spent several years in a darkened room. Here she " read almost every book worth reading in

almost every language, and gave herself heart and soul to that
poetry of which she seemed born to be the priestess." This way of
life lasted for many years : and, in the course of it, she published several volumes of noble verse. In 1846 she married Robert Browning,
also a great poet. In 1856 she brought out **Aurora Leigh,** her
longest, and probably also her greatest, poem. Mr Ruskin called
it "the greatest poem which the century has produced in any language;" but this is going too far.—Mrs Browning will probably be
longest remembered by her incomparable sonnets and by her lyrics,
which are full of pathos and passion. Perhaps her two finest poems
in this kind are the **Cry of the Children** and **Cowper's Grave.**
All her poems show an enormous power of eloquent, penetrating, and
picturesque language ; and many of them are melodious with a rich
and wonderful music. She died in 1861.

8. ROBERT BROWNING, the most daring and original poet of the
century, was born in Camberwell, a southern suburb of London, in
the year 1812. He was privately educated. In 1836 he published
his first poem **Paracelsus,** which many wondered at, but few read.
It was the story of a man who had lost his way in the mazes of
thought about life,—about its why and wherefore,—about this world
and the next,—about himself and his relations to God and his fellow-
men. Mr Browning has written many plays, but they are more fit
for reading in the study than for acting on the stage. His greatest
work is **The Ring and the Book;** and it is most probably by this
that his name will live in future ages. Of his minor poems, the best
known and most popular is **The Pied Piper of Hamelin**—a poem
which is a great favourite with all young people, from the picturesqueness and vigour of the verse. The most deeply pathetic of his
minor poems is **Evelyn Hope** :—

> " So, hush,—I will give you this leaf to keep—
>   See, I shut it inside the sweet cold hand,
>   There ! that is our secret ! go to sleep ;
>   You will wake, and remember, and understand."

9. **Browning's Style.**—Browning's language is almost always
very hard to understand ; but the meaning, when we have got at
it, is well worth all the trouble that may have been taken to reach
it. His poems are more full of thought and more rich in experience
than those of any other English writer except Shakspeare. The
thoughts and emotions which throng his mind at the same moment
so crowd upon and jostle each other, become so inextricably inter-
mingled, that it is very often extremely difficult for us to make out

any meaning at all. Then many of his thoughts are so subtle and so profound that they cannot easily be drawn up from the depths in which they lie. No man can write with greater directness, greater lyric vigour, fire, and impulse, than Browning when he chooses—write more clearly and forcibly about such subjects as love and war ; but it is very seldom that he does choose. The infinite complexity of human life and its manifold experiences have seized and imprisoned his imagination ; and it is not often that he speaks in a clear, free voice.

10. MATTHEW ARNOLD, one of the finest poets and noblest stylists of the age, was born at Laleham, near Staines, on the Thames, in the year 1822. He is the eldest son of the great Dr Arnold, the famous Head-master of Rugby. He was educated at Winchester and Rugby, from which latter school he proceeded to Balliol College, Oxford. The Newdigate prize for English verse was won by him in 1843—the subject of his poem being **Cromwell**. His first volume of poems was published in 1848. In the year 1851 he was appointed one of H.M. Inspectors of Schools ; and he held that office up to the year 1885. In 1857 he was elected Professor of Poetry in the University of Oxford. In 1868 appeared a new volume with the simple title of **New Poems**; and, since then, he has produced a large number of books, mostly in prose. He is no less famous as a critic than as a poet ; and his prose is singularly beautiful and musical.

11. **Arnold's Style.**—The chief qualities of his verse are clearness, simplicity, strong directness, noble and musical rhythm, and a certain intense calm. His lines on **Morality** give a good idea of his style :—

> " We cannot kindle when we will
>   The fire that in the heart resides :
>   The spirit bloweth and is still
>   In mystery our soul abides :
>   But tasks in hours of insight willed
>   Can be through hours of gloom fulfilled.
>
> " With aching hands and bleeding feet
>   We dig and heap, lay stone on stone ;
>   We bear the burden and the heat
>   Of the long day, and wish 'twere done.
>   Not till the hours of light return,
>   All we have built do we discern."

His finest poem in blank verse is his **Sohrab and Rustum**—a tale of the Tartar wastes.   One of his noblest poems, called **Rugby Chapel**, describes the strong and elevated character of his father, the Head-master of Rugby.—His prose is remarkable for its lucidity, its pleasant and almost conversational rhythm, and its perfection of language.

12. WILLIAM MORRIS, a great narrative poet, was born near London in the year 1834.   He was educated at Marlborough and at Exeter College, Oxford.   In 1858 appeared his first volume of poems.   In 1863 he began a business for the production of artistic wall-paper, stained glass, and furniture ; he has a shop for the sale of these works of art in Oxford Street, London ; and he devotes most of his time to drawing and designing for artistic manufacturers.   His first poem, **The Life and Death of Jason**, appeared in 1867 ; and his magnificent series of narrative poems—**The Earthly Paradise**—was published in the years from 1868 and 1870.   ' The Earthly Paradise' consists of twenty-four tales in verse, set in a framework much like that of Chaucer's 'Canterbury Tales.'   The poetic power in these tales is second only to that of Chaucer ; and Morris has always acknowledged himself to be a pupil of Chaucer's—

> "Thou, my Master still,
> Whatever feet have climbed Parnassus' hill."

Mr Morris has also translated the Æneid of Virgil, and several works from the Icelandic.

13. **Morris's Style.**—Clearness, strength, music, picturesqueness, and easy flow, are the chief characteristics of Morris's style.   Of the month of April he says :—

> " O fair midspring, besung so oft and oft,
> How can I praise thy loveliness enow?
> Thy sun that burns not, and thy breezes soft
> That o'er the blossoms of the orchard blow,
> The thousand things that 'neath the young leaves grow
> The hopes and chances of the growing year,
> Winter forgotten long, and summer near."

His pictorial power—the power of bringing a person or a scene fully and adequately before one's eyes by the aid of words alone—is as great as that of Chaucer.   The following is his picture of Edward III. in middle age :—

> " Broad-browed he was, hook-nosed, with wide grey eyes
> No longer eager for the coming prize,

But keen and steadfast : many an ageing line,
Half-hidden by his sweeping beard and fine,
Ploughed his thin cheeks ; his hair was more than grey,
And like to one he seemed whose better day
Is over to himself, though foolish fame
Shouts louder year by year his empty name.
Unarmed he was, nor clad upon that morn
Much like a king : an ivory hunting-horn
Was slung about him, rich with gems and gold,
And a great white ger-falcon did he hold
Upon his fist ; before his feet there sat
A scrivener making notes of this and that
As the King bade him, and behind his chair
His captains stood in armour rich and fair."

Morris's stores of language are as rich as Spenser's ; and he has much the same copious and musical flow of poetic words and phrases.

14. WILLIAM MAKEPEACE THACKERAY (1811-1863), one of the most original of English novelists, was born at Calcutta in the year 1811. The son of a gentleman high in the civil service of the East India Company, he was sent to England to be educated, and was some years at Charterhouse School, where one of his schoolfellows was Alfred Tennyson. He then went on to the University of Cambridge, which he left without taking a degree. Painting was the profession that he at first chose ; and he studied art both in France and Germany. At the age of twenty-nine, however, he discovered that he was on a false tack, gave up painting, and took to literary work as his true field. He contributed many pleasant articles to ' Fraser's Magazine,' under the name of **Michael Angelo Titmarsh** ; and one of his most beautiful and most pathetic stories, **The Great Hoggarty Diamond,** was also written under this name. He did not, however, take his true place as an English novelist of the first rank until the year 1847, when he published his first serial novel, **Vanity Fair.** Readers now began everywhere to class him with Charles Dickens, and even above him. His most beautiful work is perhaps **The Newcomes;** but the work which exhibits most fully the wonderful power of his art and his intimate knowledge of the spirit and the details of our older English life is **The History of Henry Esmond**—a work written in the style and language of the days of Queen Anne, and as beautiful as anything ever done by Addison himself. He died in the year 1863.

15. CHARLES DICKENS (1812-1870), the most popular writer of

this century, was born at Landport, Portsmouth, in the year 1812. His delicate constitution debarred him from mixing in boyish sports, and very early made him a great reader. There was a little garret in his father's house where a small collection of books was kept ; and, hidden away in this room, young Charles devoured such books as the 'Vicar of Wakefield,' 'Robinson Crusoe,' and many other famous English books. This was in Chatham. The family next removed to London, where the father was thrown into prison for debt. The little boy, weakly and sensitive, was now sent to work in a blacking manufactory at six shillings a-week, his duty being to cover the blacking-pots with paper. "No words can express," he says, "the secret agony of my soul, as I compared these my everyday associates with those of my happier childhood, and felt my early hopes of growing up to be a learned and distinguished man crushed in my breast. . . . The misery it was to my young heart to believe that, day by day, what I had learned, and thought, and delighted in, and raised my fancy and my emulation up by, was passing away from me, never to be brought back any more, cannot be written." When his father's affairs took a turn for the better, he was sent to school ; but it was to a school where "the boys trained white mice much better than the master trained the boys." In fact, his true education consisted in his eager perusal of a large number of miscellaneous books. When he came to think of what he should do in the world, the profession of reporter took his fancy ; and, by the time he was nineteen, he had made himself the quickest and most accurate—that is, the best reporter in the Gallery of the House of Commons. His first work, **Sketches by Boz**, was published in 1836. In 1837 appeared the **Pickwick Papers**; and this work at once lifted Dickens into the foremost rank as a popular writer of fiction. From this time he was almost constantly engaged in writing novels. His **Oliver Twist** and **David Copperfield** contain reminiscences of his own life ; and perhaps the latter is his most powerful work. "Like many fond parents," he wrote, "I have in my heart of hearts a favourite child ; and his name is *David Copperfield.*" He lived with all the strength of his heart and soul in the creations of his imagination and fancy while he was writing about them; he says himself, "No one can ever believe this narrative, in the reading, more than I believed it in the writing ;" and each novel, as he wrote it, made him older and leaner. Great knowledge of the lives of the poor, and great sympathy with them, were among his most striking gifts ; and Sir Arthur Helps goes so far as to say, "I doubt much whether there has ever been a writer of fiction who took such a real and living interest in the world about him." He died in the year 1870, and was buried in Westminster Abbey.

16. **Dickens's Style.**—His style is easy, flowing, vigorous, picturesque, and humorous; his power of language is very great; and, when he is writing under the influence of strong passion, it rises into a pure and noble eloquence. The scenery—the external circumstances of his characters, are steeped in the same colours as the characters themselves; everything he touches seems to be filled with life and to speak—to look happy or sorrowful,—to reflect the feelings of the persons. His comic and humorous powers are very great; but his tragic power is also enormous—his power of depicting the fiercest passions that tear the human breast,—avarice, hate, fear, revenge, remorse. The great American statesman, Daniel Webster, said that Dickens had done more to better the condition of the English poor than all the statesmen Great Britain had ever sent into the English Parliament.

17. John Ruskin, the greatest living master of English prose, an art-critic and thinker, was born in London in the year 1819. In his father's house he was accustomed " to no other prospect than that of the brick walls over the way; he had no brothers, nor sisters, nor companions." To his London birth he ascribes the great charm that the beauties of nature had for him from his boyhood : he felt the contrast between town and country, and saw what no country-bred child could have seen in sights that were usual to him from his infancy. He was educated at Christ Church, Oxford, and gained the Newdigate prize for poetry in 1839. He at first devoted himself to painting; but his true and strongest genius lay in the direction of literature. In 1843 appeared the first volume of his **Modern Painters**, which is perhaps his greatest work; and the four other volumes were published between that date and the year 1860. In this work he discusses the qualities and the merits of the greatest painters of the English, the Italian, and other schools. In 1851 he produced a charming fairy tale, ' The King of the Golden River, or the Black Brothers.' He has written on architecture also, on political economy, and on many other social subjects. He is the founder of a society called " The St George's Guild," the purpose of which is to spread abroad sound notions of what true life and true art are, and especially to make the life of the poor more endurable and better worth living.

18. **Ruskin's Style.**—A glowing eloquence, a splendid and full-

flowing music, wealth of phrase, aptness of epithet, opulence of ideas—all these qualities characterise the prose style of Mr Ruskin. His similes are daring, but always true. Speaking of the countless statues that fill the innumerable niches of the cathedral of Milan, he says that "it is as though a flight of angels had alighted there and been struck to marble." His writings are full of the wisest sayings put into the most musical and beautiful language. Here are a few :—

" Every act, every impulse, of virtue and vice, affects in any creature, face, voice, nervous power, and vigour and harmony of invention, at once. Perseverance in rightness of human conduct renders, after a certain number of generations, human art possible ; every sin clouds it, be it ever so little a one ; and persistent vicious living and following of pleasure render, after a certain number of generations, all art impossible."

" In mortals, there is a care for trifles, which proceeds from love and conscience, and is most holy ; and a care for trifles, which comes of idleness and frivolity, and is most base. And so, also, there is a gravity proceeding from dulness and mere incapability of enjoyment, which is most base."

His power of painting in words is incomparably greater than that of any other English author : he almost infuses colour into his words and phrases, so full are they of pictorial power. It would be impossible to give any adequate idea of this power here ; but a few lines may suffice for the present :—

" The noonday sun came slanting down the rocky slopes of La Riccia, and its masses of enlarged and tall foliage, whose autumnal tints were mixed with the wet verdure of a thousand evergreens, were penetrated with it as with rain. I cannot call it colour ; it was conflagration. Purple, and crimson, and scarlet, like the curtains of God's tabernacle, the rejoicing trees sank into the valley in showers of light, every separate leaf quivered with buoyant and burning life ; each, as it turned to reflect or to transmit the sunbeam, first a torch and then an emerald."

19. GEORGE ELIOT (the literary name for **Marian Evans, 1819-1880**), one of our greatest writers, was born in Warwickshire in the year 1819. She was well and carefully educated ; and her own serious and studious character made her a careful thinker and a most diligent reader. For some time the famous Herbert Spencer was her tutor ; and under his care her mind developed with surprising rapidity. She taught herself German, French, Italian—studied the best works in the literature of these languages ; and she was also fairly mistress of Greek and Latin. Besides all these, she was an accomplished musician.—She was for some time assistant-editor of the ' Westminster Review.' The first of her works which called the

attention of the public to her astonishing skill and power as a novelist was her **Scenes of Clerical Life.** Her most popular novel, **Adam Bede,** appeared in 1859 ; **Romola** in 1863 ; and **Middlemarch** in 1872. She has also written a good deal of poetry, among other volumes that entitled **The Legend of Jubal, and other Poems.** One of her best poems is **The Spanish Gypsy.** She died in the year 1880.

20. **George Eliot's Style.**—Her style is everywhere pure and strong, of the best and most vigorous English, not only broad in its power, but often intense in its description of character and situation, and always singularly adequate to the thought. Probably no novelist knew the English character—especially in the Midlands—so well as she, or could analyse it with so much subtlety and truth. She is entirely mistress of the country dialects. In humour, pathos, knowledge of character, power of putting a portrait firmly upon the canvas, no writer surpasses her, and few come near her. Her power is sometimes almost Shakespearian. Like Shakespeare, she gives us a large number of wise sayings, expressed in the pithiest language. The following are a few :—

" It is never too late to be what you might have been."

" It is easy finding reasons why other people should be patient."

" Genius, at first, is little more than a great capacity for receiving discipline."

" Things are not so ill with you and me as they might have been, half owing to the number who lived faithfully a hidden life, and rest in unvisited tombs."

" Nature never makes men who are at once energetically sympathetic and minutely calculating."

> " To the far woods he wandered, listening,
> And heard the birds their little stories sing
> In notes whose rise and fall seem melted speech—
> Melted with tears, smiles, glances—that can reach
> More quickly through our frame's deep-winding night,
> And without thought raise thought's best fruit, delight."

TABLES OF ENGLISH LITERATURE.

Writers.	Works.	Contemporary Events.	Centuries.
(*Author unknown*.)	**Beowulf** (brought over by Saxons and Angles from the Continent).		500
CAEDMON. A secular monk of Whitby. Died about **680**.	**Poems** on the Creation and other subjects taken from the Old and the New Testament.	Edwin (of Deira), King of the Angles, baptised 627.	600
BAEDA. **672-735.** "The Venerable Bede," a monk of Jarrow-on-Tyne.	An **Ecclesiastical History** in Latin. A translation of **St John's Gospel** into English (lost).	First landing of the Danes, 787.	700
ALFRED THE GREAT. **849-901.** King ; translator ; prose-writer.	Translated into the English of Wessex, Bede's Ecclesiastical History and other Latin works. Is said to have begun the **Anglo-Saxon Chronicle.**	The University of Oxford is said to have been founded in this reign.	800
Compiled by monks in various monasteries.	**Anglo-Saxon Chronicle,** 875-1154.		
ASSER. Bishop of Sherborne. Died **910**.	**Life of King Alfred.**	..	900
(*Author unknown*.)	A poem entitled **The Grave.**	..	1000
LAYAMON. **1150-1210.** A priest of Ernley-on-Severn.	**The Brut** (1205), a poem on Brutus, the supposed first settler in Britain.	John ascended the throne in 1199.	1100

WRITERS.	WORKS.	CONTEMPORARY EVENTS.	CEN-TURIES.
ORM OR **ORMIN.** 1187-1237. A canon of the Order of St Augustine.	**The Ormulum** (1215), a set of religious services in metre.		
ROBERT OF GLOUCESTER. 1255-1307.	Chronicle of England in rhyme (1297).	Magna Charta, 1215. Henry III. ascends the throne, 1216.	1200
ROBERT OF BRUNNE. 1272-1340. (Robert Manning of Brun.)	Chronicle of England in rhyme; *Handlyng Sinne* (1303).	University of Cambridge founded, 1231. Edward I. ascends the throne, 1272. Conquest of Wales, 1284.	
SIR JOHN MANDEVILLE. 1300-1372. Physician; traveller; prose-writer.	**The Voyaige and Travaile.** Travels to Jerusalem, India, and other countries, written in Latin, French, and English (1356). The first writer "in formed English."	Edward II. ascends the throne, 1307. Battle of Bannockburn, 1314.	1300
JOHN BARBOUR. 1316-1396. Archdeacon of Aberdeen.	**The Bruce** (1377), a poem written in the Northern English or "Scottish" dialect.	Edward III. ascends the throne, 1327.	
JOHN WYCLIF. 1324-1384. Vicar of Lutterworth, in Leicestershire.	Translation of the Bible from the Latin version; and many tracts and pamphlets on Church reform.	Hundred Years' War begins, 1338. Battle of Crecy, 1346.	1350
JOHN GOWER. 1325-1408. A country gentleman of Kent; probably also a lawyer.	**Vox Clamantis, Confessio Amantis, Speculum Meditantis** (1393); and poems in French and Latin.	The Black Death { 1349. 1361. 1369.	
WILLIAM LANGLANDE. 1332-1400. Born in Shropshire.	**Vision concerning Piers the Plowman** — three editions (1362-78).	Battle of Poitiers, 1356. First law-pleadings in English, 1362.	

WRITERS.	WORKS.	CONTEMPORARY EVENTS.	CEN-TURIES.
GEOFFREY CHAUCER. **1340-1400.** Poet; courtier; soldier; diplomatist; Comptroller of the Customs: Clerk of the King's Works; M.P.	**The Canterbury Tales** (1384-98), of which the best is the **Knightes Tale.** Dryden called him "a perpetual fountain of good sense."	Richard II. ascends the throne, 1377. Wat Tyler's insurrection, 1381.	
JAMES I. OF SCOTLAND. **1394-1437.** Prisoner in England, and educated there, in 1405-24.	**The King's Quair** (=*Book*), a poem in the style of Chaucer.	Henry IV. ascends the throne, 1399	
WILLIAM CAXTON. **1422-1492.** Mercer; printer; translator; prose-writer.	**The Game and Playe of the Chesse** (1474) — the first book printed in England; **Lives of the Fathers,** "finished on the last day of his life;" and many other works.	Henry V. ascends the throne, 1415. Battle of Agincourt, 1415. Henry VI. ascends the throne, 1422. INVENTION OF PRINTING, 1438-45.	**1400**
WILLIAM DUNBAR. **1450-1530.** Franciscan or Grey Friar; Secretary to a Scotch embassy to France.	**The Golden Terge** (1501); the **Dance of the Seven Deadly Sins** (1507); and other poems. He has been called "the Chaucer of Scotland."	Jack Cade's insurrection, 1450. End of the Hundred Years' War, 1453.	**1450**
GAWAIN DOUGLAS. **1474-1522.** Bishop of Dunkeld, in Perthshire.	**Palace of Honour** (1501); translation of **Virgil's Æneid** (1513)—the first translation of any Latin author into verse. Douglas wrote in Northern English.	Wars of the Roses, 1455-86. Edward IV. ascends the throne, 1461.	
WILLIAM TYNDALE. **1477-1536.** Student of theology; translator. Burnt at Antwerp for heresy.	**New Testament** translated (1525-34); the **Five Books of Moses** translated (1530). This translation is the basis of the Authorised Version.	Edward V. king, 1483.	

WRITERS.	WORKS.	CONTEMPORARY EVENTS.	CENTURIES.
SIR THOMAS MORE. *1480-1535.* Lord High Chancellor; writer on social topics; historian.	**History of King Edward V., and of his brother,** and of **Richard III.** (1513); **Utopia** (="The Land of Nowhere"), written in Latin; and other prose works.	Richard III. ascends the throne, 1483. Battle of Bosworth, 1485.	
SIR DAVID LYNDESAY. *1490-1556.* Tutor of Prince James of Scotland (James V.); "Lord Lyon King-at-Arms;" poet.	**Lyndesay's Dream**(1528); **The Complaint** (1529); **A Satire of the Three Estates** (1535) —a "morality-play."	Henry VII. ascends the throne, 1485. Greek began to be taught in England about 1497.	
ROGER ASCHAM. *1515-1568.* Lecturer on Greek at Cambridge; tutor to Edward VI., Queen Elizabeth, and Lady Jane Grey.	**Toxophilus** (1544), a treatise on shooting with the bow; **The Scholemastre** (1570). "Ascham is plain and strong in his style, but without grace or warmth."	Henry VIII. ascends the throne, 1509. Battle of Flodden, 1513. Wolsey Cardinal and Lord High Chancellor, 1515.	**1500**
JOHN FOXE. *1517-1587.* An English clergyman. Corrector for the press at Basle; Prebendary of Salisbury Cathedral; prose-writer.	**The Book of Martyrs** (1563), an account of the chief Protestant martyrs.	Sir Thomas More first layman who was Lord High Chancellor, 1529. Reformation in England begins about 1534.	
EDMUND SPENSER. *1552-1599.* Secretary to Viceroy of Ireland; political writer; poet.	**Shepheard's Calendar** (1579); **Faerie Queene,** in six books (1590-96).	Edward VI. ascends the throne, 1547. Mary Tudor ascends the throne, 1553.	
SIR WALTER RALEIGH. *1552-1618.* Courtier; statesman; sailor; coloniser; historian.	**History of the World** (1614), written during the author's imprisonment in the Tower of London.	Cranmer burnt, 1556.	**1550**
RICHARD HOOKER. *1553-1600.* English clergyman; Master of the Temple; Rector of Boscombe, in the diocese of Salisbury.	**Laws of Ecclesiastical Polity** (1594). This book is an eloquent defence of the Church of England. The writer, from his excellent judgment, is generally called "the judicious Hooker."	Elizabeth ascends the throne, 1558.	

Writers.	Works.	Contemporary Events.	Decades.
SIR PHILIP SIDNEY. **1554-1586.** Courtier; general; romance-writer.	**Arcadia,** a romance (1580). **Defence of Poesie,** published after his death (in 1595). **Sonnets.**	–	
FRANCIS BACON. **1561-1626.** Viscount St Albans; Lord High Chancellor of England; lawyer; philosopher; essayist.	**Essays** (1597); **Advancement of Learning** (1605); **Novum Organum** (1620); and other works on methods of inquiry into nature.	Hawkins begins slave trade in 1562. Rizzio murdered, 1566.	**1560**
WILLIAM SHAKESPEARE. **1564-1616.** Actor; owner of theatre; play-writer; poet. Born and died at Stratford-on-Avon.	Thirty - seven plays. His greatest **tragedies** are *Hamlet, Lear,* and *Othello.* His best comedies are *Midsummer Night's Dream, The Merchant of Venice,* and *As You Like It.* His best historical plays are *Julius Cæsar* and *Richard III.* Many *minor poems*—chiefly **sonnets.** He wrote no prose.	Marlowe, Dekker, Chapman, Beaumont and Fletcher, Ford, Webster, Ben Jonson, and other dramatists, were contemporaries of Shakspeare.	
BEN JONSON. **1574-1637.** Dramatist; poet; prose-writer.	**Tragedies** and **comedies.** Best plays: *Volpone or the Fox; Every Man in his Humour.*	Drake sails round the world, 1577. Execution of Mary Queen of Scots, 1578.	**1570**
WILLIAM DRUMMOND ("OF HAWTHORNDEN"). **1585-1649.** Scottish poet; friend of Ben Jonson.	**Sonnets and poems.**	Raleigh in Virginia, 1584. Babington's Plot, 1586. Spanish Armada, 1588.	**1580**
THOMAS HOBBES. **1588-1679.** Philosopher; prose-writer; translator of Homer.	**The Leviathan** (1651), a work on politics and moral philosophy.	Battle of Ivry, 1590.	**1590**

WRITERS.	WORKS.	CONTEMPORARY EVENTS.	DE-CADES.
SIR THOMAS BROWNE. 1605-1682. Physician at Norwich.	Religio Medici (= " The Religion of a Physician "); Urn - Burial ; and other prose works.	Australia discovered, 1601. James I. ascends the throne in 1603.	1600
JOHN MILTON. 1608-1674. Student ; political writer ; poet ; Foreign (or " Latin ") Secretary to Cromwell. Became blind from over-work in 1654.	Minor Poems ; Paradise Lost ; Paradise Regained ; Samson Agonistes. Many prose works, the best being Areopagitica, a speech for the Liberty of Unlicensed Printing.	Hampton Court Conference for translation of Bible, 1604-11. Gunpowder Plot, 1605.	
SAMUEL BUTLER. 1612-1680. Literary man ; secretary to the Earl of Carbery.	Hudibras, a mock - heroic poem, written to ridicule the Puritan and Parliamentarian party.	Execution of Raleigh, 1618.	1610
JEREMY TAYLOR. 1613-1667. English clergyman ; Bishop of Down and Connor in Ireland.	Holy Living and Holy Dying (1649) ; and a number of other religious books.		
JOHN BUNYAN. 1628-1688. Tinker and travelling preacher.	The Pilgrim's Progress (1678) ; the Holy War ; and other religious works.	Charles I. ascends the throne in 1625. Petition of Right, 1628.	1620
JOHN DRYDEN. 1631-1700. Poet - Laureate and Historiographer-Royal ; playwright ; poet ; prose-writer.	Annus Mirabilis (= " The Wonderful Year," 1665-66, on the Plague and the Fire of London) ; Absalom and Achitophel (1681), a poem on political parties ; Hind and Panther (1687), a religious poem. He also wrote many plays, some odes, and a translation of Virgil's Æneid. His prose consists chiefly of prefaces and introductions to his poems.	No Parliament from 1629-40. Scottish National Covenant, 1638. Long Parliament, 1640-53. Marston Moor, 1644. Execution of Charles I., 1649.	1630 1640

Writers.	Works.	Contemporary Events.	Decades.
JOHN LOCKE. **1632-1704.** Diplomatist; Secretary to the Board of Trade; philosopher; prose-writer.	**Essay concerning the Human Understanding** (1690); **Thoughts on Education;** and other prose works.	The Commonwealth, 1649-60. Cromwell Lord Protector, 1653-58.	**1650**
DANIEL DEFOE. **1661-1731.** Literary man; pamphleteer; journalist; member of Commission on Union with Scotland.	**The True-born Englishman** (1701); **Robinson Crusoe** (1719); **Journal of the Plague** (1722); and more than a hundred books in all.	Restoration, 1660. First standing army, 1661. First newspaper in England, 1663.	**1660**
JONATHAN SWIFT. **1667-1745.** English clergyman; literary man; satirist; prose-writer; poet; Dean of St Patrick's, in Dublin.	**Battle of the Books; Tale of a Tub** (1704), an allegory on the Churches of Rome, England, and Scotland; **Gulliver's Travels** (1726); a few poems; and a number of very vigorous political pamphlets.	Plague of London, 1665. Fire of London, 1666.	
SIR RICHARD STEELE. **1671-1729.** Soldier; literary man; courtier; journalist; M.P.	Steele founded the 'Tatler,' 'Spectator,' 'Guardian,' and other small journals. He also wrote some plays.	Charles II. pensioned by Louis XIV. of France, 1674.	**1670**
JOSEPH ADDISON. **1672-1719.** Essayist; poet; Secretary of State for the Home Department.	**Essays** in the 'Tatler,' 'Spectator,' and 'Guardian.' **Cato,** a Tragedy (1713). Several *Poems* and *Hymns.*	The Habeas Corpus Act, 1679.	
ALEXANDER POPE. **1688-1744.** Poet.	**Essay on Criticism** (1711); **Rape of the Lock** (1714); **Translation of Homer's Iliad and Odyssey,** finished in 1726; **Dunciad** (1729); **Essay on Man** (1739). A few prose *Essays,* and a volume of *Letters.*	James II. ascends the throne in 1685. Revolution of 1688. William III. and Mary II. ascend the throne, 1689.	**1680**
		Battle of the Boyne, 1690.	**1690**

WRITERS.	WORKS.	CONTEMPORARY EVENTS.	DE-CADES.
JAMES THOMSON. **1700-1748.** Poet.	**The Seasons ;** a poem in blank verse (1730) : **The Castle of Indolence ;** a mock - heroic poem in the Spenserian stanza (1748).	Censorship of the Press abolished, 1695. Queen Anne ascends the throne in 1702.	**1700**
HENRY FIELDING. **1707-1754.** Police - magistrate ; journalist ; novelist.	**Joseph Andrews** (1742); **Amelia** (1751). He was "the first great English novelist."	Battle of Blenheim, 1704. Gibraltar taken, 1704.	
DR SAMUEL JOHNSON. **1709-1784.** Schoolmaster ; literary man ; essayist ; poet ; dictionary-maker.	**London** (1738) ; **The Vanity of Human Wishes** (1749) ; **Dictionary of the English Language** (1755) ; **Rasselas** (1759) ; **Lives of the Poets** (1781). He also wrote **The Idler, The Rambler,** and a play called **Irené.**	Union of England and Scotland, 1707.	
DAVID HUME. **1711-1776.** Librarian ; Secretary to the French Embassy ; philosopher ; literary man.	**History of England** (1754-1762); and a number of philosophical *Essays.* His prose is singularly clear, easy, and pleasant.	George I. ascends the throne in 1714.	**1710**
THOMAS GRAY. **1716-1771.** Student ; poet ; letter-writer ; Professor of Modern History in the University of Cambridge.	**Odes ; Elegy Written in a Country Churchyard** (1750) —one of the most perfect poems in our language. He was a great stylist, and an extremely careful workman.	Rebellion in Scotland in 1715.	
TOBIAS GEORGE SMOLLETT. **1721-1771.** Doctor ; pamphleteer ; literary hack ; novelist.	**Roderick Random** (1748); **Humphrey Clinker** (1771). He also continued **Hume's History of England.** He published also some *Plays* and *Poems.*	South-Sea Bubble bursts, 1720	**1720**
OLIVER GOLDSMITH. **1728-1774.** Literary man ; play-writer ; poet.	**The Traveller** (1764) ; **The Vicar of Wakefield** (1766) ; **The Deserted Village** (1770); **She Stoops to Conquer**—a Play (1773) ; and a large number of books, pamphlets, and compilations.	George II. ascends the throne, 1727.	

Writers.	Works.	Contemporary Events.	De- cades.
ADAM SMITH. **1723-1790.** Professor in the University of Glasgow.	**Theory of Moral Sentiments** (1759); **Inquiry into the Nature and Causes of the Wealth of Nations** (1776). He was the founder of the science of political economy.	-	
EDMUND BURKE. **1730-1797.** M.P.; statesman; "the first man in the House of Commons;" orator; writer on political philosophy.	**Essay on the Sublime and Beautiful** (1757); **Reflections on the Revolution of France** (1790); **Letters on a Regicide Peace** (1797); and many other works. "The greatest philosopher in practice the world ever saw."		1730
WILLIAM COWPER. **1731-1800.** Commissioner in Bankruptcy; Clerk of the Journals of the House of Lords; poet.	**Table Talk** (1782); **John Gilpin** (1785); **A Translation of Homer** (1791); and many other *Poems.* His Letters, like Gray's, are among the best in the language.		
EDWARD GIBBON. **1737-1794.** Historian; M.P.	**Decline and Fall of the Roman Empire** (1776-87). "Heavily laden style and monotonous balance of every sentence."	Rebellion in Scotland, 1745, commonly called "The 'Forty-five."	1740
ROBERT BURNS. **1759-1796.** Farm-labourer; ploughman; farmer; excise-officer; lyrical poet.	*Poems and Songs* (1786-96). His prose consists chiefly of Letters. "His pictures of social life, of quaint humour, come up to nature; and they cannot go beyond it."	Clive in India, 1750-60. Earthquake at Lisbon, 1755. Black Hole of Calcutta, 1756.	1750

WRITERS.	WORKS.	CONTEMPORARY EVENTS.	DE-CADES.
WILLIAM WORDSWORTH. 1770-1850. Distributor of Stamps for the county of Westmoreland; poet; poet-laureate.	**Lyrical Ballads** (with Coleridge, 1798); **The Excursion** (1814); **Yarrow Revisited** (1835), and many other poems. **The Prelude** was published after his death. His prose, which is very good, consists chiefly of Prefaces and Introductions.	George III. ascends the throne in 1760. Napoleon and Wellington born, 1769.	1760
SIR WALTER SCOTT. 1771-1832. Clerk to the Court of Session in Edinburgh; Scottish barrister; poet; novelist.	**Lay of the Last Minstrel** (1805); **Marmion** (1808); **Lady of the Lake** (1810); Waverley—the first of the "Waverley Novels"—was published in 1814. The "Homer of Scotland." His prose is bright and fluent, but very inaccurate.	Warren Hastings in India, 1772-85.	1770
SAMUEL TAYLOR COLERIDGE. 1772-1834. Private soldier; journalist; literary man; philosopher; poet.	**The Ancient Mariner** (1798); **Christabel** (1816); **The Friend**—a Collection of Essays (1812); **Aids to Reflection** (1825). His prose is very full both of thought and emotion.		
ROBERT SOUTHEY. 1774-1843. Literary man; Quarterly Reviewer; historian; poet-laureate.	**Joan of Arc** (1796); **Thalaba the Destroyer** (1801); **The Curse of Kehama** (1810); **A History of Brazil; The Doctor**—a Collection of Essays; **Life of Nelson.** He wrote more than a hundred volumes. He was "the most ambitious and the most voluminous author of his age."	American Declaration of Independence, 1776.	
CHARLES LAMB. 1775-1834. Clerk in the East India House; poet; prose-writer.	*Poems* (1797); **Tales from Shakespeare** (1806); **The Essays of Elia** (1823-1833). One of the finest writers of prose in the English language.		
WALTER SAVAGE LANDOR. 1775-1864. Poet; prose-writer.	**Gebir** (1798); **Count Julian** (1812); **Imaginary Conversations** (1824-1846); **Dry Sticks Faggoted** (1858). He wrote books for more than sixty years. His style is full of vigour and sustained eloquence.	Alliance of France and America, 1778.	

WRITERS.	WORKS.	CONTEMPORARY EVENTS.	DE-CADES.
THOMAS CAMPBELL. 1777-1844. Poet; literary man; editor.	The Pleasures of Hope (1799); Poems (1803); Gertrude of Wyoming, Battle of the Baltic, Hohenlinden, etc. (1809). He also wrote some *Historical Works*.	Encyclopædia Britannica founded in 1778.	
HENRY HALLAM. 1778-1859. Historian.	View of Europe during the Middle Ages (1818); Constitutional History of England (1827); Introduction to the Literature of Europe (1839).		
THOMAS MOORE. 1779-1852. Poet; prose-writer.	Odes and Epistles (1806); Lalla Rookh (1817); History of Ireland (1827); Life of Byron (1830); Irish Melodies (1834); and many prose works.		
THOMAS DE QUINCEY. 1785-1859. Essayist.	Confessions of an English Opium-Eater (1821). He wrote also on many subjects —philosophy, poetry, classics, history, politics. His writings fill twenty volumes. He was one of the finest prose-writers of this century.	French Revolution begun in 1789.	1780
LORD BYRON (GEORGE GORDON). 1788-1824. Peer; poet; volunteer to Greece.	Hours of Idleness (1807); English Bards and Scotch Reviewers (1809); Childe Harold's Pilgrimage (1812-1818); Hebrew Melodies (1815): and many *Plays*. His prose, which is full of vigour and animal spirits, is to be found chiefly in his Letters.	Bastille overthrown, 1789.	

WRITERS.	WORKS.	CONTEMPORARY EVENTS.	DE-CADES.
PERCY BYSSHE SHELLEY. 1792-1822. Poet.	**Queen Mab** (1810); **Prometheus Unbound—a Tragedy** (1819); **Ode to the Skylark, The Cloud** (1820); **Adonaïs** (1821), and many other poems; and several prose works.	Cape of Good Hope taken, 1795.	**1790**
		Bonaparte in Italy, 1796.	
		Battle of the Nile, 1798.	
		Union of Great Britain and Ireland, 1801.	**1800**
JOHN KEATS. 1795-1821. Poet.	**Poems** (1817); **Endymion** (1818); **Hyperion** (1820). "Had Keats lived to the ordinary age of man, he would have been one of the greatest of all poets."	Trafalgar and Nelson, 1805.	
		Peninsular War, 1808-14.	**1810**
		Napoleon's Invasion of Russia; Moscow burnt, 1812.	
THOMAS CARLYLE. 1795-1881. Literary man; poet; translator; essayist; reviewer; political writer; historian.	**German Romances—a set of Translations** (1827); **Sartor Resartus — "The Tailor Repatched"** (1834); **The French Revolution** (1837); **Heroes and Hero-Worship** (1840); **Past and Present** (1843); **Cromwell's Letters and Speeches** (1845); **Life of Frederick the Great** (1858-65). "With the gift of song, Carlyle would have been the greatest of epic poets since Homer."	War with United States, 1812-14.	
		Battle of Waterloo, 1815.	
		George IV. ascends the throne, 1820.	**1820**
		Greek War of Freedom, 1822-29.	
		Byron in Greece, 1823-24.	
		Catholic Emancipation, 1829.	
LORD MACAULAY (THOMAS BABINGTON). 1800-1859. Barrister; Edinburgh Reviewer; M.P.; Member of the Supreme Council of India; Cabinet Minister; poet; essayist; historian; peer.	**Milton** (in the 'Edinburgh Review,' 1825); **Lays of Ancient Rome** (1842); **History of England**—unfinished (1849-59). "His pictorial faculty is amazing."	William IV. ascends the throne, 1830.	**1830**
		The Reform Bill, 1832.	
		Total Abolition of Slavery, 1834.	

WRITERS.	WORKS.	CONTEMPORARY EVENTS.	DE-CADES.
LORD LYTTON (EDWARD BULWER). **1805-1873.** Novelist; poet; dramatist; M. P.; Cabinet Minister; peer.	**Ismael and Other Poems** (1825); **Eugene Aram** (1831); **Last Days of Pompeii** (1834); **The Caxtons** (1849); **My Novel** (1853); **Poems** (1865).	Queen Victoria ascends the throne, 1837. Irish Famine, 1845.	**1840**
JOHN STUART MILL. **1806-1873.** Clerk in the East India House; philosopher; political writer; M.P.; Lord Rector of the University of St Andrews.	**System of Logic** (1843); **Principles of Political Economy** (1848); **Essay on Liberty** (1858); **Autobiography** (1873). "For judicial calmness, elevation of tone, and freedom from personality, Mill is unrivalled among the writers of his time."	Repeal of the Corn Laws, 1846. Revolution in Paris, 1851. Death of Wellington, 1852.	**1850**
HENRY W. LONGFELLOW. **1807-1882.** Professor of Modern Languages and Literature in Harvard University, U.S.; poet; prose-writer.	**Outre-Mer**—a Story (1835); **Hyperion**—a Story (1839); **Voices of the Night** (1841); **Evangeline** (1848); **Hiawatha** (1855); **Aftermath** (1873). "His tact in the use of language is probably the chief cause of his success."	Napoleon III. Emperor of the French, 1852. Russian War, 1854-56.	
LORD TENNYSON (ALFRED TENNYSON). **1809——.** Poet; poet-laureate; peer.	**Poems** (1830); **In Memoriam** (1850); **Maud** (1855); **Idylls of the King** (1859-73); **Queen Mary**—a Drama (1875); **Becket**—a Drama (1884). He is at present our greatest living poet.	Franco-Austrian War, 1859. Emancipation of Russian serfs, 1861.	**1860**
ELIZABETH B. BARRETT (afterwards MRS BROWNING). **1809-1861.** Poet; prose-writer; translator.	**Prometheus Bound**—translated from the Greek of Æschylus (1833); **Poems** (1844); **Aurora Leigh** (1856); and *Essays* contributed to various magazines.	Austro-Prussian "Seven Weeks' War," 1866. Suez Canal finished, 1869.	

Writers.	Works.	Contemporary Events.	De- cades.
WILLIAM MAKEPEACE THACKERAY. *1811-1863.* Novelist; writer in 'Punch'; artist.	**The Paris Sketch-Book** (1840); **Vanity Fair** (1847); **Esmond** (1852); **The New-comes** (1855); **The Virginians** (1857). The greatest novelist and one of the most perfect stylists of this century. "The classical English humorist and satirist of the reign of Queen Victoria."	Franco - Prussian War 1870-71. Third French Republic, 1870. William I. of Prussia made Emperor of the Germans at Versailles, 1871.	**1870**
CHARLES DICKENS. *1812-1870.* Novelist.	**Sketches by Boz** (1836); **The Pickwick Papers** (1837); **Oliver Twist** (1838); **Nicholas Nickleby** (1838); and many other novels and works; **Great Expectations** (1868). The most popular writer that ever lived.	Rome the new capital of Italy, 1871. Russo - Turkish War 1877-78.	
ROBERT BROWNING. *1812——.* Poet.	**Pauline** (1833); **Paracelsus** (1836); *Poems* (1865); **The Ring and the Book** (1869); and many other volumes of poetry.	Berlin Congress and Treaty, 1878. Leo XIII. made Pope in 1878.	
JOHN RUSKIN. *1819——.* Art-critic; essayist; teacher; literary man.	**Modern Painters** (1843-60); **The Stones of Venice** (1851-53); **The Queen of the Air** (1869); **An Autobiography** (1885); and very many other works. "He has a deep, serious, and almost fanatical reverence for art."	Assassination of Alexander II., 1881. Arabi Pasha's Rebellion, 1882-83. War in the Soudan, 1884.	**1880**
GEORGE ELIOT. *1819-1880.* Novelist; poet; essayist.	**Scenes of Clerical Life** (1858); **Adam Bede** (1859); and many other novels down to **Daniel Deronda** (1876); **Spanish Gypsy** (1868); **Legend of Jubal** (1874).	Murder of Gordon, 1884. New Reform Bill, 1885.	

INDEX.

PART I.

Derivations from names of persons, etc., 138.
  from names of places, 142.
  of words disguised in form, 145.
  of words greatly changed in meaning, 152.
Diphthongs, 5.

English inseparable prefixes, 104.
  roots and branches, 128.
  separable prefixes, 105.
  suffixes to adjectives, 115.
    to adverbs, 117.
    to nouns, 112.
    to verbs, 118.
English language, grammar of, 4.
  origin and development of, 4.
Etymology, 5, 8-63.
Extension of predicate, 90.

Factitive object, 22.
French derivations, etc., *included under* Latin.
Functions, words known by their, 61.

Gender, 11.
  indicated by different words, 14.
  indicated by prefixes, 13.
  indicated by suffixes, 12.
  Latin and French suffixes of, 13.
Gerund, 39.
Gerundial infinitive, 82.
Government of verbs, 78.
Grammar, 4.
  of letters, 7.
  of sounds, 5.
  of words, 8-63.
  parts of, 4
Greek prefixes, 110.
  roots, 136.
  suffixes, 125.
Gutturals, 5, 6.

Have, conjugation of, 49.

Inflexion of adjectives, 31.
  of nouns, 11.
  of pronouns, 24, 25.
  of verbs, 36.
Inseparable prefixes, English, 104.
Interjections, 60.
Interrogative pronouns, 25.
Intransitive verbs, 35.
Irregular weak verbs, 46.

Kinds of words, 8.
  known by functions, 61.

Labials, 5, 6.
Language, what it is, 3.
  spoken and written, 3.
Latin prefixes, 107.
  roots, 131.
  suffixes to adjectives, 122.
    to nouns, 118.
    to verbs, 125.
Letters, grammar of, 7.
  redundant, 8.

Moods, 38.
  syntax of, 80.
Mutes, 5, 6.

Nominative case, 20.
  absolute, 66.
  of address, 62.
  syntax of, 64.
Nouns, 9.
  abstract, 10.
  classification of, 9.
  class-names, 10.
  collective, 10.
  common, 10.
  compound, formation of, 100.
  English suffixes to, 112.
  inflexions of, 11.
  Latin and French suffixes to, 118.
  proper, 9.
  syntax of, 64-71.
Number of nouns, 15.
  of verbs, 42.
Numeral adjectives, 29.
Numerals, 30.

Object, cognate, 22.
  factitive, 22.
  reflexive, 22.
Objective case, 22.
  syntax of, 68.
Ordinal numerals, 29.
Orthography, 5.

Palatals, 6.
Participle, 40.
Passive voice, 37.
Person of verbs, 42.
Persons, words derived from names of, 138.
Places, words derived from names of, 142.
Plurals, false, 17.
  foreign, 18.
  modes of forming, 19.
  of compound words, 19.
  treated as singulars, 18.

PART II.

PART III.

PART IV.

EDINBURGH UNIVERSITY PRESS :
T. AND A. CONSTABLE, PRINTERS TO HER MAJESTY

A LIST OF

EDUCATIONAL WORKS

BY

PROFESSOR J. M. D. MEIKLEJOHN
DR. MORELL: JOHN MARKWELL
ETC. ETC. ETC.

LONDON:
SIMPKIN, MARSHALL, HAMILTON, KENT, AND CO., Lim.
ST. ANDREWS: A. M. HOLDEN

Third Edition.   Fifteenth Thousand.   Crown 8vo, pp. 550.
Price 4s. 6d.

A New Geography

ON THE COMPARATIVE METHOD

With Maps and Diagrams.

By J. M. D. MEIKLEJOHN, M.A.,

PROFESSOR OF EDUCATION IN THE UNIVERSITY OF ST. ANDREWS, FELLOW OF
THE ROYAL GEOGRAPHICAL SOCIETIES OF LONDON AND EDINBURGH.

EXTRACT FROM PREFACE.

THE Comparative Method has been employed throughout ; and the
unknown constantly referred to and compared with that which is
known.   The memory has been assisted, wherever it was possible, by
grouping, by connection, and by association ; and I have done what
I could to inform the subject through and through with thinking.

The frequent appeal to the Eye in the Maps and Diagrams will
give the matter a permanent lodging in the memory.

The Commercial Geography of each country and continent has
been treated with great fulness ; and this feature will make the book
useful in the new examinations.

The book contains all that is necessary for the Examinations of
Pupil Teachers and Students in Training Colleges ; and also for
Candidates for the Oxford and Cambridge Local Examinations.

ALSO IN TWO PARTS:

PART I.—Containing Europe, with Introduction to Geography,
              and Index, ...   2s. 6d.

PART II.—Containing Asia, Africa, the Americas, and Australasia,
              with Index and Vocabulary,   .   .   .   2s. 6d.

REVIEWS AND OPINIONS OF

A New Geography.

"The value of the Comparative Method in educational matters is comprehensively set forth, both in the arrangement of the text, and the Maps and Diagrams. The separation of facts that are of first importance from those that are secondary, the classification of subject-matter, and the systematic use of sectional paragraphs, are equally skilful, and equally conducive to simplicity, clearness, and impressiveness. The instructions in Map Drawing with illustrations are admirable."   **Saturday Review.**

"A most useful manual for examiners, and full of stimulating matter for students of Geography. Its picturesqueness of description and vividness of style make it almost as interesting and enjoyable reading as a book of travels."

    The Journal of Education.

"Professor Meiklejohn has succeeded in producing a geography which is likely to become rapidly popular. We have examined it carefully, and our admiration has increased with every perusal. Skilful arrangement of facts, the constant reference of the unknown to the known, numerous simple and illustrative diagrams, the use of distinctive ty. e to mark the varying importance of the statements, are features which combine to make the task of learning geography light and pleasant."   **Educational Times.**

"What Mr. J. R. Green did for English history Professor Meiklejohn has done for geography. Without sacrificing fulness of information he has succeeded in producing a text-book interesting and inspiring. The facts are brought down to date, and fixed in the memory by pleasant associations rather than by the weary process of reiteration."   **The English Teacher.**

"A chapter of the New Geography reads like a lively *viva voce* lesson."   **The Literary World.**

"For all that is best worth knowing, no better book than this could be studied."

    Educational News.

"Your Geography strikes us as quite first-rate, admirably arranged, accurate, clear, incisive. It is the most scientific work we know on the subject."

    Rev. H. P. Gurney, M.A. (of Messrs. Wren & Gurney), 3 Powis Square, London.

"No teacher, who desires what the age can render in this branch of study, can afford to ignore the materials you have placed in his hands."

    G. A. Christian, Esq., B.A. (Lond.), Headmaster, P. T. School, Southwark.

"I am delighted with it. I expected something very good, and the actual product in no respect falls below my anticipations."

    A. J. Wyatt, Esq., M.A. (Lond.), Univ. Corr. College, Cambridge.

"It appears to me to be admirably suited for teachers and advanced Scholars. It is full of matter, and the matter could not be more effectively arranged."

    James Ogilvie, Esq., M.A., Principal, The Church of Scotland Training College, Aberdeen.

"The contrast-and-analogy idea of the book is most happy. Visual memory is aided by the simple diagrams no less than by the maps; while the problem of stringing facts together in an inviting manner has been capitally solved."

    G. Ballantine, Esq., Headmaster, P. T. School, Peckham, London.

"It is the best geographical text-book that I know."

    David Pryde, Esq., M.A., LL.D., Principal, Ladies' College, Edinburgh.

"Your Geography is excellent, and I shall certainly recommend it to Civil Service Candidates."   **W. Baptiste Scoones, Esq., 14 Chelsea Embankment, London, S.W.**

"Incomparably the best manual in existence."   **The Private Schoolmaster.**

Crown 8vo. In Two Parts. Price 2s. 6d. each.

A New History of England

and Great Britain

By J. M. D. MEIKLEJOHN, M.A.

THIS book is an attempt to make the chief events recorded in the History of our own country vivid to the mental eye, and also easily rememberable. Those parts have been dwelt on with greatest emphasis that generally form the subjects of questions in our examinations. More than usual prominence has been given to the growth of the Constitution, and to the rise and development of Parliament. The social side of English History has also been brought out with considerable fulness. The latest authorities have always been consulted.

Every aid to the Memory that can possibly be devised has been employed—different styles of type ; tables ; maps ; diagrams ; notes ; and, above all, the excellent and inimitable scheme of Chronology invented by D. Nasmith, Esq., Q.C.

The narrative part is printed in large and clear type ; the supplementary information in smaller type ; and the illustrative notes in yet smaller—but always perfectly clear.

It is hoped that this book may be the means of interesting a large number of young learners in the story of their country, and in the constitution under which they live.

PART I.—From B.C. 55 to A.D. 1509, now ready.
PART II.—From 1509 to 1890, ready in January.

6

A NEW HISTORY OF ENGLAND—*continued.*

REVIEWS AND OPINIONS OF

A New History of England and Great Britain.

"A singularly clear compendium of the best writings and most recent research. One rarely meets with a work containing such a mass of desirable information, and not degenerating into a mere uninteresting catalogue of events. The Biographical Notices and Glossary of Historical Terms should prove particularly useful."
G. Henry Fathers, B.A., Lecturer in History at the Culham Training College, and Graduate in Historical Honours of Oxford University.

"I like it very much, and think it thoroughly adapted to the wants of Pupil-Teachers, and of junior students of History generally. The difficulty of placing in a consecutive narrative so many and such diverse facts has been admirably met; the story is told very clearly and vividly; and the original extracts in small type give further life to the whole." C. H. King, M.A., Master of Method, Training College, Cheltenham.

"It is thoroughly interesting, and made additionally valuable by the concise notes and apt quotations on every page from the greatest English historians."
F. L. Millard, Esq., M.A., Vice-Principal, Bede College, Durham.

"I like your History very much. It is suggestive, and does not ignore the social and literary side of things." Miss A. F. Andrews, Maida Vale High School for Girls, W.

"Simple and terse, scholarly and sufficient; just the book for a pupil-teacher."
J. A. Yoxall, Esq., Sharrow Lane B. School, Sheffield.

"It is very clear and nicely arranged, and provides much valuable information not found in kindred works." G. W. Davis, Esq., Mary Street School, Balsall Heath.

"Your books are simply indispensable to students preparing for the certificate examination, and to pupil-teachers." One of Her Majesty's Inspectors.

"The amount of pains of which I have already seen proofs, and the ingenuity of the methods for assisting students' memories, are fairly overwhelming."
One of Her Majesty's Inspectors.

"If a text-book is valuable in proportion as it makes everything plain and interesting for a pupil, you have succeeded admirably." The Rector of Merchiston Castle, Edinburgh.

"The difficulties of the learner are kept carefully in view throughout, and all that is possible is done to lighten the task of acquiring a thorough grip of the matter . . . . The chapter on 'Terms employed in English History' will be found specially useful."
Educational News.

"I am greatly pleased with the selection and arrangement of matter in the New History, and the Plans of Dates are excellent."
D. F. Lowe, Esq., M.A., George Heriot's Hospital, Edinburgh.

"We like the arrangement of the text, which is a distinct success for the purpose of catching the eye. We shall have much pleasure in warmly recommending it to our H.C.S. Class II. candidates." Messrs. Wren and Gurney, Powis Square, London.

"It is very attractive because of its clear, crisp style of narration and description, while the student will enjoy the comparative ease with which he can trace from it the political, social, and literary progress of our country."
A. T. Watson, Esq., M.A., Rector of Dumbarton Academy.

"I am very pleased with the concise statements and orderly marshalling of facts; such an improvement in our ordinary Histories."
R. A. Little, Esq., M.A., The College, Buxton.

"It is admirably planned. There is not too much of anything."
T. Bayns, Esq., M.A., Larchfield Academy.

"The chronological system strikes me as being a singularly happy invention."
B. F. Hall, Esq., M.A., Edinburgh Collegiate School.

"It is a model text-book. The main events of each reign are stated clearly, simply, and in the most interesting way." F. Macdougall, Esq., M.A., Rector of Bell-Baxters School.

Fourth Edition.   Crown 8vo, pp. 340.   Price 4s. 6d.

The English Language:
ITS GRAMMAR, HISTORY, AND LITERATURE.

By J. M. D. MEIKLEJOHN, M.A.,

PROFESSOR OF THE THEORY, HISTORY, AND PRACTICE OF EDUCATION IN THE UNIVERSITY OF ST. ANDREWS.

ALSO IN THREE SEPARATE VOLUMES:

1.—A New Grammar of the English Tongue.

With Chapters on COMPOSITION, VERSIFICATION, PARAPHRASING, and PUNCTUATION.   Being Parts I. and II. of 'The English Language.' With 64 pages of Exercises and Examination Questions.

Crown 8vo, 2s. 6d.

2.—A Short History of the English Language.

Being Part III. of 'The English Language.'

Crown 8vo, 1s.

3.—An Outline of the History of English Literature.

Being Part IV. of 'The English Language.'

Crown 8vo, 1s. 6d.

THIS book contains Four Parts.   The First Part consists of an easy Grammar, which contains all essential information about the inflections of the Language, its Syntax, and its Idioms.

It also contains copious chapters on Prefixes, Suffixes, Word-building, and Derivation.

The Second Part contains hints and suggestions for writing good English, with sections on the structure of Verse, etc.

The Third Part contains a short History of the English Language, from the time when it arrived in this island in the 6th century, with clear accounts of the different changes that have come over the Vocabulary, the Grammar, and the Phraseology of English.

The Fourth Part contains a brief sketch of the History of English Literature, with Tables of Literature.

This book is in use in a large number of Colleges and Higher Schools in England, Scotland, India, and the Colonies ; and the general testimony is that it is liked both by Teachers and by Pupils.

REVIEWS AND OPINIONS OF
The English Language.

"There is not a dull page in the book."
C. T. Smith, Esq., B.A., Vice-Principal, St. Mark's College, Chelsea.

"Much valuable information in a convenient and compact shape."
Joseph Landon, Esq., Saltley College, Birmingham.

"The arrangement is natural; everything touched upon is made interesting, and the style is singularly clear and terse."
David Pryde, Esq., M.A., LL.D., Principal of Edinburgh Ladies' College.

"A course in English sufficiently complete for middle-class schools. . . . A thoroughly good, practical, and sensible manual."
J. B. Charles, Esq., M.A., Chief English Master, Dundee High School.

"I know of no book generally so suitable for an ordinary student."
Alfred Barriball, Esq., B.A., Westminster Training College.

"I think it is the best thing of its kind in the market."
A. Garlick, Esq., B.A., Headmaster, P.T. School, New Road, Woolwich.

"An admirable book, adapted for pupil-teachers, training-college students, and London University matriculation students."
H. Major, Esq., B.A., B.Sc., School Board Inspector, Leicester.

"I never saw a better book on the English language of the same size."
James Sootson, Esq., Headmaster of the Central School, Manchester.

"For the first-class College of Preceptors your work is most excellent and valuable."
The Rev. F. Marshall, M.A., Almondbury Grammar School.

"As stimulating in matter as it is attractive in form. It puts life into the dry bones of fact."   A. J. Watson, Esq., M.A., Rector, the Academy, Dumbarton.

"It is the work of a master hand, and covers all the ground which has hitherto necessitated the use of several text-books."
Rev. T. Graham, D.D., St. Mary's Training College, Hammersmith.

"Exactly suited to the wants of pupil-teachers, and of candidates for the Government Certificates."   Miss M. Goddard, Training College, Warrington.

"I am struck with the methodical arrangement, and the simple manner in which the subject-matter is laid out."   W. G. Baker, Esq., M.A., The Training College, Cheltenham.

"The latter parts seem to have a special value."
Rev. Hector Nelson, M.A., Principal of the Training College, Lincoln.

"I gave it to a girl candidate for an English Scholarship; she got first place—and valued the help she got from the book."

W. Johnson, Esq., B.A., Elmfield College, York.

Will shortly be Published. Crown 8vo. 300 pp. Price 3s. 6d.

A TEXT BOOK OF
Teaching and Class Management

Intended to meet the wants of

Pupil Teachers, Students in Training Colleges, and Assistant Teachers in Middle Class and Higher Schools.

By JOSEPH LANDON, F.G.S.,

SENIOR LECTURER AND MASTER OF METHOD IN THE SALTLEY TRAINING COLLEGE ;
AUTHOR OF ' SCHOOL MANAGEMENT ' IN THE EDUCATION LIBRARY.

EXTRACT FROM PREFACE.

An attempt is here made to present in a direct and intelligible way the broader outlines and essential characteristics of the various branches of the teacher's work ; more especially the theory of oral teaching, the preparation of notes, the use of the teaching devices, and the various methods of teaching the ordinary subjects of school instruction. Organisation and discipline are discussed mainly from the point of view of the young teacher, class management receiving full attention.

The subject is treated from the *art* side rather than the *scientific*, so that it may be of as thoroughly practical and useful a character as possible ; but the underlying *science of education* has been carefully kept in mind, and it is believed that the student will have nothing to unlearn in the further prosecution of his studies for the purpose of associating his practice with the laws which govern the development of the child's mind and the modes of mental action.

I have tried throughout to make the subject suggestive rather than full, and, while laying stress upon principles and essentials, to leave room for that originality of treatment by the teacher him-self, and that elasticity and expansiveness in practice, which is the characteristic of all good method. Mere unintelligent *imitation* of the detailed plans of others is not what is required in school work, and should not be the aim of any true teacher.

J. L.

Crown 8vo.   Price 1s.

The Spelling List

(10,000 Words)

FOR CIVIL SERVICE AND OTHER EXAMINATIONS.

WITH A KEY TO CORRECT SPELLING.

THIS is a complete list of all the errors that have been made in Examination Papers of all kinds for the last five-and-twenty years. Out of every hundred failures in the Civil Service Examinations, fifty-two per cent. are for spelling.   Each candidate has his own peculiar habits of bad spelling; and he will here find them vividly and clearly corrected.

"Your Spelling List is a very decided advance in the right direction, ably conceived, and brilliantly written.   We shall certainly strongly recommend it to our pupils."
Rev. H. P. Gurney, M.A., (of Messrs. Wren and Gurney), Powis Square, London.

"There can be no question that this plan impresses the correct spelling of the word firmly on the learner's mind.   We recommend it to all Customs candidates, and to men clerk candidates, as well as to students generally."   **The Aspirant.**

"This remarkable list—"   **Publishers' Circular.**

Crown 8vo.   160 pp.   Price 1s.

Fables, Anecdotes, and Stories

FOR TEACHING COMPOSITION,

With Outline and Hints on Letter Writing.

THIS little book gives about 200 fables and anecdotes, written in a very clear style.   It begins with very short stories in short, simple sentences.   It goes on to stories a little longer, and to the use of complex sentences.   There are also letters and forms for business notes, etc. etc.

Crown 8vo. Price 1s.

A Short Geography

THIS little book gives the main features of the globe, and the most important facts regarding each country, in a clear and vivid style, and with so much connection between the statements as to make them easily remembered. It is illustrated by maps, and diagrams, which have been specially drawn for this work, and are clear, bold, and easily understood.

The commercial side of Geography is clearly brought out.

The book is so printed that the Teacher can easily see which parts are to be learned first; and it is divided into short and easy lessons.

REVIEWS AND OPINIONS.

" Its definitions are concise and to the point; and its skilful groupings will help very much in fixing the lessons on the memory." **The Educational News.**

" This book is admirably arranged; there are no half statements; there is no crowding or confusion. A better short Geography we can hardly wish for." **National Schoolmaster.**

"Terse, practical, informative and statistic. This shilling Geography is exactly what a School Geography needs to be." **Teachers' Aid.**

" Clearness and conciseness exemplified." **The Private Schoolmaster.**

Crown 8vo.   Price 1s.

A New Spelling-Book

WITH SIDE-LIGHTS FROM HISTORY.

THIS book is an attempt to solve the difficult problem of learning to spell.   All kinds of aids have been brought in for the assistance and furtherance of the learner :—*Comparison, contrast, derivation, rules,* and hints from the *history* of the language.

The First Part gives a short view of the different vowel sounds.

The Second Part contains a list of the difficult initial consonants.

The Third and Fourth Parts : Lists of words that are confounded.

The Fifth Part gives a list of Contrasted Endings Unaccented.

The Sixth Part contains Endings that are frequently confounded.

The Seventh Part gives a list of Contrasted Endings Accented Contains all those " Contrasted Derivatives "—like main*tain* main-*ten*ance—in which mistakes are frequently made.

The Eighth Part : Rules for Spelling, some new, all useful.

The Ninth Part : Side-lights from the History of English.

The Tenth Part : The Thousand most difficult words.

It is believed that this is the most complete view of the difficulties of English spelling that has yet been given to the scholastic world.

CODE 1889-90.

'Typical Test Cards'

IN ARITHMETIC

Uniformly arranged by an Assistant Inspector of Schools.

SPECIAL FEATURES.

1. These Cards are not collected " Government Sums." '

2. They have been specially prepared, and are therefore quite new. Each Card contains 16 sums, and there are 30 Cards and two sets of answers in each packet.

3. In their arrangement the object has been to vary as much as possible the form in which the same kind of sum may be set so as to develop the intelligence.

4. The true method of teaching Arithmetic, as of teaching other subjects, is always to present the same idea at different angles, and to give the maximum of repetition with the minimum of monotony. It is believed that these Cards fulfil this condition and follow this method.

STANDARDS II., III., IV., V., VI., VII., ONE SHILLING PER PACKET.

NOTICES.

" In the arrangement of the questions, the object of the compiler has been to vary as much as possible the form in which the same kind of sum may be set so as to develop the intelligence. A perusal of the questions will show that this object has been well achieved, and that a successful set of arithmetical cards has been the result. We recommend the cards to the notice of our readers." **Schoolmaster.**

" These texts are completely 'out of the rut.' A more comprehensive and thoughtful set of questions it has not fallen to our lot to see since the craze for sums *actually* set began. The ' rounded ' corners are a new fenture." **Teachers' Aid.**

" The questions are varied in character and form." **School Guardian.**

" The compiler shows considerable skill in setting the problems." **The English Teacher.**

Dr. Morell's English Series.

Works by John Markwell, M.A.

First Step in Geography, 159 pp., neatly bound in limp cloth, ... 9d.

> This little book gives the main facts of Geography in the simplest language. In addition to the usual geography, it contains the "First Step in Physical Geography," the "Railways of the World," the "Telegraphs of the World," and "A Voyage round the World."

Junior Geography, on the principles of Comparison and Contrast, with numerous Exercises, by JOHN MARKWELL, M.A.; Cr. 8vo, 206 pp., strongly bound in stiff cloth cover, ... 1s. 6d.

> This Geography gives the facts to be learned by the method of comparison and contrast. The matter is set out in short sections, written in the clearest style; and Summaries are given of all the most striking facts. Map Practice is also attached to each chapter. A few simple diagrams are also given.

Senior Geography, on the Principles of Comparison and Contrast, with 400 Exercises, by JOHN MARKWELL, M.A.; Cr. 8vo, 320 pp., strongly bound in stiff cloth cover, ... 2s. 6d.

> In this Senior Geography the objects kept in view are :—
>
> (i) The unknown is always compared with the known.
>
> (ii) The Memory is helped by Contrasts.
>
> (iii) What is required for drill is kept separate.
>
> (iv) No name is given alone ; some picturesque fact is always attached to it.
>
> (v) The page is not overcrowded with names ; and the outlines of countries are always vivid.
>
> (vi) There is connection throughout.
>
> The book also contains a sketch of Physical Geography ; Mathematical Geography ; Exercises ; etc.

Dr. Morell's English Series.

First Step in Composition, with 108 Fables, Stories, Letters, etc.; 96 pp., neatly bound in limp cloth, ... 8d.

> This little book consists chiefly of stories, which are told in the plainest and neatest language. An abridgment or skeleton of each story is given, so that the learner may dress it up in his own way and style; while a number of phrases are placed at the end of each, so that he may have a selection to choose from. First Part, stories in short, simple sentences; Second Part, stories in easy complex sentences, which gradually increase in length.

> "This seems an excellent plan and one likely to work well."   Educational Times.

> "This little treatise will admirably serve the purpose for which it is intended, and we heartily recommend it."   Civil Service Gazette.

> "This strikes us as a capital little book for its purpose, and we can readily imagine the real interest children would begin to take in that usually difficult task called 'Composition,' if its method were pursued."   Literary World.

> "The plan is very good. The First Step is a useful little work."   School Board Chronicle.

Second Step in Composition, with 200 Exercises; Cr. 8vo, 144 pp., strong cloth cover, . . . 1s. 6d.

> This book introduces the learner to Sentence Building; gives Exercises in the choice of Words; in the employ-ment of Synonymous Phrases; etc. These occupy the First and Second Courses. The Third Course gives remarks and Exercises on Prevalent Errors in style, with reasons and cautions; and also 84 subjects for short essays.

Practical Introduction to English Composition, with 300 Exercises; Cr. 8vo, 312 pp., strong cloth cover, ... 3s.

> The introduction in this book contains clear explanations, with numerous examples, of the Law of Fulness, the Law of Clearness, the Law of Plainness, etc. The Exercises consist of Narratives, each of which is accompanied by an Outline and a Phraseology (or stock of phrases to select from); Critical Lessons for

guidance in the use of words and phrases; Extracts from Old Writers to turn into Modern English; Ideas for Essays, etc. etc.

There is also a chapter on the Art of Verse, with numerous exercises and examples, and lessons on the structure of English poetry.

"One of the best manuals on the subject with which we are acquainted. The plan on which it is constructed seems to be excellent." **The Educational Times.**

"A book for students of Composition, which will be of the utmost service to them It cannot give them brains, but it will help them to make the most of what they have." **Scotsman.**

"It seems to us to supply, for the first time, an obvious gap in education." **Guardian.**

"The best and most complete manual of English composition we have ever had an opportunity of seeing." **Leeds Mercury.**

"So much sensible criticism in the present work that it cannot be perused without great profit." **National Schoolmaster.**

English Literature.

Biographical History of English Literature,

with 300 Exercises; *New Edition*, Cr. 8vo, 520 pp., strong cloth cover, ...   3s. 6d.

This book contains a brief history of English literature from the Anglo-Saxon Period down to the present time. The Lives of all the great Authors are written in full; and an account of their chief works is given. The best and most interesting extracts from their works are also presented. Chapters on the minor writers come between the more important chapters as connecting-links.

Numerous, but easy, Exercises have also been given.

ALSO IN TWO PARTS.

PART I.—From Beowulf to Milton, Cr. 8vo, 236 pp. strong cloth cover, ...   2s.

PART II.—From the "Hudibras" to "Aurora Leigh," Cr. 8vo, 270 pp., strong cloth cover, .   .   2s.

"We can confidently recommend this manual as the best we have seen of its kind. It seems to us precisely the text-book for Schools. . . . The novel feature of *Exercises* will be found to be not the least valuable part of the work." **The Nonconformist.**

"Certainly the best book of the kind we have seen." **The Glasgow Herald.**

"Candidates for appointments in the Civil Service will find a study of this book of the greatest service to them." **The Civil Service Review.**

"We are bound to say that the present effort seems thoroughly to succeed." **The Guardian.**

www.ingramcontent.com/pod-product-compliance
Lightning Source LLC
Chambersburg PA
CBHW030823110726
47900CB00006B/1718